CALDÉ

OF THE

LONG

SUN

BY GENE WOLFE FROM TOM DOHERTY ASSOCIATES

Caldé of the Long Sun
Castle of Days
Castleview
The Death of Doctor Island
Endangered Species
The Fifth Head of Cerberus
Free Live Free
Lake of the Long Sun
Nightside the Long Sun
Pandora by Holly Hollander
Seven American Nights
Soldier of Arete
Soldier of the Mist
Storeys from the Old Hotel
There Are Doors
The Urth of the New Sun

CALDÉ

OF THE

LONG

SUN

■

Gene Wolfe

TOR

A TOM DOHERTY ASSOCIATES BOOK

NEW YORK

This is a work of fiction. All the characters and events
portrayed in this book are fictitious, and any resemblance
to real people or events is purely coincidental.

CALDÉ OF THE LONG SUN

Copyright © 1994 by Gene Wolfe

All rights reserved, including the right to reproduce this
book, or portions thereof, in any form.

This book is printed on acid-free paper.

A Tor Book
Published by Tom Doherty Associates, Inc.
175 Fifth Avenue
New York, N.Y. 10010

Tor ® is a registered trademark of Tom Doherty
Associates, Inc.

Library of Congress Cataloging-in-Publication Data
Wolfe, Gene.
    Caldé of the long sun / Gene Wolfe.
        p.   cm.
    "A Tom Doherty Associates book."
    ISBN 0-312-85583-4
    I. Title.
  PS3573.O52C35   1994
  813'.54—dc20   94-12915
                                        CIP

First edition: September 1994

Printed in the United States of America

0 9 8 7 6 5 4 3 2 1

For Todd Compton, classicist and rock musician.

GODS, PERSONS, AND ANIMALS MENTIONED IN THE TEXT

N.B. In Viron, biochemical males are named after animals or animal products: Macaque, Mattak, OOSIK, and POTTO bear names of this type. Biochemical females are named for plants (most frequently flowers) or plant products: MUCOR, Nettle, ROSE, Teasel. Chemical persons, whether male or female, are named after metals and minerals: Moly, Sard, Shale. The names of major characters are given in CAPITALS in this listing.

A-man, a man representing all men.
Ah Lah, a forgotten god. (Perhaps an alternative name for the OUTSIDER.)
Aloe, a pious woman of the Sun Street Quarter.
Asphodella, a girl in the younger (prepubescent) group at the palaestra.
Aster, a girl in the older (pubescent) group at the palaestra.
AUK, the burly housebreaker who coached SILK in burglary; called "trooper" by HAMMERSTONE.
Babirousa, a smith's apprentice, one of MINT's volunteers.
Bass, the muscular bald man employed by Orchid.
Maytera *Betel,* the dark, sleepy-eyed sibyl noted by SILK during his enlightenment.

Bison, the big, black-bearded man who becomes MINT's chief lieutenant.

BLOOD, a wealthy dealer in drugs and women, at times an unpaid agent of the Ayuntamiento.

Bream, the thief who provides a white goat for Kypris at ROSE's final sacrifice.

Brocket, a distant cousin of MINT's.

Patera *Bull,* QUETZAL's prothonotary.

Bustard, AUK's older brother, now dead.

Cassava, a pious old woman of the Sun Street Quarter.

Cavy, one of the older (pubescent) boys at the palaestra.

CHENILLE, the tallest woman at Orchid's.

Major *Civet,* the officer who killed Doctor CRANE while trying to free SILK.

Doctor *CRANE,* the Trivigaunti spy who killed Councillor LEMUR, now dead.

Captain *DACE,* the skipper of the fishing boat commandeered by SCYLLA.

Dahlia, a student of MARBLE's, long ago.

Echidna, the Mother of the Gods; the most powerful goddess.

Sergeant *Eft,* Mattak's chief subordinate.

Eland, one of Urus's convict crew; he tamed and trained two tunnel gods.

Elodia, Gelada's former mistress.

Ermine, the owner of the highest-priced hotel in Viron.

Brigadier *Erne,* the commander of the Fourth Brigade of Viron's Civil Guard (formerly, the Caldé's Guard).

Femur, INCUS's much-older brother.

Gaur, one of Urus's convict crew.

Gayfeather, one of the older (pubescent) girls at the palaestra.

Captain *Gecko,* an officer on OOSIK's staff.

Gelada, the bowman in Urus's crew who shoots at CHENILLE.

Gib, the giant whose life was saved by AUK.

Ginger, one of the older (pubescent) girls at the palaestra.

Goral, an unemployed hostler, one of MINT's volunteers.

Patera *Gulo,* SILK's acolyte.

Corporal *HAMMERSTONE,* the soldier who (with Sergeant Sand) first arrested SILK in the tunnels, called "Stony" by CHENILLE.

Hart, a young layman of SILK's manteion.

Hierax, Echidna's second son, the god of death.

Holly, one of the older (pubescent) girls at the palaestra.

Horn, the student punished by ROSE for imitating SILK.

HYACINTH, the beautiful young woman at BLOOD's who persuaded CRANE to give SILK an azoth.

Patera *INCUS,* the black mechanic who repairs and reprograms HAMMERSTONE.

Iolar, the flier downed by *MUSK*'s eagle.

Patera *Jerboa,* the augur of the manteion on Brick Street.

Kingcup, the owner of a livery stable.

Kypris, the goddess of love, the first goddess to possess CHENILLE.

Councillor *LEMUR,* the leading member of the Ayuntamiento, killed by CRANE.

Liana, one of Zoril's subordinates.

Lily, AUK's mother, now dead.

Lime, MINT's chief female lieutenant.

Linsang, Liana's sweetheart.

Lion, the largest male among MUCOR's lynxes.

Councillor *LORIS,* the leader of the Ayuntamiento after the death of LEMUR.

Macaque, one of the older (pubescent) boys at the palaestra.

Mamelta, the sleeper arrested with SILK in the tunnels.

Mandrill, Gelada's cousin, now fled.

Maytera *MARBLE,* the sibyl who teaches the younger (prepubescent) children at the palaestra.

Marmot, an unemployed laborer, one of MINT's volunteers.

Cornet *Mattak,* OOSIK's son, a young cavalry officer.

Maytera *MINT,* the Sword of Echidna, the sibyl who teaches the older (pubescent) girls at the palaestra; called General MINT by the insurgents.

Maytera *Mockorange,* a sibyl at the manteion on Sun Street, now dead.

Molpe, Echidna's second daughter, goddess of the winds and of the lively arts.

Moly, HAMMERSTONE's lost sweetheart, a housemaid. (Short for Molybdenum.)

Patera *Moray,* the augur murdered by Eft.

MUCOR, the adolescent whose bedroom was invaded by SILK when he burglarized BLOOD's villa.

Murtagon, a famous artist.

MUSK, BLOOD's sadistic young killer; a competent tenor and a lover of raptorial birds.

Nettle, one of the older (pubescent) girls in Maytera MINT's class at the palaestra.

Oont, a porter.

Colonel *OOSIK,* the commander of the reserve brigade.

Orchid, the madame of a brothel owned by BLOOD.

OREB, a bird purchased by SILK as a victim but never sacrificed.

Orpine, Orchid's daughter, possessed by MUCOR and killed by CHENILLE.

The *OUTSIDER,* the god of the broken and the disparaged, whose realm lies outside the Whorl.

Pas, the Father of the Gods; the husband of Echidna and the father of SCYLLA, Molpe, TARTAROS, Hierax, Thelxiepeia, Phaea, and Sphigx.

Patera *Pike,* the elderly augur whose acolyte SILK became upon graduation from the schola, now dead.

Phaea, Echidna's fourth daughter, the goddess of food and healing.

Pork, the owner of the restaurant at which SILK dined with
AUK.

Councillor *POTTO,* the member of the Ayuntamiento who
(with Sand) interrogated SILK after his second arrest.

Patera *QUETZAL,* the ranking augur in Viron and for
thirty-three years the head of its Chapter.

Quill, a poor student at the palaestra.

Patera *REMORA,* QUETZAL's coadjutor and presumed
successor.

Rook, one of MINT's lieutenants.

Maytera *ROSE,* the sibyl who taught the older (pubescent)
boys at the palaestra, now dead.

General *Saba,* the commander of the Trivigaunti airship
and the troops it brings to Viron.

Sergeant *Sand,* HAMMERSTONE's squad leader.

Sard, the owner of a large pawnshop on Saddle Street.

Scale, one of Bison's lieutenants.

Private *Schist,* a soldier in Sand's squad.

Scleroderma, the fat woman who holds MINT's horse; the
wife of a butcher in the Sun Street Quarter.

Captain *Scup,* the fishing-boat skipper employed by CRANE
to watch the Pilgrims' Way.

SCYLLA, the firstborn of Echidna's children, and the
patroness of Viron.

Private *Shale,* a soldier in Sand's squad.

Patera *Shell,* Patera Jerboa's acolyte; he attended the schola
with SILK.

Caldé *SILK,* the augur of the manteion on Sun Street.

Generalissimo *Siyuf,* the commander of the armed forces of
Trivigaunte.

Skink, the insurgent leader who attempts an all-out assault
on the Palatine early Hieraxday night.

Sphigx, Echidna's youngest child, the patroness of
Trivigaunte and the goddess of war.

Councillor *Tarsier,* one of the members of the
    Ayuntamiento.
TARTAROS, Echidna's eldest son, the god of night.
Teasel, a girl in MARBLE's class at the palaestra.
Thetis, a minor goddess to whom lost travelers pray.
Thelxiepeia, Echidna's third daughter, the goddess of
    learning and thus of magic and witchcraft.
Lieutenant *Tiger,* OOSIK's assistant operations officer.
Caldé *TUSSAH,* SILK's predecessor; he was assassinated by
    the Ayuntamiento. (Patera *Tussah,* presumably named
    for the caldé, is a member of INCUS's circle of black
    mechanics.)
Urus, a former associate of AUK's, sentenced to the pits.
Villus, a small boy in MARBLE's class at the palaestra.
Violet, a beautiful brunet at Orchid's, a friend of
    CHENILLE's.
Wo-Man, a woman representing all women.
Maytera *Wood,* the senior sibyl at the Brick Street manteion.
Wool, one of MINT's lieutenants.
Master *XIPHIAS,* a one-legged fencing teacher.
Yapok, a stableman, one of MINT's volunteers.
Zoril, a cabinetmaker, one of MINT's lieutenants.

CALDÉ

OF THE

LONG

SUN

Chapter 1

THE SLAVES OF SCYLLA

As unruffled by the disturbances shaking the city as by the furious thunderstorm that threatened with every gust to throw down its shiprock and return its mud brick to the parent mud, His Cognizance Patera Quetzal, Prolocutor of the Chapter of This Our Holy City of Viron, studied his present sere and sallow features in the polished belly of the silver teapot.

As at this hour each day, he swung his head to the right and contemplated his nearly noseless profile, made a similar inspection of its obverse, and elevated his chin to display a lengthy and notably wrinkled neck. He had shaped and colored face and neck with care upon arising, as he did every morning; nevertheless, there remained the possibility (however remote) that something had gone awry by ten: thus the present amused but painstaking self-examination.

"For I am a careful man," he muttered, pretending to smooth one thin white eyebrow.

A crash of thunder shook the Prolocutor's Palace to its foundations at the final word, brightening every light in the room to a glare; rain and hail drummed the windowpanes.

Patera Remora, Coadjutor of the Chapter, nodded solemnly. "Yes indeed, Your Cognizance. You are indeed a most—ah—advertent man."

Yet there was always that possibility. "I'm growing old, Patera. Even we careful men grow old."

Remora nodded again, his long bony face expressive of regret. "Alas, Your Cognizance."

"As do many other things, Patera. Our city . . . The Whorl itself grows old. When we're young, we notice things that are young, like ourselves. New grass on old graves. New leaves on old trees." Quetzal lifted his chin again to study his bulging reflection through hooded eyes.

"The golden season of beauty and—um—elegiacs, Your Cognizance." Remora's fingers toyed with a dainty sandwich.

"As we notice the signs of advancing age in ourselves, we see them in the Whorl. Just a few chems today who ever saw a man who saw a man who remembered the day Pas made the Whorl."

A little bewildered by the rapid riffle through so many generations, Remora nodded again. "Indeed, Your Cognizance. Indeed not." Surreptitiously, he wiped jam from one finger.

"You become conscious of recurrences, the cyclical nature of myth. When first I received the bacculus, I had occasion to survey many old documents. I read each with care. It was my custom to devote three Hieraxdays a month to that. To that alone, and to inescapable obsequies. I gave my prothonotary the straitest instructions to make no appointments for that day. It's a practice I recommend, Patera."

Thunder rattled the room again, lightning a dragon beyond the windows.

"I will, um, reinstitute this wise usage at once, Your Cognizance."

"At once, you say?" Quetzal looked up from the silver pot, resolved to repowder his chin at the first opportunity. "You may go to young Incus and so instruct him, if you want. Tell him now, Patera. Tell him now."

"That is—ah—unfeasible, I fear, Your Cognizance. I sent

Patera Incus upon a—um—errand Molpsday. He has not—um—rejoined us.''

''I see. I see.'' With a trembling hand, Quetzal raised his cup until its gilt rim touched his lips, then lowered it, though not so far as to expose his chin. ''I want beef tea, Patera. There's no strength in this. I want beef tea. See to it, please.''

Long accustomed to the request, his coadjutor rose. ''I shall prepare it with my own hands, Your Cognizance. It will—ah—occupy only an, um, trice. Boiling water, an, um, roiling boil. Your Cognizance may rely upon me.''

Slowly, Quetzal replaced the delicate cup in its saucer as he watched Remora's retreating back; he even spilled a few drops there, for he was, as he had said, careful. The measured closing of the door. Good. The clank of the latchbar. Good again. No one could intrude now without noise and a slight delay; he had designed the latching mechanism himself.

Without leaving his chair, he extracted the puff from a drawer on the other side of the room and applied flesh-toned powder delicately to the small, sharp chin he had shaped with such care upon arising. Swinging his head from side to side as before, frowning and smiling by turns, he studied the effect in the teapot. Good, good!

Rain beat against the windows with such force as to drive trickles of chill water through crevices in the casements; it pooled invitingly on the milkstone windowsills and fell in cataracts to soak the carpet. That, too, was good. At three, he would preside at the private sacrifice of twenty-one dappled horses, the now-posthumous offering of Councillor Lemur—one to all the gods for each week since rain more substantial than a shower had blessed Viron's fields. They could be converted to a thank offering, and he would so convert them.

Would the congregation know by then of Lemur's demise? Quetzal debated the advisability of announcing the fact if they did not. It was a question of some consequence;

and at length, for the temporary relief the act afforded him, he pivoted his hinged fangs from their snug grooves in the roof of his mouth, snapping each gratefully into its socket and grinning gleefully at his distorted image.

The rattle of the latch was nearly lost in another crash of thunder, but he had kept an eye on the latchbar. There was a second and louder rattle as Remora, on the other side of the door, contended with the inconveniently shaped iron handle that would, when its balky rotation had been completed, laboriously lift the clumsy bar clear of its cradle.

Quetzal touched his lips almost absently with his napkin; when he spread it upon his lap again, his fangs had vanished. "Yes, Patera?" he inquired querulously. "What is it now? Is it time already?"

"Your beef tea, Your Cognizance." Remora set his small tray on the table. "Shall I—um—decant a cup for you? I have, er, obtained a clean cup for the purpose."

"Do, Patera. Please do." Quetzal smiled. "While you were gone, I was contemplating the nature of humor. Have you ever considered it?"

Remora resumed his seat. "I fear not, Your Cognizance."

"What's become of young Incus? You hadn't expected him to be gone so long?"

"No, Your Cognizance. I dispatched him to Limna." Remora spooned beef salts into the clean cup and added water from the small copper kettle he had brought, producing a fine plume of steam. "I am—ah—moderately concerned. An, um, modicum of civil unrest last night, eh?" He stirred vigorously. "This—ah—stripling Silk. Patera Silk, alas. I know him."

"My prothonotary told me." With the slightest of nods, Quetzal accepted the steaming cup. "I'd have thought Limna would be safer."

"As would I, Your Cognizance. As did I."

A cautious sip. Quetzal held the hot, salty fluid in his mouth, drawing it deliciously through folded fangs.

"I sent him in search of a—ah, um—individual, Your Cognizance. A, er, acquaintance of this Patera Silk's. The Civil Guard is searching for Patera himself, hey? As are, er, certain others. Other—ah—parties. So I am told. This morning, Your Cognizance, I dispatched still others to look for young Incus. The rain, however, ah, necessitous, will hamper them all, hum?"

"Do you swim, Patera?"

"I, Your Cognizance? At the—um—lakeside, you mean? No. Or at least, not for many years."

"Nor I."

Remora groped toward a point he had yet to discern. "A healthful exercise, however. For those of, um, unaugmented years, eh? A hot bath before sacrifice, Your Cognizance? Or—I have it!—springs. There are, er, reborant springs at Urbs. Healing springs, most healthful. Possibly, while—ah—affairs are so—ah—unsettled here, eh?"

Quetzal shook himself. He had a way of quivering like a fat man when he did that, although on the few occasions when Remora had been obliged to lift him into bed, his body had in fact been light and sinuous. "The gods . . ." He smiled.

"Must be served, to be sure, Your Cognizance. I would be on the spot—ah—ensuring that the Chapter's interests were vigilantly safeguarded, hey?" Remora tossed lank black hair away from his eyes. "Each rite carried out with—um—"

"You must recall the story, Patera." Quetzal swayed from side to side, perhaps with silent mirth. "A-man and Wo-man like rabbits in a garden. The—what do you call them?" He held up a thin, blue-veined hand, palm cupped.

"A cobra, Your Cognizance?"

"The cobra persuaded Wo-man to eat fruit from his tree, miraculous fruit whose taste conferred wisdom."

Remora nodded, wondering how he might reintroduce the springs. "I recollect the—um—allegory."

Quetzal nodded more vigorously, a wise teacher proffering praise to a small boy. "It's all in the Writings. Or nearly all. A god called Ah Lah barred Wo-man and her husband from the garden." He ceased to speak, apparently wandering among thoughts. "We seem to have lost sight of Ah Lah, by the way. I can't recall a single sacrifice to him. No one ever asks why the cobra wanted Wo-man to eat his fruit."

"From sheer, er, wickedness, Your Cognizance? That is what I had always supposed."

Quetzal swayed faster, his face solemn. "In order that she would climb his tree, Patera. The man likewise. Their story's not over because they haven't climbed down. That's why I asked if you had considered the nature of humor. Is Patera Incus a strong swimmer?"

"Why, I've—ah—no notion, Your Cognizance."

"Because you think you know why the woman you sent him to look for visited the lake with our scamp Silk, whose name I see on walls."

"Why, er, Your Cognizance is—ah—great penetration, as always." Remora fidgeted.

"I saw it scratched on one five floors up, yesterday," Quetzal continued as though he had not heard, "and went wide."

"Disgraceful, Your Cognizance!"

"Respect for our cloth, Patera. I myself swim well. Not so well as a fish, but very well indeed. Or I did."

"I'm pleased to hear it, Your Cognizance."

"The jokes of gods are long in telling. That's why you ought to sift the records of the past on Hieraxdays, Patera. Today's Hieraxday. You'll learn to think in new and better ways. Thank you for my beef tea. Now go."

Remora rose and bowed. "As Your Cognizance desires."

His Cognizance stared past him, lost in speculation.

Greatly daring, Remora ventured, "I have often observed that your own way of thinking is somewhat—ah—unlike, as well as much more, um, select than that of most men."

There was no reply. Remora took a step backward. "Upon every—ah—topic whatsoever, Your Cognizance's information is quite, um, marvelous."

"Wait." Quetzal had made his decision. "The riots. Has the Alambrera fallen?"

"What's that? The Alambrera? Why—ah—no. Not to my knowledge, Your Cognizance."

"Tonight." Quetzal reached for his beef tea. "Sit down, Patera. You're always jumping about. You make me nervous. It can't be good for you. Lemur's dead. Did you know it?"

Remora's mouth gaped, then snapped shut. He sat.

"You weren't. It's your responsibility to learn things."

Remora acknowledged his responsibility with a shame-faced nod. "May I inquire, Your Cognizance—?"

"How I know? In the same way I knew the woman you sent Incus after had gone to Lake Limna with Patera Caldé Silk."

"Your Cognizance!"

Once again, Quetzal favored Remora with his lipless smile. "Are you afraid I'll be arrested, Patera? Cast into the pits? You'd be Prolocutor, presumably. I've no fear of the pits." Quetzal's long-skulled, completely hairless head bobbed above his cup. "Not at my age. None."

"None the less, I implore Your Cognizance to be more—ah—circumspect."

"Why isn't the city burning, Patera?"

Caught by surprise, Remora glanced at the closest window.

"Mud brick and shiprock walls. Timbers supporting

upper floors. Thatch or shingles. Five blocks of shops burned last night. Why isn't the whole city burning today?''

"It's raining, Your Cognizance," Remora summoned all his courage. "It's been raining—ah—forcibly since early this morning."

"Exactly so. Patera Caldé Silk went to Limna on Molpsday with a woman. That same day, you sent Incus there to look for an acquaintance of his. A woman, since you were reluctant to speak of it. Councillor Loris spoke through the glass an hour before lunch."

Remora tensed. "He told you Councillor Lemur was no longer among us, Your Cognizance?"

Quetzal swung his head back and forth. "That Lemur was still alive, Patera. There are rumors. So it would appear. He wanted me to denounce them this afternoon."

"But if Councillor Loris—ah—assures—"

"Clearly Lemur's dead. If he weren't, he'd speak to me in person. Or show himself at the Juzgado. Or both."

"Even so, Your Cognizance—"

Another crash of thunder made common cause with Quetzal's thin hand to interrupt.

"Can the Ayuntamiento prevail without him? That's the question, Patera. I want your opinion."

To give himself time to consider, Remora sipped his now-tepid tea. "Munitions, the—ah—thews of contention, are stored in the Alambrera, as well as in the, um, cantonment of the Civil Guard, east of the city."

"I know that."

"It is an, er, complex of great—um—redoubtability, Your Cognizance. I am informed that the outer wall is twelve cubits in—ah—laterality. Yet Your Cognizance anticipates its surrender tonight? Before venturing an opinion, may I enquire as to the source of Your Cognizance's information?"

"I haven't any," Quetzal told him. "I was thinking out

loud. If the Alambrera doesn't fall in a day or so, Patera Caldé Silk will fail. That's my opinion. Now I want yours.''

"Your Cognizance does me honor. There is also the—um—dormant army to consider. Councillor Lemur—ah—Loris will undoubtedly issue an—ah—call to arms, should the, um, situation, in his view, become serious.''

"Your opinion, Patera.''

Remora's cup rattled in its saucer. "As long as the—ah—fidelity of the Civil Guard remains—um—unblemished, Your Cognizance," he drew a deep breath, "it would appear to me, though I am assuredly no—um—master hand at matters military, that—ah, um—Patera Caldé cannot prevail.''

Quetzal appeared to be listening only to the storm; for perhaps fifteen tickings of the coffin-shaped clock that stood beside the door, the howling of the wind and the lash of rain filled the room. At last he asked, "Suppose that you were to learn that part of the Guard's gone over to Silk already?''

Remora's eyes widened. "Your Cognizance has—?''

"No reason to think so. My question's hypothetical.''

Remora, who had much experience of Quetzal's hypothetical questions, filled his lungs again. "I should then say, Your Cognizance, that should any such unhappy circumstance—ah—circumstances eventuate, the city would find itself amongst—ah—perilous waters.''

"And the Chapter?''

Remora looked doleful. "Equally so, Your Cognizance, if not worse. As an augur, Silk could well, ah, proclaim himself Prolocutor, as well as caldé.''

"Really. He lacks reverence for you, my coadjutor?''

"No, Your Cognizance. Quite the, um, contrary.''

Quetzal sipped beef tea in silence.

"Your Cognizance—ah—intends the Chapter to support the—um—host of, er, Patera Caldé?''

"I want you to compose a circular letter, Patera. You have

nearly six hours. It should be more than enough. I'll sign it when we're through in the Grand Manteion." Quetzal stared down at the stagnant brown liquid in his cup.

"To all the clergy, Your Cognizance?"

"Emphasize our holy duty to bring comfort to the wounded and the Final Formula to the dying. Imply, but don't say—" Quetzal paused, inspired.

"Yes, Your Cognizance?"

"That Lemur's death ends the claim to rule the councillors had in the past. You say you know Patera Caldé Silk?"

Remora nodded. "I conversed with him at some—ah—extensively Scylsday evening, Your Cognizance. We discussed the financial—um—trials of his manteion, and—ah—various other matters."

"I don't, Patera. But I've read every report in his file, those of his instructors and those of his predecessor. Thus my recommendation. Diligent, sensitive, intelligent, and pious. Impatient, as is to be expected at his age. Respectful, which you now confirm. A tireless worker, a point his instructor in theonomy was at pains to emphasize. Pliable. During the past few days, he's become immensely popular. Should he succeed in subjugating the Ayuntamiento, he's apt to remain so for a year or more. Perhaps much longer. Charteral government by a young augur who'll need seasoned advisors to remain in office . . ."

"Indeed, Your Cognizance." Remora nodded energetically. "The same—ah—intuition had occurred to me."

With his cup, Quetzal gestured toward the nearest window. "We suffer a change in weather, Patera."

"An, um, profound one, Your Cognizance."

"We must acclimate ourselves to it. That's why I asked if young Incus swam. If you can reach him, tell him to strike out boldly. Have I made myself clear?"

Remora nodded again. "I will, um, strive to render the

Chapter's wholehearted endorsement of an—ah—lawful and holy government apparent, Your Cognizance.''

"Then go. Compose that letter."

"If the Alambrera doesn't—ah—hey?''

There was no indication that Quetzal had heard. Remora left his chair and backed away, at length closing the door behind him.

Quetzal rose, and an observer (had there been one) might have been more than a little surprised to see that shrunken figure grown so tall. As if on wheels, he glided across the room and threw open the broad casement that overlooked his garden, admitting pounding rain and a gust of wind that made his mulberry robe stand out behind him like a banner.

For some while he remained before the window, motionless, cosmetics streaming from his face in rivulets of pink and buff, while he contemplated the tamarind he had caused to be planted there twenty years previously. It was taller already than many buildings called lofty; its glossy, rain-washed leaves brushed the windowframe and now even, by the width of a child's hand, sidled into his bedchamber like so many timid sibyls, confident of welcome yet habitually shy. Their parent tree, nourished by his own efforts, was of more than sufficient size now, and a fount of joy to him: a sheltering presence, a memorial of home, the highroad to freedom.

Quetzal crossed the room and barred the door, then threw off his sodden robe. Even in this downpour the tree was safer, though he could fly.

The looming presence of the cliff slid over Auk as he sat in the bow, and with it a final whistling gust of icy rain. He glanced up at the beetling rock, then trained his needler on the augur standing to the halyard. "This time you didn't try anything. See how flash you're getting?'' The storm had broken at shadeup and showed no signs of slackening.

Chenille snapped, "Steer for that," and pointed. Chill tricklings from her limp crimson hair merged into a rivulet between her full breasts to flood her naked loins.

At the tiller, the old fisherman touched his cap. "Aye, aye, Scaldin' Scylla."

They had left Limna on Molpsday night. From shadeup to shadelow, the sun had been a torrent of white fire across a dazzling sky; the wind, fair and strong at morning, had veered and died away to a breeze, to an occasional puff, and by the time the market closes, to nothing. Most of that afternoon Auk had spent in the shadow of the sail, Chenille beneath the shelter of the half deck; he and she, like the augur, had gotten badly sunburned just the same.

Night had brought a new wind, foul for their destination. Directed by the old fisherman and commanded to hold ever closer by the major goddess possessing Chenille, they had tacked and tacked and tacked again, Auk and the augur bailing frantically on every reach and often sick, the boat heeling until it seemed the gunnel must go under, a lantern swinging crazily from the masthead and crashing into the mast each time they went about, going out half a dozen times and leaving the three weary men below in deadly fear of ramming or being rammed in the dark.

Once the augur had attempted to snatch Auk's needler from his waistband. Auk had beaten and kicked him, and thrown him over the side into the churning waters of the lake, from which the old fisherman had by a miracle of resource and luck rescued him with a boathook. Shadeup had brought a third wind, this out of the southeast, a storm-wind driving sheet after gray sheet of slanting rain before it with a lash of lightning.

"Down sail!" Chenille shrieked. "Loose that, you idiot! Drop the yard!"

The augur hurried to obey; he was perhaps ten years senior to Auk, with protruding teeth and small, soft hands that had begun to bleed almost before they had left Limna.

After the yard had crashed down, Auk turned in his seat to peer forward at their destination, seeing nothing but rain-wet stone and evoking indignant squawks from the meager protection of his legs. "Come on out," he told Silk's bird. "We're under a cliff here."

"No out!"

Dry by comparison though the foot of the cliff was, and shielded from the wind, it seemed colder than the open lake, reminding Auk forcibly that the new summer tunic he had worn to Limna was soaked, his baggy trousers soaked too, and his greased riding boots full of water.

The narrow inlet up which they glided became narrower yet, damp black rock to left and right rising fifty cubits or more above the masthead. Here and there a freshet, born of the storm, descended in a slender line of silver to plash noisily into the quiet water. The cliffs united overhead, and the iron mast-cap scraped stone.

"She'll go," Chenille told the old fisherman confidently. "The ceiling's higher farther in."

"I'd 'preciate ter raise up that mains'l ag'in, ma'am," the old fisherman remarked almost conversationally, "an' undo them reefs. It'll rot if it don't dry."

Chenille ignored him; Auk gestured toward the sail and stood to the halyard with the augur, eager for any exercise that might warm him.

Oreb hopped onto the gunnel to look about and fluff his damp feathers. "Bird wet!" They were gliding past impressive tanks of white-painted metal, their way nearly spent.

"A *Sacred Window!* It *is!* There's a Window and an altar *right there!* Look!" The augur's voice shook with joy, and he released the halyard. Auk's kick sent him sprawling.

"Got ter break out sweeps, ma'am, if there's more channel."

"Mind your helm. Lay alongside the Window." To the augur Chenille added, "Have you got your knife?"

He shook his head miserably.

"Your sword then," she told Auk. "Can you sacrifice?"

"I've seen it done, Surging Scylla, and I got a knife in my boot. That might work better." As daring as Remora, Auk added, "But a bird? I didn't think you liked birds."

"That?" She spat into the water.

A fender of woven cordage thumped, then ground against stone. Their side lay within a cubit of the natural quay on which the tanks and the Window stood. "Tie us up." Chenille pointed to the augur. "You, too! No, the stern, you idiot. He'll take the bow."

Auk made the halyard fast, then sprang out onto the stone quay. It was wet, and so slimed that he nearly fell; in the watery light of the cavern, he failed to make out the big iron ring at his feet until he stepped on it.

The augur had found his ring sooner. He straightened up. "I—I *am* an *augur*, Savage Scylla. I've sacrificed to you and to all the Nine *many times*. I'd be *delighted*, Savage Scylla. With his knife . . ."

"Bad bird," Oreb croaked. "Gods hate." He flapped his injured wing as if to judge how far it might carry him.

Chenille bounded onto the slippery stone and crooked a finger at the old fisherman. "You. Come up here."

"I oughter—"

"You ought to do what you're told, or I'll have my thug kill you straight off."

It was a relief to Auk to draw his needler again, a return to familiar ground.

"*Scylla!*" the augur gasped. "A *human being*? Really—"

She whirled to confront him. "What were you doing on my boat? Who sent you?"

"Bad cut," Oreb assured her.

The augur drew a deep breath. "I am H-his *Eminence's* prothonotary." He smoothed his sopping robe as if suddenly conscious of his bedraggled appearance. "H-his E-e-eminence desired me to *l-locate* a particular y-y-young woman—"

Auk trained his needler on him.

"Y-you. Tall, red hair, and so forth. I *didn't* know it was you, Savage Scylla." He swallowed and added desperately, "H-his interest was ha-wholly friendly. H-his Eminence—"

"You are to be congratulated, Patera." Chenille's voice was smooth and almost courteous; she had an alarming habit of remaining immobile in attitudes no mere human being could have maintained for more than a few seconds, and she did so now, her pivoting head and glaring eyes seemingly the only living parts of her lush body. "You have succeeded splendidly. Perhaps you identified the previous occupant? You say this woman," she touched her chest, "was described to you?"

The augur nodded rapidly. *"Yes,* Savage Scylla. Fiery hair and—and s-skill with a *knife* and . . ."

Chenille's eyes had rolled backward into her skull until only the whites could be seen. "Your Eminence. Silk addressed him like that. You attended my graduation, Your Eminence."

The augur said hurriedly, "He wished me to *assure* her of our submission. Of the *Chapter's.* To offer our *advice* and *support,* and declare our *loyalty.* Information H-his Eminence had received indicated that—that you'd *g-gone* to the lake with Patera Silk. His Eminence is Patera's *superior.* He—I— we declare our *undying loyalty,* Savage Scylla."

"To Kypris."

There was that in Chenille's tone which rendered the words unanswerable. The augur could only stare at her.

"Bad man," Oreb announced virtuously. "Cut?"

"An augur? I hadn't considered it, but . . ."

The old fisherman hawked and spat. "If'n you're really Scaldin' Scylla, ma'am, I'd like ter say somethin'." He wiped his grizzled mustache on the back of his hand.

"I am Scylla. Be quick. We must sacrifice now if we're to sacrifice at all. My slave will arrive soon."

"I been prayin' and sacrificin' ter you all my life. You an' your pa's the only ones us fishermen pay mind to. I'm not sayin' you owe me anythin'. I got my boat, an' I had a wife and raised the boys. Always made a livin'. What I'm wantin' ter say is when I go you'll be losin' one of your own. It's goin' ter be one less here for you an' ol' Pas. Maybe you figure I took you 'cause the big feller's got his stitchin' gun. Fact is, I'd of took you anywheres on the lake soon as I knowed who you was."

"I must reintegrate myself in Mainframe," Chenille told him. "There may be new developments. Are you through?"

"Pretty nigh. The big feller, he does anythin' you want him, just like what I'd do in his britches. Only he b'longs ter Hierax, ma'am."

Auk started.

"Not ter you nor your pa neither. He maybe don't know it hisself, but he do. His bird an' that needler he's got, an' the big hanger-sword, an' his knife what he tells he's got in his boots, they all show it. You got ter know it better'n me. As fer this augur you're gettin' set ter offer me up, I fished him out o' the lake last night, and t'other day I seen another fished up. They do say—"

"Describe him."

"Yes'm." The old fisherman considered. "You was down in the cuddy then, I guess. When they'd got him out, I seen him look over our way. Lookin' at the bird, seemed like. Pretty young. Tall as the big feller. Yeller hair—"

"Silk!" Auk exclaimed.

"Pulled out of the water, you said?"

The fisherman nodded. "Scup's boat. I've knowed Scup thirty year."

"You may be right," Chenille told him. "You may be too valuable to sacrifice, and one old man is nothing anyway."

She strode toward the Window before whirling to face them again. "Pay attention to what I say, all three of you. In a moment, I'll depart from this whore. My divine essence will pass from her into the Sacred Window that I have caused to be put here, and be reintegrated with my greater divine self in Mainframe. Do you understand me? All of you?"

Auk nodded mutely. The augur knelt, his head bowed.

"Kypris, my mortal enemy and the enemy of my mother, my brothers, and my sisters—of our whole family, in fact—has been mischief-making here in Viron. Already she seems to have won to her side the meager fool this idiot— What's your name, anyhow?"

"Incus, Savage Scylla. I-I'm Patera *Incus.*"

"The fool this idiot calls His Eminence. I don't doubt that she intends to win over my Prolocutor and my Ayuntamiento too, if she can. The four of you, I include the whore after I'm through with her, are to see to it that she fails. Use threats and force and the power of my name. Kill anyone you need to, it won't be held against you. If Kypris returns, do something to get my attention. Fifty or a hundred children should catch my eye, and Viron's got plenty to spare."

She glared at each man in turn. "Questions? Let's hear them now, if there are any. Objections?"

Oreb croaked in his throat, one bright black eye trained warily upon her.

"Good. You're my prophets henceforth. Keep Viron loyal, and you'll have my favor. Believe nothing Kypris may tell you. My slave should be here shortly. He'll carry you there, and assist you. See the Prolocutor and talk to the commissions in the Juzgado. Tell everyone who'll listen about me. Tell them everything I've said to you. I'd hoped that the Ayuntamiento's boat would be in this dock. It usually is. It isn't today, so you'll have to see the councillors for me. The old man can bring you back here. Tell them I mean to sink their boat and drown them all in my lake if my city goes over to Kypris.''

Incus stammered, "A *th-theophany,* S-savage S-s-scylla, w-would—''

"Not convince your councillors. They think themselves too wise. Theophanies may be useful, however. Reintegrated, I may consider them.''

She strode to the damp stone altar and sprang effortlessly to its top.

"I had this built so your Ayuntamiento might offer private sacrifices and, when I chose, confer with me. Not a trace of ash! They'll pay for that as well.

"You." She pointed to Auk. "This augur Silk's plotting to overthrow them for Kypris. Help him, but show him where his duty lies. If he can't see it, kill him. You've my permission to rule yourself as my Caldé in that case. The idiot here can be Prolocutor under similar circumstances, I suppose.''

She faced the Window and knelt. Auk knelt, too, pulling the fisherman down. (Incus was kneeling already.) Clearing his throat, Auk began the prayer that he had bungled upon the Pilgrims' Way, when Scylla had revealed her divine identity. "Behold us, lovely Scylla, woman of the waters—''

Incus and the fisherman joined in. "Behold our love and our need for thee. Cleanse us, O Scylla!''

At the name of the goddess, Chenille threw high her arms with a strangled cry. The dancing colors called the Holy Hues filled the Sacred Window with chestnut and brown, aquamarine, orange, scarlet, and yellow, cerulean blue and a curious shade of rose brushed with drab. And for a moment it seemed to Auk that he glimpsed the sneering features of a girl a year or two from womanhood.

Chenille trembled violently and went limp, slumping to the altar top and rolling off to fall to the dark and slimy stone of the quay.

Oreb fluttered over to her. "God go?"

The girl's face—if it had been a face—vanished into a wall of green water, like an onrushing wave. The Holy Hues returned, first as sun-sparkles on the wave, then claiming the entire Window and filling it with their whirling ballet before fading back to luminescent gray.

"I think so," Auk said. He rose, and discovered that his needler was still in his hand; he thrust it beneath his tunic, and asked tentatively, "You all right, Jugs?"

Chenille moaned.

He lifted her into a sitting position. "You banged your head on the rock, Jugs, but you're going to be all right." Eager to do something for her, but unsure what he should do, he called, "You! Patera! Get some water."

"She throw?"

Auk swung at Oreb, who hopped agilely to one side.

"Hackum?"

"Yeah, Jugs. Right here." He squeezed her gently with the arm that supported her, conscious of the febrile heat of her sunburned skin.

"You came back. Hackum, I'm so glad."

The old fisherman coughed, striving to keep his eyes from Chenille's breasts. "Mebbe it'd be better if me an' him stayed on the boat awhile?"

"We're all going on your boat," Auk told him. He picked up Chenille.

Incus, a battered tin cup of water in his hand, asked, "You intend to *disobey*?"

Auk dodged. "She said to go to the Juzgado. We got to get back to Limna, then there's wagons to the city."

"She was sending someone, sending her slave she said, to

take us there.'' Incus raised the cup and sipped. ''She also said *I* was to be *Prolocutor.*''

The old fisherman scowled. ''This feller she's sendin','' he'll have a boat o' his own. Have ter, ter git out here. What becomes o' mine if we go off with him? She said fer me ter fetch the rest back ter see them councillors, didn't she? How'm I s'posed ter do that if I ain't got my boat?''

Oreb fluttered onto Auk's shoulder. ''Find Silk?''

''You got it.'' Carrying Chenille, Auk strode across the quay to eye the open water between it and the boat; it was one thing to spring from the gunnel to the quay, another to jump from the quay to the boat while carrying a woman taller than most. ''Get that rope,'' he snapped to Incus. ''Pull it closer. You left too much slack.''

Incus pursed his lips. ''We cannot *possibly* disobey the instructions of the goddess.''

''You can stay here and wait for whoever she's sending. Tell him we'll meet up with him in Limna. Me and Jugs are going in Dace's boat.''

The old fisherman nodded emphatically.

''If *you* wish to disobey, my son, *I* will not attempt to prevent you. However—''

Something in the darkness beyond the last tank fell with a crash, and the scream of metal on stone echoed from the walls of the cavern. A new voice, deeper and louder than any merely human voice, roared, *''I bring her! Give her to me!''*

It was that of a talus larger than the largest Auk had ever seen; its virescent bronze face was cast in a grimace of hate, blinding yellow light glared from its eyes, and the oily black barrels of a flamer and a pair of buzz guns jutted from its open mouth. Behind it, the black dark at the back of the cavern had been replaced by a sickly greenish glow.

''I bring her! All of you! Give her to me!'' The talus extended a lengthening arm as it rolled toward them. A steel hand the size of the altar from which she had fallen closed about Che-

nille and plucked her from Auk's grasp; so a child might have snatched a small and unloved doll from the arms of another doll. *"Get on my back! Scylla commands it!"*

A half dozen widely spaced rungs of bent rod laddered the talus's metal flank. Auk scrambled up with the night chough flapping ahead of him; as he gained the top, the talus's huge hand deposited Chenille on the sloping black metal before him.

"Hang on!"

Two rows of bent rods much like the steps of the ladder ran the length of the talus's back. Auk grasped one with his left hand and Chenille with his right. Her eyelids fluttered. "Hackum?"

"Still here."

Incus's head appeared as he clambered up; his sly face looked sick in the watery light. "By—by *Hierax!*"

Auk chuckled.

"You— You— Help me *up.*"

"Help yourself, Patera. You were the one that wanted to wait for him. You won. He's here."

Before Auk had finished speaking, Incus sprang onto the talus's back with astonishing alacrity, apparently impelled by the muscular arm of the fisherman, who clambered up a moment later. "You'd make a dimber burglar, old man," Auk told him.

"Hackum, where are we?"

"In a cave on the west side of the lake."

The talus turned in place, one wide black belt crawling, the other locked. Auk felt the thump of machinery under him.

Puffs of black smoke escaped from the joint between the upright thorax and long wagonlike abdomen to which they clung. It rocked, jerked, and skewed backward. A sickening sidewise skid ended in a geyser of icy water as one belt slipped off the quay. Incus clutched at Auk's tunic as their side of the talus went under, and for a dizzying second Auk saw the boat tossed higher than their heads.

The wave that had lifted it broke over them like a blow, a suffocating, freezing whorl that at once drained away; when Auk opened his eyes again Chenille was sitting up screaming, her dripping face blank with terror.

Something black and scarlet landed with a thump upon his sopping shoulder. "Bad boat! Sink."

It had not, as he saw when the talus heaved itself up onto the quay again; Dace's boat lay on its side, the mast unshipped and tossing like driftwood in the turbulent water.

Huge as a boulder, the talus's head swiveled around to glare at them, revolving until it seemed its neck must snap. *"Five ride! The small may go!"*

Auk glanced from the augur to the fisherman, and from him to the hysterical Chenille, before he realized who was meant. "You can beat the hoof if you want to, bird. He says he won't hurt you if you do."

"Bird stay," Oreb muttered. "Find Silk."

The talus's head completed its revolution, and the talus lunged forward. Yellow light glared back at them, reflected from the curved white side of the last tank, leaving the Sacred Window empty and dead looking behind them. Sallow green lights winked into being just above the talus's helmeted head, and the still-tossing waters of the channel congealed to rough stone as the cavern dwindled to a dim tunnel.

Auk put his arm around Chenille's waist. "Fancy a bit of company, Jugs?"

She wept on, sobs lost in the wind of their passage.

He released her, got out his needler, and pushed back the sideplate; a trickle of gritty water ran onto his fingers, and he blew into the mechanism. "Should be all right," he told Oreb, "soon as it dries out. I ought to put a couple drops of oil on the needles, though."

"Good girl," Oreb informed him nervously. "No shoot."

"Bad girl," Auk explained. "Bad man, too. No shoot. No go away, either."

"Bad bird!"

"Lily." Gently, he kissed Chenille's inflamed back. "Lie down if you want to. Lay your head in my lap. Maybe you can get a little sleep."

As he pronounced the words, he sensed that they came too late. The talus was descending, the tunnel angling downward, if only slightly. The mouths of other tunnels flashed past to left and right, darker even than the damp shiprock walls. Drops of water clinging to the unchanging ceiling gleamed like diamonds, vanishing as they passed.

The talus slowed, and something struck its great bronze head, ringing it like a gong. Its buzz guns rattled and it spat a tongue of blue fire.

Chapter 2

SILK'S BACK!

"It would be better," Maytera Marble murmured to Maytera Mint, "if you did it, sib."

Maytera Mint's small mouth fell open, then firmly closed. Obedience meant obeying, as she had told herself thousands of times; obedience was more than setting the table or fetching a plate of cookies. "If you wish it, Maytera. High Hierax knows I have no voice, but I suppose I must."

Maytera Marble sighed to herself with satisfaction, a *hish* from the speaker behind her lips so soft that no ears but hers could hear it.

Maytera Mint stood, her cheeks aflame already, and studied the congregation. Half or more were certainly thieves; briefly she wondered whether even the images of the gods were safe.

She mounted the steps to the ambion, acutely conscious of the murmur of talk filling the manteion and the steady drum of rain on its roof; for the first time since early spring, fresh smelling rain was stabbing through the god gate to spatter the blackened altartop—though there was less now than there had been earlier.

Molpe, she prayed, Marvelous Molpe, for once let me have a voice. "Some—" Deep breath. "Some of you do not know me . . ."

Few so much as looked at her, and it was apparent that those who did could not hear her. How ashamed that gallant captain who had showed her his sword would be of her now!

Please Kypris! Sabered Sphigx, great goddess of war . . .

There was a strange swelling beneath her ribs; through her mind a swirl of sounds she had never heard and sights she had not seen: the rumbling hoofbeats of cavalry and the booming of big guns, the terrifying roars of Sphigx's lions, the silver voices of trumpets, and the sharp crotaline clatter of a buzz gun. A woman with a blood-stained rag about her head steadied the line: *Form up! Form up! Forward now! Forward! Follow me!*

With a wide gesture, little Maytera Mint drew a sword not even she could see. "*Fri*ends!" Her voice broke in the middle of the word.

Louder, girl! Shake these rafters!

"Friends, some of you don't know who I am. I am Maytera Mint, a sibyl of this manteion." She swept the congregation with her eyes, and saw Maytera Marble applauding silently; the babble of several hundred voices had stilled altogether.

"The laws of the Chapter permit sacrifice by a sibyl when no augur is present. Regrettably, that is the case today at our manteion. Few of you, we realize, will wish to remain. There is another manteion on Hat Street, a manteion well loved by all the gods, I'm sure, where a holy augur is preparing to sacrifice as I speak. Toward the market, and turn left. It's not far."

She waited hopefully, listening to the pattering rain; but not one of the five hundred or so lucky enough to have seats stood, and none of the several hundred standers in the aisles turned to go.

"Patera Silk did not return to the manse last night. As many of you know, Guardsmen came here to arrest him—"

The angry mutter from her listeners was like the growl of some enormous beast.

"That was yesterday, when Kind Kypris, in whose debt we shall always be, honored us for a second time. All of us feel certain that there has been a foolish error. But until Patera Silk comes back, we can only assume that he is under arrest. Patera Gulo, the worthy augur His Cognizance the Prolocutor sent to assist Patera Silk, seems to have left the manse early this morning, no doubt in the hope of freeing him."

Maytera Mint paused, her fingers nervously exploring the chipped stone of the ancient ambion, and glanced down at the attentive worshipers crouched on the floor in front of the foremost bench, and at the patchy curtain of watching faces that filled the narthex arch.

"Thus the duty of sacrifice devolves upon Maytera Marble and me. There are dozens of victims today. There is even an unspotted white bull for Great Pas, such a sacrifice as the Grand Manteion cannot often see." She paused again to listen to the rain, and for a glance at the altar.

"Before we begin, I have other news to give you, and most particularly to those among you who have come to honor the gods not only today but on Scylsday every week for years. Many of you will be saddened by what I tell you, but it is joyful news.

"Our beloved Maytera Rose has gone to the gods, in whose service she spent her long life. For reasons we deem good and proper, we have chosen not to display her mortal remains. That is her casket there, in front of the altar.

"We may be certain that the immortal gods are aware of her exemplary piety. I have heard it said that she was the oldest biochemical person in this quarter, and it may well have been true. She belonged to the last of those fortunate generations for which prosthetic devices remained, devices whose principles are lost even to our wisest. They sustained her life beyond the lives of the children of many she had taught as children, but they could not sustain it indefinitely. Nor would she have wished them to. Yesterday they failed at last, and our beloved sib was freed from the sufferings that old age had brought her, and the toil that was her only solace.''

Some men standing in the aisles were opening the windows there; little rain if any seemed to be blowing in. The storm was over, Maytera Mint decided, or nearly over.

"So our sacrifice this morning is not merely that which we offer to the undying gods each day at this time if a victim is granted us. It is our dear Maytera Rose's last sacrifice, by which I mean that it is not just that of the white bull and the other beasts outside, but the sacrifice of Maytera herself.

"Sacrifices are of two kinds. In the first, we send a gift. In the second, we share a meal. Thus my dear sib and I dare hope it will not shock you when I tell you that my dear sib has taken for her use some of the marvelous devices that sustained our beloved Maytera Rose. Even if we were disposed to forget her, as I assure you we are not, we could never do so now. They will remind us both of her life of service. Though I know that her spirit treads the Aureate Path, I shall always feel that something of her lives on in my sib."

Now, or never.

"We are delighted that so many of you have come to honor her, as it is only right you should. But there are many more outside, men and women, children too, who would honor her if they could, but were unable to find places in our manteion. It seems a shame, for her sake and for the gods' as well.

"There is an expedient, as some of you must surely know, that can be adopted on such occasions as this. It is to move the casket, the altar, and the Sacred Window itself out into the street temporarily."

They would lose their precious seats. She half expected them to riot, but they did not.

She was about to say, "I propose—" but caught herself in time; the decision was hers, the responsibility for it and its execution hers. "That is what we will do today." The thick, leather-bound Chrasmologic Writings lay on the ambion before her; she picked it up. "Horn? Horn, are you here?"

He waved his hand, then stood so she could see him.

"Horn was one of Maytera's students. Horn, I want you to choose five other boys to help you with her casket. The altar and the Sacred Window are both very heavy, I imagine. We will need volunteers to move those."

Inspiration struck. "Only the very strongest men, please. Will twenty or thirty of the strongest men present please come forward? My sib and I will direct you."

Their rush nearly overwhelmed her. Half a minute later, the altar was afloat upon a surging stream of hands and arms, bobbing and rocking like a box in the lake as a human current bore it down the aisle toward the door.

The Sacred Window was more difficult, not because it was heavier, but because the three-hundred-year-old clamps that held it to the sanctuary floor had rusted shut and had to be hammered. Its sacred cables trailed behind it as it, too, was carried out the door, at times spitting the crackling violet fire that vouched for the immanent presence of divinity.

"You did wonderfully, sib. Just wonderfully!" Maytera Marble had followed Maytera Mint out of the manteion; now she laid a hand upon her shoulder. "Taking everything outside for a viaggiatory! However did you think of it?"

"I don't know. It was just that they were still in the street, most of them, and we were in there. And we couldn't let them in as we usually do. Besides," Maytera Mint smiled impishly, "think of all the blood, sib. It would've taken us days to clean up the manteion afterward."

There were far too many victims to pen in Maytera Marble's little garden. Their presenters had been told very firmly that they would have to hold them until it was time to lead them in, with the result that Sun Street looked rather like the beast-sellers quarter in the market. How many would be here, Maytera Mint wondered, if it hadn't been for the rain? She shuddered. As it was, the victims and their presenters looked soaked but cheerful, steaming in the sunshine of Sun Street.

"You're going to need something to stand on," Maytera Marble warned her, "or they'll never hear you."

"Why not here on the steps?" Maytera Mint inquired.

"Friends . . ." To her own ears, her voice sounded weaker than ever here in the open air; she tried to imagine herself a trumpeter, then a trumpet. "Friends! I won't repeat what I said inside. This is Maytera Rose's last sacrifice. I know that she knows what you've done for her, and is glad.

"Now my sib and her helpers are going to build a sacred fire on the altar. We will need a big one today—"

They cheered, surprising her.

"We'll need a big one, and some of the wood will be wet. But the whole sky is going to be our god gate this afternoon, letting in Lord Pas's fire from the sun."

Like so many brightly colored ants, a straggling line of little girls had already begun to carry pieces of split cedar to the altar, where Maytera Marble broke the smallest pieces.

"It is Patera Silk's custom to consult the Writings before sacrificing. Let us do so too." Maytera Mint held up the book and opened it at random.

" 'Whatever it is we are, it is a little flesh, breath, and the ruling part. As if you were dying, despise the flesh; it is blood, bones, and a network, a tissue of nerves and veins. See the breath also, what kind of thing it is: air, and never the same, but at every moment sent out and drawn in. The third is the ruling part. No longer let this part be enslaved, no longer let it be pulled by its strings like a marionette. No longer complain of your lot, nor shrink from the future.'

"Patera Silk has told us often that each passage in the Writings holds two meanings at least." The words slipped out before she realized that she could see only one in this one. Her mind groped frantically for a second interpretation.

"The first seems so clear that I feel foolish explaining it, though it is my duty to explain it. All of you have seen it already, I'm sure. A part, two parts as the Chrasmologic writer would have it, of our dear Maytera Rose has perished. We must not forget that it was the baser part, the part that neither she nor we had reason to value. The better part, the part beloved by the gods and by us who knew her, will never perish. This, then, is the message for those who mourn her. For my dear sib and me, particularly."

Help me! Hierax, Kypris, Sphigx, please help!

She had touched the sword of the officer who had come to arrest Silk; her hand itched for it, and something deep within her, denied until this moment, scanned the crowd.

"I see a man with a sword." She did not, but there were scores of such men. "A fine one. Will you come forward, sir? Will you lend me your sword? It will be for only a moment."

A swaggering bully who presumably believed that she had been addressing him shouldered a path through the crowd. It was a hunting sword, almost certainly stolen, with a shell guard, a stag grip, and a sweeping double-edged blade.

"Thank you." She held it up, the polished steel dazzling in the hot sunshine. "Today is Hieraxday. It is a fitting day for final rites. I think it's a measure of the regard in which the gods held Maytera Rose that her eyes were darkened on a Tarsday, and that her last sacrifice takes place on Hieraxday. But what of us? Don't the Writings speak to us, too? Isn't it Hieraxday for us, as well as for Maytera? We know they do. We know it is.

"You see this sword?" The denied self spoke through her, so that she—the little Maytera Mint who had, for so many years, thought herself the only Maytera Mint—listened with as much amazement as the crowd, as ignorant as they of what her next word might be. "You carry these, many of you. And knives and needlers, and those little lead clubs that nobody sees that strike so hard. And only Hierax himself knows what else. But are you ready to pay the price?"

She brandished the hunting sword above her head. There was a white stallion among the victims; a flash of the blade or some note in her voice made him rear and paw the air, catching his presenter by surprise and lifting him off his feet.

"For the price is death. Not death thirty or forty years from now, but death now! Death today! These things say, *I will not cower to you! I am no slave, no ox to be led to the butcher! Wrong me, wrong the gods, and you die! For I fear not death or you!*"

The roar of the crowd seemed to shake the street.

"So say the Writings to us, friends, at this manteion. That is the second meaning." Maytera Mint returned the sword to its owner. "Thank you, sir. It's a beautiful weapon."

He bowed. "It's yours anytime you need it, Maytera, and a hard hand to hold it."

At the altar, Maytera Marble had poised the shallow bowl of polished brass that caught falling light from the sun. A curl of smoke arose from the splintered cedar, and as Maytera Mint watched, the first pale, almost invisible flame.

Holding up her long skirt, she trotted down the steps to face the Sacred Window with outstretched arms. "Accept, all you gods, the sacrifice of this holy sibyl. Though our hearts are torn, we, her siblings and her friends, consent. But speak to us, we beg, of times to come, hers as well as ours. What are we to do? Your lightest word will be treasured."

Maytera Mint's mind went blank—a dramatic pause until she recalled the sense, though not the sanctioned wording, of the rest of the invocation. "If it is not your will to speak, we consent to that, too." Her arms fell to her sides.

From her place beside the altar, Maytera Marble signaled the first presenter.

"This fine white he-goat is presented to . . ." Once again, Maytera Mint's memory failed her.

"Kypris," Maytera Marble supplied.

To Kypris, of course. The first three sacrifices were all for

Kypris, who had electrified the city by her theophany on Scylsday. But what was the name of the presenter?

Maytera Mint looked toward Maytera Marble, but Maytera Marble was, strangely, waving to someone in the crowd.

"To Captivating Kypris, goddess of love, by her devout supplicant—?"

"Bream," the presenter said.

"By her devout supplicant Bream." It had come at last, the moment she had dreaded most of all. "Please, Maytera, if you'd do it, please . . . ?" But the sacrificial knife was in her hand, and Maytera Marble raising the ancient wail, metal limbs slapping the heavy bombazine of her habit as she danced.

He-goats were supposed to be contumacious, and this one had long, curved horns that looked dangerous; yet it stood as quietly as any sheep, regarding her through sleepy eyes. It had been a pet, no doubt, or had been raised like one.

Maytera Marble knelt beside it, the earthenware chalice that had been the best the manteion could afford beneath its neck.

I'll shut my eyes, Maytera Mint promised herself, and did not. The blade slipped into the white goat's neck as easily as it might have penetrated a bale of white straw. For one horrid moment the goat stared at her, betrayed by the humans it had trusted all its life; it bucked, spraying both sibyls with its lifeblood, stumbled, and rolled onto its side.

"Beautiful," Maytera Marble whispered. "Why, Patera Pike couldn't have done it better himself."

Maytera Mint whispered back, "I think I'm going to be sick," and Maytera Marble rose to splash the contents of her chalice onto the fire roaring on the altar, as Maytera Mint herself had so often.

The head first, with its impotent horns. Find the joint between the skull and the spine, she reminded herself. Good though it was, the knife could not cut bone.

Next the hooves, gay with gold paint. Faster! Faster! They would be all afternoon at this rate; she wished that she had done more of the cooking, though they had seldom had much meat to cut up. She hissed, "You must take the next one, sib. Really, you must!"

"We can't change off now!"

She threw the last hoof into the fire, leaving the poor goat's legs ragged, bloody stumps. Still grasping the knife, she faced the Window as before. "Accept, O Kind Kypris, the sacrifice of this fine goat. And speak to us, we beg, of the days that are to come. What are we to do? Your lightest word will be treasured." She offered a silent prayer to Kypris, a goddess who seemed to her since Scylsday almost a larger self. "Should you, however, choose otherwise . . ."

She let her arms fall. "We consent. Speak to us, we beg, through this sacrifice."

On Scylsday, the sacrifices at Orpine's funeral had been ill-omened to say the least. Maytera Mint hoped fervently for better indicants today as she slit the belly of the he-goat.

"Kypris blesses . . ." Louder. They were straining to hear her. "Kypris blesses the spirit of our departed sib." She straightened up and threw back her shoulders. "She assures us that such evil as Maytera did has been forgiven her."

The goat's head burst in the fire, scattering coals: a presage of violence. Maytera Mint bent over the carcass once more, struggling frantically to recall what little she knew of augury—remarks dropped at odd moments by Patera Pike and Patera Silk, halfhearted lessons at table from Maytera Rose, who had spoken as much to disgust as to teach her.

The right side of the beast concerned the presenter and the augur who presided, the giver and the performer of the sacrifice; the left the congregation and the whole city. This red liver foretold deeds of blood, and here among its tangled veins was a knife, indicating the augur—though she was no augur—and pointing to a square, the square stem of mint almost certainly, and the hilt of a sword. Was she to die by the sword? No, the blade was away from her. She was to hold the sword, but she had already done that, hadn't she?

In the entrails a fat little fish (a bream, presumably) and a jumble of circular objects, necklaces or rings, perhaps. Certainly that interpretation would be welcomed. They lay close to the bream, one actually on top of it, so the time was very near. She mounted the first two steps.

"For the presenter. The goddess favors you. She is well pleased with your sacrifice." The goat had been a fine one, and presumably Kypris would not have indicated wealth had she not been gratified. "You will gain riches, jewels and gold particularly, within a short time."

Grinning from ear to ear, Bream backed away.

"For all of us and for our city, violence and death, from which good will come." She glanced down at the carcass, eager to be certain of the sign of addition she had glimpsed there; but it had gone, if it had ever existed. "That is all that I can see in this victim, though a skilled augur such as Patera Silk could see much more, I'm sure."

Her eyes searched the crowd around the altar for Bream. "The presenter has first claim. If he wishes a share in this meal, let him come forward."

Already the poor were struggling to get nearer the altar. Maytera Marble whispered, "Burn the entrails and lungs, sib!"

It was wise and good and customary to cut small pieces when the congregation was large, and there were two thousand in this one at least; but there were scores of victims, too, and Maytera Mint had little confidence in her own skill. She distributed haunches and quarters, receiving delighted smiles in return.

Next a pair of white doves. Did you share out doves or burn them whole? They were edible, but she remembered that Silk had burned a black cock whole at Orpine's last sacrifice. Birds could be read, although they seldom were. Wouldn't the giver be offended, however, if she didn't read these?

"One shall be read and burned," she told him firmly. "The other we will share with the goddess. Remain here if you would like it for yourself."

He shook his head.

The doves fluttered desperately as their throats were cut.

A deep breath. "Accept, O Kind Kypris, the sacrifice of these fine doves. And speak to us, we beg, of the times that are to come. What are we to do? Your lightest word will be treasured." Had she really killed those doves? She risked a peek at their lifeless bodies. "Should you, however, choose otherwise . . ."

She let her arms fall, conscious that she was getting more blood on her habit. "We consent. Speak to us, we beg, through this sacrifice."

Scraping feathers, skin, and flesh from the first dove's right shoulder blade, she scanned the fine lines that covered it. A bird with outspread wings; no doubt the giver's name was Swan or something of the sort, though she had forgotten it already. Here was a fork on a platter. Would the goddess tell a man he was going to eat dinner? Impossible! A minute drop of blood seemed to have seeped out of the bone. "Plate gained by violence," she announced to the presenter, "but if the goddess has a second message for me, I am too ignorant to read it."

Maytera Marble whispered, "The next presenter will be my son, Bloody."

Who was Bloody? Maytera Mint felt certain that she should recognize the name. "The plate will be gained in conjunction with the next presenter," she told the giver of the doves. "I hope the goddess isn't saying you'll take it from him."

Maytera Marble hissed, "He's bought this manteion, sib."

She nodded without comprehension. She felt hot and sick, crushed by the scorching sunlight and the heat from the blaze on the altar, and poisoned by the fumes of so much blood, as she bent to consider the dove's left shoulder blade.

Linked rings, frequently interrupted.

"Many who are chained in our city shall be set free," she announced, and threw the dove into the sacred fire, startling a little girl bringing more cedar. An old woman was overjoyed to receive the second dove.

The next presenter was a fleshy man nearing sixty; with him was a handsome younger one who hardly came to his shoulder; the younger man carried a cage containing two white rabbits. "For Maytera Rose," the older man said. "This Kypris is for love, right?" He wiped his sweating head with his handkerchief as he spoke, releasing a heavy fragrance.

"She is the goddess of love, yes."

The younger man smirked, pushing the cage at Maytera Mint.

"Well, roses stand for love," the older man said, "I think these should be all right."

Maytera Marble sniffed. "Victims in confinement cannot be accepted. Bloody, have him open that and hand one to me."

The older man appeared startled.

Maytera Marble held up the rabbit, pulling its head back to bare its throat. If there were a rule for rabbits, Maytera Mint had forgotten it; "We'll treat these as we did the doves," she said as firmly as she could.

The older man nodded.

Why, they do everything I tell them, she reflected. They accept anything I say! She struck off the first rabbit's head, cast it into the fire, and opened its belly.

Its entrails seemed to melt in the hot sunshine, becoming

a surging line of ragged men with slug guns, swords, and crude pikes. The buzz gun rattled once more, somewhere at the edge of audibility, as one stepped over a burning rabbit.

She mounted the steps again, groping for a way to begin. "The message is very clear. Extraordinarily clear. Unusual."

A murmur from the crowd.

"We—mostly we find separate messages for the giver and the augur. For the congregation and our city, too, though often those are together. In this victim, it's all together."

The presenter shouted. "Does it say what my reward will be from the Ayuntamiento?"

"Death." She stared at his flushed face, feeling no pity and surprised that she did not. "You are to die quite soon, or at least the presenter will. Perhaps your son is meant."

She raised her voice, listening to the buzz gun; it seemed strange that no one else heard it. "The presenter of this pair of rabbits has reminded me that the rose, our departed sib's nameflower, signifies love in what is called the language of flowers. He is right, and Comely Kypris, who has been so kind to us here on Sun Street, is the author of that language, by which lovers may converse with bouquets. My own name-flower, mint, signifies virtue. I have always chosen to think of it as directing me toward the virtues proper to a holy sibyl. I mean charity, humility, and—and all the rest. But *virtue* is an old word, and the Chrasmologic Writings tell us that it first meant strength and courage in the cause of right."

They stood in awed silence listening to her; she herself listened for the buzz gun, but it had ceased to sound if it had ever really sounded at all.

"I haven't much of either, but I will do the best I can in the fight to come." She looked for the presenter, intending to say something about courage in the face of death, but he had vanished into the crowd, and his son with him. The empty cage lay abandoned in the street.

"For all of us," she told them, "victory!" What silver

voice was this, ringing above the crowd? "We must fight for the goddess! We will win with her help!"

How many remained. Sixty or more? Maytera Mint felt she had not strength enough for even one. "But I have sacrificed too long. I'm junior to my dear sib, and have presided only by her favor." She handed the sacrificial knife to Maytera Marble and took the second rabbit from her before she could object.

A black lamb for Hierax after the rabbit; and it was an indescribable relief to Maytera Mint to watch Maytera Marble receive it and offer it to the untenanted gray radiance of the Sacred Window; to wail and dance as she had so many times for Patera Pike and Patera Silk, to catch the lamb's blood and splash it on the altar—to watch Maytera cast the head into the fire, knowing that everyone was watching Maytera too, and that no one was watching her.

One by one, the lamb's delicate hoofs fed the gods. A swift stroke of the sacrificial knife laid open its belly, and Maytera Marble whispered, "Sib, come here."

Startled, Maytera Mint took a hesitant step toward her; Maytera Marble, seeing her confusion, crooked one of her new fingers. "Please!"

Maytera Mint joined her over the carcass, and Maytera Marble murmured, "You'll have to read it for me, sib."

Maytera Mint glanced up at the senior sibyl's metal face.

"I mean it. I know about the liver, and what tumors mean. But I can't see the pictures. I never could."

Closing her eyes, Maytera Mint shook her head.

"You must!"

"Maytera, I'm afraid."

Not so distant as it had been, the buzz gun spoke again, its rattle followed by the dull boom of slug guns.

Maytera Mint straightened up; this time it was clear that people on the edge of the crowd had heard the firing.

"Friends! I don't know who's fighting. But it would ap-pear—"

A pudgy young man in black was pushing through the crowd, practically knocking down several people in his hurry. Seeing him, she knew the intense relief of passing responsi-bility to someone else. "Friends, neither my dear sib nor I will read this fine lamb for you. Nor need you endure the irregularity of sacrifice by sibyls any longer. Patera Gulo has returned!"

He was at her side before she pronounced the final word, disheveled and sweating in his wool robe, but transported with triumph. "You will, all you people—everybody in the city—have a real augur to sacrifice for you. Yes! But it won't be me. Patera Silk's back!"

They cheered and shouted until she covered her ears.

Gulo raised his arms for silence. "Maytera, I didn't want to tell you, didn't want to worry you or involve you. But I spent most of the night going around writing on walls. Talk-ing to—to people. Anybody who'd listen, really, and getting them to do it, too. I took a box of chalk from the palaestra. *Silk for caldé! Silk for caldé! Here he comes!*"

Caps and scarves flew into the air. *"SILK FOR CALDÉ!"*

Then she caught sight of him, waving, head and shoul-ders emerging from the turret of a green Civil Guard floater—one that threw up dust as all floaters did, but seemed to operate in ghostly silence, so great was the noise.

"I am come!" the talus thundered again. *"In the service of Scylla! Mightiest of goddesses! Let me pass! Or perish!"* Both buzz guns spoke together, filling the tunnel with the wild shrieking of ricochets.

Auk, who had pulled Chenille flat when the shooting began, clasped her more tightly than ever. After a half minute or more the right buzz gun fell silent, then the left. He could hear no answering fire.

Rising, he peered over the talus's broad shoulder. Chems littered the tunnel as far as the creeping lights illuminated it. Several were on fire. "Soldiers," he reported.

"Men fight," Oreb amplified. He flapped his injured wing uneasily. "Iron men."

"The Ayuntamiento," Incus cleared his throat, "must have called out the *Army.*" The talus rolled forward before he had finished, and a soldier cried out as its belts crushed him.

Auk sat down between Incus and Chenille. "I think it's time you and me had a talk, Patera. I couldn't say much while the goddess was around."

Incus did not reply or meet his eyes.

"I got pretty rough with you, and I don't like doing that to an augur. But you got me mad, and that's how I am."

"Good Auk!" Oreb maintained.

He smiled bitterly. "Sometimes. What I'm trying to say, Patera, is I don't want to have to pitch you off this tall ass. I don't want to have to leave you behind in this tunnel. But I will if I got to. Back there you said you went out to the lake looking for Chenille. If you knew about her, didn't you know about me and Silk too?"

Incus seemed to explode. "How can you sit here talking about *nothing* when *men* are *dying* down there!"

"Before I asked you, you looked pretty calm yourself."

Dace, the old fisherman, chuckled.

"I was *praying* for them!"

Auk got to his feet again. "Then you won't mind jumping off to bring 'em the Pardon of Pas."

Incus blinked.

"While you're thinking that over," Auk frowned for effect and felt himself grow genuinely angry, "maybe you could tell me what your jefe wanted with Chenille."

The talus fired, a deafening report from a big gun he had

not realized it possessed; the concussion of the bursting shell followed without an interval.

"You're *correct.*" Incus stood up. His hand trembled as he jerked a string of rattling jet prayer beads from a pocket of his robe. "You're right, because Hierax has *prompted* you to recall *me* to my duty. I—I *go.*"

Something glanced off the talus's ear and ricocheted down the tunnel, keening like a grief-stricken spirit. Oreb, who had perched on the crest of its helmet to observe the battle, dropped into Auk's lap with a terrified squawk. "Bad fight!"

Auk ignored him, watching Incus, who with Dace's help was scrambling over the side of the talus. Behind it, the tunnel stretched to the end of sight, a narrowing whorl of spectral green varied by fires.

When he caught sight of Incus crouched beside a fallen solder, Auk spat. "If I hadn't seen it . . . I didn't think he had the salt." A volley pelted the talus like rain, drowning Dace's reply.

The talus roared, and a gout of blue flame from its mouth lit the tunnel like lightning; a buzz gun supported its flamer with a long, staccato burst. Then the enormous head revolved, an eye emitting a pencil of light that picked out Incus's black robe. *"Return to me!"*

Still bent over the soldier, Incus replied, although Auk could not make out his words. Ever curious, Oreb fluttered up the tunnel toward them. The talus stopped and rolled backward, one of its extensile arms reaching for Incus.

This time his voice carried clearly. *"I'll* get back on if you take *him,* too."

There was a pause. Auk glanced behind him at the metal mask that was the talus's face.

"Can he speak!"

"Soon, I hope. I'm *trying* to repair him."

The huge hand descended, and Incus moved aside for it.

Perched on the thumb, Oreb rode jauntily back to the talus's back. "Still live!"

Dace grunted doubtfully.

The hand swept downward; Oreb fluttered to Auk's shoulder. "Bird home!"

With grotesque tenderness fingers as thick as the soldier's thighs deposited him between bent handholds.

"Still live?" Oreb repeated plaintively.

Certainly it did not seem so. The fallen soldier's arms and legs, of painted metal now scratched and lusterless, lay motionless, bent at angles that appeared unnatural; his metal face, designed as a model of valor, was filled with the pathos that attaches to all broken things. Singled out inquiringly by one of Oreb's bright, black eyes, Auk could only shrug.

The talus rolled forward again as Incus's head appeared above its side. "I'm going to—he's not *dead,*" the little augur gasped. "Not completely."

Auk caught his hand and pulled him up.

"I was—was just reciting the *liturgy,* you know. And I saw— The gods provide us such graces! I looked into his *wound,* there where the chest plate's sprung. They train us, you know, at the schola, to repair Sacred Windows."

Afraid to stand near the edge of the talus's back, he crawled across it to the motionless soldier, pointing. "I was quite good at it. And— And I've had occasion since to—to *help* various chems. *Dying* chems, you understand."

He took the gammadion from about his neck and held it up for Auk's inspection. "This is Pas's voided cross. You've seen it many times, I'm sure. But you can undo the catches and open up a chem with the pieces. *Watch.*"

Deftly he removed the sprung plate. There was a ragged hole near its center, through which he thrust his forefinger. "Here's where a flechette went in."

Auk was peering at the mass of mechanisms the plate had concealed. "I see little specks of light."

"Certainly you do!" Incus was triumphant. "What you're seeing is what *I* saw under this plate when *I* was bringing him the Pardon of Pas. His primary cable had been severed, and those are the ends of the fibers. It's *exactly* as if your spinal cord were cut."

Dace asked, "Can't you splice her?"

"Indeed!" Incus positively glowed. "Such is the mercy of Pas! Such is his *concern* for us, his adopted sons, that here upon the back of this valiant talus is the one man who can *in actual fact* restore him to health and strength."

"So he can kill us?" Auk inquired dryly.

Incus hesitated, his eyes wary, one hand upraised. The talus was advancing even more slowly now, so that the chill wind that had whistled around them before the shooting began had sunk to the merest breeze. Chenille (who had been lying flat on the slanted plate that was the talus's back) sat up, covering her bare breasts with her forearms.

"Why, ah, *no,*" Incus said at last. He took a diminutive black device rather like a pair of very small tongs or large tweezers from a pocket of his robe. "This is an opticsynapter, an *extremely* valuable tool. With it— Well, look there."

He pointed again. "That black cylinder is the triplex, the part corresponding to *your* heart. It's idling right now, but it pressurizes *his* working fluid so that he can move his limbs. The primary cable runs to his microbank—this big silver thing below the triplex—conveying instructions from his postprocessor."

Chenille asked, "Can you really bring him back to life?"

Incus looked frightened. "If he were *dead,* I could not, Superlative Scylla—"

"I'm not her. I'm me." For a moment it seemed that she might weep again. "Just me. You don't even know me, Patera, and I don't know you."

"I don't know you either," Auk said. "Remember that? Only I'd like to meet you sometime. How about it?"

She swallowed, but did not speak.

"Good girl!" Oreb informed them. Neither Incus nor Dace ventured to say anything, and the silence became oppressive.

With an arm of his gammadion, Incus removed the soldier's skull plate. After a scrutiny Auk felt sure had taken half an hour at least, he worked one end of a second gamma between two threadlike wires.

And the soldier spoke: "K-thirty-four, twelve. A-thirty-four, ninety-seven. B-thirty-four . . ."

Incus removed the gamma, telling Dace, "He was *scanning,* do you follow me? It's as if *you* were to consult a physician. He might listen to your chest and tell you to cough."

Dace shook his head. "You make this sojer well, an' he could kill all on board, like the big feller says. I says we shoves him over the side."

"He *won't.*" Incus bent over the soldier again.

Chenille extended a hand to Dace. "I'm sorry about your boat, Captain, and I'm sorry I hit you. Can we be friends? I'm Chenille."

Dace took it in his own large, gnarled hand, then released it to tug the bill of his cap. "Dace, ma'am. I never did hold nothin' agin you."

"Thank you, Captain. Patera, I'm Chenille."

Incus glanced up from the soldier. "You asked whether I could restore *life,* my daughter. He isn't dead, merely unable to actuate those parts that require fluid. He's unable to move his head, his arms, and his legs, in other words. He can *speak,* as you've heard. He *doesn't* because of the shock he's suffered. That is my *considered* opinion. The problem is to reconnect all the severed fibers correctly. Otherwise, he'll move his *arms* when he *intends* to take a step." He tittered.

"I still says—" Dace began.

"In *addition,* I'll attempt to render him *compliant.* For our safety. It's not *legal*, but if we're to do as *Scylla* has commanded . . ." He bent over the recumbent soldier again.

Chenille said, "Hi, Oreb."

Oreb hopped from Auk's shoulder to hers. "No cry?"

"No more crying." She hesitated, nibbling her lower lip. "Other girls are always telling me how tough I am, because I'm so big. I think I better start trying to live up to it."

Incus glanced up again. "Wouldn't you like to borrow my *robe*, my daughter?"

She shook her head. "It hurts if anything touches me, and my back and shoulders are the worst. I've had men see me naked lots. Usually I've had a couple, though, or a pinch of rust. Rust makes it easy." She turned to Auk. "My name's Chenille, Bucko. I'm one of the girls from Orchid's."

Auk nodded, not knowing what to say, and at length said, "I'm Auk. Real pleased, Chenille."

That was the last thing he could remember. He was lying face down on a cold, damp surface, aware of pervasive pain and soft footsteps hastening to inaudibility. He rolled onto his back and sat up, then discovered that blood from his nose was dribbling down his chin.

"Here, trooper." The voice was unfamiliar, metallic and harshly resonant. "Use this."

A wad of whitish cloth was pressed into his hand; he held it gingerly to his face. "Thanks."

From some distance, a woman called, "Is that you?"

"Jugs?"

The tunnel was almost pitch dark to his left, a rectangle of black relieved by a single remote fleck of green. To his right, something was on fire—a shed or a big wagon, as well as he could judge.

The unfamiliar voice asked, "Can you stand up, trooper?"

Still pressing the cloth to his face, Auk shook his head.

There was someone nearer the burning structure, whatever it was: a short stocky figure with one arm in a sling. Others, men with dark and strangely variegated skins . . . Auk blinked and looked again.

They were soldiers, chems that he had sometimes seen in parades. Here they lay dead, their weapons beside them, eerily lit by the flames.

A small figure in black materialized from the gloom and gave him a toothy grin. *"I* had sped you to the *gods,* my son. I see *they* sent you back."

Through the cloth, Auk managed to say, "I don't remember meeting any," then recalled that he had, that Scylla had been their companion for the better part of two days, and that she had not been in the least as he had imagined her. He risked removing the cloth. "Come here, Patera. Have a seat. I got to have a word with you."

"Gladly. *I* must speak with *you,* as well." The little augur lowered himself to the shiprock floor. Auk could see the white gleam of his teeth.

"Was that really Scylla?"

"You know better than *I,* my son."

Auk nodded slowly. His head ached, and the pain made it difficult to think. "Yeah, only I don't know. Was it her, or just a devil pretending?"

Incus hesitated, grinning more toothily than ever. "This is *rather* difficult to explain."

"I'll listen." Auk groped his waistband for his needler; it was still in place.

"My son, if a devil were to *personate* a goddess, it would *become* that goddess, in a way."

Auk raised an eyebrow.

"Or that *god.* Pas, let us say, or *Hierax.* It would run a grave risk of merging into the total god. Or so the science of *theodaimony* teaches us."

"That's abram." His knife was still in his boot as well, his hanger at his side.

"Such are the *facts,* my son." Incus cleared his throat impressively. "That is to say, the facts as far as they can be expressed in purely *human* terms. It's there averred that devils do not often dare to personate the gods for *that very reason,* while the immortal gods, for their part, *never* stoop to personating devils."

"Hornbuss," Auk said. The man with the injured arm was circling the fire. Changing the subject, Auk asked, "That's our talus, ain't it? The soldiers got it?"

The unfamiliar voice said, "That's right, we got it."

Auk turned. There was a soldier squatting behind him. "I'm Auk," Auk said; he had reintroduced himself to Chenille with same words, he remembered, before whatever had happened had happened. He offered his hand.

"Corporal Hammerstone, Auk." The soldier's grip stopped just short of breaking bones.

"Pleased." Auk tried to stand, and would have fallen if Hammerstone had not caught him. "Guess I'm still not right."

"I'm a little rocky myself, trooper."

"Dace and *that young woman* have been after me to have Corporal Hammerstone carry you, my son. I've *resisted* their importunities for *his* sake. He would *gladly* do it if I asked. He and I are the *best of friends.*"

"More than friends," Hammerstone told Auk; there was no hint of humor in his voice. "More than brothers."

"He would do *anything* for me. I'm tempted to *demonstrate* that, though I refrain. I prefer you to think about it for a while, always with some element of *doubt.* Perhaps I'm teasing you, merely *blustering.* What do you think?"

Auk shook his head. "What I think don't matter."

"Exactly. Because you *thought* that you could throw me from that filthy little boat with *impunity.* That I'd *drown,* and you would be well rid of me. We see *now,* don't we, how *misconceived* that was. You have forfeited any right to have your opinions heard with the *slightest* respect."

Chenille strode out of the darkness carrying a long weapon with a cylindrical magazine. "Can you walk now, Hackum? We've been waiting for you."

From his perch on the barrel, Oreb added, "All right?"

"Pretty soon," Auk told them. "What's that you got?"

"A launcher gun." Chenille grounded it. "This is what did for our talus, or that's what we think. Stony showed me how to shoot it. You can look, but don't touch."

Although pain prevented Auk from enjoying the joke, he managed, "Not till I pay, huh?"

She grinned wickedly, making him feel better. "Maybe not even then. Listen here, Patera. You too, Stony. Can I tell all of you what I've been thinking?"

"Smart girl!" Oreb assured them.

Incus nodded; Auk shrugged and said, "I'm not getting up for a while yet. C'mere, bird."

Oreb hopped onto his shoulder. "Bad hole!"

Chenille nodded. "He's right. We heard some real funny noises while I was back there looking for something to shoot, and there's probably more soldiers farther on. There's more lights up that way too though, and that might help."

Hammerstone said, "Not if we want to dodge their patrols."

"I guess not. But the thing is, Oreb could say what he did about anyplace down here, and he wouldn't be wrong. Auk, what I was going to tell you is I used to have a cute little dagger that I strapped onto my leg. It had a blade about as long as my foot, and I thought it was just right. I thought your knife or your needler or whatever should fit you, like shoes. You know what I'm saying?"

He did not, but he nodded nevertheless.

"Remember when I was Scylla?"

"It's whether you remember. That's what I want to know."

"I do a little bit. I remember being Kypris, too, maybe a little better. You didn't know about that, did you, Patera? I was. I was them, but underneath I was still me. I think it's like a donkey feels when somebody rides him. He's still him, Snail or whatever his name is, but he's you, too, going where you want to and doing what you want to do. And if he doesn't want to, he gets kicked till he does it anyhow."

Oreb cocked his head sympathetically. "Poor girl!"

"So pretty soon he gives up. Kick him and he goes, pull up and he stops, not paying a lot of attention either way. It was like that with me. I wanted rust really bad, and I kept thinking about it and how shaggy tired I was. And all at once it was like I'd been dreaming. I was in a manteion in Limna, then up on an altar in a cave and fit for sod. And I didn't remember anything, or if I did I wouldn't think about it. But when I was bumping out to the shrine, up on those high rocks, stuff started coming back. About being Kypris, I mean."

Incus sighed. "*Scylla* mentioned it, my daughter, so I did know. Sharing your *body* with the *goddess of love!* How I *envy* you! It must have been *wonderful!*"

"I guess it was. It wasn't nice. It wasn't fun at all. But the more I think, the more I think it really was wonderful in a abram sort of way. I'm not exactly like I used to be, either. I think when they left, the goddesses must have left some crumbs behind, and maybe they took some with them, too."

She picked up the launcher, running her fingers along the pins protruding from its magazine. "What I started to say was that after the talus got hit I saw I'd been wrong about things fitting, my dagger and all that. This stuff isn't really like shoes at all. The smaller somebody is, the bigger a shiv she needs. Scylla left that behind, I think, or maybe something I could use to see it myself.

"Anyway, Auk here plucks a dimber needler, but I doubt he needs it much. If I lived the way he does, and I close to do, I'd need it just about every day. So I found this launcher gun, and it's bigger. It was empty, but I found another one with the barrel flat where the talus had gone over it, and it was full. Stony showed me how you load and unload them."

Auk said, "I think I'll get something myself, a slug gun, anyhow. There's probably a bunch of 'em lying around."

Incus shook his head and reached for Auk's waist. "You'd better allow me to take your needler this time, my son."

At once Auk's arms were pinned from behind by a grip that was quite literally of steel.

With evident distaste, Incus lifted the front of Auk's tunic and took his needler from his waistband. "This wouldn't harm Corporal Hammerstone, but it would *kill* me, I suppose." He gave Auk a toothy smile. "Or *you*, my son."

"No shoot," Oreb muttered; it was a moment or two before Auk understood that he was addressing Chenille.

"If you see him with a *slug gun*, Corporal, you're to take it from him and break it *immediately*. A slug gun or any other such weapon."

"Ahoy, Ahoy there!" The old fisherman was shouting and waving, silhouetted by orange flames from the burning talus. *"He says he's dyin'! Wants to talk to us!"*

Silk lifted himself until he could sit almost comfortably upon the turret, then waved both hands. His face was smeared with the mud of the storm, mud that was cracking and falling away now; the gaudy tunic that Doctor Crane had brought him in Limna was daubed with mud as well, and he wondered how many of those who waved and cheered and jumped and shouted around the floater actually recognized him.

SILK FOR CALDÉ!
SILK FOR CALDÉ!

Was there really to be a caldé again, and was this new

caldé to be himself? Caldé was a title that his mother had mentioned occasionally, a carved head in her closet.

He looked up Sun Street, then stared. That was, surely, the silver-gray of a Sacred Window, nearly lost in the bright sunshine—a Window in the middle of the street.

The wind carried the familiar odor of sacrifice—cedar smoke, burning fat, burning hair, and burning feathers, the mixture stronger than that of hot metal, hot fish-oil, and hot dust that wrapped the floater. Before the silver shimmer of the Window, a black sleeve slid down a thin arm of gray metal, and a moment later he caught sight of Maytera Marble's shining, beloved face below the waving, fleshlike hand. It seemed too good to be true.

"Maytera!" In the tumult of the crowd he could scarcely hear his own voice; he silenced them with a gesture, arms out, palms down. *"Quiet! Quiet, please!"*

The noise diminished, replaced by the troubled bleating of sheep and the angry hissing of geese; as the crowd parted before the floater, he located the animals themselves.

"Maytera! You're holding a viaggiatory sacrifice?"

"Maytera Mint is! I'm helping!"

"Patera!" Gulo was back, trotting alongside the floater, his black robe fallow with dust. "There are dozens of victims, Patera! Scores!"

They would have to sacrifice alternately if the ceremony were not to be prolonged till shadelow—which was what Gulo wanted, of course; the glory of offering so many victims, of appearing before so large a congregation. Yet he was not (as Silk reminded himself sharply) asking for more than his due as acolyte. Furthermore, Gulo could begin immediately, while he, Silk, would have to wash and change. "Stop," he called to the driver. "Stop right here." The floater settled to the ground before the altar.

Silk swung his legs from the turret to stand at the edge of the deck before it, admonished by a twinge from his ankle.

"Friends!" A voice he felt he should recognize at once, shrill yet thrilling, rang from the walls of every building on Sun Street. "This is Patera Silk! This is the man whose fame has brought you to the poorest manteion in the city. To the Window through which the gods look upon Viron again!"

The crowd roared approval.

"Hear him! Recall your holy errand, and his!"

Silk, who had identified the speaker at the fourth word, blinked and shook his head, and looked again. Then there was silence, and he had forgotten what he had been about to say.

An antlered stag among the waiting victims (an offering to Thelxiepeia, the patroness of divination, presumably) suggested an approach; his fingers groped for an ambion. "No doubt there are many questions you wish to ask the gods concerning these unsettled times. Certainly there are many questions I need to ask. Most of all, I wish to beg the favor of every god; and most of all to beg Stabbing Sphigx, at whose order armies march and fight, for peace. But before I ask the gods to speak to us, and before I beg their favor, I must wash and change into suitable clothes. I've been in a battle, you see—one in which good and brave men died; and before I return to our manse to scrub my face and hands and throw these clothes into the stove, I must tell you about it."

They listened with upturned faces, eyes wide.

"You must have wondered at seeing me in a Guard floater. Some of you surely thought, when you saw our floater, that the Guard intended to prevent your sacrifice. I know that, because I saw you drawing weapons and reaching for stones. But you see, these Guardsmen have endorsed a new government for Viron."

There were cheers and shouts.

"Or as I should have said, a return to the old one. They wish us to have a caldé—"

"Silk is caldé!" someone shouted.

"—and a return to the forms laid down in our Charter. I encountered some of these brave and devout Guardsmen in Limna, and because I was afraid we might be stopped by other units of the Guard, I foolishly suggested that they pretend I was their prisoner. Many of you will have anticipated what happened as a result. Other Guardsmen attacked us, thinking that they were rescuing me." He paused for breath.

"Remember that. Remember that you must not assume that every Guardsman you see is our enemy, and remember that even those who oppose us are Vironese." His eyes sought out Maytera Marble again. "I've lost my keys, Maytera. Is the garden gate unlocked? I should be able to get into the manse that way."

She cupped her hands (hands that might have belonged to a bio woman) around her mouth. "I'll open it for you, Patera!"

"Patera Gulo, proceed with the sacrifice, please. I'll join you as soon as I can."

Clumsily, Silk vaulted from the floater, trying to put as much weight as he could on his sound left leg; at once he found himself surrounded by well-wishers, some of them in green Civil Guard uniforms, some in mottled green conflict armor, most in bright tunics or flowing gowns, and more than a few in rags; they touched him as they might have touched the image of a god, in speeches blurted in a second or two declared themselves his disciples, partisans, and supporters forever, and carried him along like the rush of a rain-swollen river.

Then the garden wall was at his elbow, and Maytera Marble at the gate waving to him while the Guardsmen swung the butts of the slug guns to keep back the crowd. A voice at his ear said, "I shall come with you, My Caldé. Always now, you must have someone to protect you." It was the captain with whom he had breakfasted at four in the morning in Limna.

The garden gate banged shut behind them; on the other

side Maytera Marble's key grated in the lock. "Stay here," the captain ordered a Guardsman in armor. "No one is to enter." He turned back to Silk, pointed toward the cenoby. "Is that your house, My Caldé?"

"No. It's over there. The triangular one." Belatedly, he realized that it did not appear triangular from the garden; the captain would think him mad. "The smaller one. Patera Gulo won't have locked the door. Potto got my keys."

"Councillor Potto, My Caldé?"

"Yes, Councillor Potto." Yesterday's pain rushed back: Potto's fists and electrodes, Sand's black box. Scrupulous answers that brought further blows and the electrodes at his groin. Silk pushed the memories away as he limped along the graveled path, the captain behind him and five troopers behind the captain, passing the dying fig in whose shadow the animals that were to die for Orpine's spirit had rested, the arbor in which he had spoken to Kypris and chatted with Maytera Marble, her garden and his own blackberries and wilting tomato vines, all in less time than his mind required to recognize and love them.

"Leave your men outside, Captain. They can rest in the shade of the tree beside the gate if they like." Were they doomed, too? From the deck of the floater he had talked of Sphigx; and those who perished in battle were accounted her sacrifices, just as those struck by lightning were said to have been offered to Pas.

The kitchen was exactly as he recalled it; if Gulo had eaten since moving into the manse, he had not done it here. Oreb's water cup still stood on the kitchen table beside the ball snatched from Horn. "If it hadn't happened, the big boys would have won," he murmured.

"I beg pardon, My Caldé?"

"Pay no attention—I was talking to myself." Refusing the captain's offer of help, he toiled at the pump handle until he could splash his face and disorderly yellow hair with cold water that he could not help imagining smelled of the tunnels, soap and rinse them, and rub them dry with a dish towel.

"You'll want to wash up a bit, too, Captain. Please do so while I change upstairs."

The stair was steeper than he remembered; the manse, which he had always thought small, smaller than ever. Seated on the bed that he had left unmade on Molpseday morning, he lashed its wrinkled sheets with Doctor Crane's wrapping.

He had told the crowd he would burn his tunic and loose brown trousers, but although soaked and muddy they were still practically new, and of excellent quality; washed, they might clothe some poor man for a year or more. He pulled the tunic off and tossed it into the hamper.

The azoth he had filched from Hyacinth's boudoir was in the waistband of the trousers. He pressed it to his lips and carried it to the window to examine it again. It had never been Hyacinth's, from what Crane had told him; Crane had merely had her keep it, feeling that her rooms were less likely to be searched than his own. Crane himself had received it from an unnamed khanum in Trivigaunte who had intended it as a gift for Blood. Was it Blood's, then? If so, it must be turned over to Blood without fail. There must be no more theft from Blood; he had gone too far in that direction on Phaesday.

On the other hand, if Crane had been authorized to dispose of it (as it seemed he had), it was his, since Crane had given it to him as Crane lay dying. It might be sold for thousands of cards and the money put to good use—but a moment's self-examination convinced him that he could never exchange it for money if he had any right to it.

Someone in the crowd beyond the garden wall had seen him standing at the window. People were cheering, nudging each other, and pointing. He stepped back, closed the curtains, and examined Hyacinth's azoth again, an object of severe beauty and a weapon worth a company of the Civil Guard—the weapon with which he had slain the talus in the tunnels, and the one she had threatened him with when he would not lie with her.

Had her need really been so great? Or had she hoped to make him love her by giving herself to him, as he had hoped (he recognized the kernel of truth in the thought) to make her love him by refusing? Hyacinth was a prostitute, a woman rented for a night for a few cards—that was to say, for the destruction of the mind of some forsaken, howling monitor like the one in the buried tower. He was an augur, a member of the highest and holiest of professions. So he had been taught.

An augur ready to steal to get just such cards as her body sold for. An augur ready to steal by night from the man from whom he had already bullied three cards at noon. One of those cards had bought Oreb and a cage to keep him in. Would three have bought Hyacinth? Brought her to this old three-sided cage of a manse, with its bolted doors and barred windows?

He placed the azoth on his bureau, put Hyacinth's needler and his beads beside it, and removed his trousers. They were muddier even than the tunic, the knees actually plastered with mud, though their color made their state less obvious. Seeing them, it struck him that augurs might wear black not in order that they might eavesdrop on the gods while concealed by the color of Tartaros, but because it made a dramatic background for fresh blood, and masked stains that could not be washed out.

His shorts, cleaner than the trousers but equally rain-soaked, followed them into the hamper.

Rude people called augurs butchers for good reason, and there was butchery enough waiting for him. Leaving aside his proclivity toward theft, were augurs really any better in the eyes of a god such as the Outsider than a woman like Hyacinth? Could they be better than the people they represented before the gods and still represent them? Bios and chems alike were contemptible creatures in the eyes of the gods, and ultimately those were the only eyes that mattered.

Eyes in the foggy little mirror in which he shaved caught his. As he stared, Mucor's deathly grin coalesced below them; in a travesty of coquetry, she simpered, "This isn't the first time I've seen you with no clothes on."

He spun around, expecting to see her seated on his bed; she was not there.

"I wanted to tell you about my window and my father. You were going to tell him to lock my window so I couldn't get out and bother you any more."

By that time he had recovered his poise. He got clean undershorts from the bureau and pulled them on, then shook his head. "I wasn't. I hoped that I wouldn't have to."

From beyond the bedroom door: *"My Caldé?"*

"I'll be down in a moment, Captain."

"I heard voices, My Caldé. You are in no danger?"

"This manse is haunted, Captain. You may come up and see for yourself if you like."

Mucor tittered. "Isn't this how you talk to them? In the glasses?"

"To a monitor, you mean?" He had been thinking of one; could she read his thoughts? "Yes, it's very much like this. You must have seen them."

"They don't look the same to me."

"I suppose not." With a considerable feeling of relief, Silk pulled on clean black trousers.

"I thought I'd be one for you."

He nodded in recognition of her consideration. "Just as you use your window and the gods their Sacred Windows. I had not thought of the parallel, but I should have."

Unreflected, her face in his mirror bobbed up and down. "I wanted to tell you it's no good any more, telling my father to lock my window. He'll kill you if he sees you, now. Potto said he had to, and he said he would.''

The Ayuntamiento had learned that he was alive and in the city, clearly; it would learn that he was here soon, if it had not already. It would send loyal members of the Guard, might even send soldiers.

"So it doesn't matter. My body will die soon anyway, and I'll be free like the others. Do you care?"

"Yes. Yes, I do. Very much. Why will your body die?"

"Because I don't eat. I used to like it, but I don't any more. I'd rather be free."

Her face had begun to fade. He blinked, and nothing but the hollows that had been her eyes remained. A breath of wind stirred the curtains, and those hollows, too, were gone.

He said, "You must eat, Mucor. I don't want you to die." Hoping for a reply, he waited. "I know you can hear me. You have to eat." He had intended to tell her that he had wronged her and her father. That he would make amends, although Blood might kill him afterward. But it was too late.

Wiping his eyes, he got out his last clean tunic. His prayer beads and a handkerchief went into one trouser pocket, Hyacinth's needler into the other. (He would return it when he could, but that problematic moment at which they might meet again seemed agonizingly remote.) His waistband claimed the azoth; it was possible that augury would provide some hint of what he ought to do with it. He considered selling it again, and thought again of the howling face that had been so like Mucor's in his mirror, and shuddered.

Clean collar and cuffs on his second-best robe would have to do. And here was the captain, waiting at the foot of the stair and looking nearly as spruce as he had in that place— what had it been called? In the Rusty Lantern in Limna.

"I was concerned for your safety, My Caldé."

"For my reputation, you mean. You heard a woman's voice."

"A child's, I thought, My Caldé."

"You may search the upper floor if you wish, Captain. If you find a woman—or a child, either—please let me know."

"Hierax have my bones if I have thought of such a thing, My Caldé!"

"She is a child of Hierax's, certainly."

The Silver Street door was barred, as it should have been; Silk rattled the handle to make certain it was locked as well. The window was shut, and locked behind its bars.

"I can station a trooper in here, if you wish, My Caldé."

Silk shook his head. "We'll need every trooper you have and more, I'm afraid. That officer in the floater—"

"Major Civet, My Caldé."

"Tell Major Civet to station men to give the alarm if the Ayuntamiento sends its troopers to arrest me. They should be a street or two away, I suppose."

"Two streets or more, My Caldé, and there must be patrols beyond them."

"Very well, Captain. Arrange it. I'm willing to stand trial if I must, but only if it will bring peace."

"You are willing, My Caldé. We are not. Nor are the gods."

Silk shrugged and went into the sellaria. The Sun Street door was locked and barred. Two letters on the mantel, one sealed with the Chapter's knife and chalice, one with a flame between cupped hands; he dropped them into the large pocket of his robe. Both the Sun Street windows were locked.

As they hurried through the garden again and into the street, he found himself thinking of Mucor. And of Blood, who had adopted her; then of Highest Hierax, who had dropped from the sky a few hours ago for Crane and the solemn young trooper with whom he and Crane had talked in the Rusty Lantern. Mucor wanted to die, to yield to Hierax;

and he, Silk, would have to save her if he could. Had it been wrong of him, then, to call her a child of Hierax?

Perhaps not. Women as well as men were by adoption the children of the gods, and no other god so suited Mucor.

Chapter 3

A TESSERA FOR THE TUNNEL

"Bad thing," Oreb muttered, watching the burning talus to see whether it could hear him. When it did not react, he repeated more loudly, "Bad thing!"

"Shut up." Auk, too, watched it warily.

Chenille addressed it, stepping forward with her launcher ready. "We'd put out the fire if we could. If we had blankets or—or anything we could beat it out with."

"I die! Hear me!"

"I just wanted to say we're sorry." She glanced back at the four men, and Dace nodded.

"I serve Scylla! You must!"

Incus drew himself up to his full height. "You may rely upon *me* to do everything in my power to carry out the goddess's will. I speak here for my friend Corporal Hammerstone, as well as for myself."

"The Ayuntamiento has betrayed her! Destroy it!"

Hammerstone snapped to attention. "Request permission to speak, Talus."

The slender black barrel of one buzz gun trembled and the gun fired, its burst whistling five cubits above their heads and sending screaming ricochets far down the tunnel.

"Maybe you better not," Auk whispered. He raised his

voice. "Scylla told us Patera Silk was trying to overthrow them, and ordered us to help him. We will if we can. That's Chenille and me, and his bird."

"Tell the Juzgado!"

"Right, she said to." Dace and Incus nodded.

A tongue of flame licked the talus's cheek. *"The tessera! Thetis! To the subcellar . . ."* An interior explosion rocked it.

Needlessly, Auk shouted, "Get back!" As they fled down the tunnel, fire veiled the great metal face.

"She's done fer now! She's goin' down!" Dace was slower even than Auk, who tottered on legs weaker than he had known since infancy.

A second muffled explosion, then silence except for the sibilation of the flames. Hammerstone, who had been matching strides with Auk, broke step to snatch up a slug gun. "This was a sleeper's," he told Auk cheerfully. "See how shiny the receiver is? Probably never been fired. I couldn't go back for mine 'cause I was supposed to watch you. Mine's had about five thousand rounds through it." He put the new slug gun to his shoulder and sighted down the barrel.

Oreb squawked, and Auk said, "Careful there! You might hit Jugs."

"Safety's on." Hammerstone lowered the gun. "You knew her before, huh?"

Auk nodded and slowed his pace enough to allow Dace to catch up. "Since spring, I guess it was."

"I had a girl myself once," Hammerstone told him. "She was a housemaid, but you'd never have guessed it to look at her. Pretty as a picture."

Auk nodded. "What happened?"

"I had to go on reserve. I went to sleep, and when I woke up I wasn't stationed in the city any more. Maybe I should've gone looking for Moly." He shrugged. "Only I figured by then she'd found somebody else. Just about all of them had."

"You'll find somebody, too, if you want to," Auk assured

him. He paused to look back up the tunnel; the talus was still in view but seemed remote, a dot of orange fire no larger than the closest light. "You could be dead," he said. "Suppose Patera hadn't fixed you up?"

Hammerstone shook his head. "I can't ever pay him. I can't even show how much I love him, really. We can't cry. You know about that?"

"Poor thing!" Oreb sounded shocked.

Auk told him, "You can't cry either, cully."

"Bird cry!"

"You meatheads are always talking about how good us chems have it," Hammerstone continued. "Good means not being able to eat, and duty seventy-four, maybe a hundred and twenty, hours at a stretch. Good means sleeping so long the *Whorl* changes, and you got to learn new procedures for everything. Good means seven or eight tinpots after every woman. You want to try it?"

"Shag, no!"

Dace caught Auk's arm. "Thanks for waitin' up."

Auk shook him off. "I can't go all that fast myself."

More cheerfully Hammerstone said, "I could carry you both, only I'm not supposed to. Patera wouldn't like it."

Dace's grin revealed a dark gap from which two teeth were missing. "Mama, don't put me on no boat!"

Auk chuckled.

"He means well," Hammerstone assured them. "He cares about me. That's one reason I'd die for him."

Auk suppressed his first thought and substituted, "Don't you think about your old knot any more? The other soldiers?"

"Sure I do. Only Patera comes first."

Auk nodded.

"You got to consider the whole setup. Our top commander ought to be the caldé. That's our general orders. Only there isn't one, and that means all of us are stuck. Nobody's got the right to give an order, only we do it 'cause we've got to, to keep the brigade running. Sand's my sergeant, see?''

"Uh-huh.''

"And Schist and Shale are privates in our squad. He tells me and I tell them. Then they go sure, Corporal, whatever you say. Only none of us feels right about it.''

"Girl wait?" Oreb inquired. He had been eyeing Chenille's distant, naked back.

"Sooner or later,'' Auk told him. "Snuff your jaw. This is interesting.''

"Take just the other day,'' Hammerstone continued, "I was watching a prisoner. A flap broke and I tried to handle it, and he got away from me. If everything was right, I'd've lost my stripes over that, see? Only it's not, so all I got was a chewing out from Sand and double from the major. Why's that?'' He leveled a pipe-sized finger at Auk, who shook his head.

"I'll tell you. 'Cause both of them know Sand wasn't authorized to give anybody orders in the first place, and I could've told him dee-dee if I'd wanted to.''

"Dee-dee?" Oreb peered quizzically at Hammerstone.

"You want the straight screw? I felt pretty bad when it happened, but it was a lot worse when I was talking to them. Not 'cause of anything they said. I've heard all that till I could sing it. 'Cause they didn't take my stripes. I never thought I'd say that, but that's what it was. They could've done it, only they didn't 'cause they knew they didn't have authority from the caldé, and I kept thinking, you don't have to tell me to wipe them off, I'll wipe them off myself. Only that would just have made them feel worse.''

"I never liked working for anybody but me,'' Auk told him.

"You got to have somebody outside. Or anyhow I do. You feeling pretty good now?''

"Better'n I did.''

"I been watching you, 'cause that's what Patera wants. And you can't hardly walk. You hit your head when the talus bought it, and we figured you were KIA. Patera sort of liked it at first. Only then, not so much. His essential nobility of character coming out. Know what I'm saying?"

Dace put in, "That big gal cryin' an' yellin' at him."

"Yeah, that too. Look here—"

"Wait a minute," Auk told them. "Chenille. She cried?"

Dace chuckled. "I felt sorrier fer her than fer you."

"She wasn't even there when I woke up!"

"She run off. I was over talkin' ter that talus, but I seen her."

"She was around when I came to," Hammerstone told Auk. "She had that launcher, only it was empty. There was another one, all smashed up, where we were. Maybe she brought it, I don't know. Anyhow, after I talked to Patera about you and a couple other things, I showed her how to disarm the bad one's magazine and load the SSMs in the good one."

Dace told Hammerstone, "She got her'n up the tunnel whilst the augur was fixin' you. This big feller, he was off watch, an' didn't nobody know rightly how bad he'd got hurt. When she come back an' seen he wasn't comin' 'round, she foundered."

Auk scratched his ear.

"You've broke your head-bone, big feller, don't let nobody tell you no different. I seen it afore. Feller on my boat got a rap from the boom. He laid in the cuddy couple nights 'fore we could fetch him ashore. He'd open the point an' talk, then sheer off down weather. We fetched him the doctor an' I guess he done all he was able but that feller died next day. You're in luck you wasn't hit no worse."

"What makes it good luck?" Hammerstone asked him.

"Why, stands ter reason, don't it? He don't want ter be dead, no more'n me!"

"All you meatheads talk like that. Only look at it. No more trouble and no more work. No more patrols through these tunnels looking everywhere for nothing and lucky to get a shot at a god. No more—"

"Shot god?" Oreb inquired.

"Yeah," Auk said. "What the shag are you talking about?"

"That's just what we call them," Hammerstone explained. "They're really animals. Kind of like a dog, only ugly where a real dog's all right, so we say it backwards."

"I've never seen any kind of shaggy animal down here."

"You haven't been down here long, either. You just think you have. There's bats and big blindworms, out under the lake especially. There's gods all around here, only there's five of us and me a soldier, and quite a few lights on this stretch. When we get to someplace darker, watch out."

"You don't mind dyin'," Dace reminded him. "That's what you says a little back."

"Now I do." Hammerstone pointed up the tunnel to Incus, a hundred cubits ahead. "That's what I was trying to tell you. Auk said he didn't need an outfit or a leader like Patera, or anything like that."

"I don't," Auk declared. "It's the shaggy truth."

"Then sit down right here. Go to sleep. Dace and me will keep going. You feel pretty sick, I can tell. You don't like walking. Well, there's no reason you've got to. I'll wait till we're about to lose sight of you, then I'll put a couple slugs in you."

"No shoot!" Oreb protested.

"I'll wait till you've settled down, see? You won't know it's coming. You'll get to thinking I'm not going to. What do you say?"

"No thanks."

"All right, here's what I been trying to get across. It doesn't sound that good to you. If I kept on about it, you'd say you had to take care of your girl, even when you're hurt so bad you can't hardly take care of yourself. Or maybe look out for your talking bird or something. Only it'd all be gas, 'cause you really don't want to, even when you know it makes more sense than what you're doing.''

Sick and weak, Auk shrugged. "If you say so."

"It's not like that for us. Just sitting down somewhere down here and letting everything slow down till I go to sleep, and sleeping, with nobody ever coming by to wake me up, that sounds pretty good. It would sound all right to my sergeant, too, or the major. The reason we don't is we're supposed to look out for Viron. That means the caldé, 'cause he's the one that says what's good for Viron and what's not."

"Silk's supposed to be the new caldé," Auk remarked. "I know him, and that's what Scylla said."

Hammerstone nodded. "That'll be great if it happens, but it hasn't happened yet and maybe it never will. Only I've got Patera now, see? Right now I can walk in back of him like this and keep looking at him just about all the time, and he isn't even telling me not to look like he did at first. So I don't want to sit down and die any more than you do."

Oreb bobbed his approval. "Good! Good!"

Farther along the tunnel, Incus asked with some asperity, "Are you *sure* that's all, my daughter?"

"That's everything since Patera Silk shrived me, like I said," Chenille declared, "everything that I remember, anyhow." Apologetically she added, "That was Sphixday, so there wasn't time for a lot, and you said things I did when I was Kypris or Scylla don't count."

"Nor *do* they. The gods *can* do no evil. At least, not on *our* level." Incus cleared his throat and made sure that he was holding his prayer beads correctly. "That being the case, I bring to you, my daughter, the pardon of all the gods. In the name of *Lord Pas,* you are forgiven. In the name of *Divine*

Echidna, you are forgiven. In the *glorious ever-efficacious* name of *Sparkling Scylla, loveliest* of goddesses and *firstborn* of the Seven and *ineffable patroness* of *this,* our—"

"I'm not her any more, Patera. That's lily."

Incus, who had been seized by a sudden, though erroneous, presentiment, relaxed. "You are forgiven. In the name of *Molpe,* you are forgiven. In the name of *Tartaros,* you are forgiven. In the name of *Hierax,* you are forgiven."

He took a deep breath. "In the name of *Thelxiepeia,* you are forgiven. In the name of *Phaea,* you are forgiven. In the name of *Sphigx,* you are forgiven. And in the name of *all lesser gods,* you are forgiven. Kneel now, my daughter. I must trace the sign of addition over your head."

"I'd sooner Auk didn't see. Couldn't you just—"

"Kneel!" Incus told her severely, and by way of merited discipline added, *"Bow* your head!" She did, and he swung his beads forward and back, then from side to side.

"I hope he didn't see me," Chenille whispered as she got to her feet, "I don't think he's jump for religion."

"I dare say *not."* Incus thrust his beads back into his pocket. "While you *are,* my daughter? If that's so, you've deceived me most completely."

"I thought I'd better, Patera. Get you to shrive me, I mean. We could've been killed back there when our talus fought the soldiers. Auk just about was, and the soldiers could have killed us afterwards. I don't think they knew we were on his back, and when he caught fire they were afraid he'd blow up, maybe. If they'd been right, we'd have got killed by that."

"They will return for their *dead,* eventually. I must say the prospect *concerns* me. What if we *encounter* them?"

"Yeah. We're supposed to get rid of the councillors?"

Incus nodded. "So *you,* possessed by Scylla, instructed us, my daughter. We are to displace *His Cognizance* as well."

Incus permitted himself a smile, or perhaps could not resist it. "I am to have the office."

"You know what happens to people that go up against the Ayuntamiento, Patera? They get killed or thrown in the pits. All of them I ever heard of."

Incus nodded gloomily.

"So I thought I'd better get you to do it. Shrive me. I've got a day left, maybe. That's not a whole lot of time."

"Women, and *augurs,* are usually spared the ignominy of execution, my daughter."

"When they go up against the Ayuntamiento? I don't think so. Anyhow, I'd be locked up in the Alambrera or tossed in a pit. They eat the weak ones in the pits."

Incus, a full head shorter than she, looked up at her. "You've *never* struck me as *weak,* my daughter. And you *have* struck me, you know."

"I'm sorry, Patera. It wasn't personal, and anyhow you said it doesn't count." She glanced over her shoulder at Auk, Dace, and Hammerstone. "Maybe we'd better slow down, huh?"

"Gladly!" He had been hard put to keep up with her. "As I said, my daughter, what you did to me is not to be accounted *evil. Scylla* has every right to strike me, as a mother her child. Contrast that with that man *Auk's* behavior toward me. He seized me *bodily* and cast me into the lake."

"I don't remember that."

"Scylla did not order it, my daughter. He acted upon his own *evil impulse,* and were I to be asked to shrive him for it *again,* I am *far* from confident I could bring myself to do so. Do you find him attractive?"

"Auk? Sure."

"I confess *I* thought him a fine specimen when I first saw him. His features are *by no means* handsome, yet his *muscular masculinity* is both real and impressive." Incus sighed. "One *dreams* . . . I mean *a young woman* such as yourself, my daughter, not infrequently dreams of such a man. *Rough,* yet, one hopes, not entirely lacking inner *sensitivity.* When the *actual object* is encountered, however, one is *invariably* disappointed.''

"He lumped me a couple of times while we were hoofing out to that shrine. Did he tell you about that?"

"About visiting a *shrine?*"Incus's eyebrows shot up. "Auk and yourself? No *indeed.*"

"Lumping me, I meant. I thought maybe . . . Never mind. Once I sat down on one of those white rocks, and he kicked me. Kicked my leg, you know. I got pretty sore about that."

Incus shook his head, dismayed at Auk's brutality. "I should imagine *so,* my daughter. I, for one, am disinclined to criticize you for it."

"Only by-and-by I figured it out. See, Kypris had—you know, what Scylla did. It was at Orpine's funeral. Orpine's a dell I used to know." Transfering the launcher to her other hand, Chenille wiped her eyes. "I still feel really bad about her. I always will."

"Your grief does you *credit,* my daughter."

"Now she's lying in a box in the ground, and I'm walking in this one, only mine's a whole lot deeper. I wonder whether this is what being dead seems like to her? Maybe it is."

"Her *spirit* has doubtless united itself with the gods in Mainframe," Incus said kindly.

"Her spirit, sure, but what about her? What do you call this tunnel stuff? They make houses out of it, sometimes."

"The ignorant say *shiprock,* the learned *navislapis.*"

"A big shiprock box. That's what we're in, and we're just as buried as Orpine. What I was going to say is Kypris never told Auk, Patera. Not like Scylla. She told him right away, but he thought Kypris was me, and he liked her a lot. He gave me this ring, see? Then she talked to people in Limna and went in the manteion and went away. Went clear out of me and left me all alone in front of the Window. I was scared to death. I had some money and I kept buying red ribbon—''

"Brandy, my daughter?"

"Yeah. Throwing it down, trying to pretend it was rust because it's about the same color. It took a lot before I got over being scared, and then I still was, a little, way back in my head and deep down in my tripes. Then I saw Auk, this was still in Limna, so I hooked him because I was out of gelt, and I was just some drunk, some old drunk trull. So naturally he lumped me. He never did lump me as hard as Bass did once, and I'm sorry I lumped you. Aren't the gods supposed to care about us, Patera?"

"They *do,* my daughter."

"Well, Scylla didn't. She could've kept me out of the sun and kept my clothes so I wouldn't get so burned. We got hot when I was running for her and they got in our way, so she just tore them off and threw them down. My best winter gown."

Incus cleared his throat. "I have been meaning to speak to you about *that,* my daughter. Your *nudity.* Perhaps I ought to have done so when I shrove you. I foresaw, however, that you might misunderstand. I, *myself,* am sunburned, and nudity *is* wrong, you know."

"It gets bucks hot. Mine does, I mean, or Violet. I saw a buck practically jump the wall once when Violet took off her gown, and she wasn't really naked, either. She had on one of those real good bandeaus that hike up your tits when they look like they're just shoving them back."

"*Nudity,* my daughter," Incus continued gamely, "is wrong not only because it engenders concupiscent thoughts in weak men, but because it is *often* the occasion of *violent* attacks. Concupiscent thoughts are wrong in themselves, as I suggested, though they are not *seriously* evil. Violent *attacks,* on the other hand, *are* seriously evil. In the matter of concupiscent thoughts, the fault lies with you when by *intentional*

nudity you give rise to them. In that of *violent attacks,* the fault
lies with the *attacker.* He is obliged to *restrain* himself, no matter *how severe* a provocation is offered him. But I ask you to
consider, my daughter, whether you wish *any* human spirit to
be rejected by the immortal gods.''

''Getting beat over the head the way they do,'' Chenille
said positively, ''that's the part I'd really hate.''

Incus nodded, gratified. ''There is *that,* as well. You must
consider that the *men* most inclined to these attacks are *by no
means* the most noble of my sex. To the *contrary!* You might
actually be *killed.* Women frequently *are.*''

''I guess you're right, Patera.''

''Oh, I *am,* my daughter. You may *rely* upon it. In our present company, your nudity does *little* harm, I would say. *I,* at
least, am *proof* against it. So is the solder whose life I, by the
grace and aid of *Fairest Phaea,* contrived to save. The captain
of our boat—''

''Dace.''

''Yes, *Dace.* Dace is *also* proof against it, or *nearly* so, I
would imagine, by virtue of his advanced age. *Auk,* of whom I
had entertained the gravest fears for your sake has *now,* by
the intercession of *Divine Echidna,* who ever strives to safe-
guard the chastity of your sex as well as *my own,* been so
severely injured that he is *most unlikely* to attack you or—''

''Auk? He wouldn't have to.''

Incus cleared his throat again. ''I forbear to dispute the
matter, my daughter. Your reason or mine, though I *greatly*
prefer *my own.* But consider this, *also.* We are to enter the
Juzgado, using the tessera the talus supplied. Once there—''

''Is that what we're supposed to do when we get back? I
guess it is, but I haven't been thinking about it, just about
getting Auk to a doctor and all that. I know a good one. And
sitting down and getting somebody nice to wash my feet,
and some powder and rouge and some decent perfume, and

drinks and something to eat. Aren't you hungry, Patera? I'm starving."

"I am not *wholly* unaccustomed to fasting, my daughter. To *revert* to our topic, we are to enter the Juzgado, or so that *talus* informed us as the claws of Hierax closed upon him. His instructions were *Scylla's,* he said, and I credit him. He told us the Ayuntamiento must be *destroyed,* as Scylla *herself* did upon that *unforgettable* occasion when she announced that she has chosen *me* her Prolocutor. The *talus* indicated that we were to announce her decision to the commissioners, and provided a *tessera* by which we are to *penetrate* the subcellar for that purpose. I must confess *I* had not known that such a subcellar existed, but presumably it does. *Consider* then, my daughter, that you will soon—"

"Thetis, that was it, wasn't it? I wondered what he meant when he said that. Does it work like a key? I've heard there are doors like that."

"Ancient doors," Incus informed her. "Doors constructed by *Great Pas* at the time he built the Whorl. The *Prolocutor's Palace* has such a door. Its tessera is known to me, though I may not reveal it."

"Thetis sounds like a god's name. Is it? I don't really know very much about any of the gods except the Nine. And the Outsider. Patera Silk told me a little about him."

"It is *indeed."* Incus glowed with satisfaction. "In the *Writings,* my daughter, the mechanism by which we augurs are chosen is described in *beautiful* though *picturesque* terms. It is there said . . ." He paused. "I regret that I cannot *quote* the passage. I must paraphrase it, I'm afraid. But it is written there that *each* new year Pas brings is like a *fleet.* You are familiar with boats, my daughter. You were upon that *wretched* little fishing boat with *me,* after all."

"Sure."

"Each year, as I have indicated, is likened to a fleet of

boats that are its days, *gallant* craft loaded with the *young men* of that year. Each of these day-boats is *obliged* to pass *Scylla* on its voyage to *infinity*. Some sail very near to her, while others remain at a greater *distance,* their youthful crews crowding the side *most distant* from her loving embrace. None of which *signifies*. From each of these boats, she selects the young men who most *please* her.''

''I don't see—''

''But,'' Incus continued impressively, ''how is it that these *boats* pass her at all? Why do they not remain safe in harbor? Or sail *someplace else?* It is because there is a minor goddess whose function it is to direct them to her. *Thetis* is that goddess, and thus a most suitable *tessera* for us. A *key,* as you said. A *ticket* or *inscribed tile* that will admit *us* to the Juzgado, and incidentally *release* us from the cold and dark of these *horrid* tunnels.''

''You think we might be close to the Juzgado now, Patera?''

Incus shook his head. ''I do not know, my daughter. We traveled *some distance* on that *unfortunate* talus, and he went *very* fast. I dare *hope* we are beneath the city now.''

''I doubt if we're much past Limna,'' Chenille told him.

Auk's head ached. Sometimes it seemed to him that a wedge had been pounded into it, sometimes it felt more like a spike; in either case, it hurt so much at times that he could think of nothing else, forcing himself to take one step forward like an automaton, one more weary step in a progression of weary steps that would never be over. When the ache subsided, as it did now and then, he became aware that he was as sick as he had ever been in his life and might vomit at any moment.

Hammerstone stalked beside him, his big, rubber-shod feet making less noise than Auk's boots as they padded over the damp shiprock of the tunnel floor. Hammerstone had his needler, and when the pain in his head subsided, Auk schemed to recover it, illusory schemes that were more like nightmares. He would push Hammerstone from a cliff into the lake, snatching his needler as Hammerstone fell, trip him as they scaled a roof, break into Hammerstone's house, find him asleep, and take his needler from Hammerstone's strong room. . . . Hammerstone falling headlong, somersaulting, rolling down the roof as he, Auk, fired needle after needle at him, viscous black fluid spurting from every wound to paint the snowy sheets and turn the water of the lake to black blood in which they drowned.

No, Incus had his needler, had it under his black robe; but Hammerstone had a slug gun, and even soldiers could be killed with slugs, which could and often did penetrate the mud-brick walls of houses, the thick bodies of horses and oxen as well as men, slugs that left horrible wounds.

Oreb fluttered on his shoulders, climbing with talon and crimson beak from one to the other. Peering though his ears Oreb glimpsed his thoughts; but Oreb could not know, no more than he himself knew, what those thoughts portended. Oreb was only a bird, and Incus could not take him from him, no more than his hanger, no more than his knife.

Dace had a knife as well. Under his tunic Dace had the old thick-bladed spear-pointed knife he had used to gut and fillet the fish they had caught from his boat, the knife that had worked so quickly, so surely, though it looked so unsuited to its task. Dace was not an old man at all, but a flunky and a toady to that old knife, a thing that carried it as Dace's old boat had carried them all when there was nothing inside it to make it go, carrying them as they might have been carried by a child's toy, toys that can shoot or fly because they are the right shape though hollow and empty as Dace's boat, as crank as the boat or solid as a potato; but Bustard would see to Dace.

His brother Bustard had taken his sling because he had slung stones at cats with it, and had refused to give it back.

Nothing about Bustard had ever been fair, not his being born first though his name began with *B* and Auk's with *A,* not his dying first either. Bustard had cheated to the end and past the end, cheating Auk as he always did and cheating himself of himself. That was the way life was, the way death was. A man lived as long as you hated him and died on you as soon as you began to like him. No one but Bustard had been able to hurt him when Bustard was around; it was a privilege that Bustard reserved for himself, and Bustard was back and carrying him, carrying him in his arms again, though he had forgotten that Bustard had ever carried him. Bustard was only three years older, four in winter. Had Bustard himself been the mother that he, Bustard, professed to remember, that he, Auk, could not? Never could, never quite, Bustard with this big black bird bobbing on his head like a bird upon a woman's hat, its eyes jet beads, twitching and bobbing with every movement of his head, a stuffed bird mocking life and cheating death.

Bustards were birds, but bustards could fly—that was the Lily truth, for Bustard's mother had been Auk's mother had been Lily whose name had meant truth, Lily who had in truth flown away with Hierax and left them both; therefore he never prayed to Hierax, to Death or the God of Death, or anyhow very seldom and never in his heart, though Dace had said that he belonged to Hierax and therefore Hierax had snatched Bustard, the brother who had been a father to him, who had cheated him of his sling and of nothing else that he could remember.

"How you feelin', big feller?"

"Fine. I'm fine," he told Dace. And then, "I'm afraid I'm going to puke."

"Figure you might walk some?"

"It's all right, I'll carry him," Bustard declared, and by the timbre of his harsh baritone revealed Hammerstone the soldier. "Patera said I could."

"I don't want to get it on your clothes," Auk said, and Hammerstone laughed, his big metal body shaking hardly at all, the slug gun slung behind his shoulder rattling just a little against his metal back.

"Where's Jugs?"

"Up there. Up ahead with Patera."

Auk raised his head and tried to see, but saw only a flash of fire, a thread of red fire through the green distance, and the flare of the exploding rocket.

The white bull fell, scarlet arterial blood spilling from its immaculate neck to spatter its gilded hooves. Now, Silk thought, watching the garlands of hothouse orchids slide from the gold leaf that covered its horns.

He knelt beside its fallen head. Now if at all.

She came with the thought. The point of his knife had begun the first cut around the bull's right eye when his own glimpsed the Holy Hues in the Sacred Window: vivid tawny yellow iridescent with scales, now azure, now dove gray, now rose and red and thunderous black. And words, words that at first he could not quite distinguish, words in a voice that might almost have been a crone's, had it been less resonant, less vibrant, less young.

"Hear me. You who are pure."

He had assumed that if any god favored them it would be Kypris. This goddess's unfamiliar features overfilled the Window, her burning eyes just below its top, her meager lower lip disappearing into its base when she spoke.

"Whose city is this, augur?" There was a rustle as all who heard her knelt.

Already on his knees beside the bull, Silk contrived to bow. "Your eldest daughter's, Great Queen." The serpents around her face—thicker than a man's wrist but scarcely larger than hairs in proportion to her mouth, nose, and eyes, and pallid, hollow cheeks—identified her at once. "Viron is Scalding Scylla's city."

"Remember, all of you. You most of all, Prolocutor."

Silk was so startled that he nearly turned his head. Was it possible that the Prolocutor was in fact here, somewhere in this crowd of thousands?

"I have watched you," Echidna said. "I have listened."

Even the few remaining animals were silent.

"This city must remain my daughter's. Such was the will of her father. I speak everywhere for him. Such is my will. Your remaining sacrifices must be for her. For no one else. Disobedience invites destruction."

Silk bowed again. "It shall be as you have said, Great Queen." Momentarily he felt that he was not so much honoring a deity as surrendering to the threat of force; but there was no time to analyze the feeling.

"There is one here fit to lead. She shall be your leader. Let her step forth."

Echidna's eyes, hard and black as opals, had fastened on Maytera Mint. She rose and walked with small, almost mincing steps toward the awful presence in the Window, her head bowed. When she stood beside Silk, that head was scarcely higher than his own, though he was on his knees.

"You long for a sword."

If Maytera Mint nodded, her nod was too slight to be seen.

"You are a sword. Mine. Scylla's. You are the sword of the Eight Great Gods."

Of the thousands present, it was doubtful if five hundred had been able to hear most of what Maytera Marble, or Patera Gulo, or Silk himself had said; but everyone—from men so near the canted altar that their trouser legs were speckled with blood, to children held up by mothers themselves scarcely taller than children—could hear the goddess, could hear the peal of her voice and to a limited degree understand her, Great Echidna, the Queen of the Gods, the highest and most proximal representative of Twice-Headed Pas. As she spoke they stirred like a wheatfield that feels the coming storm.

"The allegiance of this city must be restored. Those who have suborned it must be cast out. This ruling council. Kill them. Restore my daughter's Charter. The strongest place in the city. The prison you call the Alambrera. Pull it down."

Maytera Mint knelt, and again the silver trumpet sounded. "I will, Great Queen!" Silk could hardly believe that it had emanated from the small, shy sibyl he had known.

At her reply the theophany was complete. The white bull lay dead beside him, one ear touching his hand; the Window was empty again, though Sun Street was still filled with kneeling worshipers, their faces blank or dazed or ecstatic. Far away—so distant that he, standing, could not see her—a woman screamed in an agony of rapture.

He raised his hands as he had when he had stood upon the floater's deck. "People of Viron!"

Half, perhaps, showed some sign of having heard.

"We have been honored by the Queen of the Whorl! Echidna herself—"

The words he had planned died in his throat as a searing incandescence smashed down upon the city like a ruinous wall. His shadow, blurred and diffused as shadows had always been under the beneficent radiance of the long sun, solidified to a pitch-black silhouette as sharp as one cut from paper.

He blinked and staggered beneath the weight of the white-hot glare; and when he opened his eyes again, it was no more. The dying fig (whose upper branches could be seen above the garden wall) was on fire, its dry leaves snapping and crackling and sending up a column of sooty smoke.

A gust fanned the flames, twisting and dissolving their smoke column. Nothing else seemed to have changed. A brutal-looking man, still on his knees by the casket before the altar, inquired, "W-was that more word from the gods, Patera?"

Silk took a deep breath. "Yes, it was. That was word from a god who is not Echidna, and I understand him."

Maytera Mint sprang to her feet—and with her a hundred or more; Silk recognized Gayfeather, Cavy, Quill, Aloe, Zoril, Horn and Nettle, Holly, Hart, Oont, Aster, Macaque, and scores of others. The silver trumpet that Maytera Mint's voice had become summoned all to battle. "Echidna has spoken! We have felt the wrath of Pas! To the Alambrera!"

The congregation became a mob.

Everyone was standing now, and it seemed that everyone was talking and shouting. The floater's engine roared. Guardsmen, some mounted, most on foot, called, "To me, everyone!" "To me!" "To the Alambrera!" One fired his slug gun into the air.

Silk looked for Gulo, intending to send him to put out the burning tree; he was already some distance away, at the head of a hundred or more. Others led the white stallion to Maytera Mint; a man bowed with clasped hands, and she sprang onto its back in a way Silk would not have thought possible. It reared, pawing the wind, at the touch of her heels.

And he felt an overwhelming sense of relief. "Maytera! *Maytera!*" Shifting the sacrificial knife to his left hand and forsaking the dignity augurs were expected to exhibit, he ran to her, his black robe billowing in the wind. "Take this!"

Silver, spring-green, and blood-red, the azoth Crane had given him flashed through the air as he flung it over the heads of the mob. The throw was high and two cubits to her left—yet she caught it, as he had somehow known she would.

"Press the bloodstone," he shouted, "when you want the blade!"

A moment later that endless aching blade tore reality as it

swept the sky. She called, "Join us, Patera! As soon as you've completed the sacrifices!"

He nodded, and forced himself to smile.

The right eye first. It seemed to Silk that a lifetime had passed between the moment he had first knelt to extract the eye from its socket and the moment that he laid it in the fire, murmuring Scylla's short litany. By the time he had completed it, the congregation had dwindled to a few old men and a gaggle of small children watched by elderly women, perhaps a hundred persons in all.

In a low and toneless voice, Maytera Marble announced, "The tongue for Echidna. Echidna has spoken to us."

Echidna herself had indicated that the remaining victims were to be Scylla's, but Silk complied. "Behold us, Great Echidna, Mother of the Gods, Incomparable Echidna, Queen of this whorl—" (Were there others, where Echidna was not Queen? All that he had learned in the schola argued against it, yet he had altered her conventional compliment because he felt that it might be so.) "Nurture us, Echidna. By fire set us free."

The bull's head was so heavy that he could lift it only with difficulty; he had expected Maytera Marble to help, but she did not. Vaguely he wondered whether the gold leaf on the horns would merely melt, or be destroyed by the flames in some way. It did not seem likely, and he made a mental note to make certain it was salvaged; thin though gold leaf was, it would be worth something. A few days before, he had been planning to have Horn and some of the others repaint the front of the palaestra, and that would mean buying paint and brushes.

Now Horn, the captain, and the toughs and decent family men of the quarter were assaulting the Alambrera with Maytera Mint, together with boys whose beards had not yet sprouted, girls no older, and young mothers who had never held a weapon; but if they lived . . .

He amended the thought to: if some lived.

"Behold us, lovely Scylla, wonderful of waters, behold our love and our need for thee. Cleanse us, O Scylla. By fire set us free."

Every god claimed that final line, even Tartaros, the god of night, and Scylla, the goddess of water. While he heaved the bull's head onto the altar and positioned it securely, he reflected that "by fire set us free" must once have belonged to Pas alone. Or perhaps to Kypris—love was a fire, and Kypris had possessed Chenille, whose hair was dyed flaming red. What of the fires that dotted the skylands beneath the barren stone plain that was the belly of the Whorl?

Maytera Marble, who should have heaped fresh cedar around the bull's head, did not. He did it himself, using as much as they would have used in a week before Kypris came.

The right front hoof. The left. The right rear and the left, this last freed only after a struggle. Doubtfully, he fingered the edges of his blade; they were still very sharp.

Not to read a victim as large as the bull would have been unthinkable, even after a theophany; he opened the great paunch and studied the entrails. "War, tyranny, and terrible fires." He pitched his voice as low as he dared, hoping that the old people would be unable to hear him. "It's possible I'm wrong. I hope so. Echidna has just spoken to us directly, and surely she would have warned us if such calamities awaited us." In a corner of his mind, Doctor Crane's ghost snickered. *Letters from the gods in the guts of a dead bull, Silk? You're getting in touch with your own subconscious, that's all.*

"More than possible that I'm wrong—that I'm reading my own fears into this splendid victim." Silk elevated his voice. "Let me repeat that Echidna said nothing of the sort." Rather too late, he realized that he had yet to transmit her precise words to the congregation. He did so, interspersing every fact he could recall about her place at Pas's side and her vital role in superintending chastity and fertility. "So you see that Great Echidna simply urged us to free our city. Since those who have left to fight have gone at her behest, we may confidently expect them to triumph."

He dedicated the heart and liver to Scylla.

A young man had joined the children, the old women, and the old men. There was something familiar about him, although Silk, nearsightedly peering at his bowed head, was unable to place him. A small man, his primrose silk tunic gorgeous with gold thread, his black curls gleaming in the sunshine.

The bull's heart sizzled and hissed, then burst loudly—fulminated was the euchologic term—projecting a shower of sparks. It was a sign of civil unrest, but a sign that came too late; riot had become revolution, and it seemed entirely possible that the first to fall in this revolution had fallen already.

Indeed, laughing Doctor Crane had fallen already, and the solemn young trooper. This morning (only this morning!) he had presumed to tell the captain that nonviolent means could be employed to oust the Ayuntamiento. He had envisioned refusals to pay taxes and refusals to work, possibly the Civil Guard arresting and detaining officials who remained obedient to the four remaining councillors. Instead he had helped unleash a whirlwind; he reminded himself gloomily that the whirlwind was the oldest of Pas's symbols, and strove to forget that Echidna had spoken of "the Eight Great Gods."

With a last skillful cut he freed the final flap of hide from the bull's haunch; he tossed it into the center of the altar fire. "The benevolent gods invite us to join in their feast. Freely, they return to us the food we offer them, having made it holy. I take it that the giver is no longer present? In that case, all those who honor the gods may come forward."

The young man in the primrose tunic started toward the

bull's carcass; an old woman caught his sleeve, hissing, "Let the children go first!" Silk reflected that the young man had probably not attended sacrifice since he had been a child himself.

For each, he carved a slice of raw bull-beef, presenting it on the point of the sacrificial knife—the only meat many of these children would taste for some time, although all that remained would be cooked tomorrow for the fortunate pupils at the palaestra.

If there was a tomorrow for the palaestra and its pupils.

The last child was a small girl. Suddenly bold, Silk cut her a piece substantially thicker than the rest. If Kypris had chosen to possess Chenille because of her fiery hair, why had she chosen Maytera Mint as well, as she had confided to him beneath the arbor before they went to Limna? Had Maytera Mint loved? His mind rejected the notion, and yet . . . Had Chenille, who had stabbed Orpine in a nimiety of terror, loved something beyond herself? Or did self-love please Kypris as much as any other sort? She had told Orchid flatly that it did not.

He gave the first old woman an even larger slice. These women, then the old men, then the lone young man, and finally, to Maytera Marble (the only sibyl present) whatever remained for the palaestra and the cenoby's kitchen. Where was Maytera Rose this morning?

The first old man mumbled thanks, thanking him and not the gods; he remembered then that others had done the same thing at Orpine's final rites, and resolved to talk to the congregation about that next Scylsday, if he remained free to talk.

Here was the last old man already. Silk cut him a thick slice, then glanced past him and the young man behind him to Maytera Marble, thinking she might disapprove—and abruptly recognized the young man.

For a moment that seemed very long, he was unable to move. Others were moving, but their motions seemed as labored as the struggles of so many flies in honey. Slowly, Maytera Marble inched toward him, her face back-tilted in a delicate smile; evidently she felt as he did: palaestra tomorrow was worse than problematical. Slowly, the last old man bobbed his head and turned away, gums bared in a toothless grin. Ardently, Silk's right hand longed to enter his trousers pocket, where the gold-plated needler Doctor Crane had given Hyacinth awaited it; but it would have to divest itself of the sacrificial knife first, and that would take weeks if not years.

The flash of oiled metal as Musk drew his needler blended with the duller gleam of Maytera Marble's wrists. The report was drowned by the screech of a wobbling needle, unbalanced by its passage through the sleeve of Silk's robe.

Maytera Marble's arms locked around Musk. Silk slashed at the hand that grasped the needler. The needler fell, and Musk shrieked. The old women were hurrying away (they would call it running), some herding children. A small boy dashed past Silk and darted around the casket, reappearing with Musk's needler precariously clutched in both hands and ridiculously trained upon Musk himself.

Two insights came to Silk simultaneously. The first was that Villus might easily fire by accident, killing Musk. The second, that he, Silk, did not care.

Musk's thumb dangled on a rag of flesh, and blood from his hand mingled with the white bull's. Still trying to comprehend the situation, Silk asked, "He sent you to do this, didn't he?" He pictured the flushed, perspiring face of Musk's employer vividly, although at that moment he could not recall his name.

Musk spat thick, yellow phlegm that clung to Silk's robe as Maytera Marble wrestled him toward the altar. Horribly, she bent him over the flames. Musk spat again, this time into her face, and struggled with such desperate strength that she was lifted off her feet.

Villus asked, "Should I shoot him, Maytera?" When she did not answer, Silk shook his head.

"This fine and living man," she pronounced slowly, "is presented to me, to Divine Echidna." Her hands, the bony blue-veined hands of a elderly bio, glowed crimson in the flames. "Mother of the Gods. Incomparable Echidna, Queen of the *Whorl*. Fair Echidna! Smile upon us. Send us beasts for the chase. Great Echidna! Put forth thy green grass for our kine . . ."

Musk moaned. His tunic was smoking; his eyes seemed ready to start from their sockets.

An old woman tittered.

Surprised, Silk looked for her and from her death's-head grin knew who watched through her eyes. "Go home, Mucor."

The old woman tittered again.

"Divine Echidna!" Maytera Marble concluded. "By fire set us free."

"Release him, Echidna," Silk snapped.

Musk's silk tunic was burning; so were Maytera Marble's sleeves.

"Release him!"

The perverse self-forged discipline of the Orilla broke at last; Musk screamed and continued to scream, each pause and gasp followed by a scream weaker and more terrible. To Silk, tugging futilely at Maytera Marble's relentless arms, those screams seemed the creakings of the wings of death, of the black wings of High Hierax as he flapped down the whorl from Mainframe at the East Pole.

Musk's needler spoke twice, so rapidly it seemed almost to stammer. Its needles scarred Maytera Marble's cheek and chin, and fled whimpering into the sky.

"Don't," Silk told Villus. "You might hit me. It won't do any good."

Villus started, then stared down in astonishment at the dusty black viper that had fastened upon his ankle.

"Don't run," Silk told him, and turned to come to his aid, thereby saving himself. A larger viper pushed its blunt head from Maytera Marble's collar to strike at his neck, missing by two fingers' width.

He jerked the first viper off Villus's ankle and flung it to one side, crouching to mark the punctures made by its fangs with the sign of addition, executed in shallow incisions with the point of the sacrificial knife. "Lie down and stay quiet," he told Villus. When Villus did, he applied his lips to the bleeding crosses.

Musk's screams ceased, and Maytera Marble faced them, her blazing habit slipping from her narrow shoulders; in each hand she brandished a viper. "I have summoned these children to me from the alleys and gardens of this treacherous city. Do you not know who I am?"

The familiarity of her voice left Silk feeling that he had gone mad. He spat a mouthful of blood.

"The boy is mine. I claim him. Give him to me."

Silk spat a second time and picked up Villus, cradling him in his arms. "None but the most flawless may be offered to the gods. This boy has been bitten by a poisonous snake and so is clearly unsuitable."

Twice Maytera Marble waved a viper before her face as if whisking away a fly. "Are you to judge that? Or am I?" Her burning habit fell to her feet.

Silk held out Villus. "Tell me why Pas is angry with us, O Great Echidna."

She reached for him, saw the viper she held as if for the first time, and raised it again. "Pas is dead and you a fool. Give me Auk."

"This boy's name is Villus," Silk told her. "Auk was a boy

like this about twenty years ago, I suppose." When she said nothing more, he added, "I knew you gods could possess bios like us. I didn't know you could possess chems as well."

Echidna whisked the writhing viper before her face. "They are easier what mean these numbers? Why should we let you . . . ? My husband . . ."

"Did Pas possess someone who died?"

Her head swiveled toward the Sacred Window. "The prime calcula . . . His citadel."

"Get away from that fire," Silk told her, but it was too late. Her knees would no longer support her; she crumpled onto her burning habit, seeming to shrink as she fell.

He laid Villus down and drew Hyacinth's needler. His first shot took a viper behind the head, and he congratulated himself; but the other escaped, lost in the scorching yellow dust of Sun Street.

"You're to forget everything you just overheard," he told Villus as he dropped Hyacinth's needler back into his pocket.

"I didn't understand anyway, Patera." Villus was sitting up, hands tight around his bitten leg.

"That's well." Silk pulled her burning habit from under Maytera Marble.

The old woman tittered. "I could kill you, Silk." She was holding the needler that had been Musk's much as Villus had, and aiming it at Silk's chest. "There's councillors at our house now. They'd like that."

The toothless old man slapped the needler from her hand with his dripping slab of raw beef, saying sharply, "Don't, Mucor!" He put his foot on the needler.

As Silk stared, he fished a gammadion blazing with gems from beneath his threadbare brown tunic. "I ought to have made my presence known earlier, Patera, but I'd hoped to do it in private. I'm an augur too, as you see. I'm Patera Quetzal."

*   *   *

Auk stopped and looked back at the last of the bleared green lights. It was like leaving the city, he thought. You hated it—hated its nasty ugly ways, its noise and smoke and most of all its shaggy shitty itch for gelt, gelt for this and gelt for that until a man couldn't fart without paying. But when you rode away from it with the dark closing in on you and skylands you never noticed much in the city sort of floating around up there, you missed it right away and pulled up to look back at it from just about any place you could. All those tiny lights so far away, looking just like the lowest skylands after the market closed, over where it was night already.

From the black darkness ahead, Dace called, "You comin'?"

"Yeah. Don't get the wind up, old man."

He still held the arrow someone had shot at Chenille; its shaft was bone, not wood. A couple long strips of bone, Auk decided, running his fingers along it for the tenth or twelfth time, scarfed and glued together, most likely strips from the shinbone of a big animal or maybe even a big man. The nock end was fletched with feathers of bone, but the wicked barbed point was hammered metal. Country people hunted with arrows and bows, he had heard, and you saw arrows in the market. But not arrows like this.

He snapped it between his hands and let the pieces fall, then hurried down the tunnel after Dace. "Where's Jugs?"

"Up front ag'in with the sojer." Dace sounded as though he was still some distance ahead.

"Well, by Hierax! They almost got her the first time."

"They very nearly killed *me.*" Incus's voice floated back through the darkness. "Have you forgotten *that*?"

"No," Auk told him, "only it don't bother me as much."

"No care," Oreb confirmed from Auk's shoulder.

Incus giggled. "Nor do *you* bother *me,* Auk. When I sent Corporal Hammerstone ahead of us, my *first* thought was that you would have to accompany him. Then I realized that there was no harm in *your* laggling behind. Hammerstone's task is not to *nurse you,* but to protect *me* from your *brutal* treatment.''

''And thresh me out whenever you decide I need it.''

''Indeed. Oh, *indeed.* But *mercy* and *forbearance* are much dearer to the *immortal gods* than sacrifice, Auk. If you wish to stay where you are, *I* will not seek to prevent you. Neither will my tall friend, who is, as we have seen, so much stronger than *yourself.* ''

''Chenille ain't stronger than me, not even now. I doubt she's much stronger than you.''

''But she possesses the best *weapon.* She insisted for *that* reason. For my own part, *I* was glad to have her *and* her weapon near the *redoubtable* corporal, and remote from *yourself.* ''

Auk kicked himself mentally for having failed to realize that the launcher Chenille carried would flatten Hammerstone as effectively as any slug gun. Bitterly he mumbled, ''Always thinking, ain't you.''

''You refuse to call me *Patera,* Auk? Even *now,* you refuse me my title of respect?''

Auk felt weak and dizzy, afraid for Chenille and even for himself; but he managed to say, ''It's supposed to mean you're my father, like Maytera meant this teacher I used to have was my mother. Anytime you start acting like a father, I'll call you that.''

Incus giggled again. ''We *fathers* are expected to curb the violent behavior of our offspring, and to teach them—I *do* hope you'll excuse a trifling bit of vulgarity—to teach them to wipe their *dirty, snotty little noses.* ''

Auk drew his hanger; it felt unaccustomedly heavy in his hand, but the weight and the cold, hard metal of the hilt were reassuring. Hoarsely, Oreb advised, ''No, no!''

Incus, having heard the hiss of the blade as it cleared the scabbard, called, *''Corporal!''*

Hammerstone's voice came from a distance, echoing through the tunnel. "Right here, Patera. I started dropping back as soon as I heard you and him talking."

"Hammerstone has no *light,* I fear. He tells me he lost it when he was *shot.* But he can see in the dark better than *we,* Auk. Better than *any* biological person, in fact."

Auk, who could see nothing in the pitch blackness, said, "I got eyes like a cat."

"Do you really. What have I in my *hand,* in that case?"

"My needler." Auk sniffed; there was a faint stench, as though someone were cooking with rancid fat.

"You're guessing." Hammerstone sounded closer. "You can't see Patera's needler 'cause he's not holding it. You can't see my slug gun either, but I see you and I got it aimed at you. Try to stick Patera with that thing, and I'll shoot you. Put it up or I'll take it away from you and bust it."

Faintly, Auk heard the big soldier's rapid steps. He was running, or at least trotting.

"Bird see," the night chough muttered in Auk's ear.

"You don't have to do that," Auk told Hammerstone. "I'm putting it up." To Oreb he whispered, "Where is he?"

"Come back."

"Yeah, I know. Is he as close as that shaggy butcher?"

"Near men. Men wait."

Auk called, "Hammerstone! Stop! Watch out!"

The running steps halted. "This better be good."

"How many men, bird?"

"Many." The night chough's bill clacked nervously. "Gods too. Bad gods!"

"Hammerstone, listen up! You can't see much better'n Patera. I know that."

"Spit oil!"

"Only I can. Between you and him, there's a bunch of culls, waiting quiet up against the wall. They got—"

The sound that filled the tunnel was half snarl and half

howl. It was followed by a boom from Hammerstone's slug gun, and the ring of a hard blow on metal.

"Hit head," Oreb explained, and elaborated, "Iron man."

Hammerstone fired twice in quick succession, the echoing thunders succeeded by a series of hard, flat reports and the tortured shriekings of ricocheting needles.

"Get down!" Auk reached for a place where he thought Dace might be, but his hand met only air.

A scream. Auk shouted, "I'm coming, Jugs!" and found that he was running already, sprinting sightless through darkness thicker than the darkest night, his hanger blade probing the blackness before him like a beggar's white stick.

Oreb flapped overhead. "Man here!"

Auk slashed wildly again and again, half crouched, still advancing, his left hand groping frantically for the knife in his boot. His blade struck something hard that was not the wall, then bit deep into flesh. Someone who was not Chenille yelped with pain and surprise.

Hammerstone's slug gun boomed, close enough that the flash lit the vicinity like lightning: a naked skeletal figure reeled backward with half its face gone. Auk slashed again and again and again. The third slash met no resistance.

"Man dead!" Oreb announced excitedly. "Cut good!"

"Auk! Auk, help me! Help!"

"I'm coming!"

"Watch out!" Oreb warned, *sotto voce*. "Iron man."

"Get outta my way, Hammerstone!"

From his left, Oreb croaked, "Come Auk."

His blade rang upon metal. He ducked, certain Hammerstone would swing at him. Then he was past, and Oreb exclaiming from some distance, "Here girl! Here Auk! Big fight!"

"Auk! Get him off me!"

A new voice nearly as harsh as Oreb's demanded, "Auk? Auk from the Cock?"

"Shag yes!"

"Pas piss. Wait a minute."

Auk halted. "Jugs, you all right?"

There was no reply.

Someone moaned, and Hammerstone fired again. Auk yelled, "Don't fight unless they do, anybody. Old man, where are you?" His own fighting frenzy had drained away, leaving him weaker and sicker than ever. "Jugs?"

Oreb seconded him. "Girl say. All right? No die?"

"No! I'm not all right." Chenille gasped for breath. "He hit me with something, Auk. He knocked me down and tried to . . . You know. Get it free. I'm pretty beat up, but I'm still alive, I guess."

The darkness faded, as sudden as shadeup and as faint. A dozen stades along the tunnel, one of the crawling lights was slowly rounding a corner. As Auk watched fascinated, it came into full view, a gleaming pinprick that rendered plain all that had been concealed.

Chenille was sitting up some distance away. Seeing Auk, the naked, starved-looking man standing over her raised both hands and backed off. Auk went to her and tried to help her up, discovering (just as Silk had a moment before) that his hand was encumbered by his knife. Gritting his teeth against pain that seemed about to tear his head to bits, he stooped and returned the knife to his boot.

"He grabbed my launcher in the dark. Hit me with a club or something."

Examining her scalp in the dim light, Auk decided the dark splotch was a bleeding bruise. "You're shaggy lucky he didn't kill you."

The naked man smirked. "I could of. I wasn't tryin' to."

"I ought to kill you," Auk told him. "I think I will. Go get your launcher, Jugs."

Behind Auk, Incus said, "He intended to take her by *force,* I dare say. I warned her on that *very* point. To force *any* woman is wrong, my son. To force yourself upon a *prophetess*—" Striding forward, the little augur leveled Auk's big needler. "I *too* am of half a mind to kill you, for *Scylla's* sake."

"Patera got both gods," Hammerstone announced proudly. "A couple of you meatheads, too."

"Wait up, Patera. We got to talk to him." Auk indicated the naked man by a jab of his gory hanger. "What's your name?"

"Urus. Look, Auk, we used to be a dimber knot. Remember that sweatin' ken? You went in through the back while I kept the street for you."

"Yeah. I remember you. You got the pits. That was—" Auk tried to think, but found only pain.

"Only a couple months ago, 'n I got lucky." Urus edged closer, hands supplicating. "If I'd of knowed it was you, Auk, this whole lay would of gone different. We'd of helped you, me 'n my crew. Only I never had no way to know, see? This cully Gelada, all he said was her 'n him." He indicated Chenille and Incus by quick gestures. "A tall piece out of the piece pit 'n a runt cull with her, see, Auk? He never said nothin' about no sojer. Nothin' about you. Soon's I twigged the sojer walkin', I was fit to beat hoof, only by then he was goin' back."

Chenille began, "How come—"

"Because you ain't got anything on, Jugs." Auk sighed. "They take their clothes before they shove 'em in. I thought everybody knew that. Sit down. You too, Patera, Hammerstone. Old man, you coming?"

Oreb added his own throaty summons. "Old man!"

There was no reply from the ebbing darkness.

"Sit down," Auk told them again. "We're all tired out—shaggy Hierax knows I am—and we've probably got a long way to go before we find dinner or a place to sleep. I got a few questions for Urus here. Most likely the rest of you got some too."

"*I* do, certainly."

"All right, you'll get your chance." Auk seated himself gingerly on the cold floor of the tunnel. "First, I ought to tell you that what he said's lily, but it don't mean a lot. I know maybe a hundred culls I can trust a little, only not too much. Before they threw him in the pits, he used to be one of 'em, and that's all it ever was."

Incus and Hammerstone had sat down together as he spoke; cautiously, Urus sat, too, after receiving a permissive nod.

Auk leaned back, his eyes shut and his head spinning. "I said everybody'd get their chance. I only got this one first, then the rest of you can go ahead. Where's Dace, Urus?"

"Who's that?"

"The old man. We had a old man with us, a fisherman. His name's Dace. You do for him?"

"I didn't do for anybody." Urus might have been a league away. Hammerstone's voice: "Why'd they throw you in the pit?" Chenille's: "That doesn't matter now. What are you doing here? That's what I want to know. You're supposed to be in a pit, and you thought I'd been in one. Was it no clothes, like Auk said?" Incus: "My son, I have been *considering* this. You could *hardly* have foreseen that I, an augur, would be *armed*." "I didn't even know you was one. That cully Geiada, he said there was this long mort, and a little cull with her. That's all we knew when we started pullin' lights down." "It was this *Gelada* who shot the bone arrow at *me*, I take it." "Not at you, Patera. At her. She had a launcher, he said, so he shot, only he missed. He's got this bow pasted up out of bones, only he's not as good with it as he thinks. Auk, all I want's to get out, see? You take me up, anyplace, 'n that's it. I'll do anythin' you say.''

"I was wondering," Auk murmured.

Incus: "I *fired* twenty times at least. There were *beastly animals,* and *men* as well." Chenille: "You could've killed all of us, you know that? Just shooting Auk's needler like that in the dark. That was abram." Hammerstone: "Not me." "If I had *not,* my daughter, I might very well have died *myself.* Nor was I firing at *random.* I *knew!* Though I might as well have been *blind.* That was *wonderful.* Truly *miraculous. Scylla* must have been at my side. They *rushed* upon me to kill me, all of them, but *I* killed *them* instead."

Auk opened his eyes to squint into the darkness behind them. "They killed Dace, maybe. I dunno. In a minute I'm going to see."

Chenille prepared to rise. "You feel awful, don't you? I'll go."

"Not now, Jugs. It's still dark back there. Urus, you said your culls took down lights. That was to make a dark stretch here so you could get behind us, right?"

"That's it, Auk. Gelada got up on my shoulders to pull four down, 'n Gaur run them on back. They spread out lookin' for dark. You know about that?"

Auk grunted.

"Only they don't go real fast. So we figured we'd wait flat to the side till you went by. Her, I mean, 'n this runt augur cully. That's all we figured there was." "And jump on me from in back!" "What'd you of done?" (Auk sensed, though he could not see, Urus's outspread hands.) "You shot a rocket at Gelada. If it hadn't been for the bend, you coulda done for our whole knot." "Bad man!" (That was Oreb.)

Auk opened his eyes once more. "Three or four, anyhow. Hammerstone, didn't you say something about a couple animals Patera shot?"

"Tunnel gods," Hammerstone confirmed. "Like dogs, like I told you, only not nice like dogs."

"I got to go back," Auk muttered. "I got to see what's happened to the old man, and I want to have a look at these gods. Urus, you're one, and I did for one, so that makes two. Hammerstone says Patera got a couple, that's four. Anybody else do for any?"

Hammerstone: "Me. One. And one Patera'd shot was still flopping around, so I shot him again."

"Yeah, I think I heard that. So that's five. Urus, don't give me clatter, I'm telling you. How many'd you have?"

"Six, Auk, 'n the two bufes."

"Counting you?"

"That's right, countin' me, 'n that's the lily word."

"I'm going back there," Auk repeated, "soon as the lights get there and I feel better. Anybody that wants to come with me, that's all right. Anybody that wants to go on, that's all right, too. But I'm going to look at the gods and see about Dace." He closed his eyes again.

"Good man!"

"Yeah, bird, he was." Auk waited for someone to speak, but no one did. "Urus, they threw you in the pits. Do they really throw them? I always wondered."

"Only if you get their backs up. If you don't, you can ride down in the basket."

"That's how they feed you? Put your slum in this basket and let it down?"

"'N water jars, sometimes. Only mostly we got to catch our own when it rains."

"Keep talking."

"It ain't as bad as you think. Anyhow mine ain't. Mostly we get along, see? 'N the new ones comin' in are stronger."

"Unless they get thrown. They'd have broken legs and so forth, I guess."

"That's lily, Auk."

"Then you kill 'em right off and eat 'em while they're still fat?"

Someone (Incus, Auk decided) gasped.

"Not all the time, 'n that's lily. Not if it's somebody that somebody knows. We wouldn't of et you, see."

"So you got stuck in a pit, riding down in this basket, and you're a bully cull, or used to be. Found out they'd been digging, didn't you?" Auk opened his eyes, resolving to keep them open.

"That's it. They meant to dig out, see? Over till they fetched the big wall, then down underneath, deep as they had to. Ours is about the deepest, see? One of the real old 'uns 'n one that's near the wall. They'd dig with bones, two culls at once, 'n more carryin' it out in their hands. The rest'd watch for Hoppy 'n tramp it down when it was scattered 'round. They told me all about it."

Hammerstone asked, "You hit this tunnel when you went to go under the wall?"

Urus nodded eagerly. "They did, that's the right of it. They told me. And the shiprock—it's shiprock there, it is in lots of places—it was cracked, see? 'N they scraped the dirt out, hopin' to get through, 'n saw the lights. They got wild then, that's what they said. So they fetched rocks 'n chipped away at the shiprock, just a snowflake, like, for your wap, till you can wiggle through."

Incus grinned, exposing his protruding teeth more than ever. "I *begin* to comprehend your plight, my son. When you had *accessed* these horrid tunnels, you found yourself *unable* to reach the *surface*. Is that not correct? The fact of the matter? *Pas's* justice on you?"

"Yeah, that's it, Patera." With an ingratiating grimace, Urus leaned toward Incus, appearing almost to abase himself. "Only look at it, Patera. You shot a couple friends of mine just a minute ago, didn't you? You didn't lend 'em no horse to Mainframe, did you?"

Incus shook his head, plump cheeks quivering. "I thought it best to let the gods judge for *themselves* in this instance, my son. As I would in *yours,* as well."

"All right, I was fixin' to kill you. That's lily, see? I'm not tryin' to bilk you over it. Only now you 'n me ought to forget about all that, see Patera? Put it right behind us like what Pas'd want us to do. So how about it?" Urus held out his hand.

"My son, when you possess such a needler as *this,* I shall consent to a truce *gladly.*"

Auk chuckled. "How far you gone, Urus? Looking for a way out?"

"Pretty far. Only there's queer cheats in these tunnels, see? 'N there's various ones, too. Some's full of water, or there's cave-ins. Some ends up against doors."

Chenille said, "I can tell you something about the doors, Hackum, next time we're alone."

"That's the dandy, Jugs. You do that." Painfully, Auk clambered to his feet. Seeing that the blade of his hanger was still fouled with blood, he wiped it on the hem of his tunic and sheathed it. "Things in these tunnels, huh? What kinds of things?"

"There's sojers like him down this way." Urus pointed to Hammerstone. "They'll shoot if they see you, so you got to keep listenin' for 'em. That was how I knowed he was a sojer in the dark, see? They don't make much noise, not even when they're marchin', but they don't sound like you 'n me, neither, 'n sometimes you can hear when their guns hit up against 'em. Then there's bufes, what he calls gods, 'n they can be devils. Only this cull Eland caught a couple little 'uns 'n kind of tamed 'em, see? We had 'em with us. There's big machines, sometimes, too. Some's tall asses, only not all. Some won't row you if you don't rouse 'em."

"That all?"

"All I ever seen, Auk. There's stories 'bout ghosts 'n things, but I don't know."

"All right." Auk turned to address Incus, Hammerstone, and Chenille. "I'm going to go back there and have a look for Dace, like I said."

He strolled slowly along the tunnel toward the lingering darkness, not stopping until he reached the point at which the men and beasts shot by Incus lay. Squatting to examine them more closely, he contrived to glance toward the group he had left. No one had followed him, and he shrugged. "Just you and me, Oreb."

"Bad things!"

"Yeah, they sure are. He called 'em bufes, but a bufe's a watchdog, and Hammerstone was right. These ain't real dogs at all."

A crude bludgeon, a stone lashed with sinew to a fire-blackened bone, lay near one of the convicts Incus had shot. Auk picked it up to look at, then tossed it away, wondering how close the man had gotten to Incus before he fell. If Incus had been killed, he, Auk, would have gotten his needler back. But what might Hammerstone have done?

He examined more curiously the one he had cut down with his hanger. He had stolen the hanger originally, had worn it largely for show, had sharpened it once only because he used it now and then to cut rope or prize open drawers, had taken two lessons from Master Xiphias out of curiosity; now he felt that he possessed a weapon he had never known was his.

The radiance of the creeping lights was noticeably dimmer here; it would be some time before the section in which he had left the old fisherman was well lit. He drew his hanger and advanced cautiously. "You sing out if you see anything, bird."

"No see."

"But you can see in this, can't you? Shag, I can see, too. I just can't see good."

"No men." Oreb snapped his bill and fluttered from Auk's right shoulder to his left. "No things."

"Yeah, I don't see much either. I wish I could be sure this was the spot."

Most of all, he wished that Chenille had come. Bustard was walking beside him, big and brawny; but it was not the same. If Chenille had not cared enough to come, there was no point going—no point in anything.

How'd you get yourself into this, sprat, Bustard wanted to know.

"I dunno," Auk muttered. "I forget."

Give me the pure keg, sprat. You want me to winnow you out? If I'm going to help, I got to know.

"Well, I liked him. Patera, I mean. Patera Silk. I think the Ayuntamiento got him. I thought, well, I'll go out to the lake tonight, meet 'em in Limna, and they'll be glad to see me for the gelt, for a dimber dinner and drinks, and maybe a couple uphill rooms for us after. He won't touch her, he's a augur—"

"Bad talk!"

"He's a augur, and she'll have a couple with her dinner and feel like she owes me for it and the ring, owes for both, and it'll be nice."

What'd I tell you about hooking up with some dell, sprat?

"Yeah, sure, brother. Whatever you say. Only then he was gone and she was fuddled, and I got hot and lumped her and went looking. Only everybody say's he's going to be caldé, the new caldé—Patera. That would be somebody to know, if he pulls it off."

"Girl come!"

Never mind that. So now you're going back here, back the way we come, for this Silk butcher?

"Yeah, for Silk, because he'd want me to. And for him, too, for Dace, the old man that owned our boat."

You've snaffled a sackful like him. You don't even have his shaggy boat.

"Patera'd want me to, and I liked him."

This much?

"Hackum? Hackum!"

He's waitin', you know. That buck Gelada's waitin' for us in the dark next to the old man's body, sprat. He had a bow. Didn't any of 'em back there have no bow.

"Girl come," Oreb repeated.

Auk swung around to face her. "Stand clear, Jugs!"

"Hackum, there's something I've got to tell you, but I can't yell it."

"He can see us, Jugs. Only we can't see him. Not even the bird can see him from here where it's brighter, looking into the dark. Where's your launcher?"

"I had to leave it with Stony. Patera didn't want me to go. I think he thought I might try to kill them with it once I got off a ways."

Auk glanced to his right, hoping to consult Bustard; but Bustard had gone.

"So I said, we're not going to do anything like that. We don't hate you. But he said you did."

Auk shook his head, the pain there a crimson haze. "He hates me, maybe. I don't hate him."

"That's what I told him. He said very well my daughter— you know how he talks—leave *that* with us, and I shall believe you. So I did. I gave it to Stony."

"And came after me without it to tell me about the shaggy doors."

"Yes!" She drew nearer as she spoke. "It's important, really important, Hackum, and I don't want that cully that knocked me down to hear it."

"Is it about what the tall ass said?"

Chenille halted, dumbfounded.

"I heard, Jugs. I was right there behind you, and doors are my business. Doors and windows and walls and roofs. You think I'd miss that?"

She shook her head. "I guess not."

"I guess not, too. Stay back where you'll be safe." He turned away, hoping she had not seen how sick and dizzy he was; the darkening tunnel seemed to spin as he stared into its black maw, a pinwheel that had burned out, or the high rear wheel of a deadcoach, all ebony and black iron, rolling down a tarred road to nowhere. "I know you're in there, Gelada, and you got the old man with you. You listen here. My name's Auk, and I'm a pal of Urus's. I'm not here for a row. Only I'm a pal of the old man's, too."

His voice was trailing away. He tried to collect such strength as remained. "What we're going to do pretty soon now, we're going to go back to your pit with Urus."

"Hackum!"

"Shut up." He did not bother to look at her. "That's 'cause I can get you through one of these iron doors down here that you can't solve. I'm going to talk to 'em in your pit. I'm going to say anybody that wants out, you come with me and I'll get you out. Then we'll go to that door and I'll open it, and we'll go on out. Only that's it. I ain't coming back for anybody."

He paused, waiting for some reply. Oreb's bill clacked nervously.

"You and the old man come here and you can come with us. Or let him go and head back to the pit yourself, and you can come along with the rest if you want to. But I'm going to look for him."

Chenille's hand touched his shoulder, and he started.

"You in this, Jugs?"

She nodded and put her arm through his. They had taken perhaps a hundred more steps into the deepening darkness when an arrow whizzed between their heads; she gasped and held him more tightly than ever.

"That's just a warning," he told her. "He could have put it in us if he'd wanted to. Only he won't, because we can get him out and he can't get out himself."

He raised his voice as before. "The old man's finished, ain't he, Gelada? I got you. And you think when I find out, it's all in the tub. That's not how it'll be. Everything I said still goes. We got a augur with us, the little cull you saw with Jugs here when you shot at her. Just give us the old man's body. We'll get him to pray over it and maybe bury it somewhere proper, if we can find a place. I never knew you, but maybe you knew Bustard, my brother. Buck that nabbed the gold Molpe Cup? You want us to fetch Urus? He'll cap for me."

Chenille called, "He's telling the truth, Gelada, really he is. I don't think you're here any more, I think you ran off down the tunnel. That's what I'd have done. But if you are, you can trust Auk. You must have been down in the pit a real long time, because everybody in the Orilla knows Auk now."

"Bird see!" Oreb muttered.

Auk walked slowly into the deepening twilight of the tunnel. "He got his bow?"

"Got bow!"

"Put it down, Gelada. You shoot me, you're shooting the last chance you'll ever get."

"Auk?" The voice from the darkness might have been that of Hierax himself, hollow and hopeless as the echo from a tomb. "That your name? Auk?"

"That's me. Bustard's brother. He was older than me."

"You got a needler? Lay it down."

"I don't have one." Auk sheathed his hanger, pulled off his tunic, and dropped it to the tunnel floor. With uplifted arms, he turned in a complete circle. "See? I got the whin, and that's all I got." He drew his hanger again and held it up. "I'm leaving it right here on my gipon. You can see Jugs don't have anything either. She left her launcher back there with the soldier." Slowly he advanced into the darkness, his hands displayed.

There was a sudden glimmer a hundred paces up the tunnel. "I got a darkee," Gelada called. "Burns bufe drippin's."

He puffed the flame again, and this time Auk could hear the soft exhalation of his breath. "I should've figured," he muttered to Chenille.

"We don't like to use 'um much." Gelada stood, a stick figure not much taller than Incus. "Keep 'um shut up mostly. Wick 'bout snuffed. Culls bring 'um down 'n leave 'um."

When Auk, walking swiftly through the dark, said nothing, he repeated, "Burn drippin's when the oil's gone."

"I was thinking you'd make 'em out of bones," Auk said conversationally. "Maybe twist the wicks out of hair." He was close now, near enough to see Dace's shadowy body lying at Gelada's feet.

"We do that sometimes, too. Only hair's no good. We braid 'um out o' rags."

Auk halted beside the body. "Got him back there, didn't you? His kicks are messed some."

"Dragged 'im far as I could. 'E's a grunter."

Auk nodded absently. Silk had once told him, as the two had sat at dinner in a private room in Viron, that Blood had a daughter, and that Blood's daughter's face was like a skull, was like talking to a skull though she was living and Bustard was dead (Bustard whose face really was a skull now) was not like that. Her father's face, Blood's flabby face, was not like that either, was soft and red and sweating even when he was saying that this one or that one must pay.

But this Gelada's too was a skull, as if he and not Blood were the mort Mucor's father, was as beardless as any skull or nearly, the grayish white of dirty bones even in the stinking yellow light of the dark lantern—a talking cadaver with a little round belly, elbows bigger than its arms, and shoulders like a towel horse, the dark lantern in its hand and its small bow, like a child's bow, of bone wound with rawhide, lying at its feet, with an arrow next to it, with Dace's broad-bladed old knife next to that, and Dace's old head, the old cap it always wore gone, his wild white hair like a crone's and the clean white bones of his arm half-cleaned of flesh and whiter than his old eyes, whiter than anything.

"You crank, Auk?"

"Yeah, a little." Auk crouched beside Dace's body.

"Had the shiv on 'im." Stooping swiftly, Gelada snatched it up. "I'm keepin' it."

"Sure." The sleeve of Dace's heavy, worn blue tunic had been cut away, and strips cut from his forearm and upper arm. Oreb hopped from Auk's shoulder to scrutinze the work, and Auk warned him, "Not your peck."

"Poor bird!"

"Had a couple bits, too. You can have 'um when you get me out."

"Keep 'em. You'll need 'em up there."

From the corner of his eye, Auk saw Chenille trace the sign of addition. "High Hierax, Dark God, God of Death . . ."

"He show much fight?"

"Not much. Got behind 'im. Got my spare string 'round 'is neck. There a art to that. You know Mandrill?"

"Lit out," Auk told him without looking up. "Palustria's what I heard."

"My cousin. Used to work with 'im. How 'bout Elodia?"

"She's dead. You, too." Auk straightened up and drove his knife into the rounded belly, the point entering below the ribs and reaching upward for the heart.

Gelada's eyes and mouth opened wide. Briefly, he sought to grasp Auk's wrist, to push away the blade that had already ended his life. His dark lantern fell clattering to the naked shiprock with Dace's old knife, and darkness rushed upon them.

"Hackum!"

Auk felt Gelada's weight come onto the knife as Gelada's legs went limp. He jerked it free and wiped the blade and his right hand on his thigh, glad that he did not have to look at Gelada's blood at that moment, or meet a dead man's empty, staring eyes.

"Hackum, you said you wouldn't hurt him!"

"Did I? I don't remember."

"He wasn't going to do anything to us."

She had not touched him, but he sensed the nearness of her, the female smell of her loins and the musk of her hair. "He'd already done it, Jugs." He returned his knife to his boot, located Dace's body with groping fingers, and slung it across his shoulders. It felt no heavier than a boy's. "You want to bring that darkee? Could be good if we can figure a way to light it."

Chenille said nothing, but in a few seconds he heard the tinny rattle of the lantern.

"He killed Dace. That'd be enough by itself, only he ate him some, too. That's why he didn't talk at first. Too busy chewing. He knew we'd want the old man's body, and he wanted to fill up."

"He was starving. Starving down here." Chenille's voice was barely above a whisper.

"Sure. Bird, you still around?"

"Bird here!" Feathers brushed Auk's fingers; Oreb was riding atop Dace's corpse.

"If you were starving, you might have done the same thing, Hackum."

Auk did not reply, and she added, "Me, too, I guess."

"It don't signify, Jugs." He was walking faster, striding along ahead of her.

"I don't see why not!"

"Because I had to. He'd have done it too, like I said. We're going to the pit. I told him so."

"I don't like that, either." Chenille sounded as though she were about to weep.

"I got to. I got too many friends that's been sent there, Jugs. If some's in this pit and I can get 'em out, I got to do it. And everybody in the pit's going to find out. Maybe Patera wouldn't tell 'em, if I asked nice. Maybe Hammerstone wouldn't. Only Urus would for sure. He'd say this cull, he did for a pal of Auk's and ate him, too, and Auk never done a thing. When I got 'em out, it'd be all over the city."

A god laughed behind them, faintly but distinctly, the meaningless, humorless laughter of a lunatic; Auk wondered whether Chenille had heard it. "So I had to. And I did it. You would've too, in my shoes."

The tunnel was growing lighter already. Ahead, where it was brighter still, he could see Incus, Hammerstone, and Urus still seated on the tunnel floor, Hammerstone with Chenille's launcher across his steel lap, Incus telling his beads, Urus staring back up the tunnel toward them.

"All right, Hackum."

Here were his hanger and his tunic. He laid down Dace's corpse, sheathed the hanger, and put on his tunic again.

"Man good!" Oreb's beak snapped with appreciation.

"You been eating off him? I told you about that."

"Other man," Oreb explained. "My eyes."

Auk shrugged. "Why not?"

"Let's get out of here. Please, Hackum." Chenille was already several steps ahead.

He nodded and picked up Dace.

"I've got this bad feeling. Like he's still alive back there or something."

"He ain't." Auk reassured her.

As they reached the three who had waited, Incus pocketed his beads. "I would gladly have brought the *Pardon of Pas* to our late comrade. But his spirit has *flown.*"

"Sure," Auk said. "We were just hoping you'd bury him, Patera, if we can find a place."

"It's *Patera* now?"

"And before. I was saying Patera before. You just didn't notice, Patera."

"Oh, but I *did,* my son." Incus motioned for Hammerstone and Ursus to rise. "I would do what I *can* for our unfortunate comrade in any case. Not for your sake, my son, but for *his.*"

Auk nodded. "That's all we're asking, Patera. Gelada's dead. Maybe I ought to tell everybody."

Incus was eyeing Dace's body. "You cannot bear such a weight *far,* my son. Hammerstone will have to carry him, I suppose."

"No," Auk said, his voice suddenly hard. "Urus will. Come're, Urus. Take it."

Chapter 4

THE PLAN OF PAS

"I'm sorry you did that, Mucor," Silk said mildly.

The old woman shook her head. "I wasn't going to kill you. But I could've."

"Of course you could."

Quetzal had picked up the needler; he brushed it with his fingers, then produced a handkerchief with which to wipe off the white bull's blood. The old woman turned to watch him, her eyes widening as her death's-head grin faded.

"I'm sorry, my daughter," Silk repeated. "I've noticed you at sacrifice now and then, but I don't recall your name."

"Cassava." She spoke as though in a dream.

He nodded solemnly. "Are you ill, Cassava?"

"I . . ."

"It's the heat, my daughter." To salve his conscience, he added, "Perhaps. Perhaps it's the heat, in part at least. We should get you out of the sun and away from this fire. Do you think you can walk, Villus?"

"Yes, Patera."

Quetzal held out the needler. "Take this, Patera. You may need it." It was too large for a pocket; Silk put it in his waistband beneath his tunic, where he had carried the azoth. "Farther back, I think," Quetzal told him. "Behind the point of the hip. It will be safer there and just as convenient."

"Yes, Your Cognizance."

"This boy shouldn't walk." Quetzal picked up Villus. "He has poison in his blood at present, and that's no little thing, though we may hope there's only a little poison. May I put him in your manse, Patera? He should be lying down, and this poor woman, too."

"Women are not—but of course if Your Cognizance—"

"They are with my permission," Quetzal told him. "I give it. I also permit you, Patera, to go into the cenoby to fetch a sibyl's habit. Maytera here," he glanced down at Maytera Marble, "may regain consciousness at any moment. We must spare her as much embarrassment as we can." With Villus over his shoulder, he took Cassava's arm. "Come with me, my daughter. You and this boy will have to nurse each other for a while."

Silk was already through the garden gate. He had never set foot in the cenoby, but he thought he had a fair notion of its plan: sellaria, refectory, kitchen, and pantry on the lower floor; bedrooms (four at least, and perhaps as many as six) on the upper floor. Presumably one would be Maytera Marble's, despite the fact that Maytera Marble never slept.

As he trotted along the graveled path, he recalled that the altar and Sacred Window were still in the middle of Sun Street. They should be carried back into the manteion as soon as possible, although that would take a dozen men. He opened the kitchen door and found himself far from certain of even that necessity. Pas was dead—no less a divine personage than Echidna had declared it—and he, Silk, could not imagine himself sacrificing to Echidna again, or so much as attending a sacrifice honoring her. Did it actually matter, save to those gods, if the altar of the gods or the Window through which they so rarely condescended to communicate were ground beneath the wheels of dung carts and tradesmen's wagons?

Yet this was blasphemy. He shuddered.

The cenoby kitchen seemed almost familiar, in part, he decided, because Maytera Marble had often mentioned this stove and this woodbox, these cupboards and this larder; and in part because it was, although cleaner, very much like his own.

Upstairs he found a hall that was an enlarged version of the landing at the top of the stair in the manse, with three faded pictures decorating its walls: Pas, Echidna, and Tartaros bringing gifts of food, progeny, and prosperity (here mawkishly symbolized by a bouquet of marigolds) to a wedding; Scylla spreading her beautiful unseen mantle over a traveler drinking from a pool in the southern desert; and Molpe, perfunctorily disguised as a young woman of the upper classes, approving a much older and poorer woman's feeding pigeons.

Momentarily he paused to examine the last. Cassava might, he decided, have posed for the old woman; he reflected bitterly that the flock she fed could better have fed her, then reminded himself that in a sense they had—that the closing years of her life were brightened by the knowledge that she, who had so little left to give, could still give something.

A door at the end of the hall was smashed. Curious, he went in. The bed was neatly made and the floor swept. There was water in a ewer on the nightstand, so this was certainly Maytera Mint's room or Maytera Rose's, or perhaps the room in which Chenille had spent Scylsday night. An icon of Scylla's hung on the wall, much darkened by the votive lamps of the small shrine before it. And here was—yes—what appeared to be a working glass. This was Maytera Rose's room, surely. Silk clapped, and a monitor's bloodless face appeared in its gray depths.

"Why has Maytera Rose never told me she had this glass?" Silk demanded.

"I have no idea, sir. Have you inquired?"

"Of course not!"

"That may well be the reason, sir."

"If you—" Silk rebuked himself, and found that he was smiling. What was this, compared to the death of Doctor Crane or Echidna's theophany? He must learn to relax, and to think.

When the manteion had been built, a glass must have been provided for the use of the senior sibyl as well as the senior augur; that was natural enough, and in fact praiseworthy. The senior augur's glass, in what was now Patera Gulo's room, was out of order and had been for decades; this one, the senior sibyl's, was still functioning, perhaps only because it had been less used. Silk ran his fingers through his disorderly yellow hair. "Are there more glasses in this cenoby, my son?"

"No, sir."

He advanced a step, wishing that he had a walking stick to lean upon. "In this manteion?"

"Yes, sir. There is one in the manse, sir, but it is no longer summonable."

Silk nodded to himself. "I don't suppose you can tell me whether the Alambrera has surrendered?"

Immediately the monitor's face vanished, replaced by the turreted building and its flanking walls. Several thousand people were milling before the grim iron doors, where a score of men attempted to batter their way in with what seemed to be a building timber. As Silk watched, two Guardsmen thrust slug guns over the parapet of a turret on the right and opened fire.

Maytera Mint galloped into view, her black habit billowing about her, looking no bigger than a child on the broad back of her mount. She gestured urgently, the newfound silver trumpet that was her voice apparently sounding retreat, although Silk could not distinguish her words; the terrible discontinuity that was the azoth's blade sprang from her upraised hand, and the parapet exploded in a shower of stones.

"Another view," the monitor announced smoothly.

From a vantage point that appeared to be fifteen or twenty cubits above the street, Silk found himself looking down at the mob before the doors; some turned and ran; others were still raging against the Alambrera's stone and iron. The sweating men with the timber gathered themselves for a new assault, but one fell before they began it, his face a pulpy mask of scarlet and white.

"Enough," Silk said.

The monitor returned. "I think it safe to say, sir, that the Alambrera has not surrendered. If I may, I might add that in my judgment it is not likely to do so before the arrival of the relief force, sir."

"A relief force is on the way?"

"Yes, sir. The First Battalion of the Second Brigade of the Civil Guard, sir, and three companies of soldiers." The monitor paused. "I cannot locate them at the moment, sir, but not long ago they were marching along Ale Street. Would you care to see it?"

"That's all right. I should go." Silk turned away, then back. "How were you—there's an eye high up on a building on the other side of Cage Street, isn't there? And another over the doors of the Alambrera?"

"Precisely, sir."

"You must be familiar with this cenoby. Which room is Maytera Marble's?"

"Less so than you may suppose, sir. There are no other glasses in this cenoby, sir, as I told you. And no eyes save mine, sir. However, from certain remarks of my mistress's, I infer that it may be the second door on the left, sir."

"By your mistress you mean Maytera Rose? Where is she?"

"Yes, sir. My mistress has abandoned this land of trials

and sorrows for a clime infinitely more agreeable, sir. That is to say, for Mainframe, sir. My lamented mistress has, in short, joined the assembly of the immortal gods.''

''She's dead?''

''Precisely so, sir. As to the present whereabouts of her remains, they are, I believe, somewhat scattered. This is the best I can do, sir.''

The monitor's face vanished again, and Sun Street sprang into view: the altar (from which Musk's fire-blackened corpse had partially fallen); and beyond it, Maytera Marble's naked metal body, sprawled near a coffin of softwood stained black.

''Those were her final rites,'' Silk muttered to himself. ''Maytera Rose's last sacrifice. I never knew.''

''Yes, sir, I fear they were.'' The monitor sighed. ''I served her for forty-three years, sir, eight months, and five days. Would you care to view her as she was in life, sir? Or the last scene it was my pleasure to display to her? As a species of informal memorial, sir? It may console your evident grief, sir, if I may be so bold.''

Silk shook his head, then thought better of it. ''Is some god prompting you, my son? The Outsider, perhaps?''

''Not that I'm aware of, sir.''

''Last Phaesday I encountered a very cooperative monitor,'' Silk explained. ''He directed me to his mistress's weapons, something that I wouldn't—in retrospect—have supposed a monitor would normally do. I have since concluded that he had been ordered to assist me by the goddess Kypris.''

''A credit to us all, sir.''

''He would not say so, of course. He had been enjoined to silence. Show me that scene, the last your mistress saw.''

The monitor vanished. Choppy blue water stretched to the horizon; in the mid-distance, a small fishing boat ran close-hauled under a lowering sky. A black bird (Silk edged closer) fluttered in the rigging, and a tall woman, naked or nearly so, stood beside the helmsman. A movement of her left hand was accompanied by a faint crimson flash.

Silk stroked his cheek. "Can you repeat the order Maytera Rose gave you that led you to show her this?"

"Certainly, sir. It was, 'Let's see what that slut Silk foisted on us is doing now.' I apologize, sir, as I did to my mistress, for the meager image of the subject. There was no nearer point from which to display it, and the focal length of the glass through which I viewed it was at its maximum."

Hearing Silk's approach, Maytera Marble turned away from the Window and tried to cover herself with her new hands. With averted eyes, he passed her the habit he had taken from a nail in the wall of her room, saying, "It doesn't matter, Maytera. Not really."

"I know, Patera. Yet I feel . . . There, it's on."

He faced her and held out his hand. "Can you stand up?"

"I don't know, Patera. I—I was about to try when you came. Where is everyone?" Harder than flesh, her fingers took his. He heaved with all his strength, reawakening the half-healed wounds left by the beak of the white-headed one.

Maytera Marble stood, almost steadily, and endeavored to shake the dust from her long, black skirt, murmuring, "Thank you, Patera. Did you get—? Thank you very much."

He took a deep breath. "I'm afraid you must think I've acted improperly. I should explain that His Cognizance the Prolocutor personally authorized me to enter your cenoby to bring you that. His Cognizance is here; he's in the manse at the moment, I believe."

He waited for her to speak, but she did not.

"Perhaps if you got out of the sun."

She leaned heavily on his arm as he led her through the arched gateway and the garden to her accustomed seat in the arbor.

In a voice not quite like her own, she said, "There's something I should tell you. Something I should have told you long ago.''

Silk nodded. ''There's something I should have told you long ago, too, Maytera—and something new that I must tell you now. Please let me go first; I think that will be best.''

It seemed she had not heard him. ''I bore a child once, Patera. A son, a baby boy. It was . . . Oh, very long ago.''

''Built a son, you mean. You and your husband.''

She shook her head. ''Bore him in blood and pain, Patera. Great Echidna had blinded me to the gods, but it wasn't enough. So I suffered, and no doubt he suffered, too, poor little mite, though he had done nothing. We nearly died, both of us.''

Silk could only stare at her smooth, metal face.

''And now somebody's dead, upstairs. I can't remember who. It will come to me in a moment. I dreamt of snakes last night, and I hate snakes. If I tell you now, I think perhaps I won't have that dream again.''

''I hope not, Maytera,'' he told her. And then, ''Think of something else, if you can.''

''It was . . . Was not an easy confinement. I was forty, and had never borne a child. Maytera Betel was our senior then, an excellent woman. But fat, one of those people who lose nothing when they fast. She became horribly tired when she fasted, but never thinner.''

He nodded, increasingly certain that Maytera Marble was possessed again, and that he knew who possessed her.

''We pretended I was becoming fat, too. She used to tease me about it, and our sibs believed her. I'd been such a small woman before.''

Watching carefully for her reaction, Silk said, ''I would have carried you, Maytera, if I could; but I knew you'd be too heavy for me to lift.''

She ignored it. ''A few bad people gossiped, but that was all. Then my time came. The pains were awful. Maytera had arranged for a woman in the Orilla to care for me. Not a good woman, Maytera said, but a better friend in time of need than many good women. She told me she'd delivered children often, and washed her hands, and washed me, and told me what to do, but it would not come forth. My son. He wouldn't come into this world, though I pressed and pressed until I was so tired I thought I must die."

Her hand—he recognized it now as Maytera Rose's—found his. Hoping it would reassure her, he squeezed it as hard as he could.

"She cut me with a knife from her kitchen that she dipped in boiling water, and there was blood everywhere. Horrible! Horrible! A doctor came and cut me again, and there he was, covered with my blood and dripping. My son. They wanted me to nurse him, but I wouldn't. I knew that she'd blinded me, Ophidian Echidna had blinded me to the gods for what I'd done, but I thought that if I didn't nurse it she might relent and let me see her after all. She never has."

Silk said, "You don't have to tell me this, Maytera."

"They asked me to name him, and I did. They said they'd find a family that wanted a child and would take him, and he'd never find out, but he did, though it must have taken him a long while. He spoke to Marble, said she must tell me he'd bought it, and his name. When I heard his name, I knew."

Silk said gently, "It doesn't matter any more, Maytera. That was long ago, and now the whole city's in revolt, and it no longer matters. You must rest. Find peace."

"And that is why," Maytera Marble concluded. "Why my son Bloody bought our manteion and made all this trouble."

The wind wafted smoke from the fig tree to Silk's nose, and he sneezed.

"May every god bless you, Patera." Her voice sounded normal again.

"Thank you," he said, and accepted the handkerchief she offered.

"Could you bring me water, do you think? Cool water?"

As sympathetically as he could, he told her, "You can't drink water, Maytera."

"Please? Just a cup of cool water?"

He hurried to the manse. Today was Hieraxday, after all; no doubt she wished him to bless the water for her in Hierax's name. Later she would sprinkle it upon Maytera Rose's coffin and in the corners of her bedroom to prevent Maytera's spirit from troubling her again.

Cassava was sitting in the kitchen, in the chair Patera Pike had used at meals. Silk said, "Shouldn't you lie down, my daughter? It would make you feel better, I'm sure, and there's a divan in the sellaria."

She stared at him. "That was a needler, wasn't it? I gave you a needler. Why'd I have a thing like that?"

"Because someone gave it to you to give me." He smiled at her. I'm going to the Alambrera, you see, and I'll need it." He worked the pump-handle vigorously, letting the first rusty half-bucketful drain away, catching the clear, cold flood that followed in a tumbler, and presenting it to Cassava. "Drink this, please, my daughter. It should make you feel better."

"You called me Mucor," she said. "Mucor." She set the untasted tumbler on the kitchen table and rubbed her forehead. "Didn't you call me Mucor, Patera?"

"I mentioned Mucor, certainly; she was the person who gave you the needler to give to me." Studying her puzzled frown, Silk decided it would be wise to change the subject. "Can you tell me what has become of His Cognizance and little Villus, my daughter?"

"He carried him upstairs, Patera. He wanted him to lie down, like you wanted me."

"Doubtless he'll be down shortly." Silk reflected that the

Prolocutor had probably intended to bandage Villus's leg, and lost some time searching for medical supplies. "Drink that water, please. I'm sure it will make you feel better." He filled a second tumbler and carried it outside.

Maytera Marble was sitting in the arbor just as he had left her. Pushing aside the vines, he handed her the tumbler, saying, "Would you like me to bless this for you, Maytera?"

"It won't be necessary, Patera."

Water spilled from the lip; rills laced her fingers, and rain pattered upon the black cloth covering her metal thighs. She smiled.

"Does that make you feel better?" he asked.

"Yes, much better. Much cooler, Patera. Thank you."

"I'll be happy to bring you another, if you require it."

She stood. "No. No, thank you, Patera. I'll be all right now, I think."

"Sit down again, Maytera, please. I'm still worried about you, and I have to talk to you."

Reluctantly, she did. "Aren't there others hurt? I seem to remember others—and Maytera Rose, her coffin."

Silk nodded. "That's a part of what I must talk to you about. Fighting has broken out all over the city."

She nodded hesitantly. "Riots."

"Rebellion, Maytera. The people—some at least—are rising against the Ayuntamiento. There won't be any burials for several days, I'm afraid; so when you're feeling better, you and I must carry Maytera's coffin into the manteion. Is it very heavy?"

"I don't think so, Patera."

"Then we should be able to manage it. But before we go, I ought to tell you that Villus and an old woman named Cassava are in the manse with His Cognizance. I can't stay here, nor will he be able to, I'm sure; so I intend to ask him to allow you to enter to care for them."

Maytera Marble nodded.

"And our altar and Window are still out in the street. I doubt that it will be possible for you to get enough help to move them back inside until the city is at peace. But if you can, please do."

"I certainly will, Patera."

"I want you to stay and look after our manteion, Maytera. Maytera Mint's gone; she felt it her duty to lead the fighting, and she answered duty's call with exemplary courage. I'll have to go soon as well. People are dying—and killing others—to make me caldé, and I must put a stop to that if I can."

"Please be careful, Patera. For all our sakes."

"Yet this manteion is still important, Maytera. Terribly important." (Doctor Crane's ghost laughed aloud in a corner of Silk's mind.) "The Outsider told me so, remember? Someone must care for it, and there's no one left but you."

Maytera Marble's sleek metal head bobbed humbly, oddly mechanical without her coif. "I'll do my best, Patera."

"I know you will." He filled his lungs. "I said there were two things I had to tell you. You may not recall it, but I did. When you began to speak, I found there were a great many more. Now I must tell you those two, and then we'll carry Maytera into the manteion, if we can. The first is something I should have said months ago. Perhaps I did; I know I've tried. Now I believe—I believe it's quite likely I may be killed, and I must say it now, or be silent forever."

"I'm anxious to hear it, Patera." Her voice was soft, her metal mask expressionless and compassionate; her hands clasped his, hard and wet and warm.

"I want to say—this is the old thing—that I could never have stood it here if it hadn't been for you. Maytera Rose and Maytera Mint tried to help, I know they did. But you have been my right arm, Maytera. I want you know that."

Maytera Marble was staring at the ground. "You're too kind, Patera."

"I've loved three women. My mother was the first. The

third . . ." He shrugged. "It doesn't matter. You don't know her, and I doubt that I'll ever see her again." A pillar of swirling dust rose above the top of the garden wall, to be swept away in a moment.

"The second thing, the new one, is that I can't remain the sort of augur I've been. Pas—Great Pas, who ruled the whole Whorl like a father—is dead, Maytera. Echidna herself told us. Do you remember that?"

Maytera Marble said nothing.

"Pas built our whorl, as we learn from the Writings. He built it, I believe, to endure for a long, long time, but not to endure indefinitely in his absence. Now he's dead, and the sun has no master. I believe that the Fliers have been trying to tame it, or perhaps only trying to heal it. A man in the market told me once that his grandfather had spoken of them, saying their appearance presaged rain; so all my life, and my mother's, and her parents', too, have been lived under their protection, while they wrestled the sun."

Silk peered through the wilting foliage overhead at the dwindling golden line, already narrowed by the shade. "But they've failed, Maytera. A flier told me yesterday, with what was almost his final breath. I didn't understand then; but I do now, or at least I believe I may. Something happened in the street that made it unmistakable. Our city, and every other, must help if it can, and prepare for worse times than we've ever known."

Quetzal's tremulous old voice came from outside the arbor. "Excuse me, Patera. Maytera." The wilting vines parted, and he stepped inside. "I overheard what you said. I couldn't help it, it's so quiet. You'll pardon me, I hope?"

"Of course, Your Cognizance." Both rose.

"Sit down, my daughter. Sit, please. May I sit beside you, Patera? Thank you. Everyone's hiding indoors, I imagine, or gone off to join the fighting. I've been upstairs in your manse, Patera, and I looked out your window. There isn't a cart in the street, and you can hear shooting."

Silk nodded. "A terrible thing, Your Cognizance."

"It is, as I overheard you say earlier, Patera. Maytera, you are, from all I've heard and read in our files, a woman of sound sense. A woman outstanding for that valuable quality, in fact. Viron's at war with itself. Men and women, and even children, are dying as we speak. They call us butchers for offering animal blood to the gods, though they're only animals and die quickly for the highest of purposes. Now the gutters are running with wasted human blood. If we're butchers, what will they call themselves when it's over?" He shook his head. "Heroes, I suppose. Do you agree?"

Maytera Marble nodded mutely.

"Then I ask you, how can it be ended? Tell me, Maytera. Tell us both. My coadjutor fears my humor, and I myself fear at times that I overindulge it. But I was never more serious."

She muttered something inaudible.

"Louder, Maytera."

"Patera Silk must become our caldé."

Quetzal leaned back in the little rustic seat. "There you have it. Her reputation for good sense is entirely justified, Patera Caldé."

"Your Cognizance!"

Maytera Marble made Quetzal a seated bow. "You're too kind, Your Cognizance."

"Maytera. Suppose I maintain that yours isn't the only solution. Suppose I say that the Ayuntamiento has governed us before and can govern us again. We need only submit. What's wrong with that?"

"There'd be another rebellion, Your Cognizance, and more riots." Maytera Marble would not meet Silk's eyes. "More fighting, new rebellions every few years until the Ayuntamiento was overthrown. I've watched discontent grow for twenty years, Your Cognizance, and now they're killing, Patera says. They'll be quicker to fight next time, and quicker again until it never really stops. And—and . . ."

"Yes?" Quetzal motioned urgently. "Tell us."

"The soldiers will die, Your Cognizance, one by one. Each time the people rise, there will be fewer soldiers."

"So you see." His head swung about on its wrinkled neck as he spoke to Silk. "Your supporters must win, Patera Caldé. Stop wincing when I call you that, you've got to get used to it. They must, because only their victory will bring Viron peace. Tell Loris and the rest they can save their lives by surrendering now. Lemur's dead, did you know that?"

Swallowing, Silk nodded.

"With Lemur gone, a few smacks of your quirt will make the rest trot anywhere you want. But you must be caldé, and the people must see you are."

"If I may speak, Your Cognizance?"

"Not to tell me that you, an anointed augur, will not do what I, your Prolocutor, ask you to, I trust."

"You've been Prolocutor for many years, Your Cognizance. Since long before I was born. You were Prolocutor in the days of the last caldé."

Quetzal nodded. "I knew him well. I intend to know you better, Patera Caldé."

"I was a child when he died, Your Cognizance, a child just learning to walk. A great many things must have happened then that I've never heard of. I mention it to emphasize that I'm asking out of ignorance. If you would prefer not to answer, no more will be said about the matter."

Quetzal nodded. "If it were Maytera here inquiring, or your acolyte, let's say, or even my coadjutor, I might refuse exactly as you suggest. I can't imagine a question asked by our caldé that I wouldn't feel it was my duty to answer fully and clearly, however. What's troubling you?"

Silk ran his fingers through his hair. "When the caldé

died, Your Cognizance, did you—did anyone—protest the Ayuntamiento's decision not to hold an election?''

Quetzal nodded, as if to himself, and passed a trembling hand across his hairless scalp, a gesture similar to Silk's yet markedly different. ''The short answer, if I intended nothing more than a short answer, would be yes. I did. So did various others. You deserve more than a short answer, though. You deserve a complete explanation. In the meantime, that lucky young man's body lies half consumed on the altar. I saw it from your window. You indicate that you're not inclined to plead your office to excuse disobedience. Will you follow me into the street and help me do what can be done there? When we're finished, I'll answer you fully.''

Crouched behind the remaining wall of a fire-gutted shop, Maytera Mint studied her subordinates' faces. Zoril looked fearful, Lime stunned, and the big, black-bearded man (she found she had forgotten his name, if she had ever heard it) resolute. ''Now, then,'' she said.

Why it's just like talking to the class, she thought. No different at all. I wish I had a chalkboard.

''Now then, we've just had news, and it's bad news, I don't intend to deny that. But it isn't unexpected news. Not to me, and I hope to none of you. We've got Guards penned up in the Alambrera, where they're supposed to pen up other people.''

She smiled, hoping they appreciated the irony. ''Anyone would expect that the Ayuntamiento would send its people help. Certainly I expected it, though I hoped it wouldn't be quite so prompt. But it's come, and it seems to me that we can do any of three things.'' She held up three fingers. ''We can go on attacking the Alambrera, hoping we can take it before they get here.'' One finger down. ''We can withdraw.'' Another finger down. ''Or we can leave the Alambrera as it is and fight the reinforcements before they can get inside.'' The last finger down. ''What do you suggest, Zoril?''

''If we withdraw, we won't be doing what the goddess said for us to.''

The black-bearded man snorted.

''She told us to capture the Alambrera and tear it down,'' Maytera Mint reminded Zoril. ''We've tried, but we haven't been able to. What we've got to decide, really, is should we go on trying until we're interrupted? Or rest awhile until we feel stronger, knowing that they'll be stronger too? Or should we see to it that we're not interrupted. Lime?''

She was a lank woman of forty with ginger-colored hair that Maytera Mint had decided was probably dyed. ''I don't think we can think *only* about what the goddess said. If she just wanted it torn down, she could have done it herself. She wants *us* to do it.''

Maytera Mint nodded. ''I'm in complete agreement.''

''We're mortals, so we've got to do it as mortals.'' Lime gulped. ''I don't have as many people following me as the rest of you, and most of mine are women.''

''There's nothing wrong with that,'' Maytera Mint assured her. ''So am I. So is the goddess, or at least she's female like us. We know she's Pas's wife and seven times a mother. As for your not having lots of followers, that's not the point. I'd be happy to listen to somebody who didn't have any, if she had good, workable ideas.''

''What I was trying to say—'' A gust of wind carried dust and smoke into their council; Lime fanned her face with one long, flat hand. ''Is most of mine don't have much to fight with. Just kitchen knives, a lot of them. Eight, I think it is, have needlers, and there's one who runs a stable and has a pitchfork.''

Maytera Mint made a mental note.

''So what I was going to say is they're feeling left out. Discouraged, you know?''

Maytera Mint assured her that she did.

"So if we go home, I think some will stay there. But if we can beat these new Hoppies that're coming, they could get slug guns. They'd feel better about themselves, and us, too."

"A very valid point."

"Bison here—"

Maytera Mint made another note: "Bison" was clearly the black-bearded man; she resolved to use his name whenever she could until it was fixed in her memory.

"Bison thinks they won't fight. And they won't, not the way he wants them to. But if they had slug guns, they'd shoot all day if you told them to, Maytera. Or if you told them to go someplace and Hoppies tried to stop them."

"You're for attacking the relief column, Lime?"

Lime nodded.

Bison said, "She's for it as long as somebody else does the fighting. I'm for it, too, and we'll do the fighting."

"The fighting among ourselves, you mean, Bison?" Maytera Mint shook her head. "That sort of fighting will never bring back the Charter, and I'm quite sure it isn't what the goddess intended. But you're in favor of attacking the relief column? Good, so am I! I'm not sure I know what Zoril wants, and I'm not sure he knows. Even so, that's a clear majority. Where would you suggest we attack it, Bison?"

He was silent, fingering his beard.

"We'll lose some stragglers. I realize that. But there are steps we can take to keep from losing many, and we might pick up some new people as well. Zoril?"

"I don't know, Maytera. I think you ought to decide."

"So do I, and I will. But it's foolish to make decisions without listening to advice, if there's time for it. I think we should attack right here, when they reach the Alambrera."

Bison nodded emphatically.

"In the first place, we don't have much time to prepare, and that will give us the most."

Bison said, "People are throwing stones at them from the

rooftops. The messenger told us that, too, remember? Maybe they'll kill a few Hoppies for us. Let's give them a chance."

"And perhaps some of their younger men will come over to us. We ought to give them as much opportunity as we can to do that." Inspired by the memory of games at the palaestra, she added, "When somebody changes sides, it counts twice, one more for us and one fewer for them. Besides, when they get here the Guards in the Alambrera will have to open those big doors to let them in." Their expressions showed that none of them had thought of that, and she concluded, "I'm not saying that we'll be able to get inside ourselves. But we might. Now them, how are we going to attack?"

"Behind and before, with as many men as we can," Bison rumbled.

Lime added, "We need to take them by surprise, Maytera."

"Which is another reason for attacking here. When they get to the Alambrera, they'll think they've reached their goal. They may relax a little. That will be the time for us to act."

"When the doors open." Bison drove a fist into his palm.

"Yes, I think so. What is it, Zoril?"

"I shouldn't say this. I know what everybody's going to think, but they've been shooting down on us from the walls and the high windows. Just about everybody we've lost, we've lost like that." He waited for contradiction, but there was none.

"There's buildings across the street as high as the wall, Maytera, and one just a little up the street that's higher. I think we ought to have people in there to shoot at the men on the wall. Some of mine that don't have needlers or slug guns could be on the roofs, too, throwing stones like the messenger talked about. A chunk of shiprock falling that far ought to hit as hard as a slug, and these Hoppies have got armor."

Maytera Mint nodded again. "You're right. I'm putting

you in charge of that. Get some people—not just your own, some of the older boys and girls particularly—busy right away carrying stones and bricks up there. There must be plenty around after the fires.

"Lime, Your women are no longer fighters unless they've got needlers or slug guns. We need people to get our wounded out of the fight and take care of them. They can use their knives or whatever they have on anyone who tries to interfere with them. And that woman with the pitchfork? Go get her. I want to talk to her."

A fragment of broken plaster caught Maytera Mint's eye. "Now, Bison, look here." Picking it up, she scratched two widely spaced lines on the fire-blackened wall behind her. "This is Cage Street." With speed born of years of practice, she sketched in the Alambrera and the buildings facing it.

There was still a good deal of cedar left, and the fire on the altar had not quite gone out. Silk heaped fresh wood on it and let the wind fan it for him, sparks streaking Sun Street.

Quetzal had taken charge of Musk's corpse, arranging it decently beside Maytera Rose's coffin. Maytera Marble, who had gone to the cenoby for a sheet, had not yet returned.

"He was the most evil man I've ever known." Silk had not intended to speak aloud, but the words had come just the same. "Yet I can't help feeling sorry for him, and for all of us, as well, because he's gone."

Quetzal murmured, "Does you credit, Patera Caldé," and wiped the blade of the manteion's sacrificial knife, which he had rescued from the dust.

Vaguely, Silk wondered when he had dropped it. Maytera Rose had always taken care of it, washing and sharpening it after each sacrifice, no matter how minor; but Maytera Rose was gone, as dead as Musk.

After he had cut the sign of addition in Villus's ankle, of course, when he had knelt to suck out the poison.

When he had met Blood on Phaesday, Blood had said that he had promised someone—had promised a woman—that he would pray at this manteion for her. Suddenly Silk knew (without in the least understanding how he knew) that the "woman" had been Musk. Was Musk's spirit lingering in the vicinity of Musk's body and prompting him in some fashion? Whispering too softly to be heard? Silk traced the sign of addition, knowing that he should add a prayer to Thelxiepeia, the goddess of magic and ghosts, but unable to do so.

Musk had bought the manteion for Blood with Blood's money; and Musk must have felt, in some deep part of himself that all his evil actions had not killed, that he had done wrong—that he had by his purchase offended the gods. He had asked Blood to pray for him, or perhaps for them both, in the manteion that he had bought; and Blood had promised to do it.

Had Blood kept his promise?

"If you'd help with the feet, Patera Caldé?" Quetzal was standing at the head of Maytera Rose's coffin.

"Yes, of course, Your Cognizance. We can carry that in."

Quetzal shook his head. "We'll lay it on the sacred fire, Patera Caldé. Cremation is allowed when burial is impractical. If you would . . . ?"

Silk picked up the foot of the coffin, finding it lighter than he had expected. "Shouldn't we petition the gods, Your Cognizance? On her behalf?"

"I already have, Patera Caldé. You were deep in thought. Now then, as high as you can, then quickly down upon the fire. Without dropping it, please. One, two, *three!*"

Silk did as he was told, then stepped hurriedly away from the lengthening flames. "Possibly we ought to have waited for Maytera, Your Cognizance."

Quetzal shook his head again. "This way is better, Patera Caldé. It would be better for you to keep from looking at the fire, too. Do you know why coffins have that peculiar shape, by the way? Look at me, Patera Caldé."

"To allow for the shoulders, Your Cognizance, or so I've heard."

Quetzal nodded. "That's what everyone's told. Would this sibyl of yours need extra room for her shoulders? Look at me, I said."

Already the thin, stained wood was blackening honestly, charring as the flames that licked it brought forth new flames. "No," Silk said, and looked away again. (It was strange to think that this bent, bald old man was in fact the Prolocutor.) "No, Your Cognizance. Nor would most women, or many men."

There was a stench of burning flesh.

"They do it so that we, the living, will know at which end the head lies, when the lid's on. Coffins are sometimes stood on end, you see. Patera!"

Silk's gaze had strayed to the fire again. He turned away and covered his eyes.

"I would have saved you that if I could," Quetzal told him, and Maytera Marble, arriving with the sheet, inquired, "Saved him from what, Your Cognizance?"

"Saved me from seeing Maytera Rose's face as the flames consumed it," Silk told her. He rubbed his eyes, hoping that she would think he had been rubbing them before, that he had gotten smoke in them.

She held out one end of the sheet. "I'm sorry I took so long, Patera. I—I happened to see my reflection. Then I looked for Maytera Mint's mirror. My cheek is scratched."

Silk took corners of the sheet in tear-dampened fingers; the wind tried to snatch it from him, but he held it fast. "So it is, Maytera. How did you do it?"

"I have no idea!"

To his surprise, Quetzal lifted Musk's half-consumed

body easily. Clearly, this venerable old man was stronger than he appeared. "Spread it flat and hold it down," he told them. "We'll lay him on it and fold it over him."

A moment more, and Musk, too, rested among the flames.

"It's our duty to tend the fire until both have burned. We don't have to watch, and I suggest we don't." Quetzal had positioned himself between Silk and the altar. "Let us pray privately for the repose of their spirits."

Silk shut his eyes, bowed his head, and addressed himself to the Outsider, without much confidence that this most obscure of gods heard him or cared about what he said, or even existed.

"And yet I know this." (His lips moved, although no sound issued from them.) *"You are the only god for me. It is better for me that I should give you all my worship, though you are not, than that I should worship Echidna or even Kypris, whose faces I have seen. Thus I implore your mercy on these, our dead. Remember that I, whom once you signally honored, ought to have loved them both but could not, and so failed to provide the impetus that might have brought them to you before Hierax claimed them. Mine therefore is the guilt for any wrong they have done while they have known me. I accept it, and pray you will forgive them, who burn, and forgive me also, whose fire is not yet lit. Obscure Outsider, be not angry with us, though we have never sufficiently honored you. All that is outcast, discarded, and despised is yours. Are this man and this woman, who have been neglected by me, to be neglected by you as well? Recall the misery of our lives and their deaths. Are we never to find rest? I have searched my conscience, Outsider, to discover that in which I have displeased you. I find this: That I avoided Maytera Rose whenever I could, though she might have been to me the grandmother I have never known; and that I hated Musk, and feared him too, when he had not done me the least wrong. Both were yours, Outsider, as I now see; and for your sake I should have been loving with both. I renounce*

my pride, and I will honor their memories. This I swear. My life to you, Outsider, if you will forgive this man and this woman whom we burn today.''

Opening his eyes he saw that Quetzal had already finished, if he had ever prayed. Soon Maytera Marble raised her head as well, and he inquired, "Would Your Cognizance, who knows more about the immortal gods than anyone else in the Whorl, instruct me regarding the Outsider? Though he's enlightened me, as I informed your coadjutor, I would be exceedingly grateful if you could tell me more.''

"I have no information to give, Patera Caldé, regarding the Outsider or any other god. What little I have learned in the course of a long life, regarding the gods, I have tried to forget. You saw Echidna. After that, can you ask me why?''

"No, Your Cognizance." Silk looked nervously at Maytera Marble.

"I didn't, Your Cognizance. But I saw the Holy Hues and heard her voice, and it made me wonderfully happy. I remember that she exhorted all of us to purity and confirmed Scylla's patronage, nothing else. Can you tell me what else she said?''

"She told your sib to overthrow the Ayuntamiento. Let that be enough for you, Maytera, for the present.''

"Maytera Mint? But she'll be killed!''

Quetzal's shoulders rose and fell. "I think we can count on it, Maytera. Before Kypris manifested here on Scylsday, the Windows of our city had been empty for decades. I can't take credit for that, it wasn't my doing. But I've done everything in my power to prevent theophanies. It hasn't been much, but I've done what I could. I proscribed human sacrifice, and got it made law, for one thing. I admit I'm proud of that.''

He turned to Silk. "Patera Caldé, you wanted to know if I protested when the Ayuntamiento failed to hold an election to choose a new caldé. You were right to ask, more right than you knew. If a new caldé had been elected when the last died, we wouldn't have had that visit from Echidna today."

"If Your Cognizance—"

"No, I want to tell you. There are many things you have to know as caldé, and this is one. But the situation wasn't as simple as you may think. What do you know about the Charter?"

"Next to nothing, Your Cognizance. We studied when I was a boy—that is to say, our teacher read it to us and answered our questions. I was ten, I think."

Maytera Marble said, "We're not supposed to teach it now. It was dropped from all the lesson plans years ago."

"At my order," Quetzal told them, "when even mentioning it became dangerous. We have copies at the Palace, however, and I've read it many times. It doesn't say, Patera Caldé, that an election must be held on the death of the caldé, as you seem to believe. What it really says is that the caldé is to hold office for life, that he may appoint his successor, and that a successor is to be elected if he dies without having done it. You see the difficulty?"

Uneasily, Silk glanced up and down the street, seeing no one near enough to overhear. "I'm afraid not, Your Cognizance. That sounds quite straightforward to me."

"It does *not* say that the caldé must announce his choice, you'll notice. If he wants to keep it secret, he can do it. The reasons are so obvious I hesitated to explain them."

Silk nodded. "I can see that it would put them both in an uncomfortable position."

"In a very dangerous one, Patera Caldé. Partisans of the successor might assassinate the caldé, while those who'd hoped to become caldé would be tempted to murder the successor. When the last caldé's will was read, it was found to designate a successor. I remember the exact wording. It said, 'Though he is not the son of my body, my son will succeed me.' What do you make of that?"

Silk stroked his cheek. "It didn't name this son?"

"No. I've given you the entire clause. The caldé had never married, as I should have told you sooner. As far as anybody knew, he had no sons."

Maytera Marble ventured, "I never knew about this, Your Cognizance. Didn't the son tell them?"

"Not that I know of. It's possible he did and was killed secretly by Lemur or one of the other councillors, but I doubt it." Quetzal selected a long cedar split and poked the sinking fire. "If they'd done that, I'd have heard about it by this time. Probably much sooner. No public announcement was made, you understand. If there'd been one, pretenders would have put themselves forward and made endless trouble. The Ayuntamiento searched in secret. To be frank, I doubt that the boy would have lived if they'd found him."

Silk nodded reluctantly.

"If it had been a natural son, they could've used medical tests. As it was, the only hope was turn up a record. The monitors of every glass that could be located were queried. Old documents were read and reread, and the caldé's relatives and associates interrogated, all without result. An election should have been held, and I urged one repeatedly because I was afraid we'd have a theophany from Scylla unless something was done. But an election would have been illegal, as I had to admit. The caldé had designated his successor. They simply couldn't find him."

"Then I'll have no right to office if it's forced on me."

"Hardly. In the first place, that was a generation ago. It's likely the adopted son's dead if he ever existed. In the second, the Charter was written by the gods. It's a document expressing their will regarding our governance, nothing more. It's clear they're displeased with the present state of things, and you're the only alternative, as Maytera told you."

Quetzal handed the sacrificial knife to Maytera Marble. "I think we can go now, Maytera. You must stay. Watch the fire until it goes out. When it does, carry the ashes into your manteion and dispose of them as usual. You may notice bones or teeth among them. Don't touch them, or treat them differently from the rest of the ashes in any way."

Maytera Marble bowed.

"Purify the altar as usual. If you can get people to help you, take it back into the manteion. Your Sacred Window, too."

She bowed again. "Patera has already instructed me to do so, Your Cognizance."

"Fine. You're a good sensible woman, Maytera, as I said. I was glad to see that you had resumed your coif when you went back to your cenoby. You've my permission to enter the manse. There's an old woman there. I think you'll find she's well enough to go home. There's a boy on one of the beds upstairs. You can leave him there or carry him into your cenoby to nurse, if that will be more convenient. See to it that he doesn't exert himself, and that he drinks a lot of water. Get him to eat, if you can. You might cook some of this meat for him."

Quetzal turned to Silk. "I want to look in on him again, Patera, while Maytera's busy with the fire. I'm also going to borrow a spare robe I saw up there, your acolyte's, I suppose. It looked too short for you, but it should fit me, and when we meet the rebels—perhaps we should call them servants of the Queen of the Whorl, some such. When we meet them, it may help if they know who I am as well as who you are."

Silk said, "I feel certain Patera Gulo would want you to have anything that can be of any assistance whatsoever to you, Your Cognizance."

As Quetzal tottered away, Maytera Marble asked, "Are you going to help Maytera Mint, Patera? You'll be in frightful danger, both of you. I'll pray for you."

"I'm much more worried about you than about myself," Silk told her. "More, even, than I am about her—she must be under Echidna's protection, in spite of what His Cognizance said.''

Maytera Marble lifted her head in a slight, tantalizing smile. "Don't fret about me. Maytera Marble's taking good care of me." Unexpectedly, she brushed his cheek with warm metal lips. "If you should see my boy Bloody, tell him not to worry either. I'll be all right."

"I certainly will, Maytera." Silk took a hasty step back. "Good-bye, Maytera Rose. About those tomatoes—I'm sorry, truly sorry about everything. I hope you've forgiven me."

"She passed away yesterday, Patera. Didn't I tell you?"

"Yes," Silk mumbled. "Yes, of course."

Auk lay on the floor of the tunnel. He was tired—tired and weak and dizzy, he admitted to himself. When had he slept last? Dayside on Molpsday, after he'd left Jugs and Patera, before he went to the lake, but he'd slept on the boat a dog's right before the storm. Her and the butcher had been tired, too, tireder than him though they hadn't been knocked on the head. They'd helped in the storm, and Dace was dead. Urus hadn't done anything, would kill him if he got the chance. He pictured Urus standing over him with a bludgeon like the one he had seen, and sat up and stared around him.

Urus and the soldier were talking quietly. The soldier called, "I'm keeping an eye out. Go back to sleep, trooper."

Auk lay down again, though no soldier could be a friend to somebody like him, though he'd sooner trust Urus though he didn't trust Urus at all.

What day was it? Thelxday. Phaesday, most likely. Grim Phaea, for food and healing. Grim because eating means killing stuff to eat, and it's no good pretending it don't. Stuff like Gelada'd killed Dace with his bad arm and the string around his neck. That's why you ought to go to manteion once in a while. Sacrifice showed you, showed the gray ram dying and its blood thrown in the fire, and poor people thanking Phaea or whatever god it was for "this good food." Grim because healing hurts more than dying, the doctor cuts you to make you well, sets the bone and it hurts. Dace said a bone in his head was broken, was cracked or something, he was cracked for sure and it was probably true because he got awful dizzy sometimes, couldn't see good sometimes, even stuff right in front of him. A white ram, Phaea, if I get over this.

It should've been a black ram. He'd promised Tartaros a black ram, but the only one in the market had cost more than he had, so he'd bought the gray one. That was before last time, before Kypris had promised them it'd be candy, before the ring for Jugs, the anklet for Patera. It had been why his troubles started, maybe, because his ram had been the wrong color. They dyed those black rams anyhow. . . .

Up the tree and onto the roof, then in through the attic window, but he was dizzy, dizzy and the tree already so high its top touched the shade, brushed the shaggy shade with dead leaves rustling, rustling, and the roof higher, Urus whistling, whistling from the corner because the Hoppies were practically underneath this shaggy tree now.

He stood on a limb, walked out on it watching the roof sail away with all the black peaked roofs of Limna as the old man's old boat put out with Snarling Scylla at the helm, Scylla up in Jugs's head not taking up room but pulling her strings, jerking her on reins, digging spurred heels in, Spurred Scylla a gamecock spurring Jugs to make her trot. A little step and another and the roof farther than ever, higher than the top of the whole shaggy tree and his foot slipped where Gelada's blood wet the slick silvery bark and he fell.

He woke with a start, shaking. Something warm lay beside him, close but not quite touching. He rolled over, bringing his legs up under her big soft thighs, his chest against her back, an arm around her to warm her and it, cupping her breast. "By Kypris, I love you, Jugs. I'm too sick to shag you, but I love you. You're all the woman I'll ever want."

She didn't talk, but there'd been a little change in her breathing, so he knew she wasn't asleep even if she wanted him to think so. That was dimber by him, she wanted to look at it and he didn't blame her, wouldn't want a woman who wouldn't look because a women like that got you nabbed sooner or later even if she didn't mean to.

Only he'd looked at it already, had looked all that he'd ever need to while he was rolling over. And he slept beside her quite content.

"I shocked you, Patera Caldé. I know I did. I could see it in your face. My eyes aren't what they were, I'm afraid. I'm no longer good at reading expressions. But I read yours."

"Somewhat, Your Cognizance." Together, they were walking up a deserted Sun Street, a tall young augur and a stooped old one side-by-side, Silk taking a slow step for two of Quetzal's lame and unsteady ones.

"Since you left the schola, Patera Caldé, since you came to this quarter, you've prayed that a god would come to your Window, haven't you? I feel sure you have. All of you do, or nearly all. Who did you hope for? Pas or Scylla?"

"Scylla chiefly, Your Cognizance. To tell the truth, I scarcely thought about the minor gods then. I mean the gods outside the Nine—no god is truly minor, I suppose. Scylla seemed the most probable. It was only on Scylsdays that we had a victim, for one thing; and she's the patroness of the city, after all."

"She'd tell you what to do, which was what you wanted." Quetzal squinted up at Silk with a toothless smile he found disconcerting. "She'd fill your cash box, too. You could fix up those old buildings, buy books for your palaestra, and sacrifice in the grand style every day."

Reluctantly, Silk nodded.

"I understand. Oh, I understand. It's perfectly normal, Patera Caldé. Even commendable. But what about me? What about me, not wanting gods to come at all? That isn't, is it? It isn't, and it's bothering you."

Silk shook his head. "It's not my place to judge your acts or your words, Your Cognizance."

"Yet you will." Quetzal paused to peer along Lamp Street, and seemed to listen. "You will, Patera Caldé. You can't help it. That's why I've got to tell you. After that, we're going to talk about something you probably think that you learned all about when you were a baby. I mean the Plan of Pas. Then you can go off to Maytera what'shername."

"Mint, Your Cognizance."

"You can go off to help her overthrow the Ayuntamiento for Echidna, and I'll be going off to find you more people to do it with, and better weapons. To begin—"

"Your Cognizance?" Silk ran nervous fingers through his haystack hair, unable to restrain himself any longer. "Your Cognizance, did you know Great Pas was dead? Did you know it already, before she told us today?"

"Certainly. We can start there, Patera Caldé, if that's troubling you. Would you have talked about it from the ambion of the Grand Manteion if you'd been in my place? Made a public announcement? Conducted ceremonies of mourning and so forth?"

"Yes," Silk said firmly. "Yes, I would."

"I see. What do you suppose killed him, Patera Caldé? You're an intelligent young fellow. You studied hard at the schola, I know. Your instructors' reports are very favorable. How could the Father of the Gods die?"

Faintly, Silk could hear the booming of slug guns, then a long, concerted roar that might almost have been thunder.

"Building falling," Quetzal told him. "Don't worry about that now. Answer my question."

"I can't conceive of such a thing, Your Cognizance. The

gods are immortal, ageless. It's their immortality that makes them gods, really, more than anything else.''

"A fever," Quetzal suggested. "We mortals die of fevers every day. Perhaps he caught a fever?"

"The gods are spiritual beings, Your Cognizance. They're not subject to disease."

"Kicked in the head by a horse. Don't you think that could have been it?"

Silk did not reply.

"I'm mocking you, Patera Caldé, of course I am. But not idly. My question's perfectly serious. Echidna told you Pas is dead, and you can't help believing her. I've known it for thirty years, since shortly after his death, in fact. How did he die? How could he?"

Silk combed his disorderly yellow hair with his fingers again.

"When I was made Prolocutor, Patera Caldé, we had a vase at the Palace that had been thrown on the Short Sun Whorl, a beautiful thing. They told me it was five hundred years old. Almost inconceivable. Do you agree?"

"And priceless, I would say, Your Cognizance."

"Lemur wanted to frighten me, to show me how ruthless he could be. I already knew, but he didn't know I did. I think he thought that if I did I'd never dare oppose him. He took that vase from its stand and smashed it at my feet."

Silk stared down at Quetzal. "You—you're serious, Your Cognizance? He actually did that?"

"He did. Look, now. That vase was immortal. It didn't age. It was proof against disease. But it could be destroyed, as it was. So could Pas. He couldn't age, or even fall sick. But he could be destroyed, and he was. He was murdered by his family. Many men die like that, Patera Caldé. When you're half my age, you'll know it. Now a god has, too."

"But, Your Cognizance . . ."

"Viron's isolated, Patera Caldé. All the cities are. He gave us floaters and animals. No big machines that could carry heavy loads. He thought that would be best for us, and I dare say he was right. But the Ayuntamiento's not isolated. The caldé wasn't either, when we had one. Did you think he was?''

Silk said, ''I realize we have diplomats, Your Cognizance, and there are traveling traders and so forth—boats on the rivers, and even spies.''

''That's right. As Prolocutor, I'm no more isolated than he was. Less, but I won't try to prove that. I'm in contact with religious leaders in Urbs, Wick, and other cities, cities where his children have boasted of killing Pas.''

''It was the Seven, then, Your Cognizance? Not Echidna? Was Scylla involved?''

Quetzal had found prayer beads in a pocket of Gulo's robe; he ran them through his fingers. ''Echidna was at the center. You've seen her, can you doubt it? Scylla, Molpe, and Hierax were in it. They've said so at various times.''

''But not Tartaros, Thelxiepeia, Phaea, or Sphigx, Your Cognizance?'' Silk felt an irrational surge of hope.

''I don't know about Tartaros and the younger gods, Patera Caldé. But do you see why I didn't announce it? There would have been panic. There will be, if it becomes widely known. The Chapter will be destroyed and the basis of morality gone. Imagine Viron with neither. As for public observances, how do you think Pas's murderers would react to our mourning him?''

''We—'' Something tightened in Silk's throat. ''We, you and I, Your Cognizance. Villus and Maytera Marble, all of us are—were his children too. That is to say, he built the whorl for us. Ruled us like a father. I . . . .''

''What is it, Patera Caldé?''

''I just remembered something, Your Cognizance. Kypris—you must know there was a theophany of Kypris at our manteion on Scylsday.''

"I've had a dozen reports. It's the talk of the city."

"She said she was hunted, and I didn't understand. Now I believe I may."

Quetzal nodded. "I imagine she is. The wonder is that they haven't been able to corner her in thirty years. She can't be a tenth as strong as Pas was. But it can't be easy to kill even a minor goddess who knows you're trying to. Not like killing a husband and father who trusts you. Now you see why I've tried to prevent theophanies, don't you, Patera Caldé? If you don't, I'll never be able to make it clear."

"Yes, Your Cognizance. Of course. It's—horrible. Unspeakable. But you were right. You are right."

"I'm glad you realize it. You understand why we go on sacrificing to Pas? We must. I've tried to downgrade him somewhat. Make him seem more remote than he used to. I've emphasized Scylla at his expense, but you're too young to have realized that. Older people complain, sometimes."

Silk said nothing, but stroked his cheek as he walked.

"You have questions, Patera Caldé. Or you will have when you've digested all this. Don't fear you may offend me. I'm at your disposal whenever you want to question me."

"I have two," Silk told him. "I hesitate to pose the first, which verges upon blasphemy."

"Many necessary questions do." Quetzal cocked his head. "This isn't one, but do you hear horses?"

"Horses, Your Cognizance? No."

"I must be imagining it. What are your questions?"

Silk walked on in silence for a few seconds to collect his thoughts. At length he said, "My original two questions have become three, Your Cognizance. The first, for which I apologize in advance, is, isn't it true that Echidna and the Seven love us just as Pas did? I've always felt, somehow, that Pas loved them, while they love us; and if that is so, will his death—terrible though it is—make a great deal of difference to us?''

"You have a pet bird, Patera Caldé. I've never seen it, but so I've been told."

"I had one, Your Cognizance, a night chough. I've lost him, I'm afraid, although it may be that he's with a friend. I'm hoping he'll return to me eventually."

"You should have caged him, Patera Caldé. Then you'd still have him."

"I liked him too much for that, Your Cognizance."

Quetzal's small head bobbed upon its long neck. "Just so. There are people who love birds so much they free them. There are others who love them so much they cage them. Pas's love of us was of the first kind. Echidna's and the Seven's is of the other. Were you going to ask why they killed Pas? Is that one of your questions?"

Silk nodded, "My second, Your Cognizance."

"I've answered it. What's the third?"

"You indicated that you wished to discuss the Plan of Pas with me, Your Cognizance. If Pas is dead, what's the point of discussing his plan?"

Hoofbeats sounded faintly behind them.

"A god's plans do not die with him, Patera Caldé. He is dead, as Serpentine Echidna told us. We are not. We were to carry Pas's plan out. You said he ruled us as a father. Do a father's plans benefit him? Or his children?"

"Your Cognizance, I just remembered something! Another god, the Outsider—"

"*Pateras!*" The horseman, a lieutenant of the Civil Guard in mottled green conflict armor, pushed up his visor. "Are you—you there, Patera. The young one. Aren't you Patera Silk?"

"Yes, my son," Silk said. "I am."

The lieutenant dropped the reins. His hand appeared

slow as it jerked his needler from the holster, yet it was much too quick to permit Silk to draw Musk's needler. The flat crack of the shot sounded an instant after the needle's stinging blow.

Chapter 5

MAIL

They had insisted she not look for herself, that she send one of them to do it, but she felt she had already sent too many others. This time she would see the enemy for herself, and she had forbidden them to attend her. She straightened her snowy coif as she walked, and held down the wind-tossed skirt of her habit—a sibyl smaller and younger than most, gowned (like all sibyls) in black to the tops of her worn black shoes, out upon some holy errand, and remarkable only for being alone.

The azoth was in one capacious pocket, her beads in the other; she got them out as she went around the corner onto Cage Street, wooden beads twice the size of those Quetzal fingered, smoothed and oiled by her touch to glossy chestnut.

First, Pas's gammadion: *"Great Pas, Designer and Creator of the Whorl, Lord Guardian of the Aureate Path, we—"*

The pronoun should have been *I*, but she was used to saying them with Maytera Rose and Maytera Marble; and they, praying together in the sellaria of the cenoby, had quite properly said "we." She thought: But I'm praying for all of us. For all who may die this afternoon, for Bison and Patera Gulo and Bream and that man who let me borrow his sword.

For the volunteers who'll ride with me in a minute, and Patera Silk and Lime and Zoril and the children. Particularly for the children. For all of us, Great Pas.

"We acknowledge you the supreme and sovereign . . ."

And there it was, an armored floater with all its hatches down turning onto Cage Street. Then another, and a third. A good big space between the third and the first rank of marching Guardsmen because of the dust. A mounted officer riding beside his troopers. The soldiers would be in back (that was what the messenger had reported) but there was no time to wait until they came into view, though the soldiers would be the worst of all, worse even than the floaters.

Beads forgotten, she hurried back the way she had come.

Scleroderma was still there, holding the white stallion's reins. "I'm coming too, Maytera. On these two legs since you won't let me have a horse, but I'm coming. You're going, and I'm bigger than you."

Which was true. Scleroderma was no taller, but twice as wide. "Shout," she told her. "You're blessed with a good, loud voice. Shout and make all the noise you can. If you can keep them from seeing Bison's people for one second more, that may decide it."

A giant with a gape-toothed grin knelt, hands clasped to help her mount; she put her left foot in them and swung into the saddle, and although she sat a tall horse, the giant's head was level with her own. She had chosen him for his size and ferocious appearance. (Distraction—distraction would be everything.) Now it struck her that she did not know his name. "Can you ride?" she asked. "If you can't, say so."

"Sure can, Maytera."

He was probably lying; but it was too late, too late to quiz him or get somebody else. She rose in her stirrups to consider the five riders behind her, and the giant's riderless horse. "Most of us will be killed, and it's quite likely that all of us will be."

The first floater would be well along Cage Street already, halted perhaps before the doors of the Alambrera; but if they were to succeed, their diversion would have to wait until the marching men behind the third floater had closed the gap. It might be best to fill the time.

"Should one of us live, however, it would be well for him—or her—to know the names of those who gave their lives. Scleroderma, I can't count you among us, but you are the most likely to live. Listen carefully."

Scleroderma nodded, her pudgy face pale.

"All of you. Listen, and try to remember."

The fear she had shut out so effectively was seeping back now. She bit her lip; her voice must not quaver. "I'm Maytera Mint, from the Sun Street manteion. But you know that. You," she pointed to the rearmost rider. "Give us your name, and say it loudly."

"Babirousa!"

"Good. And you?"

"Goral!"

"Kingcup!" The woman who had supplied horses for the rest.

"Yapok!"

"Marmot!"

"Gib from the Cock," the giant grunted, and mounted in a way that showed he was more accustomed to riding donkeys.

"I wish we had horns and war drums," Maytera Mint told them. "We'll have to use our voices and our weapons instead. Remember, the idea is to keep them, the crews of the floaters especially, looking and shooting at us for as long as we can."

The fear filled her mind, horrible and colder than ice; she felt sure her trembling fingers would drop Patera Silk's azoth if she tried to take it from her pocket; but she got it out anyway, telling herself that it would be preferable to drop it here, where Scleroderma could hand it back to her.

Scleroderma handed her the reins instead.

"You have all volunteered, and there is no disgrace in reconsidering. Those who wish may leave." Deliberately she faced forward, so that she would not see who dismounted.

At once she felt that there was no one behind her at all. She groped for something that would drive out the fear, and came upon a naked woman with yellow hair—a wild-eyed fury who was not herself at all—wielding a scourge whose lashes cut and tore the gray sickness until it fled her mind.

Perhaps because she had urged him forward with her heels, perhaps only because she had loosed his reins, the stallion was rounding the corner at an easy canter. There, still streets ahead though not so far as they had been, were the floaters, the third settling onto the rutted street, with the marching troopers closing behind it.

"For Echidna!" she shouted. "The gods will it!" Still she wished for war drums and horns, unaware that the drumming hooves echoed and re-echoed from each shiprock wall, that her trumpet had shaken the street. "Silk is Caldé!"

She jammed her sharp little heels in the stallion's sides. Fear was gone, replaced by soaring joy. *"Silk is Caldé!"* At her right the giant was firing two needlers as fast as he could pull their triggers.

"Down the Ayuntamiento! Silk is Caldé!"

The shimmering horror that was the azoth's blade could not be held on the foremost floater. Not by her, certainly not at this headlong gallop. Slashed twice across, the floater wept silvery metal as the street before it erupted in boiling dust and stones exploded from the gray walls of the Alambrera.

Abruptly, Yapok was on her right. To her left, Kingcup flailed a leggy bay with a long brown whip, Yapok bellowing obscenities, Kingcup shrieking curses, a nightmare witch, her loosed black hair streaming behind her.

The blade again, and the foremost floater burst in a ball of orange flame. Behind it, the buzz guns of the second were firing, the flashes from their muzzles mere sparks, the rattle of their shots lost in pandemonium. "Form up," she shouted, not knowing what she meant by it. Then, *"Forward! Forward!"*

Thousands of armed men and women were pouring from the buildings, crowding through doorways and leaping from windows. Yapok was gone, Kingcup somehow in front of her by half a length. Unseen hands snatched off her coif and plucked one flapping black sleeve.

The shimmering blade brought a gush of silver from the second floater, and there were no more flashes from its guns, only an explosion that blew off the turret—and a rain of stones upon the second floater, the third, and the Guardsmen behind it, and lines of slug guns booming from rooftops and high windows. But not enough, she thought. Not nearly enough, we must have more.

The azoth was almost too hot to hold. She took her thumb off the demon and was abruptly skyborn as the white stallion cleared a slab of twisted, smoking metal at a bound. The guns of the third floater were firing, the turret gun not at her but at the men and women pouring out of the buildings, the floater rising with a roar and a cloud of dust and sooty smoke that the wind snatched away, until the blade of her azoth impaled it and the floater crashed on its side, at once pathetic and comic.

To Silk's bewilderment, his captors had treated him with consideration, bandaging his wound and letting him lie unbound in an outsized bed with four towering posts which only that morning had belonged to some blameless citizen.

He had not lost consciousness so much as will. With mild surprise, he discovered that he no longer cared whether the Alambrera had surrendered, whether the Ayuntamiento remained in power, or whether the long sun would nourish Viron for ages to come or burn it to cinders. Those things had mattered. They no longer did. He was aware that he might die, but that did not matter either; he would surely die, whatever happened. If eventually, why not now? It would be over—over and done forever.

He imagined himself mingling with the gods, their humblest servitor and worshiper, yet beholding them face-to-face; and found that there was only one whom he desired to see, a god who was not among them.

"Well, well, well!" the surgeon exclaimed in a brisk, professional voice. "So you're Silk!"

He rolled his head on the pillow. "I don't think so."

"That's what they tell me. Somebody shoot you in the arm, too?"

"No. Something else. It doesn't matter." He spat blood.

"It does to me, that's an old dressing. It ought to be changed." The surgeon left, returning at once (it seemed) with a basin of water and a sponge. "I'm taking that ultrasonic diathermic wrapping on your ankle. We've got men who need it a lot more than you do."

"Then take it, please," Silk told him.

The surgeon looked surprised.

"What I mean is that 'Silk' has become someone a great deal bigger than I am—that I'm not what is meant when people say, 'Silk.' "

"You ought to be dead, Patera," the surgeon informed him somewhat later. "It'll do less damage if I open up the exit wound, instead of going in where the needle did. I'm going to turn you over. Did you hear that? I'm going to turn you over. Keep your nose and mouth to the side so you can breathe."

He did not, but the surgeon moved his head for him.

Abruptly he was sitting almost upright with a quilt around him while the surgeon stabbed him with another needle.

"It's not as bad as I thought, but you need blood. You'll feel a lot better with more blood in you."

A dark flask dangled from the bedpost like a ripe fruit.

Someone he could not see was seated beside his bed. He turned his head and craned his neck to no avail. At last he extended a hand toward the visitor; and the visitor took it between his own, which were large and hard and warm. As soon as their hands touched, he knew.

You said you weren't going to help, he told the visitor. You said I wasn't to expect help from you, yet here you are.

The visitor did not reply, but his hands were clean and gentle and full of healing.

"Are you awake, Patera?"

Silk wiped his eyes. "Yes."

"I thought you were. Your eyes were closed, but you were crying."

"Yes," Silk said again.

"I brought a chair. I thought we might talk for a minute. You don't mind?" The man with the chair was robed in black.

"No. You're an augur, like me."

"We were at the schola together, Patera. I'm Shell—Patera Shell now. You sat behind me in canonics. Remember?"

"Yes. Yes, I do. It's been a long time."

Shell nodded. "Nearly two years." He was thin and pale, but his small shy smile made his face shine.

"It was good of you to come and see me, Patera—very good." Silk paused for a moment to think. "You're on the other side, the Ayuntamiento's side. You must be. You're taking a risk by talking to me, I'm afraid."

"I was." Shell coughed apologetically. "Perhaps— I don't know, Patera. I—I haven't been fighting, you know. Not at all."

"Of course not."

"I brought the Pardon of Pas to our dying. To your dying, too, Patera, when I could. When that was done, I helped nurse a little. There aren't enough doctors and nurses, not nearly enough, and there was a big battle on Cage Street. Do you know about it? I'll tell you if you like. Nearly a thousand dead."

Silk shut his eyes.

"Don't cry, Patera. Please don't. They've gone to the gods. All of them, from both sides, and it wasn't your fault, I'm sure. I didn't see the battle, but I heard a great deal about it. From the wounded, you know. If you'd rather talk about something else—"

"No. Tell me, please."

"I thought you'd want to know, that I could describe it to you and it would be something that I could do for you. I thought you might want me to shrive you, too. We can close the door. I talked to the captain, and he said that as long as I didn't give you a weapon it would be all right."

Silk nodded. "I should have thought of it myself. I've been involved with so many secular concerns lately that I've been getting lax, I'm afraid." There was a bow window behind Shell; noticing that it displayed only black night and their own reflected images, Silk asked, "Is this still Hieraxday, Patera?"

"Yes, but its after shadelow. It's about seven-thirty, I think. There's a clock in the captain's room, and it was seven-twenty-five when I went in. Seven-twenty-five by that clock, I mean, and I wasn't there long. He's very busy."

"Then I haven't neglected Thelxiepeia's morning prayers." Briefly, he wondered whether he could bring himself to say them when morning came, and whether he should. "I won't have to ask forgiveness for that when you shrive me. But first, tell me about the battle."

"Your forces have been trying to capture the Alambrera, Patera. Do you know about that?"

"I knew they had gone to attack it. Nothing more."

"They were trying to break down the doors and so on. But they didn't, and everybody inside thought they had gone away, probably to try to take over the Juzgado."

Silk nodded again.

"But before that, the government—the Ayuntamiento, I mean—had sent a lot of troopers, with floaters and so on and a company of soldiers, to drive them away and help the Guards in the Alambrera."

"Three companies of soldiers," Silk said, "and the Second Brigade of the Guard. That's what I was told, at any rate."

Shell nearly bowed. "Your information will be much more accurate than mine, I'm sure, Patera. They had trouble getting through the city, even with soldiers and floaters, although not as much as they expected. Do you know about that?"

Silk rolled his head from side to side.

"They did. People were throwing things. One man told me he was hit by a slop jar thrown out of a fourth-floor window." Shell ventured an apologetic laugh. "Can you imagine? What will the people who live up there do tonight, I wonder? But there wasn't much serious resistance, if you know what I mean. They expected barricades in the street, but there was nothing like that. They marched through the city and stopped in front of the Alambrera. The troopers were supposed to go in while the soldiers searched the buildings along Cage Street."

Silk allowed his eyes to close again, visualizing the column described by the monitor in Maytera Rose's glass.

"Then," Shell paused for emphasis, "General Mint herself charged them down Cage Street, riding like a devil on a big white horse. From the other way, you see. From the direction of the market.''

Surprised, Silk opened his eyes. *''General* Mint?''

''That's what they call her. The rebels—your people, I mean.'' Shell cleared his throat. ''The fighters loyal to the Caldé. To you.''

''You're not offending me, Patera.''

''They call her General Mint and she's got an azoth. Just imagine! She chopped up the Guard's floaters horribly with it. This trooper I talked to had been the driver of one, and he'd seen everything. Do you know how the Guard's floaters are on the inside, Patera?''

''I rode in one this morning.'' Silk shut his eyes again, striving to remember. ''I rode inside until the rain stopped. Later I rode on it, sitting on the . . . Up on that round part that has the highest buzz gun. It was crowded inside, not at all comfortable, and we'd put the bodies in there—but it was better than being out in the rain, perhaps.''

Shell nodded eagerly, happy to agree. ''There are two men and an officer. One of the men drives the floater. He was the one I talked to. The officer's in charge. He sits beside the driver, and there's a glass for the officer, though some don't work any more, he said. The officer has a buzz gun, too, the one that points ahead. There's another man, the gunner, up in the round thing you sat on. It's called the turret.''

''That's right. I remember now.''

''General Mint's azoth cut right into their floater and killed their officer, and stopped one of the rotors. That's what this driver said. It had seemed to me that if an azoth could do that, it could cut right through the doors of the Alambrera and kill everyone in there, but he said they won't. That's because the doors are steel and three fingers thick, but a floater's armor is aluminum because it couldn't lift that much. It couldn't float at all, if it were made out of iron or steel.''

"I see. I didn't know that."

"There was cavalry following General Mint. About a troop is what he said. I asked how many that was, and it's a hundred or more. The others had needlers and swords and things. His floater had fallen on its side, but he crawled out through the hatch. The gunner had already gotten out, he said, and their officer was dead, but as soon as he got out himself, someone rode him down and broke his arm. That's why he's here, and without the gods' favor he would've been killed. When he got up again, there were rebels— I mean—''

"I know what you mean, Patera. Go on, please."

"They were all around him. He said he would have climbed back in their floater, but it was starting to burn, and he knew that if the fire didn't go out their ammunition would explode, the bullets for the buzz guns. He wasn't wearing armor like the troopers outside, just a helmet, so he pulled it off and threw it away, and the—your people thought he was one of them, most of them. He said that sometimes swords would cut the men's armor. It's polymeric, did you know that, Patera? Sometimes they silver it, private guards and so on do, like a glazier silvers the back of a mirror. But it's still polymeric under that, and the troopers' is painted green like a soldier.''

"It will stop needles, won't it?"

Shell nodded vigorously. "Mostly it will. Practically always. But sometimes a needle will go through the opening for the man's eyes, or where he breathes. When it does that, he's usually killed, they say. And sometimes a sword will cut right through their armor, if it's a big heavy sword, and the man's strong. Or stabbing can split the breastplate. A lot of your people had axes and hatchets. For firewood, you know. And some had clubs with spikes through them. A big club can knock down a trooper in armor, and if there's a spike in it, the spike will go right through." Shell paused for breath.

"But the soldiers aren't like that at all. Their skin's all metal, steel in the worst places. Even a slug from a slug gun will bounce off a soldier sometimes, and nobody can kill or even hurt a soldier with a club or a needler."

Silk said, I know, I shot one once, then realized that he had not spoken aloud. I'm like poor Mamelta, he thought—I have to remember to speak, to breathe out while I move my lips and tongue.

"One told me she saw two men trying to take a soldier's slug gun. They were both holding onto it, but he lifted them right off their feet and threw them around. This wasn't the driver but a woman I talked to, one of your people, Patera. She had her washing stick, and she got behind him and hit him with it, but he shook off the two men and hit her with the slug gun and broke her shoulder. A lot of your people had gotten slug guns from troopers by then, and they were shooting at the soldiers with them. Somebody shot the one fighting her. She would've been killed if it hadn't been for that she said. But the soldiers shot a lot of them, too, and chased them up Cheese Street and a lot of other streets. She tried to fight, but she didn't have a slug gun, and with her shoulder she couldn't have shot one if she'd had it. A slug hit her leg, and the doctors here had to cut it off."

"I'll pray for her," Silk promised, "and for everyone else who's been killed or wounded. If you see her again, Patera, please tell her how sorry I am that this happened. Was Maytera—was General Mint hurt?"

"They say not. They say she's planning another attack, but nobody really knows. Were you wounded very badly, Patera?"

"I don't believe I'm going to die." For seconds that grew to a minute or more, Silk stared in wonder at the empty flask hanging from the bedpost. Was life such a simple thing that it could be drained from a man as red fluid, or poured into him? Would he eventually discover that he held a different life, one which longed for a wife and children, in a house that he had never seen? It had not been his own blood—not his own life—surely. "I believed I was, not long ago. Even when you came, Patera. I didn't care. Consider the wisdom and mercy of the god who made us so that when we're about to die we no longer fear death!"

"If you don't think you're going to die—"

"No, no. Shrive me. The Ayuntamiento certainly intends to kill me. They can't possibly know I'm here; if they did, I'd be dead already." Silk pushed aside his quilt.

Hurriedly, Shell replaced it. "You don't have to kneel, Patera. You're still ill, terribly ill. You've been badly hurt. Turn your head toward the wall, please."

Silk did so, and the familiar words seemed to rise to his lips of their own volition. "Cleanse me, Patera, for I have given offense to Pas and to other gods." It was comforting, this return to ritual phrases he had memorized in childhood; but Pas was dead, and the well of his boundless mercy gone dry forever.

"Is that all, Patera?"

"Since my last shriving, yes."

"As penance for the evil you have done, Patera Silk, you are to perform a meritorious act before this time tomorrow." Shell paused and swallowed. "I'm assuming that your physical condition will permit it. You don't think it's too much? The recitation of a prayer will do."

"Too much?" With difficulty, Silk forced himself to keep his eyes averted. "No, certainly not. Too little, I'm sure."

"Then I bring to you, Patera Silk, the pardon of all the gods—"

Of *all* the gods. He had forgotten that aspect of the Pardon, fool that he was! Now the words brought a huge sense of relief. In addition to Echidna and her dead husband, in addition to the Nine and truly minor gods like Kypris, Shell was empowered to grant amnesty for the Outsider. For all the gods. Hence he, Silk, was forgiven his doubt.

He turned his head so that he could see Shell. "Thank you, Patera. You don't know—you can't—how much this means to me."

Shell's hesitant smile shone again. "I'm in a position to do you another favor, Patera. I have a letter for you from His Cognizance." Seeing Silk's expression, he added quickly, "It's only a circular letter, I'm afraid. All of us get a copy." He reached into his robe. "When I told Patera Jerboa you had been captured, he gave me yours, and it's about you."

The folded sheet Shell handed him bore the seal of the Chapter in mulberry-colored wax; beside it, a clear, clerkly hand had written: "Silk, Sun Street."

"It's a very important letter, really," Shell said.

Silk broke the seal and unfolded the paper.

30th Nemesis 332
To the Clergy of the Chapter,
Both Severally and Collectively

Greetings in the name of Pas, in the name of Scylla, and in the names of all gods! Know that you are ever in my thoughts, as in my heart.

The present disturbed state of Our Sacred City obliges us to be even more conscious of our sacred duty to minister to the dying, not only to those amongst them with whose recent actions we may sympathize, but to all those to whom, as we apprehend, Hierax may swiftly reveal his compassionate power. Thus it is that I implore you this day to cultivate the perpetual and indefatigable—

Patera Remora composed this, Silk thought; and as
though Remora sat before him, he saw Remora's long, sallow, uplifted face, the tip of the quill just brushing his lips as
he sought for a complexity of syntax that would satisfy his
insatiate longing for caution and precision.

> The perpetual and indefatigable predisposition toward
> mercy and pardon whose conduit you so frequently
> must be.
>
> Many of you have appealed for guidance in these
> most disturbing days. Nay, many appeal so still, even
> hourly. Most of you will have learned before you read
> this epistle of the lamented demise of the presiding
> officer of the Ayuntamiento.
>
> The late Councillor Lemur was a man of extra-
> ordinary gifts, and his passing cannot but leave a void in
> every heart. How I long to devote the remainder of this
> necessarily curtailed missive to mourning his passing.
> Instead, for such are the exactions of this sad whorl, the
> whorl that passes, my duty to you requires that I
> forewarn you without delay against the baseless pretexts
> of certain vile insurgents who would have you to believe
> that they act in the late Councillor Lemur's name.
>
> Let us set aside, my beloved clergy, all fruitless
> debate regarding the propriety of an intercaldéan
> caesura spanning some two decades. That the press of
> unhappy events then rendered an interval of that kind,
> if not desirable, then unquestionably attractive, we can
> all agree. That it represented, to judgments not daily
> schooled to the nice discriminations of the law, a severe
> strain upon the elasticity of our Charter, we can agree
> likewise, can we not? The argument is wholly historical
> now. O beloved, let us resign it to the historians.
>
> What is inarguable is that this caesura, to which I
> have had reason to refer above, has attained to its
> ordained culmination. It cannot, O my beloved clergy,

as it should not, survive the grievous loss which it has so recently endured. What, then, we may not illegitimately inquire, is to succeed that just, beneficent and ascendant government so sadly terminated?

Beloved clergy, let us not be unmindful of the wisdom of the past, wisdom which lies in no less a vehicle than our own Chrasmologic Writings. Has it not declared, *"Vox populi, vox dei"*? Which is to say, in the will of the masses we may discern words of Pas's. At the present critical moment in the lengthy epic of Our Sacred City, Pas's grave words are not to be mistaken. With many voices they cry out that the time has arrived for a precipitate return to that Charteral guardianship which once our city knew. Shall it be said of us that we stop our ears to Pas's words?

Nor is their message so brief, and so less than mistakable. From forest to lake, from the proud crown of the Palatine to the humblest of alleys they proclaim him. O my beloved clergy, with what incommunicable joy shall I do so additionally. For Supreme Pas has, as never previously, espoused for our city a caldé from within our own ranks, an anointed augur, holy, pious, and redolent of sanctity.

May I name him? I shall, yet surely I need not. There is not one amongst you, Beloved Clergy, who will not know that name prior to mine overjoyed acclamation. It is Patera Silk.

Again I say, Patera Silk!

How readily here might I inscribe, let us welcome him and obey him as one of ourselves. With what delight shall I inscribe in its place, let us welcome him and obey him, for he is one of ourselves!

May every god favor you, beloved clergy. Blessed be you in the Most Sacred Name of Pas, Father of the Gods, in that of Gracious Echidna, His Consort, in those of their Sons and their Daughters alike, this day and forever, in the name of their eldest child, Scylla, Patroness of this, Our Holy City of Viron. Thus say I, Pa. Quetzal, Prolocutor.

As Silk refolded the letter, Shell said, "His Cognizance has come down completely on your side, you see, and brought the Chapter with him. You said—I hope you were mistaken in this, Patera, really I do. But you said a minute ago that if the Ayuntamiento knew you were here they'd have you shot. If that's true—" He cleared his throat nervously. "If it's true, they'll have His Cognizance shot too. And—and some of the rest of us."

"The coadjutor," Silk said, "he drafted this. He'll die as well, if they can get their hands on him." It was strange to think of Remora, that circumspect diplomatist, tangled and dead in his own web of ink.

Of Remora dying for him.

"I suppose so, Patera." Shell hesitated, plainly ill at ease. "I'd call you—use the other word. But it might be dangerous for you."

Silk nodded slowly, stroking his cheek.

"His Cognizance says you're the first augur, ever. That— it came as a shock to—to a lot of us, I suppose. To Patera Jerboa, he said. He says it's never happened before in his life-time. Do you know Patera Jerboa, Patera?"

Silk shook his head.

"He's quite elderly. Eighty-one, because we had a little party for him just a few weeks ago. But then he thought, you know, sort of getting still and pulling at his beard the way he does, and then he said it was sensible enough, really. All the others, the previous—the previous—"

"I know what you mean, Patera."

"They'd been chosen by the people. But you, Patera, you were chosen by the gods, so naturally their choice fell upon an augur, since augurs are the people they've chosen to serve them.''

"You yourself are in danger, Patera," Silk said. "You're in nearly as much danger as I am, and perhaps more. You must be aware of it.''

Shell nodded miserably.

"I'm surprised they let you in here after this.''

"They—the captain, Patera. I—I haven't . . .''

"They don't know.''

"I don't think so, Patera. I don't think they do. I didn't tell them.''

"That was wise, I'm sure.'' Silk studied the window as he had before, but as before saw only their reflections, and the night. "This Patera Jerboa, you're his acolyte? Where is he?''

"At our manteion, on Brick Street.''

Silk shook his head.

"Near the crooked bridge, Patera.''

"Way out east?''

"Yes, Patera.'' Shell fidgeted uncomfortably. "That's where we are now, Patera. On Basket Street. Our manteion's that way," he pointed, "about five streets.''

"I see. That's right, they lifted me into something—into some sort of cart that jolted terribly. I remember lying on sawdust and trying to cough. I couldn't, and my mouth and nose kept filling with blood.'' Silk's index finger drew small circles on his cheek. "Where's my robe?''

"I don't know. The captain has it, I suppose, Patera.''

"The battle, when General Mint attacked the floaters on Cage Street, was that this afternoon?''

Shell nodded again.

"About the time I was shot, perhaps, or a little later. You brought the Pardon to the wounded. To all of them? All those in danger of death, I mean?''

"Yes, Patera.''

"Then you went back to your manteion—?"

"For something to eat, Patera, a bite of supper." Shell looked apologetic. "This brigade—it's the Third. They're in reserve, they say. They don't have much. Some were going into people's houses, you know, and taking any food they could find. There's supposed to be food coming in wagons, but I thought—"

"Of course. You returned to your manse to eat with Patera Jerboa, and this letter had arrived while you were gone. There would have been a copy for you, too, and one for him."

Shell nodded eagerly. "That's right, Patera."

"You would have read yours at once, of course. My copy—this one—it was there as well?"

"Yes, Patera."

"So someone at the Palace knew I had been captured, and where I'd been taken. He sent my copy to Patera Jerboa instead of to my own manteion in the hope that Patera Jerboa could arrange to get to me, as he did. His Cognizance was with me when I was shot; there's no reason to conceal that now. While my wounds were being treated, I was wondering whether he had been killed. The officer who shot me may not have recognized him, but if he did . . ." Silk let the thought trail away. "If they don't know about this already—and I think you're right, they can't know yet, not here at any rate—they're bound to find out soon. You realize that?"

"Yes, Patera."

"You must leave. It would probably be wise for you and Patera Jerboa to leave your manteion, in fact—to go to a part of the city controlled by General Mint, if you can."

"I—" Shell seemed to be choking. He shook his head desperately.

"You what, Patera?"

"I don't want to leave you as long as I can be of—of help to you. Of service. It's my duty."

"You have been of help," Silk told him. "You've rendered invaluable service to me and to the Chapter already. I'll see you're recognized for it, if I can." He paused, considering.

"You can be of further help, too. On your way out, I want you to speak to this captain for me. There were two letters in a pocket of my robe. They were on the mantel this morning; my acolyte must have put them there yesterday. I haven't read them, and your giving me this one has reminded me of them." Somewhat tardily, he thrust the letter under his quilt. "One had the seal of the Chapter. It may have been another copy of this, though that doesn't seem very likely, since this one has today's date. Besides, they wouldn't have sent this to Patera Jerboa this evening, in that case."

"I suppose not, Patera."

"Don't mention them to the captain. Just say I'd like to have my robe—all of my clothes. Ask for my clothes and see what he gives you. Bring them to me, my robe particularly. If he mentions the letters, say that I'd like to see them. If he won't give them to you, try to find out what was in them. If he won't tell you, return to your manteion. Tell Patera Jerboa that I, the caldé, order him to get himself and you—are there sibyls, too?"

Shell nodded. "There's Maytera Wood—"

"Never mind their names. That you and he and they are to lock up the manteion and leave as quickly as possible."

"Yes, Patera." Shell stood, very erect. "But I won't go back to our manteion straight away, no matter what the captain says. I—I'm coming back. Back here to see you and tell you what he said, and try to do something more for you, if I can. Don't tell me not to, please, Patera. I'll only disobey."

To his surprise, Silk found that he was smiling. "Your disobedience is better than the obedience of many people I've known, Patera Shell. Do what you think right; you will anyway, I feel certain."

Shell left, and the room seemed empty as soon as he was out the door. Silk's wound began to throb, and he made himself think of something else. How proudly Shell had announced his intention to disobey, while his lip trembled! It reminded Silk of his mother, her eyes shining with tears of joy at some only too ordinary childhood feat. *Oh, Silk! My son, my son!* That was how he felt now. These boys!

Yet Shell was no younger. They had entered the schola together, and Shell had sat at the desk in front of his own when an instructor insisted on alphabetical seating; they had been anointed on the same day, and both had been assigned to assist venerable augurs who were no longer able to attend to all the demands of their manteions.

Shell, however, had not been enlightened by the Outsider—or had not had a vein burst in his head, as Doctor Crane would have had it. Shell had not been enlightened, had not hurried to the market, had not encountered Blood. . . .

He had been as young as Shell when he had talked to Blood and plucked three cards out of Blood's hand, not knowing that somewhere below a monitor was mad and howling for want of those cards—as young or nearly, because Shell might have done it, too. Again Silk smelled the dead dog in the gutter and the stifling dust raised by Blood's floater, saw Blood wave his stick, tall, red faced, and perspiring. Silk coughed, and felt that a poker had been plunged into his chest.

Somewhat unsteadily, he crossed the room to the window and raised the sash to let in the night wind, then surveyed his naked torso in the mirror over the bureau, a much larger one than his shaving mirror back at the manse.

A dressing half concealed the multicolored bruise left by Musk's hilt. From what little anatomy he had picked up from the victims he had sacrificed, he decided that the needle had missed his heart by four fingers. Still, it must have been good shooting by a mounted man.

With his back to the mirror, he craned his neck to see as much as possible of the dressing on his back; it was larger, and his back hurt more. He was conscious of a weak wrongness deep in his chest, and of the effort he had to make to breathe.

Clothing in the drawers of the bureau: underwear, tunics, and carelessly folded trousers—under these last, a woman's perfumed scarf. This was a young man's room, a son's; the couple who owned the house would have a bedroom on the ground floor, a corner room with several windows.

Chilled, he returned to the bed and drew up the quilt. The son had left without packing, otherwise the drawers would be half empty. Perhaps he was fighting in Maytera Mint's army.

Some part of Kypris had entered her, and that fragment had made the shy sibyl a general—that, and Echidna's command. For a moment he wondered what fragment it had been, and whether Echidna had realized Maytera possessed it. It was the element that had freed Chenille from rust, presumably; they would be part and parcel of the same thing. Kypris had told him she was hunted, and His Cognizance had called it a wonder that she had not been killed long ago. Echidna and her children, hunting the goddess of love, must soon have learned that love is more than perfumed scarves and thrown flowers. That there is steel in love.

A young woman had thrown that scarf from a balcony, no doubt. Silk tried to visualize her, found she wore Hyacinth's face, and thrust the vision back. Blood had wiped his face with a peach-colored handkerchief, a handkerchief more heavily perfumed than the scarf. And Blood had said . . .

Had said there were people who could put on a man like a tunic. He had been referring to Mucor, though he, Silk, had not known it then—had not known that Mucor existed, a girl who could dress her spirit in the flesh of others just as he, a few moments before, had been considering putting on the clothes of the son whose room this was.

Softly he called, "Mucor? Mucor?" and listened; but there was no phantom voice, no face but his own in the mirror above the bureau. Closing his eyes, he composed a long formal prayer to the Outsider, thanking him for his life, and for the absence of Blood's daughter. When it was complete, he began a similar prayer to Kypris.

Beyond the bedroom door, a sentry sprang to attention with an audible clash of his weapon and click of his heels.

Shadeup woke Auk, brilliant beams of the long sun piercing his tasseled awnings, his gauze curtains, his rich draperies of puce velvet, and the grimed glass of every window in the place, slipping past his lowered blinds of split bamboo, the warped old boards someone else had nailed up, his colored Scylla, and his shut and bolted shutters; through wood, paper, and stone.

He blinked twice and sat up, rubbing his eyes. "I feel better," he announced, then saw that Chenille was still asleep, Incus and Urus both sleeping, Dace and Bustard sound asleep as well, and only big Hammerstone the soldier already up, sitting crosslegged with Oreb on his shoulder and his back against the tunnel wall. "That's good, trooper," Hammerstone said.

"Not good," Auk explained. "I don't mean that. Better. Better than I did, see? That feels better than good, 'cause when you're feeling good you don't even think about it. But when you feel the way I do, you pay more attention than when you're feeling good. I'm a dimberdamber nanny nipper." He nudged Chenille with the toe of his boot. "Look alive, Jugs. Time for breakfast!"

"What's the matter with *you?*" Incus sat up as though it had been he and not Chenille who had been thus nudged.

"Not a thing," Auk told him. "I'm right as rain." He considered the matter. "If it does, I'll go to the Cock. If it don't, I'll do some business on the hill. Slept with my boots on." He seated himself beside Chenille. "You too? You shouldn't do that, Patera. Bad on the feet."

Untying their laces, he tugged off his boots, then pulled off his stockings. "Feel how wet these are. Still wet from the boat. Wake up, old man! From the boat and the rain. If we had that tall ass again, I'd make him squirt fire for me so I could dry 'em. Phew!" He hung the stockings over the tops of his boots and pushed them away.

Chenille sat up and began to take off her jade earrings. "Ooh, did I dream!" She shuddered. "I was lost, see? All alone down here, and this tunnel I was in kept going deeper both ways. I'd walk one way for a long, long while, and it would just keep going down. So I'd turn around and walk the other way, only that way went down, too, deeper and deeper all the time."

"Recollect that the *immortal gods* are always with you, my daughter," Incus told her.

"Uh-huh. Hackum, I've got to get hold of some clothes. My sunburn's better. I could wear them, and it's too cold down here without any." She grinned. "A bunch of new clothes, and a double red ribbon. After that, I'll be ready for ham and half a dozen eggs scrambled with peppers."

"Watch out," Hammerstone warned her, "I don't think your friend's ready for inspection."

Auk rose, laughing. "Look at this," he told Hammerstone, and kicked Urus expertly, bending up his bare toes so that Urus's ribs received the ball of his foot.

Urus blinked and rubbed his eyes just as Auk had, and Auk realized that he himself was the long sun. He had awakened himself with his own light, light that filled the whole tunnel, too dazzlingly bright for Urus's weak eyes.

"The way you been carrying the old man," he told Urus,

"I don't like it." He wondered whether his hands were hot enough to burn Urus. It seemed possible; they were ordinary when he wasn't looking at them, but when he did they glowed like molten gold. Stooping, he flicked Urus's nose with a forefinger, and when Urus did not cry out, jerked him to his feet.

"When you carry the old man," Auk told him, "you got to do it like you love him. Like you were going to kiss him." It might be a good idea to make Urus really kiss him, but Auk was afraid Dace might not like it.

"All right," Urus said. "All right."

Bustard inquired, How you feelin', sprat?

Auk pondered. "There's parts of me that work all right," he declared at length, "and parts that don't. A couple I'm not set about. Remember old Marble?"

Sure.

"She told us she could pull out these lists. Out of her sleeve, like. What was right and what wasn't. With me, it's one thing at a time."

"I can do that," Hammerstone put in. "It's perfectly natural."

Chenille had both earrings off, and was rubbing her ears. "Can you put these in your pocket, Hackum? I got no place to carry them."

"Sure," Auk said. He did not turn to look at her.

"I could get a couple cards for them at Sard's. I could buy a good worsted gown and shoes, and eat at the pastry cook's till I was ready to split."

"Like, there's this dimber punch," Auk explained to Urus. "I learned it when I wasn't no bigger than a cobbler's goose, and I always did like it a lot. You don't swing, see? Culls always talk about swinging at you, and they do. Only this is better. I'm not sure it still works, though."

His right fist caught Urus square in the mouth, knocking him backward into the shiprock wall. Incus gasped.

"You sort of draw your arm up and straighten it out," Auk explained. Urus slumped to the tunnel floor. "Only with your weight behind it, and your knuckles level. Look at them." He held them out. "If your knuckles go up and down, that's all right, too. Only it's a different punch, see?" Not as good, Bustard said. "Only not as good," Auk confirmed.

I kin walk, big feller, he don't have to carry me, nor kiss me neither.

The dead body at his feet, Auk decided, must be somebody else. Urus, maybe, or Gelada.

Maytera Marble tried to decide how long it had been since she had done this, entering *roof,* and when that evoked only a flood of dripping ceilings and soaked carpets, *attic.*

A hundred and eighty-four years ago.

She could scarcely believe it—did not wish to believe it. A graceful girl with laughing eyes and industrious hands had climbed this same stair, as she still did a score of times every day, walked along this hall, and halted beneath this odd-looking door overhead, reaching up with a tool that had been lost now for more than a century.

She snapped her new fingers in annoyance, producing a loud and eminently satisfactory clack, then returned to one of the rooms that had been hers and rummaged through her odds-and-ends drawer until she found the big wooden crochet hook that she had sometimes plied before disease had deprived her of her fingers. Not these fingers, to be sure.

Back in the hall, she reached up as the girl who had been herself had and hooked the ring, wondering whimsically whether it had forgotten how to drop down on its chain.

It had not. She tugged. Puffs of dust emerged from the edges of the door above her head. The hall would have to be swept again. She hadn't been up there, no one had—

A harder tug, and the door inclined reluctantly downward, exposing a band of darkness. "Am I going to have to swing on you?" she asked. Her voice echoed through all the empty rooms, leaving her sorry she had spoken aloud.

Another tug evoked squeals of protest, but brought the bottom of the door low enough for her to grasp it and pull it down; the folding stair that was supposed to slide out when she did yielded to a hard pull.

I'll oil this, she resolved. I don't care if there isn't any oil. I'll cut up some fat from that bull and boil it, and skim off the grease and strain it, and use that. Because this *isn't* the last time. It *is not.*

She trotted up the folding steps in an energetic flurry of black bombazine.

Just look how good my leg is! Praise to you, Great Pas!

The attic was nearly empty. There was never much left when a sibyl died; what there was, was shared among the rest in accordance with her wishes, or returned to her family. For half a minute, Maytera Marble tried to recall who had owned the rusted trunk next to the chimney, eventually running down the whole list—every sibyl who had ever lived in the cenoby—without finding a single tin trunk among the associated facts.

The little gable window was closed and locked. She told herself that she was being foolish even as she wrestled its stubborn catch. Whatever it was that she had glimpsed in the sky while crossing the playground was gone, must certainly be gone by this time if it had ever existed.

Probably it had been nothing but a cloud.

She had expected the window to stick, but the dry heat of the last eight months had shrunk its ancient wood. She heaved at it with all her strength, and it shot up so violently that she thought the glass must break.

Silence followed, with a pleasantly chill wind through the window. She listened, then leaned out to peer up at the sky, and at last (as she had planned the whole time, having a lively appreciation of the difficulty of proving a negative after so many years of teaching small boys and girls) she stepped over the sill and out onto the thin old shingles of the cenoby roof.

Was it necessary to climb to the peak? She decided that it was, necessary for her peace of mind at least, though she wondered what the quarter would say if somebody saw her there. Not that it mattered, and most were off fighting anyhow. It wasn't as noisy as it had been during the day, but you could still hear shots now and then, like big doors shutting hard far away. Doors shutting on the past, she thought. The cold wind flattened her skirt against her legs as she climbed, and would have snatched off her coif had not one hand clamped it to her smooth metal head.

There were fires, as she could see easily from the peak, one just a few streets away. Saddle Street or String Street, she decided, probably Saddle Street, because that was where the pawnbrokers were. More fires beyond it, right up to the market and on the other side, as was to be expected. Darkness except for a few lighted windows up on Palatine Hill.

Which meant, more surely than any rumor or announcement, that Maytera Mint had not won. Hadn't won yet. Because the Hill would burn, would be looted and burned as predictably as the sixth term in a Fibonacci series of ten was an eleventh of the whole. With the Civil Guard beaten, nothing—

Before she could complete the thought, she caught sight of it, way to the south. She had been looking west toward the market and north to the Palatine, but it was over the Orilla . . . No, leagues south of that, way over the lake. Hanging low in the southern sky and, yes, opposing the wind in some fashion, because the wind was in the north, was blowing cold out of the north where night was new, because the wind must have come up, now that she came to think of it, only a few minutes before while she had been in the palaestra cutting up the last of the meat and carrying it down to the root cellar.

She had come upstairs again and found her hoarded wrapping papers blown all over the kitchen, and shut the window.

So this thing—this huge thing, whatever it might be—had been over the city or nearly over it when she had glimpsed it above the back wall of the ball court. And it wasn't being blown south any more, as a real cloud would be; if anything, it was creeping north toward the city again, was creeping ever so slowly down the sky.

She watched for a full three minutes to make sure.

Was creeping north like a beetle exploring a bowl, losing heart at times and retreating, then inching forward again. It had been here, had been over the city, before. Or almost over it, when the wind had risen—had been taken unawares, as it seemed, and blown away over the lake; and now it had collected its strength to return, wind or no wind.

So briefly that she was not sure she had really seen it, something flashed from the monstrous dark flying bulk, a minute pinprick of light, as though someone in the shadowy skylands behind it had squeezed an igniter.

Whatever it might be, there was no way for her to stop it. It would come, or it would not, and she had work to do, as she always did. Water, quite a lot of it, would have to be pumped to fill the wash boiler. She picked her way back to the gable, wondering how much additional damage she had done to a roof by no means tight to begin with.

She would have to carry wood in, enough for a big fire in the stove. Then she could wash the sheets from the bed she had died in and hang them out to dry. If Maytera Mint came back (and Maytera Marble prayed very fervently that she would) she could cook breakfast for her on the same fire, and Maytera Mint might even bring friends with her. The men, if there were any, could eat in the garden; she would carry one of the long tables and some chairs out of the palaestra for them. Luckily there was still plenty of meat, though she had cooked some for Villus and given more to his family when she had carried him home.

She stepped back into the attic and closed the window.

Her sheets would be dry by shadeup. She could iron them and put them back on her bed. She was still senior sibyl—or rather, was again senior sibyl, so both rooms were hers, though she probably ought to move everything into the big one.

Descending the folding steps, she decided that she would leave them down until she oiled them. She could cut off some fat and boil it in a saucepan while the wash water was getting hot; the boiler wouldn't take up the whole stove. By shadeup, the thing in the air would be back, perhaps; if she stood in the middle of Silver Street she might be able to see it quite clearly then, if she had time.

Auk felt sure they had been tramping through this tunnel forever, and that was funny because he could remember when they had turned off the other one to go down this one that they had been going down since Pas built the Whorl, Urus spitting blood and carrying the body, himself behind them in case Urus needed winnowing out, Dace and Bustard so they could talk to him, then Patera with the big soldier with the slug gun who had told them how to walk and made him do it, and last Chenille in Patera's robe, with Oreb and her launcher. Auk would rather have walked with her and had tried to, but it was no good.

He looked around at her. She waved friendly, and Bustard and Dace had gone. He thought of asking Incus and the soldier what had become of them but decided he didn't want to talk to them, and she was too far in back for a private chat. Bustard had most likely gone on ahead to look things over and taken the old man with him. It would be like Bustard, and if Bustard found something to eat he'd bring him back some.

Pray to Phaea, Maytera Mint instructed him. Phaea is the food goddess. Pray to her, Auk, and you will surely be fed. He grinned at her. "Good to see you, Maytera! I been worried about you." May every god smile upon you, Auk, this day and every day. Her smile turned the cold damp tunnel into a palace and replaced the watery green glow of the crawling light with the golden flood that had awakened him. Why should you worry about me, Auk? I have served the gods faithfully since I was fifteen. They will not abandon me. No one has less reason to worry than I. "Maybe you could get some god to come down here and walk with us," Auk suggested.

Behind him, Incus protested, *"Auk, my son!"*

He made a rude noise and looked around for Maytera Mint, but she was gone. For a minute he thought she might have run ahead to talk to Bustard, then realized that she had gone to fetch a god to keep him company. That was the way she'd always been. The least little thing you happened to mention, she'd jump up and do it if she could.

He was still worried about her, though. If she was going to Mainframe to fetch a god, she'd have to pass the devils that made trouble for people on the way, telling lies and pulling them off the Aureate Path. He should have asked her to go get Phaea. Phaea and maybe a couple pigs. Jugs would like some ham, and he still had his hanger and knife. He could kill a pig and cut it up, and dish up her ham. Shag, he was hungry himself and Jugs couldn't eat a whole pig. They'd save the tongue for Bustard, he'd always liked pig's tongue. It was Phaesday, so Maytera would most likely bring Phaea, and Phaea generally brought at least one pig. Gods generally brought whatever animal theirs was, or anyhow, pretty often.

Pigs for Phaea. (You had to get them all right if you wanted to learn the new stuff next year.) Pigs for Phaea and lions or anyhow cats for Sphinx. Who'd eat a cat? Fish for Scylla, but some fish would be all right. Little birds for Molpe, and the old 'un had limed perches for 'em, salted 'em, and made sparrow pie when he'd got enough. Bats for Tartaros, and owls and moles.

Moles?

Suddenly and unpleasantly it struck Auk that Tartaros was the underground god, the god for mines and caves. So this was his place, only Tartaros was supposed to be a special friend of his and look what had happened to him down here, he had made Tartaros shaggy mad at him somehow because his head hurt, his head wasn't right, something kept sliding and slipping up there like a needler that wouldn't chamber right no matter how much you oiled it and made sure every last needle was as straight as the sun. He reached under his tunic for his, but it wasn't right at all—was so wrong, in fact, that it wasn't there, though Maytera Mint was his mother and in need of him and it.

"Poor Auk! Poor Auk!" Oreb circled above his head. The wind from his laboring wings stirred Auk's hair, but Oreb would not settle on his shoulder, and soon flew back to Chenille.

It wasn't there any more and neither was she. Auk wept.

The captain's salute was much smarter than his torn and soiled green uniform. "My men are in position, My General. My floater is patrolling. To reinforce the garrison by stealth is no longer possible. Nor will reinforcement at the point of the sword be possible, until we are dead."

Bison snorted, tilting back the heavy oak chair that was temporarily his.

Maytera Mint smiled. "Very good, Captain. Thank you. Perhaps you had better get some rest now."

"I have slept, My General, though not long. I have eaten

as well, as you, I am told, have not. Now I inspect my men at their posts. When my inspection is complete, perhaps I shall sleep another hour, with my sergeant to wake me.''

''I'd like to go with you,'' Maytera Mint told him. ''Can you wait five minutes?''

''Certainly, My General. I am honored. But . . .''

She looked at him sharply. ''What is it, Captain? Tell me, please.''

''You yourself must sleep, My General, and eat as well. Or you will be fit for nothing tomorrow.''

''I will, later. Please sit down. We're tired, all of us, and you must be exhausted.'' She turned back to Bison. ''We have a principle in the Chapter, for sibyls like me and augurs like Patera Silk. Discipline, it's called, and it comes from an old word for pupil or student. If you're a teacher, as I am, you must have discipline in the classroom before you can teach anything. If you don't, they'll be so busy talking among themselves that they won't hear a thing that you say, and draw pictures instead of doing the assignment.''

Bison nodded.

Recalling an incident from the year before, Maytera Mint smiled again. ''Unless you've *told* them to draw pictures. If you've told them to draw, they'll write each other notes.''

The captain smoothed his small mustache. ''My General. We have discipline also, we officers and men of the Civil Guard. The word is the same. The practice, I dare say, not entirely different.''

''I know, but I can't use you to patrol the streets and stop the looting. I wish I could, Captain. It would be very convenient, and no doubt effective. But to many people the Guard is the enemy. There would be a rebellion against our rebellion, and that's exactly what we cannot afford.''

She turned back to Bison. ''You understand why this is needed, don't you? Tell me.''

''We're robbing ourselves,'' he said.

His beard made it difficult to read his expression, but she tried and decided he was uncomfortable. "What you say is true. The people whose houses and shops are being looted are our people, too, and if they have to stay there to defend them, they can't fight for us. But that isn't all, is it? What else did you want to say?"

"Nothing, General."

"You must tell me everything." She wanted to touch him, as she would have touched one of the children at that moment, but decided it might be misconstrued. "Telling me everything when I ask you to is discipline as well, if you like. Are we going to let the Guard be better than we are?"

Bison did not reply.

"But it's really more important than discipline. Nothing is more important to us now than my knowing what you think is important. You and the captain here, and Zoril, and Kingcup, and all the rest."

When he still said nothing, she added, "Do you want us to fail, so you won't be embarrassed, Bison? That is what is going to happen if we won't share concerns and information: we will fail the gods and die. All of us, probably. Certainly I will, because I will fight until they kill me. What is it?"

"They're burning, too," he blurted. "The burning's worse than the looting, a lot worse. With this wind, they'll burn down the city if we don't stop them. And—and . . ."

"And what?" Maytera Mint nibbled her underlip. "And put out the fires that are raging all around the city already, of course. You're right, Bison. You always are." She glanced at the door. "Teasel? Are you still out there? Come in, please. I need you."

"Yes, Maytera."

"We're telling one another we should rest, Teasel. It seems to be the convention of this night. You're not exempt. You were quite ill only a few days ago. Didn't Patera Silk bring you the Peace of Pas?"

Teasel nodded solemnly; she was a slender, pale girl of thirteen, with delicate features and lustrous black hair. "On Sphixday, Maytera, and I started getting better right away."

"Sphixday, and this is Hieraxday." Maytera Mint glanced at the blue china clock on the sideboard. "Thelxday in a few hours, so we'll call it Thelxday. Even so, less than a week ago you were in imminent danger of death, and tonight you're running errands for me when you ought to be in bed. Can you run one more?"

"I'm fine, Maytera."

"Then find Lime. Tell her where I am, and that I want to see her just as soon as she can get away. Then go home and go to bed. *Home,* I said. Will you do that, Teasel?"

Teasel curtsied, whirled, and was gone.

"She's a good, sensible girl," Maytera Mint told Bison and the captain. "Not one of mine. Mine are older, and they're off fighting or nursing, or they were. Teasel's one of Maytera Marble's, very likely the best of them."

Both men nodded.

"Captain, I won't keep you waiting much longer. Bison, I had begun to talk about discipline. I was interrupted, which served me right for being so long-winded. I was going to say that out of twenty boys and girls, you can make eighteen good students with discipline. I can, and you could too. In fact you would probably be better at it than I am, with a little practice." She sighed, then forced herself to sit up straight with her shoulders back.

"Of the remaining two, one will never be a good student. He doesn't have it in him, and all you can do is stop him from unsettling the others. The other one doesn't need discipline at all, or at least that's how it seems. Pas's own truth is that he's already disciplined himself before you ever called the class to order. Do you understand me?"

Bison nodded.

"You're one of those. If you weren't, you wouldn't be my surrogate now. Which you are, you know. If I am killed, you must take charge of everything."

Bison grinned, big white teeth flashing in the thicket of his black beard. "The gods love you, General. Your getting killed's one thing I don't have to worry about."

She waited for a better answer.

"Hierax forbid," Bison said at last. "I'll do my best if it happens."

"I know you will, because you always do. What you have to do is find others like yourself. We don't have enough time to establish real discipline, though I wish very much that we did. Choose men with needlers, we won't need slug guns for this—older men, who won't loot themselves when they're sent to stop looters. Organize them in groups of four, designate a leader for each group, and have them tell— Don't forget this, it's extremely important. Have them tell everyone they meet that looting and burning have to stop, and they'll shoot anyone they find doing either."

She rose. "We'll go now, Captain. I want to see how you've arranged this. I've a great deal to learn and very little time to learn it in."

Horn and Nettle, he with a captured slug gun and she with a needler, had stationed themselves outside the street door.

"Horn, go in the house and find yourself a bed," Maytera Mint told him. "That is an order. When you wake up, come back here and relieve Nettle if she's still here. Nettle, I'm going around the Alambrera with the captain. I'll be back soon."

The wind that chilled her face seemed almost supernatural after so many months of heat; she murmured thanks to Molpe, then recalled that the wind was fanning the fires Bison feared, and that it might—that in some cases it most certainly would—spread fire from shop to stable to manufactory. That there was a good chance the whole city would burn while she fought the Ayuntamiento for it.

"The Ayuntamiento. They aren't divine, Captain."

"I assure you, I have never imagined that they were, My General." He guided her down a crooked street whose name she had forgotten, if she had ever known it; around its shuttered store fronts the wind whispered of snow.

"Since they aren't," she continued, "they can't possibly resist the will of the gods for long. It is Echidna's will, certainly. I think we can be sure it's Scylla's too."

"Also that of Kypris," he reminded her. "Kypris spoke to me, My General, saying that Patera Silk must be caldé. I serve you because you serve him, him because he serves her."

She had scarcely heard him. "Five old men. Four, if His Cognizance is right, and no doubt he is. What gives them the courage?"

"I cannot guess, My General. Here is our first post. Do you see it?"

She shook her head.

"Corporal!" the captain called. Hands clapped, and lights kindled across the street; a gleaming gun barrel protruded from a second-floor window. The captain pointed. "We have a buzz gun for this post, as you see, My General. A buzz gun because the street offers the most direct route to the entrance. The angle affords us a longitudinal field of fire. Down there," he pointed again, "a step or two more, and we could be fired upon from an upper window of the Alambrera."

"They could come down this street, straight across Cage, and go into the Alambrera?"

"That is correct, My General. Therefore we will not go farther. This way, please. You do not object to the alley?"

"Certainly not."

How strange the service of the gods was! When she was

only a girl, Maytera Mockorange had told her that the gods'
service meant missing sleep and meals, and had made her
give that response each time she was asked. Now here she
was; she hadn't eaten since breakfast, but by Thelxiepeia's
grace she was too tired to be hungry.

"The boy you sent off to bed." The captain chuckled.
"He will sleep all night. Did you foresee that, My General?
The poor girl will have to remain at her post until morning."

"Horn? No more than three hours, Captain, if that."

The alley ended at a wider steet. Mill Street, Maytera Mint
told herself, seeing the forlorn sign of a dark coffee shop
called the Mill. Mill Street was where you could buy odd
lengths of serge and tweed cheaply.

"Here we are out of sight, though not hidden from sentries on the wall. Look." He pointed again. "Do you recognize it, My General?"

"I recognize the wall of the Alambrera, certainly. And I
can see a floater. Is it yours? No, it can't be, or they'd be
shooting at it, and the turret's missing."

"It is one of those you destroyed, My General. But it is
mine now. I have two men in it." He halted. "Here I leave
you for perhaps three minutes. It is too dangerous for us to
proceed, but I must see that all is well with them."

She let him trot away, waiting until he had almost reached
the disabled floater before she began to run herself, running
as she had so often pictured herself running in games with
the children at the palaestra, her skirt hiked to her knees and
her feet flying, the fear of impropriety gone who could say
where.

He jumped, caught the edge of the hole where the turret
had been, pulled himself up and rolled over, vanishing into
the disabled floater. Seeing him, she felt less confident that
she could do it too.

Fortunately she did not have to; when she was still half a
dozen strides away, a door opened in its side. "I did not think

you would remain behind, My General," the captain told her, "though I dared hope. You must not risk yourself in this fashion."

She nodded, too breathless to speak, and ducked into the floater. It was cramped yet strangely roofless, the crouching Guardsmen clearly ill at ease, trained to snap to attention but compressed by circumstance. "Sit down," she ordered them, "all of you. We can't stand on formality in here."

That word *stand* had been unwisely chosen, she reflected. They sat anyway, with muttered thanks.

"This buzz gun, you see, My General," the captain patted it, "once it belonged to the commander of this floater. He missed you, so it is yours."

She knew nothing about buzz guns and was curious despite her fatigue. "Does it still operate? And do you have," at a loss, she waved a vague hand, "whatever it shoots?"

"Cartridges, My General. Yes, there are enough. It was the fuel that exploded in this floater, you see. They are not like soldiers, these floaters. They are like taluses and must have fish oil or palm-nut oil for their engines. Fish oil is not so nice, but we employ it because it is less costly. This floater carried sufficient ammunition for both guns, and there is sufficient still."

"I want to sit there." She was looking at the officer's seat. "May I?"

"Certainly, My General." The captain scrambled out of her way.

The seat was astonishingly comfortable, deeper and softer than her bed in the cenoby, although its scorched upholstery smelled of smoke. Not astonishing, Maytera Mint told herself, not really. To be expected, because it had been an officer's seat, and the Ayuntamiento treated officers well, knowing that its power rested on them; that was something to keep in mind, one more thing she must not forget.

"Do not touch the trigger, My General. The safety catch

is disengaged.'' The captain reached over her shoulder to push a small lever. ''Now it is engaged. The gun will not fire.''

''This spiderweb thing.'' She touched it instead. ''Is it what you call the sight?''

''Yes, the rear sight, My General. The little post you see at the end of the barrel, that is the front sight. The gunner aligns the two, so that he sees the top of the post in one or another of the small rectangles.''

''I see.''

''Higher rectangles, My General, if the target is distant. To left or right if there is a strong wind, or because the gun favors one side or another.''

She leaned back in the seat and allowed herself, for no more than a second or two, to close her eyes. The captain was saying something about night vision, short bursts hitting more than long ones, about fields of fire.

Fire was eating up somebody's home while he talked, and Lime (if Teasel had found her quickly and she hadn't been far) was looking for her right now, going from sentry post to post to post. Looking for her and asking people at each post whether they had seen her, whether they knew where the next one was and whether they would take her there because of the fires, because Bison had known, had rightly known that the fires must be put out but had been afraid to say it because he had known his people couldn't do it, could not, men and women who had fought so long and hard already all day, fight fires tonight and fight again tomorrow. Bison who made her feel so strong and competent, whose thick and curling black beard was longer than her hair. Maytera Mockorange had warned her about going without her coif, which was not just against the rule but stimulating to a great many men who were aroused by the sight of women's hair, particularly if long. She had lost her coif somewhere, had gone without it though her hair was short, though it had been cropped short on the first day, all of it.

She fled Maytera Mockorange's anger down dark cold halls full of sudden turnings until she found Auk, who reminded her that she was to bring him the gods.

"I am Colonel Oosik, Caldé," Silk's visitor informed him. He was a big man, so tall and broad that Shell was hidden by his green-uniformed bulk.

"The officer who directs this brigade," Silk offered his hand. "In command. Is that what you say? I'm Patera Silk."

"You have familiarized yourself with our organization." Oosik sat down in the chair Shell had carried in earlier.

"Not really. Are those my clothes you have?"

"Yes." Oosik held them up, an untidy black bundle. "We will speak of them presently, Caldé. If you have made no study of our organization charts, how is it you know my position?"

"I saw a poster." Silk paused, remembering. "I was going to the lake with a woman named Chenille. The poster announced the formation of a reserve brigade. It was signed by you, and it told anyone who wanted to join it to apply to Third Brigade Headquarters. Patera Shell was kind enough to look in on me a few minutes ago, and he happened to mention that this was the Third Brigade. After he had gone, I recalled your poster."

Shell said hurriedly, "The colonel was in the captain's room when I got there, Patera. I told them I'd wait, but he made me come in and asked what I wanted, so I told him."

"Thank you," Silk said. "Please return to your manteion at once, Patera. You've done everything that you can do here tonight." Trying to freight the words with significance, he added, "It's already late. Very late."

"I thought, Patera—"

"Go," Oosik tugged his drooping mustache. "Your caldé and I have delicate matters to discuss. He understands that. So should you."

"I thought—"

"Go!" Oosik had scarcely raised his voice, yet the word was like the crack of a whip. Shell hurried out.

"Sentry! Shut the door."

The mustache was tipped with white, Silk observed; Oosik wound it about his index finger as he spoke. "Since you have not studied our organization, Caldé, you will not know that a brigade is the command of a general, called a brigadier."

"No." Silk admitted. "I've never given it any thought."

"In that case no explanation is necessary. I had planned to tell you, so that each of us would know where we stand, that though I am a mere colonel, an officer of field grade," Oosik released his mustache to touch the silver osprey on his collar, "I command my brigade exactly as a brigadier would. I have for four years. Do you want your clothes?"

"Yes. I'd like to get dressed, if you'll let me."

Oosik nodded, though it was not clear whether his nod was meant to express permission or understanding. "You are nearly dead, Caldé. A needle passed through your lung."

"Nevertheless, I'd feel better if I were up and dressed." It was a lie, although he wished fervently that it were true. "I'd be sitting on this bed then, instead of lying in it; but I've got nothing on."

Oosik chuckled. "You wish your shoes as well?"

"My shoes and my stockings. My underwear, my trousers, my tunic, and my robe. Please, Colonel."

The corners of the mustache tilted upward. "Dressed, you might easily escape, Caldé. Isn't that so?"

"You say I'm near death, Colonel. A man near death might escape, I suppose; but not easily."

"We have handled you roughly here in the Third, Caldé. You have been beaten. Tortured."

Silk shook his head. "You shot me. At least, I suppose that it was one of your officers who shot me. But I've been treated by a doctor and installed in this comfortable room. No one has beaten me.''

"With your leave." Oosik peered at him. "Your face is bruised. I assumed that we had beaten you."

Silk shook his head, pushing back the memory of hours of interrogation by Councillor Potto and Sergeant Sand.

"You do not wish to explain the source of your bruises. You have been fighting, Caldé, a shameful thing for an augur. Or boxing. Boxing would be permissible, I suppose."

"Through my own carelessness and stupidity, I fell down a flight of stairs," Silk said.

To his surprise, Oosik roared with laughter, slapping his knee. "That is what our troopers say, Caldé," he wiped his eyes, still chuckling, "when one has been beaten by the rest. He says he fell down the barracks stairs, almost always. They don't want to confess that they've cheated their comrades, you see, or stolen from them."

"In my case it's the truth." Silk considered. "I had been trying to steal, though not to cheat, two days earlier. But I really did fall down steps and bruise my face."

"I am happy to hear you haven't been beaten. Our men do it sometimes without orders. I have known them to do it when it was contrary to their orders, as well. I punish them for that severely, you may be sure. In your case, Caldé," Oosik shrugged. "I sent out an officer because I required better information concerning the progress of the battle before the Alambrera than my glass could give me. I had made provisions for wounded and for prisoners. I needed to learn whether they would be sufficient."

"I understand."

"He came back with you." Oosik sighed. "Now he expects a medal and a promotion for putting me in this very difficult position. You understand my problem, Caldé?"

"I'm not sure I do."

"We are fighting, you and I. Your followers, a hundred

thousand or more, against the Civil Guard, of which I am a senior officer, and a few thousand soldiers. Either side may win. Do you agree?''

"I suppose so," Silk said.

"Let us say, for the moment, that it is mine. I do not intend to be unfair to you, Caldé. We will discuss the other possibility in a moment. Say that the victory is ours, and I report to the Ayuntamiento that you are my prisoner. I will be asked why I did not report it earlier, and I may be court-martialed for not having reported it. If I am fortunate, my career will be destroyed. If I am not, I may be shot.''

"Then report it," Silk told him, "by all means."

Oosik shook his head again, his big face gloomier than ever. "There is no right course for me in this, Caldé. No right course at all. But there is one that is clearly wrong, that can lead only to disaster, and you have advised it. The Ayuntamiento has ordered that you be killed on sight. Do you know that?''

"I had anticipated it." Silk discovered that his hands were clenched beneath the quilt. He made himself relax.

"No doubt. Lieutenant Tiger should have killed you at once. He didn't. May I be frank? I don't think he had the stomach for it. He denies it, but I don't think he had the stomach. He shot you. There you lay, an augur in an augur's robe, gasping like a fish and bleeding from the mouth. One more shot would be the end." Oosik shrugged. "No doubt he thought you would die while he was bringing you in. Most men would have.''

"I see," Silk said. "He'll be in trouble now if you tell the Ayuntamiento that you have me, alive.''

"*I* will be in trouble." Oosik tapped his chest with a thick forefinger. "I will be ordered to kill you, Caldé, and I will have to do it. If we lose after that, your woman Mint will have me shot, if she doesn't light upon something worse. If we win, I will be marked for life. I will be the man who killed Silk, the augur who was, as the city firmly believes, chosen by Pas to be caldé. If it is wise, the Ayuntamiento will disavow my actions, court-martial me, and have me shot. No, Caldé, I will not report that I hold you. That is the last thing that I will do."

"You said that the Guard and the Army—I've been told there are seven thousand soldiers—are fighting the people. What is the strength of the Guard, Colonel?" Silk strove to recall his conversation with Hammerstone. "Thirty thousand, approximately?"

"Less."

"Some Guardsmen have deserted the Ayuntamiento. I know that for a fact."

Oosik nodded gloomily.

"May I ask how many?"

"A few hundred, perhaps, Caldé."

"Would you say a thousand?"

For half a minute or more, Oosik did not speak; at last he said, "I am told five hundred. If that is correct, almost all have come from my own brigade."

"I have something to show you," Silk said, "but I have to ask you for a promise first. It's something that Patera Shell brought me, and I want you to give me your word that you won't harm him or the augur of his manteion, or any of their sibyls. Will you promise?"

Oosik shook his head. "I cannot disobey if I am ordered to arrest them, Patera."

"If you're not ordered to." It should give them ample time to leave, Silk thought. "Promise me that you won't do anything to them on your own initiative."

Oosik studied him. "You are offering your information very cheaply, Caldé. We don't bother you religious, except under the most severe provocation."

"Then I have your word as an officer?"

Oosik nodded, and Silk took the Prolocutor's letter from under his quilt and handed it to him. He unbuttoned a shirt pocket and got out a pair of silver-rimmed glasses, shifting his position slightly so that the light fell upon the letter.

In the silence that followed, Silk reviewed everything Oosik had said. Had he made the right decision? Oosik was ambitious—had probably volunteered to take charge of the reserve brigade as well as his own in the hope of gaining the rank and pay to which his position entitled him. He might be, in fact he almost certainly was, underestimating the fighting capabilities of soldiers like Sand and Hammerstone; but he was sure to know a great deal about those of the Civil Guard, in which he had spent his adult life; and he was considering the possibility that the Ayuntamiento would lose. The Prolocutor's letter, with its implications of increased support for Maytera Mint, might tilt the balance.

Or so Silk hoped.

Oosik looked up. "This says Lemur's dead."

Silk nodded.

"There have been rumors all day. What if your Prolocutor is simply repeating them?"

"He's dead." Silk made the statement as forceful as he could, fortified by the knowledge that for once there was no need to hedge the truth. "You've got a glass, Colonel. You must. Ask it to find Lemur for you."

"You saw him die?"

Silk shook his head, saying, "I saw his body, however," and Oosik returned to the letter.

Too much boldness could ruin everything; it would be worse than useless to try to make Oosik say or do anything that could be brought up against him later.

Oosik put down the letter. "The Chapter is behind you, Caldé. I suspected as much, and this makes it very plain."

"It is now, apparently." Here was a chance for Oosik to declare himself. "If you suspected it before you read that letter, Colonel, it was doubly kind of you to let Patera Shell in to see me."

"I didn't, Caldé. Captain Gecko did."

"I see. But you'll keep your promise?"

"I am a man of honor, Caldé." Oosik refolded the letter and put it in his pocket with his glasses. "I will also keep this. Neither of us would want anyone else to read it. One of my officers, particularly."

Silk nodded. "You're welcome to."

"You want your clothes back. No doubt you would like to have the contents of your pockets as well. Your beads are in there, I think. I imagine you would like to tell them as you lie here."

"I would, yes. Very much."

"There are needlers, too. One is like the one with which you were shot. There is also a smaller one that seems to have belonged to a woman named Hyacinth."

"Yes," Silk said again.

"I see. I know her, if she is the Hyacinth I'm thinking of. An amiable girl, as well as a very beautiful one. I lay with her on Phaesday."

Silk shut his eyes.

"I did not set out to give you pain, Caldé. Look at me. I'm old enough to be your father, or hers. Do you imagine she sends me love letters?"

"Is that . . . ?"

"What one of the letters in your pocket is?" Oosik nodded solemnly. "Captain Gecko told me the seals had not been broken when he found them. Quite frankly, I doubted him. I see that I should not have. You have not read them."

"No," Silk said.

"Captain Gecko has, and I. No one else. Gecko can be discreet if I order it, and a man of honor must be a man of discretion, also. Otherwise he is worse than useless. You did not recognize her seal?"

Silk shook his head. "I've never gotten a letter from her before."

"Caldé, I have never gotten one at all." Oosik tugged his mustache. "You would be well advised to keep that before you. Many letters from women over the years, but never one from her. I say again, I envy you."

"Thank you," Silk said.

"You love her." Oosik leaned back in his chair. "That is not a question. You may not know it, but you do." His voice softened. "I was your age once, Caldé. Do you realize that in a month it may be over?"

"In a day it may be over," Silk admitted. "Sometimes I hope it will be."

"You fear it, too. You need not say so. I understand. I told you I knew her and it gave you pain, but I do not want you to think, later, that I have been less than honest. I am being equally honest now. Brutally honest with myself. My pride. I am nothing to her."

"Thank you again," Silk said.

"You are welcome. I do not say that she is nothing to me. I am not a man of stone. But there are others, several who are much more. To explain would be offensive."

"Certainly you don't have to go into details unless you want me to shrive you. May I see her letter?"

"In a moment, Caldé. Soon I will give it to you to keep. I think so, at least. There is one further matter to be dealt with. You chanced to mention a woman called Chenille. I know a woman of that name, too. She lives in a yellow house."

Silk smiled and shook his head.

"That does not pain you at all. She is not the Chenille you took to the lake?"

"I was amused at myself—at my stupidity. She told me she had entertained colonels; but until you said you knew her, it had never entered my mind that you were almost certain to be one of them. There can't be a great many."

"Seven besides myself." Oosik rummaged in the bundle of clothing and produced Musk's big needler and Hyacinth's small, gold-plated one. After holding them up so that Silk could see them, he laid them on the windowsill.

"The little one is hers," Silk said. "Hyacinth's. Could you see that it's returned to her?"

Oosik nodded. "I shall send it by a mutual acquaintance. What about the large one?"

"The owner's dead. I suppose it's mine now."

"I am too well mannered to ask if you killed him, but I hope he was not one of our officers."

"No," Silk said, "and no. I confess I was tempted to kill him several times—as he was undoubtedly tempted to kill me—but I didn't. I've only killed once, in self-defense. May I read Hyacinth's letter now?"

"If I can find it." Oosik fumbled through Silk's clothes again, then held up both the letters Silk had taken from the mantel in the manse that morning. "This other is from another augur. You have no interest in it?"

"Not as much, I'm afraid. Who is it?"

"I have forgotten." Oosik extracted the letter from its envelope and unfolded it. " 'Patera Remora, Coadjutor.' He wishes to see you, or he did. You were to come to his suite in the Prolocutor's Palace yesterday at three. You are more than a day late already, Caldé. Do you want it?"

"I suppose so," Silk said; and Oosik tossed it on the bed.

Oosik rose, holding out Hyacinth's letter. "This one you will not wish to read while I watch, and I have urgent matters to attend to. I may look in on you again, later this evening. Much later. If I am too busy, I will see you in the morning, perhaps." He tugged his mustache. "Will you think me a fool if I say I wish you well, Caldé? That if we were no longer opponents I should consider your friendship an honor?"

"I'd think you were an estimable, honorable man," Silk told him, "which you are."

"Thank you, Caldé!" Oosik bowed, with a click of his booted heels.

"Colonel?"

"Your beads. I had forgotten. You will find them in a pocket of the robe, I feel sure." Oosik turned to go, but turned back. "A matter of curiosity. Are you familiar with the Palatine, Caldé?"

Silk's right hand, holding Hyacinth's letter, had begun to tremble; he pressed it against his knee so that Oosik would not see it. "I've been there." By an effort of will, he kept his voice almost steady. "Why do you ask?"

"Often, Caldé?"

"Three times, I believe." It was impossible to think of anything but Hyacinth; he could as easily have said fifty, or never. "Yes, three times—once to the Palace, and twice to attend sacrifice at the Grand Manteion."

"Nowhere else?"

Silk shook his head.

"There is a place having a wooden figure of Thelxiepeia. As an augur, you may know where it is."

"There's an onyx image in the Grand Manteion—"

Oosik shook his head. "In Ermine's, to the right as one enters the sellaria. One sees an arch with greenery beyond it. At the rear, there is a pool with goldfish. She stands by it holding a mirror. The lighting is arranged so that the pool is reflected in her mirror, and her mirror in the pool. It is mentioned in that letter." Oosik turned upon his heel.

"Colonel, these needlers—"

He paused at the door. "Do you intend to shoot your way to freedom, Caldé?" Without waiting for Silk's reply he went out, leaving the door ajar behind him. Silk heard the sentry come to attention, and Oosik say, "You are dismissed. Return to the guardroom immediately."

Silk's hands were still shaking as he unfolded Hyacinth's letter; it was on stationery the color of heavy cream, scrawled in violet ink, with many flourishes.

O My Darling Wee Flea:

 I call you so not only because of the way you sprang from my window, but because of the way you hopped into my bed! How your lonely bloss has longed for a note from you!!! You might have sent one by the kind friend who brought you my gift, you know!

That had been Doctor Crane, and Doctor Crane was dead—had died in his arms that very morning.

Now you have to tender me your thanks and so much more, when next we meet! Don't you know that little place up on the Palatine where Thelx holds up a mirror? *Hieraxday.*

Hy

Silk closed his eyes. It was foolish, he told himself. Utterly foolish. The semiliterate scribbling of a woman whose education had ended at fourteen, a girl who had been given to her father's superior as a household servant and concubine, who had scarcely read a book or written a letter, and was trying to flirt, to be arch and girlish and charming on paper. How his instructors at the schola would have sneered!

 Utterly foolish, and she had called him darling, had said she longed for him, had risked compromising herself and Doctor Crane to send him this.

 He read it again, refolded it, and returned it to its envelope, then pushed aside the quilt and got up.

 Oosik had intended him to go, of course—had intended him to escape, or perhaps to be killed escaping. For a few seconds he tried to guess which. Had Oosik been insincere in speaking of friendship? Oosik was capable of any quantity of double-dealing, if he was any judge of men.

 It did not matter.

 He took his clothing from the chair and spread it on the

bed. If Oosik intended him to escape, he must escape as Oosik intended. If Oosik intended him to be killed escaping, he must escape just the same, doing his best to remain alive.

His tunic was crusted with his own blood and completely unwearable; he threw it down and sat on the bed to pull on his undershorts, trousers, and stockings. When he had tied his shoes, he rose and jerked open a drawer of the bureau.

Most of the tunics were cheerful reds and yellows; but he found a blue one, apparently never worn, so dark that it might pass for black under any but the closest scrutiny. He laid it on the pillow beside the letters, and put on a yellow one. The closet yielded a small traveling bag. Slipping both letters into a pocket, he rolled up his robe, stuffed it into the bag, and put the dark blue tunic on top of it.

The magazine status pin of the big needler indicated it was loaded; he opened the action anyway, trying to recall how Auk had held his that night in the restaurant, and remembering at the last moment Auk's adjuration to keep his finger off the trigger. The magazine appeared to be full of long, deadly looking needles, or nearly full. Auk had said his needler held how many? A hundred or more, surely; and this big needler that had been Musk's must hold at least as many if not more. It was possible, of course, that it had been disabled in some way.

There was no one in the hall outside. Silk closed the door, and after a moment's thought put the quilt against its bottom and shut the window, then sat down on the bed, sick and horribly weak. When had he eaten last?

Very early that morning, in Limna, with Doctor Crane and that captain whose name he had never learned or had forgotten, and the captain's men. Kypris had granted another theophany, had appeared to them, and to Maytera Marble and Patera Gulo, and they had been full of the wonder of it, all three of them newly come to religious feeling, and feeling that no one had ever come to it before. He had eaten a very good omelet, then several slices of hot, fresh bread with country butter, because the cook, roused from sleep by a trooper, had popped the loaves that had been rising overnight into the oven. He had drunk hot, strong coffee, too; coffee lightened with cream the color of Hyacinth's stationery and sweetened with honey from a white, blue-flowered bowl passed to him by Doctor Crane, who had been putting honey on his bread. Now Doctor Crane was dead, and so was one of the troopers, the captain and the other trooper most likely dead too, killed in the fighting before the Alambrera.

Silk lifted the big needler.

Someone had told him that he, too, should be dead—he could not remember whether it had been the surgeon or Colonel Oosik. Perhaps it had been Shell, although it did not seem the sort of thing that Shell would say.

The needler would not fire. He tugged its trigger again and returned it to the windowsill, congratulating himself on having resolved to test it; saw that he had left the safety catch on, pushed it off, took aim at a large bottle of cologne on the dresser, and squeezed the trigger. The needler cracked in his hand like a bullwhip and the bottle exploded, filling the room with the clean scent of spruce.

He reapplied the safety and thrust the needler into his waistband under the yellow tunic. If Musk's needler had not been disabled, there was no point in testing Hyacinth's small one, too. He made sure its safety catch was engaged, forced himself to stand, and dropped it into his trousers pocket.

One thing more, and he could go. Had the young man whose bedroom this was never written anything here? Looking around, he saw no writing materials.

What of the owner of the perfumed scarf? She would write to him, almost certainly. A woman who cared enough to drop a silk scarf from her window would write notes and letters. And he would keep them, concealing them somewhere in this room and replying in notes and letters of his own, though perhaps less frequently. The study, if there was one, would belong to his father. Even a library would not be sufficiently private. He would write to her here, surely, sitting—where?

There had been no chair in the room until Shell brought one. The occupant could only have sat on the bed or the floor, assuming that he had sat at all. Silk sat down again, imagined that he held a quill, pushed aside the chair Shell had put in front of the little night table, and pulled it over to him. Its shallow drawer held a packet of notepaper, a discolored scrap of flannel, a few envelopes, four quills, and a small bottle of ink.

Choosing a quill, he wrote:

> Sir, events beyond my control have forced me to occupy your bedchamber for several hours, and I fear I have broken a bottle of your cologne, and stained your sheets. In extreme need, I have, in addition, appropriated two of your tunics and your smallest traveling bag. I am heartily sorry to have imposed on you in this fashion. I am compelled, as I indicated.
>
> When peace and order return to our city, as I pray that they soon will, I will endeavor to locate you, make restitution, and return your property. Alternately, you may apply to me, at any time you find convenient. I am Pa. Silk, of Sun Street

For a long moment he paused, considering, the feathery end of the gray goose-quill tickling his lips. Very well.

With a final dip into the ink, he added a comma and the word *Caldé* after "Sun Street," and wiped the quill.

Restoring the quilt to the bed, he opened the door. The hall was still empty. Back stairs brought him to the kitchen, in which it appeared at least a company had been foraging for food. The back door opened on what seemed, from what he could see by skylight, to be a small formal garden; a white-painted gate was held shut by a simple hook.

Outside on Basket Street, he stopped to look back at the house he had left. Most of its windows were lit, including one on the second floor whose lights were dimming; his, no doubt. Distant explosions indicated the center of the city as well as anything could.

An officer on horseback who might easily have been the one who had shot him galloped past without taking the least notice. Two streets nearer the Palatine, a hurrying trooper carrying a dispatch box touched his cap politely.

The box might contain an order to arrest every augur in the city, Silk mused; the galloping officer might be bringing Oosik word of another battle. It would be well, might in fact be of real value, for him to read those dispatches and hear the news that the galloping officer brought.

But he had already heard, as he walked, the most important news, news pronounced by the muzzles of guns: the Ayuntamiento did not occupy all the city between this remote eastern quarter and the Palatine. He would have to make his way along streets in which Guardsmen and Maytera Mint's rebels were slaughtering each other, return to the ones that he knew best—and then, presumably, cross another disputed zone to reach the Palatine.

For the Guard would hold the Palatine if it held anything, and in fact the captain had indicated only that morning that a full brigade had scarcely sufficed to defend it Molpsday night. Combatants on both sides would try to prevent him; he might be killed, and the exertions he was making this moment might kill him as surely as any slug. Yet he had to try, and if he lived he would see Hyacinth tonight.

His free hand had begun to draw Musk's needler. He forced it back to his side, reflecting grimly that before shadeup he might learn some truths about himself that he would not prefer to ignorance. Unconsciously, he increased his pace.

Men thought themselves good or evil; but the gods—the Outsider especially—must surely know how much depended upon circumstance. Would Musk, whose needler he had nearly drawn a few seconds before, have been an evil man if he had not served Blood? Might not Blood, for that matter, be a better man with Musk gone? He, Silk, had sensed warmth and generosity in Blood beneath his cunning and his greed, potentially at least.

Something dropped from the sky, lighting on his shoulder so heavily he nearly fell. " 'Lo Silk! Good Silk!"

"Oreb! Is it really you?"

"Bird back." Oreb caught a lock of Silk's hair in his beak and gave it a tug.

"I'm very glad—immensely glad you've returned. Where have you been? How did you get here?"

"Bad place. Big hole!"

"It was I who went into the big hole, Oreb. By the lake, in that shrine of Scylla's, remember?"

Oreb's beak clattered. "Fish heads?"

Chapter 6

THE BLIND GOD

Oreb had eyed Dace's corpse hopefully when Urus let it fall to the tunnel floor and spun around to shout at Hammerstone. "Why we got to find him? Tell me that! Tell me, an' I'll look till I can't shaggy walk, till I got to crawl—"

"Pick it up, you." Without taking his eyes off Urus, Hammerstone addressed Incus. "All right if I kill him, Patera? Only I won't be able to carry them both and shoot."

Incus shook his head. "He has a *point,* my son, so let us consider it. *Ought* we, as he inquires, continue to search for our friend Auk?"

"I'll leave it up to you, Patera. You're smarter than all of us, smarter than the whole city'd be if you weren't living there. I'd do anything you say, and I'll see to it these bios do, too."

"*Thank* you, my son." Incus, who was exceedingly tired already, lowered himself gratefully to the tunnel floor. "Sit *down,* all of you. We shall discuss this."

"I don't see why." Tired herself, Chenille grounded her launcher. "Stony there does whatever you tell him to, and he could do for me and Urus like swatting flies. You say it and we'll do it. We'll have to."

"Sit *down.* My daughter, can't you see how very *illogical* you're being? You *maintain* that you're forced to obey in *all things,* yet you will not oblige even the simplest request.''

''All right.'' She sat; and Hammerstone, laying a heavy hand on Urus, forced him to sit, too.

''Where Auk?'' Oreb hopped optimistically across the damp gray shiprock. ''Auk where?'' Although he could not have put the feeling into words, Oreb felt that he was nearer Silk when he was with Auk than in any other company. The red girl was close to Silk as well, but she had once thrown a glass at him, and Oreb had not forgotten.

''Where indeed?'' Incus sighed. ''My daughter, you invite me to be a *despot,* but what you say is true. I might lord it over you both if I chose. I need not lord it over our friend. *He* obeys me very willingly, as you have seen. But I am *not,* by inclination, training, or *native character* inclined toward despotism. A holy augur's part is to lead and to advise, to *conduct* the laity to rich fields and *unfailing* springs, if I may put it thus *poetically.*

''So *let us* review our position and take *council,* one with another. Then I will lead us in prayer, a fervent and *devout* prayer, let it be, to all the Nine, *imploring* their guidance.''

''Then we'll decide?'' Urus demanded.

''Then *I* will decide, my son.'' By an effort, Incus sat up straighter. ''But *first,* allow me to dispel certain fallacies that have already crept into our deliberations.'' He addressed himself to Chenille. *''You,* my daughter, seek to accuse me of despotism. It is *impolite,* but courtesy itself must at times give way to the *sacred duty* of *correction.* May I remind you that *you,* for the space of nearly *two days, tyrannized* us all aboard that miserable boat? Tyrannized *me* largely by means of our unfortunate friend, for whom we have already searched, as I would think, for nearly half a day?''

''I'm not saying we ought to stop, Patera. That was him.'' She pointed to Urus. ''I want to find him.''

''Be *quiet,* my daughter. I am not yet finished with *you.* I shall come to *him* soon enough. *Why,* I inquire, did you so tyrannize us? I say—''

''I was possessed! Scylla was in me. You know that.''

''No, no, my daughter. It won't *do.* It is what you have *maintained,* deflecting all criticism of your conduct with the same *shabby* defense. It shall serve you no longer. You were *domineering, oppressive,* and *brutal.* Is that characteristic of *Our Surging Scylla?* I affirm that it is *not.* As we have trudged on, I have reviewed all that is recorded of *her,* both in the *Chrasmologic Writings* and in our *traditions* likewise. *Imperious?* One can but agree. *Impetuous* at times, perhaps. But *never* brutal, oppressive, or *domineering.''* Incus sighed again, removed his shoes, and caressed his blistered feet.

''*Those* evil traits, I say, my daughter, *cannot* have been *Scylla's.* They were present *in you* when she arrived, and so deeply rooted that she found it, I dare say, quite impossible to *expunge* them. *Some* there are, or so I have heard it said, who actually *prefer* domineering women, *unhappy* men twisted by nature beyond the natural. Our poor friend Auk, with all his manifest excellencies of *strength* and *manly* courage, is one of those unfortunates, so it would seem. I am *not,* my daughter, and I thank Sweet Scylla for it! Understand that for *my* part, and for our tall friend's here, as I dare to say, we have not sought Auk for your sake, but for *his own.''*

''Talk talk,'' Oreb muttered.

''As for *you,''* Incus shifted his attention to Urus, *''you* appear to believe that it is only because of my loyal friend *Hammerstone* that you obey me. It that not so?''

Urus stared sullenly at the tunnel wall to the left of Incus's face.

''You are *silent,''* Incus continued. ''Talk and more talk, complains our small *feathered* companion, and again, talk, talk and *talk.* Not impossibly you concur. No, my son, you *deceive* yourself, as you have deceived yourself throughout what I feel *certain* must have been a most unhappy life.'' Incus drew Auk's needler and leveled it at the silent Urus. "I have but little *need* of my tall friend Hammerstone, where *you* are concerned, and should this endless *talk* that you complain of end, you may find yourself less pleased *than ever* with that which succeeds it. I invite a *comment.*"

Urus shook his head. Hammerstone clenched his big fists, clearly itching to batter him insensible.

"Nothing? In that case, my son, I am going to take the opportunity to tell you something of *myself,* because I have been pondering *that,* with many other things, while we walked, and it will bear upon what I mean to do, as you will see.

"I was born to poor yet *upright* parents, their *fifth* and *final* child. At the time they were *wed,* they had made *solemn pledge* to Echidna that they would furnish the immortal gods with an augur or a sibyl, the ripest *fruit* of their union and the most *perfect* of all *thank offerings* for it. Of my older brothers and sisters, I shall say nothing. *Nothing,* that is to say, except that there was nothing to be hoped for from *them.* No more *holy piety* was to be discovered in the four of them than in four of those *horrid beasts* with which you, my son, proposed to attack us. I was born some *seven years* after my youngest sibling, Femur. Conceive of my parents' *delight,* I invite you, when the passing *days, weeks, months,* and *years* showed ever more plainly my *predilection* for a life of *holy contemplation,* of *worship* and *ritual,* far from the *bothersome exigencies* that trouble the hours of most men. The schola, if I may say it, welcomed me with *arms outspread.* Its *warmth* was no less than that with which I, in my turn, rushed to *it.* I was together *pious* and *brilliant,* a combination not often found. *Thus endowed,* I gained the friendship of *older men* of tastes like to *my own,* who were to extend themselves *without stint* in my behalf following my *designation.*

"I was informed, and you may conceive of my *rapture,* my *delight,* that no less a figure than the *coadjutor* had agreed to make me his prothonotary. With all my heart I entered into my *duties,* drafting and summarizing letters and depositions, stamping, filing, and retrieving files, managing his *calendar of appointments,* and a hundred like tasks.''

Incus fell silent until Chenille said, ''By Thelxiepeia I could sleep for a week!'' She leaned back against the tunnel wall and closed her eyes.

''Where Auk?'' Oreb demanded, but no one paid him the least attention.

''We are all *exhausted,* my daughter. I not *less* than you, and perhaps with more *reason,* because my legs are not so *long,* nor am I, by a decade and *more,* so young, nor so well fed.''

''I'm not even a little bit well fed, Patera.'' Chenille did not open her eyes. ''I guess none of us are. I haven't had anything but water since forever.''

''When we were on that *wretched* little fishing boat, you *appropriated* to yourself what food you *wished,* and *all* that you wished, my daughter. You left to *Auk* and Dace, and even to *me,* an anointed augur, only such *scraps* as you disdained. But you have *forgotten* that, or say you have. I wish that I might forget it, too.''

''Fish heads?''

Chenille shrugged, her eyes still closed. ''All right, Patera, I'm sorry. I don't suppose we'll ever find any food down here, but if we do, or when we get back home, I'll let you have first pick.''

''I would *refuse* it, my daughter. That is the *point* I am *striving* to make. I became His Eminence's prothonotary, as I said. I entered the *Prolocutor's Palace,* not as an awestruck *visitor,* but as an *inhabitant.* Each morning I sacrificed *one squab* in the *private chapel* below the reception hall, chanting my prayers to empty chairs. Afterward, I enjoyed that same *bird* at my luncheon. *Upon a monthly basis,* I shrove Patera Bull, His

Cognizance's prothonotary, as *he me*. That was the whole compass of my duties as an augur.

"But from time to time, His Eminence assigned to *me* such errands as he felt, or *feigned* to feel, overdifficult for a *boy*. One such brought me to that miserable village of *Limna*, as you know. I was to search for *you*, my daughter, and it was my *ill luck* to succeed. Your own life, I suppose, has been, I will not say *adventurous*, but *tumultuous*. Is that not so?"

"It's had its ups and downs," Chenille conceded.

"Mine had not, with the result that I had assumed myself *incapable*. Had some god informed me," Incus paused to thrust Auk's needler back into his waistband, then contemplated his scabbed hands, "that I should be forced to serve as the *entire crew* of a fishing vessel, *bailing, making sail, reefing,* and all the rest, and this during a *tempest* as severe as any the Whorl has ever seen, I should have called it *quite impossible,* declaring roundly that I should *die* within an hour. I would have informed this wholly supposititious divinity that I was a man of *intellect,* now largely affecting to be a man of prayer, for my early piety had long since given way to an advancing *skepticism.* Had he suggested that I might *yet* become a man of action, I would have declared it to be *beneath* me, and thought myself profound."

Urus said, "Well, if you didn't have a needler 'n this big chem, we'd see."

Incus nodded his agreement, his round, plump little face serious and his protuberant teeth giving him something of the look of a resolute chipmunk. "We would *indeed.* Therefore, I shall *kill* you, Urus my son, or order Hammerstone to, whenever it appears that I am liable to lose either."

"Bad man!" It was not immediately apparent whether Oreb intended Incus or Urus.

Chenille said, "You don't really mean that, Patera."

"Oh, but I *do*, my daughter. Tell them, Corporal. Do I mean what I say?"

"Sure, Patera. See, Chenille, Patera's a bio like you, and bios like you and him are real easy to kill. You can't take chances, or him either. You got a prisoner, he's got to toe the line every minute, 'cause if you let him get away with anything, that's it. If it was up to me, I'd kill him right now, and not chance something happening to Patera."

"We need him to show us how to get to the pit, and that door that opens into the cellar of the Juzgado."

"Only we're not going to either one now, are we? And I know where the Juzgado is if I can get myself located. So why shouldn't I quiet him down?" As if by chance, Hammerstone's slug gun was pointing in Urus's direction; his finger found its trigger.

"We *have not* been going to the pit, I am happy to say," Incus told them. "It was *Auk* who wished to go there, for no good reason that *I* could ever understand. *Unfortunately*, we haven't been going to the Juzgado, *either*, though it was to the Juzgado that Surging Scylla directed us. *I* am the sole person present who *recollects* her instructions, possibly. But I *assure* you it is so."

"All right," Chenille said wearily, "I believe you."

"As you *ought*, my daughter, because it was *through your mouth* that Scylla spoke. That very *fact* brings me to another point. She made Auk, Dace, and *myself* her prophets, specifying that I am to replace His Cognizance as *Prolocutor*. Dace has *departed* this whorl, so grievously infected by *evil*, for the richer life of Mainframe. Succoring Scylla might recall him *if she chose*, perhaps. I *cannot*. If our search for *Auk* is to be given up, or at least *postponed*, and I confess there is *much* that appeals to *me* in that, only *I* remain of Scylla's three.

"Earlier, *bedeviled* by multiple interruptions, I *strove* to explain my position. Because neither of you has *patience* for that explanation, though it would occupy but a *few moments* at most, I shall *state* it. Pay *attention,* both of you.''

Incus's voice strengthened. "I have awakened to *myself,* both as *man* and as *augur.* A servant of *Men,* if you will. A servant of the *gods,* most particularly. You are three. One loves, two *hate* me. I am not unaware of it.''

"I don't hate you,'' Chenille protested. "You let me wear this when I got cold. Auk doesn't hate you either. You just think that.''

"Thank you, my daughter. I was about to remark that from what I've learned from my brother augurs concerning manteions, the proportion implied is the one most frequently seen, though our *congregation* is so much less numerous. Very well, *my good people,* I accept it. I shall do my best for each and for all, nonetheless, trusting in a reward from the east.''

"See?'' Hammerstone nudged Chenille. "What'd I tell you? The greatest man in the *Whorl.* "

Oreb cocked his head at Incus. "Where Auk?''

"Nowhere to be found in that shining city we name *Reason,* I fear,'' Incus told him half humorously. "He hailed someone. *I* saw him do it, though there was no one to be seen. After saluting this *unseen being,* he dashed away. Our good corporal pursued him, as you saw, but lost him in the *darkness.* "

"These green lights don't work the way people think, see, Chenille. People think they just crawl around all the time and don't care where they're at, only they're not really like that. If it's bright one way and dark the other, they'll head for the dark, see? Real slow, but that's how they go. It's what keeps them spread out.''

Chenille nodded. "Urus said something about that.''

"In a little place, they get everything worked out among themselves after a while and don't hardly move except to get away from the windows in the daytime, but in a big place like this they don't ever settle down completely. Only they don't ever go down much, 'cause if they did, they'd get stepped on and broken real fast.''

"Lots of these tunnels slope down besides the one Auk ran down," she objected, "and I've seen lights in them."

"Depends on how dark it is down there, and how steep the slope is. If it's too steep, they won't go in there at all."

"It was pretty steep," Chenille conceded, "and we went down it quite a ways, but later we took that one that went up, remember? It didn't go up as steep as the dark one went down, and it had lights, but it climbed like that for a long time."

"I *think,* my daughter—"

"So what I've been wondering is would Auk have gone back up like we did? He was kind of out of it."

"He was *deranged,*" Incus declared positively. "I would hope that condition was only temporary, but temporary or *not,* he was not *rational.*"

"Yeah, and that's why we took the tunnel that angled back up that I was talking about, Patera. We're not abram and we knew we wanted to get back up to the surface, besides finding Auk. But if Auk was abram . . . To let you have the lily word, all you bucks seem pretty abram to me, mostly, so I didn't pay much attention. Only if he was, maybe he'd just keep on going down, because that's easier. He was running like you say, and it's pretty easy to run downhill."

"There *may* be something in what you suggest, my daughter. We must keep it in mind, *if* our discussion concludes that we should continue our pursuit.

"Now, may *I* sum up? The *question* is whether we are to continue, or to break off our search, *at least temporarily,* and attempt to return to the surface. Allow *me,* please, to state both cases. I shall strive for *concision.* If any of you has an *additional point,* you are free to advance it when I have *concluded.*

"It would seem to me that there is only one *cogent* reason to *protract* our search, and I have touched upon that *already*. It is that Auk is one of the *triune prophets* commissioned by *Scylla*. As a *prophet* he is a *theodidact* of *inestimable* value, as was Dace. It is for that reason, and for it alone, that I *instructed* Hammerstone to pursue him following his precipitate departure. It is for that reason *solely* that I have prolonged the pursuit so far. For *I*, also, am such a prophet. The only such prophet remaining, as I have said."

"He's one of us," Chenille declared. "I was with him at Limna before Scylla possessed me, and I remember him a little on the boat. We can't just go off and leave him."

"Nor do *I* propose to do so, my daughter. Hear me out, I beg you. We are *exhausted and famished*. When we return to the *surface* with Scylla's messages, in *fulfillment* of her will, we can gain rest and food. *Furthermore*, we can enlist others in the search. We will—"

Urus interrupted. "You said we could put in stuff of our own, right? All right, how about me? Do I get to talk, or are you goin' to have the big chem shoot me?"

Incus smiled gently. "You must understand, my son, that as your spiritual guide, I love *you* no less and no more than the others. I have threatened your life only as the *law* does, for your correction. *Speak.*"

"Well, I don't love Auk, only if you want to get him back it looks to me like you're goin' about it wrong. He wanted us to go to the pit, remember? So maybe now that he's gone off by himself that's where. We could go 'n see, 'n there's lots of bucks there that know these tunnels as well as me, so why not tell 'em what happened 'n get 'em to look too?"

Incus nodded, his face thoughtful. "It *is* a suggestion worthy of consideration."

"They'll eat us," Chenille declared.

"Fish head?" Oreb fluttered to her shoulder.

"Yeah, like you'd eat a fish head, Oreb. Only we'd have to have fish heads to do it."

"They won't eat me," Hammerstone told her. "They won't eat anybody I say not to eat, either, while I'm around."

"Now let us *pray.*" Incus was on his knees, hands clasped behind him. "Let us petition the *immortal gods,* and Scylla *particularly,* to rescue both Auk and *ourselves,* and to guide us in the ways they would have us go."

"I twigged you don't buy that any more."

"I have *encountered* Scylla," Incus told Urus solemnly. "I have seen for myself the *majesty* and *power* of that very great goddess. How could I lack belief now?" He contemplated the voided cross suspended from his prayer beads as if he had never seen it before. "I have suffered, too, on that wretched boat and in these *detestable* tunnels. I have been in terror of my life. It is hunger and fear that direct us toward the gods, my son. I have learned that, and I wonder that *you,* suffering as you clearly have, have not turned to them long ago."

"How do you know I haven't, huh? You don't know a shaggy thing about me. Maybe I'm holier than all of you."

Tired as she was, Chenille giggled.

Incus shook his head. "No, my son. It won't do. I am a *fool,* perhaps. Beyond dispute I have not infrequently been a fool. But not such a fool as that." More loudly he added, "On your *knees.* Bow your heads."

"Bird pray! Pray Silk!"

Incus ignored Oreb's hoarse interruption, his right hand making the sign of addition with the voided cross. "Behold us, lovely Scylla, *wonderful* of *waters.* Behold our love and our need for thee. Cleanse us, O Scylla!" He took a deep breath, the inhalation loud in the whispering silence. "Your prophet is bewildered and dismayed, Scylla. Wash clear my *eyes* as I implore you to cleanse my *spirit.* Guide me in this confusion of darkling passages and obscure responsibilities." He looked up, mouthing: *"Cleanse us, O Scylla."*

Chenille, Hammerstone, and even Urus dutifully repeated, "Cleanse us, O Scylla."

Bored, Oreb had flown up to grip a rough stone protrusion in his red claws. He could see farther even than Hammerstone through the yellow-green twilight that filled the tunnel, and clinging thus to the ceiling, his vantage point was higher; but look as he might, he saw neither Auk or Silk. Abandoning the search, he peered hungrily at Dace's corpse; its half-open eyes tempted him, though he felt sure he would be chased away.

Below, the black human droned on: "Behold us, fair Phaea, *lady of the larder*. Behold our love and our need for thee. *Feed* us, O Phaea! Famished we wander in need of your nurture." All the humans squawked, "Feed us, O Phaea!"

"Talk talk," Oreb muttered to himself; he could talk as well as they, but it seemed to him that talking was of small benefit in such situations.

"Behold us, fierce Sphigx, *woman of war*. Behold our love and our need for thee. *Lead* us, O Sphigx! We are lost and dismayed, O Sphigx, hemmed *all about* by danger. Lead us in the ways we should go." And all the humans, "Lead us, O Sphigx!"

The black one said, "Let us now, with heads bowed, put ourselves in *personal communion* with the Nine." He and the green one and the red one looked down, and the dirty one got up, stepped over the dead one, and trotted softly away.

"Man go," Oreb muttered, congratulating himself on having hit on the right words; and because he liked announcing things, he repeated more loudly, "Man go!"

The result was gratifying. The green one sprang to his feet and dashed after the dirty one. The black one shrieked and fluttered after the green one, and the red one jiggled after them both, faster than the black one but not as fast as the first two. For as long as it might have taken one of his feathers to float to the tunnel floor, Oreb preened, weighing the significance of these events.

He had liked Auk and had felt that if he remained with Auk, Auk would lead him to Silk. But Auk was gone, and the others were not looking for him any more.

Oreb glided down to a convenient perch on Dace's face and dined, keeping a wary eye out. One never knew. Good came of bad, and bad of good. Humans were both, and changeable in the extreme, sleeping by day yet catching fish whose best parts they generously shared.

And—so on. His crop filled, Oreb meditated on these points while cleaning his newly bright bill with his feet.

The dead one had been good. There could be no doubt about that. Friendly in the reserved fashion Oreb preferred alive, and delicious, dead. There was another one back there, but he was no longer hungry. It was time to find Silk in earnest. Not just look. Really find him. To leave this green hole and its living and dead humans.

Vaguely, he recalled the night sky, the gleaming upside-down country over his head, and the proper country below.

The wind in trees. Drifting along with it looking for things of interest. It was where Silk would be, and where he could be found. Where a bird could fly high, see everything, and find Silk.

Flying was not as easy as riding the red one's launcher, but flying downwind through the tunnel permitted rests in which he had only to keep his wings wide and sail along. There were twinges at times, reminding him of the blue thing that had been there. He had never understood what it was or why it had stuck to him.

Downwind along this hole and that, through a little hole (he landed and peered into it cautiously before venturing in himself) and into a big one where dirty humans stretched on the ground or prowled like cats, a hole lidded like a pot with the remembered sky of night.

*   *   *

Sword in hand, Master Xiphias stood at the window looking at the dark and empty street. Go home. That was what they'd told him.

Go home, though it had not been quite so bluntly worded. That dunce Bison, a fool who couldn't hold a sword correctly! That dunce Bison, who seemed in charge of everything, had come by while he was arguing with that imbecile Scale. Had smiled like friend and admired his sword, and had only pretended—pretended!—to believe him when he had stated (not boasting, just supplying a plain, straightforward answer in response to direct, uninvited questions) that he had killed five troopers in armor in Cage Street.

Then Bison had—the old fencing master grinned gleefully—had gaped like a carp when he, Xiphias, had parted a thumb-thick rope dangling from his, Bison's, hand. Had admired his sword and waved it around like the ignorant boy he was, and had the gall to say in many sweet words, go home like Scale says, old man. We don't need you tonight, old man. Go home and eat, old man. Go home and sleep. Get some rest, old man, you've had a big day.

Bison's sweet words had faded and blown away, lighter and more fragile than the leaves that whirled up the empty street. Their import, bitter as gall, remained. He had been fighting—had been a famous fighting man—when Bison was in diapers. Had been fighting before Scale's mother had escaped her kennel to bump tails with some filthy garbage-eating cur.

Xiphias turned his back to the window and sat on the sill, his head in his hands, his sword at his feet. He was no longer what he had been thirty years ago, perhaps. No longer what he had been before he lost his leg. But there wasn't a man in the city—not one!—who dared cross blades with him.

A knock at the front door, floating up the narrow stair from the floor below.

There would be no students tonight; his students would be fighting on one side or the other; yet somebody wanted to see him. Possibly Bison had realized the gravity of his error and come to implore him to undertake some almost suicidal mission. He'd go, but by High Hierax they'd have to beg first!

He picked up his sword to return it to its place on the wall, then changed his mind. In times like these—

Another knock.

There had been somebody. A new student down for tonight, came with Auk, tall, left-handed. Had studied with somebody else but wouldn't admit it. Good though. Talented! Gifted, in fact. Couldn't be here for his lesson, could he? With the city like this?

A third knock, almost cursory. Xiphias returned to the window and peered out.

Silk sighed. The house was dark; when he had been here before, the second floor had blazed with light. He had been foolish to think that the old man might be home after all.

He knocked for the last time and turned away, only to hear a window thrown open above him. "It's you! Good! Good!" The window banged down. With speed that was almost comic, the door flew wide. "Inside! Inside! Bolt it, will you? Is that a bird? A pet bird? Upstairs!" Xiphias gestured largely with a saber, his shadow leaping beside him; whipped by the night wind, his wild white hair seemed to possess a life of its own.

"Master Xiphias, I need your help."

"Good man?" Oreb croaked.

"A very good man," Silk assured him, hoping he was right; he caught the good man's arm as he turned away. "I know I was supposed to come tonight for another lesson, Master Xiphias. I haven't. I can't, but I need your advice."

"Been called out? Have to fight? What did I tell you? What weapons?"

"I'm very tired. Is there a place where we can sit down?"

"Upstairs!" The old man bounded up them himself just as he had on Sphixday night. Wearily, Silk followed.

"Lesson first!" Lights kindled at the sound of the old man's voice, brightened as he beat the wall with a foil.

The traveling bag now held only the yellow tunic, yet it seemed as heavy as a full one; Silk dropped it into a corner. "Master Xiphias—"

He snatched down another foil and beat the wall with that as well. "Been fighting?"

"Not really. In a manner of speaking I have, I suppose."

"Me too!" Xiphias tossed Silk the second foil. "Killed five. Ruins you, fighting! Ruins your technique!"

Oreb squawked, "Look out!" and flew as Silk ducked.

"Don't cringe!" Another whistling cut, this one rattling on the bamboo blade of Silk's foil. "What do you need, lad?"

"A place to sit." He was tired, deadly tired; his chest throbbed and his ankle ached. He parried and parried again, sickened by the realization that the only way to get this mad old man to listen was to defeat him or lose to him; and to lose (it was as if a god had whispered it) tonight was death: the thing in him that had kept him alive and functioning since he had been shot would die at his defeat, and he soon after.

Feinting and lunging, Silk fought for his life with the bamboo sword.

Its hilt was just long enough for him to grip it with both hands, and he did. Cut right and left and right again, beating down the old man's guard. He was still stronger than any old man, however strong, however active, and he drove him back and again back, slashing and stabbing with frenzied speed.

"Where'd you learn that two-handed thrust, lad? Aren't you left-handed?"

Dislodged from his waistband, Musk's needler fell to the mat. Silk kicked it aside and snatched a second foil from the wall, parrying with one, then the other, attacking with the

free foil, right, left, and right again. A vertical cut, and suddenly Xiphias's foot was on his right-hand foil. The blunt tip
of Xiphias's foil thumped his wound, bringing excruciating
pain.

"What'll you charge, lad? For the lesson?"

Silk shrugged, trying to hide the agony that lightest of
blows had brought. "I should pay you, sir. And you won."

"Silk win!" Oreb proclaimed from the grip of a yataghan.

Silk die, Silk thought. So be it.

"I learned, lad! Know how long it's been since I had a
student who could teach me anything? I'll pay! Food? You
hungry?"

"I think so." Silk leaned upon his foil; in the same way
that faces from his childhood swam into his consciousness,
he recalled that he had once had a walking stick with the
head of a lioness carved on its handle—had leaned upon it
like this the last time he had been here, although he could
not remember where he had acquired such a thing or what
had become of it.

"Bread and cheese? Wine?"

"Wonderful." Retrieving the traveling bag, he followed
the old man downstairs.

The kitchen was at once disorderly and clean, glasses and
dishes and bowls, pots and ladles anywhere and everywhere,
an iron bread-pan already in the chair Xiphias offered, as if it
fully expected to join in their conversation, though it found
itself banished to the woodbox. Mismatched glasses crashed
down on the table so violently that for a moment Silk felt sure
they had broken.

"Have some? Red wine from the veins of heroes! Care for
some?" It was already gurgling into Silk's glass. "Got it from
a student! Fact! Paid wine! Ever hear of such a thing? Swore it
was all good! Not so! What do you think?"

Silk sipped, then half emptied his glass, feeling that he

was indeed drinking from the flask that had dangled from his bedpost, drinking new life.

"Bird drink?"

He nodded, and when he could find no napkin patted his mouth with his handkerchief. "Could we trouble you for a cup of water, Master Xiphias, for Oreb here?"

The pump at the sink wheezed into motion. "You been out? City in an uproar! Dodging! Throwing stones! Haven't thrown stones since I was a sprat! Had a sling! You too? Better armed!" Crystal water rushed forth like the old man's words until he had filled a battered tankard. "This new cull, Silk! Going to show 'em! We'll see . . . Fighting, fighting! Threw stones, ducked and yelled! Five with my sword. I tell you? Know how to make a sling?"

Silk nodded again, certain that he was being gulled but unresentful.

"Me too! Used to be good with one!" The tankard arrived with a cracked green plate holding a shapeless lump of white-rinded cheese only slightly smaller than Silk's head. "Watch this!" Thrown from across the room, a big butcher knife buried its blade in the cheese.

"You asked whether I'd been out much tonight."

"Think there's any real fighting now?" Abruptly, Xiphias found himself siding with Bison. "Nothing! Nothing at all! Snipers shooting shadows to keep awake." He paused, his face suddenly thoughtful. "Can't see the other man's blade in the dark, can you? Interesting. Interesting! Have to try it! A whole new field! What do you think?"

The sight and the rich, corrupt aroma of the cheese had awakened Silk's appetite. "I think that I'll have a piece," he replied with sudden resolution. He was about to die—very well, but no god had condemned him to die hungry. "Oreb, you like cheese, too, I know. It was one of the first things you told me, remember?"

"Want a plate?" It came with a quarter of what must have been a gargantuan loaf on a nicked old board, and a bread knife nearly as large as Auk's hanger. "All I've got! You eat at cookshops, mostly? I do! Bad now! All shut!"

Silk swallowed. "This is delicious cheese and wonderful wine. I thank you for it, Master Xiphias and Feasting Phaea." Impelled by habit, the last words had left his lips before he discovered that he did not mean them.

"For my lesson!" The old man dropped into a chair. "Can you throw, lad? Knives and whatnot? Like I just did?"

"I doubt it. I've never tried."

"Want me to teach you? You're an augur?"

Silk nodded again as he sliced bread.

"So's this Silk! You know Bison? He told me! Told us all!" Xiphias raised his glass, discovered he had neglected to fill it, and did so. "Funny, isn't it? An augur! Heard about him? He's an augur too!"

Although his mouth watered for the bread, Silk managed, "That's what they say."

"He's here! He's there! Everybody knows him! Nobody knows where he is! Going to do away with the Guard! Half's on his side already! Ever hear such nonsense in your life? No taxes, but he'll dig canals!" Master Xiphias made a rude noise. "Pas and the rest! Could they do all that people want by this time tomorrow? You know they couldn't!"

Oreb hopped back onto Silk's shoulder. "Good drink!"

He chewed and swallowed. "You should have some of this cheese, too, Oreb. It's marvelous."

"Bird full."

Xiphias chortled. "Me too, Oreb! That's his name? Ate when I got home! Ever see a shoat? Like that! All the meat, half the bread, and two apples! Why'd you go out?"

Silk patted his lips. "That was what I came to talk to you about, Master Xiphias. I was on the East Edge—"

"You walked?"

"Walked and ran, yes."

"No wonder you're limping! Wanted to sit, didn't you? I remember!"

"There was no other way by which I might hope to reach the Palatine," Silk explained, "but there were Guardsmen all along one side of Box Street, and the rebels—General Mint's people—had three times as many on the other, young men mostly, but women and even children, too, though the children were mostly sleeping. I had trouble getting across."

"I'll lay you did!"

"Maytera—General Mint's people wanted to take me to her when they found out who I was. I had a hard time getting away from them, but I had to. I have an appointment at Ermine's."

"On the Palatine? You should've stayed with the Guard! Thousands there! Know Skink? Tried about suppertime! Took a pounding! Two brigades! Taluses, too!"

Silk persevered. "But I must go there, without fighting if I can. I must get to Ermine's." Before he could rein in his tongue he added, "She might actually be there."

"See a woman, eh, lad?" Xiphias's untidy beard rearranged itself in a smile. "What if I tell old what'shisname? Old man, purple robe?"

"I had hoped—"

"I won't! I won't! Forget everything anyhow, don't I? Ask anybody! We going tomorrow? Need a place to sleep?"

"Day sleep," Oreb advised.

"Tonight," Silk told the old man miserably, "and only I am going. But it has to be tonight. Believe me, I would postpone it until morning if I could."

"Drinking wine? No more for us!" Xiphias recorked the bottle and set it on the floor beside his chair. "Watch your bird! Watch and learn! Knows more than you, lad!"

"Smart bird!"

"Hear that? There you are!" Xiphias bounced out of his

chair. "Have an apple? Forgot 'em! Still a few." He opened the oven door and banged it shut. "Not in there! Had to move 'em! Cooked the meat! Where's Auk?"

"I've no idea, I'm afraid." Silk cut himself a second, smaller piece of cheese. "I hope he's home in bed. May I put that apple you're looking for in my pocket? I appreciate it very much—I feel a great deal better—but I must go. I wanted to ask whether you knew a route to the Palatine that might be safer than the principal streets—"

"Yes, lad! I do, I do!" Triumphantly, Xiphias displayed a bright red apple snatched from the potato bin.

"Good man!"

"And whether you could teach me a trick that might get me past the fighters on both sides. I knew there must be such things, and Auk would certainly know them; but it's a long way to the Orilla, and I wasn't sure that I'd be able to find him. It occurred to me that he'd probably learned many from someone else, and that you were a likely source."

"Need a teacher? Yes, you do! Glad you know it! Where's your needler, lad?"

For a moment Silk was nonplussed. "My—? Right here in my pocket." He held it up much as Xiphias had the apple. "It isn't actually mine, however. It belongs to the young woman I'm to meet at Ermine's."

"Big one! I saw it! Fell out of your pants! Left it upstairs! Want me to get it? Eat your cheese!"

Xiphias darted through the kitchen door, and Silk heard him clattering up the stair. "We must go, Oreb." He rose and dropped the apple into a pocket of his robe. "He intends to go with us, and I can't permit it." For a second his head spun; the walls of the kitchen shook like jelly and revolved like a carousel before snapping back into place.

A dark little hallway beyond the kitchen door led to the stair, and the door by which they had entered the house. He steadied himself against the newel post, half hoping to hear the old man on the floor above or even to see him descending again, but the old house could not have been more silent if he and Oreb had been alone in it; it puzzled him until he recalled the canvas mats on the floor of the salon.

Unbolting the door, he stepped into the empty, skylit street. The tunnels through which he had trudged for so many weary hours presumably underlay the Palatine, as they seemed to underlie everything; but they would almost certainly be patrolled by soldiers like the one from whom he had escaped. He knew of no entrance except Scylla's lakeshore shrine in any case, and was glad at that moment that he did not. A big hole, Oreb had said. Was it possible that Oreb, also, had wandered in those dread-filled tunnels?

Shuddering at the memories he had awakened, Silk limped away toward the Palatine with renewed determination, telling himself that his ankle did not really hurt half so much as he believed it did. His gaze was on the rutted pot-holed street, for he knew that despite what he might tell himself, twisting his ankle would put an end to walking; but regardless of all the self-discipline he brought to bear, his thoughts threaded the tunnels once more, and hand-in-hand with Mamelta reentered that curious structure (not unlike a tower, but a tower thrust into the ground instead of rising into the air) that she had called a ship, and again beheld below it emptiness darker than any night and gleaming points of light that the Outsider—at his enlightenment!—had indicated were whorls, whorls outside the whorl, to which dead Pas and deathless Echidna, Scylla and her siblings had never penetrated.

You was goin' to get me out. Said you would. Promised.

Auk, who could not quite see Gelada, heard him crying in the wind that filled the pitch-black tunnel, while Gelada's tears dripped from the rock overhead. The two-card boots he had always kept well greased were sodden above the ankle now. "Bustard?" he called hopefully. "Bustard?"

Bustard did not reply.

You had the word, you said. Get me out o' here. "I saw you that time, off to one side." Unable to remember when or where he had said it last, Auk repeated, "I got eyes like a cat."

It was not quite true because Gelada had vanished when he had turned his head, yet it seemed a good thing to say. Gelada might walk wide if he thought he was being watched.

Auk? That your name? Auk? "Sure. I told you." Where's the Juzgado, Auk? Lot o' doors down here. Which 'uns that 'un, Auk? "I dunno. Maybe the same word opens 'em all."

This was the widest tunnel he had seen, except he couldn't see it. The walls to either side were lost in the dark, and he might, for all he knew, be walking at a slant, might run into the wall slantwise with any step. From time to time he waved his arms, touching nothing. Oreb flapped ahead, or maybe it was a bat, or nothing.

(Far away a woman's voice called, *"Auk? Auk?"*)

The tunnel wall was aglow now, but still dark, dark with a peculiar sense of light—a luminous blackness. The toe of one boot kicked something solid, but his groping fingers found nothing.

"Auk, my noctolater, are you lost?"

The voice was near yet remote, a man's, deep and laden with sorrow.

"No, I ain't. Who's that?"

"Where are you going, Auk? Truthfully."

"Looking for Bustard." Auk waited for another question, but none came. The thing he had kicked was a little higher than his knees, flat on top, large and solid feeling. He sat on it facing the luminous dark, drew up his legs, and untied his boots. "Bustard's my brother, older than me. He's dead now, took on a couple Hoppies and they killed him. Only he's been down here with me a lot, giving me advice and telling me stuff, I guess because this is under the ground and it's where he lives on account of being dead."

"He left you."

"Yeah, he did. He generally does that if I start talking to somebody else." Auk pulled off his right boot; his foot felt colder than Dace had after Gelada killed him. "What's a noctolater?"

"One who worships by night, as you worship me."

Auk looked up, startled. "You a god?"

"I am Tartaros, Auk, the god of darkness. I have heard you invoke me many times, always by night."

Auk traced the sign of addition in the air. "Are you standing over there in the dark talking to me?"

"It is always dark where I stand, Auk. I am blind."

"I didn't know that." Black rams and lambs, the gray ram when Patera Silk got home safely, once a black goat, first of all the pair of bats he'd caught himself, surprised by day in the dark, dusty attic of the palaestra and brought to Patera Pike, all for this blind god. "You're a god. Can't you make yourself see?"

"No." The hopeless negative seemed to fill the tunnel, hanging in the blackness long after its sound had faded. "I am an unwilling god, Auk. The only unwilling god. My father made me do this. If, as a god, I might have healed myself, I would have obeyed very willingly, I believe."

"I asked my mother . . . Asked Maytera to bring a god down here to walk with us. I guess she brought you."

"No," Tartaros said again; then, "I come here often, Auk. It is the oldest altar we have."

"This I'm sitting on? I'll get off."

(Again the woman's voice: *"Auk? Auk?"*)

"You may remain. I am also the sole humble god, Auk, or nearly."

"If it's sacred . . ."

"Wood was heaped upon it, and the carcasses of animals. You profane it no more than they. When the first people came, Auk, they were shown how we desired to be worshiped. Soon, they were made to forget. They did, but because they had seen what they had seen, a part of them remembered, and when they found our altars on the inner surface, they sacrificed as we had taught them. First of all, here."

"I haven't got anything," Auk explained. "I used to have a bird, but he's gone. I thought I heard a bat a little while ago. I'll try to catch one, if you'd like that."

"You think me thirsty for blood, like my sister Scylla."

"I guess. I was with her awhile." Auk tried to remember when that had been; although he recalled incidents—seeing her naked on a white stone and cooking fish for her—the days and the minutes slipped and slid.

"What is it you wish, Auk?"

Suddenly he was frightened. "Nothing really, Terrible Tartaros."

"Those who offer us sacrifice always wish something, Auk. Often, many things. Rain, in your city and many others."

"It's raining down here already, Terrible Tartaros."

"I know, Auk."

"If you're blind . . . ?"

"Can you see it, Auk?"

He shook his head. "It's too shaggy dark."

"But you hear it. Hear the slow splash of the falling drops kissing the drops that fell."

"I feel it, too," Auk told the god. "Every once in a while one goes down the back of my neck."

"What is it you wish, Auk?"

"Nothing, Terrible Tartaros." Shivering, Auk wrapped himself in his own arms.

"All men wish for something, Auk. Most of all, those who say they wish for nothing."

"I don't, Terrible Tartaros. Only if you want me to, I'll wish for something for you. I'd like something to eat."

Silence answered him.

"Tartaros? Listen, if this's a altar I'm sitting on and you're here talking to me, shouldn't there be a Sacred Window around here someplace?"

"There is, Auk. You are addressing it. I am here."

Auk took off his left boot. "I got to think about that."

Maytera Mint had taught him all about the gods, but it seemed to him that there were really two kinds, the ones she had told about, the gods in his copybook, and the real ones like Scylla when she'd been inside Chenille, and this Tartaros. The real kind were a lot bigger, but the ones in his copybook had been better, and stronger somehow, even if they were not real.

"Terrible Tartaros?"

"Yes, Auk, my noctolater, what is it you wish?"

"The answers to a couple questions, if that's all right. Lots of times you gods answer questions for augurs. I know I'm not no augur. So is it all right for me to ask you, 'cause we haven't got one here?"

Silence, save for the ever-present splashings, and the woman's voice, sad and hoarse and very far away.

"How come I can't see your Window, Terrible Tartaros? That's my first one, if that's all right. I mean, usually they're sort of gray, but they shine in the dark. So am I blind, too?"

Silence fell again. Auk chafed his freezing feet with his hands. Those hands had glowed like molten gold, not long ago; now they were not even warm.

"I guess you're waiting for the other question? Well, what I wanted to know is how come I hear words and everything? At this palaestra I went to, Maytera said when we got bigger we wouldn't be able to make sense out of the words if a god ever came to our Sacred Window, just sort of know what he meant and maybe catch a couple of words once in a while.

Then when Kypris came, it was just like what Maytera'd said it was going to be. Sometimes I felt like I could practically see her, and there was a couple words she said that I heard just as clear as I ever heard anybody, Terrible Tartaros. She said *love* and *robbery*, and I knew it. I knew both those words. And I knew she was telling us it was all right, she loved us and she'd protect us, only we had to believe in her. But when you talk, it's like you were a man just like me or Bustard, standing right here with me."

No voice replied. Auk let out his breath with a whoosh, and put his freezing fingers in armpits for a moment or two, and then began to wring out his stockings.

"You yourself have never seen a god in a Window, Auk my noctolater?"

Auk shook his head. "Not real clear, Terrible Tartaros. I sort of saw Kindly Kypris just a little, though, and that's good enough for me."

"Your humility becomes you, Auk."

"Thanks." Lost in thought, Auk reflected on his own life and character, the limp stocking still in his hand. At length he said, "It's never done me a lot of good, Terrible Tartaros, only I guess I never really had much."

"If an augur sees the face and hears the words of a god, Auk, he sees and hears because he has never known Woman. A sibyl, also, may see and hear a god, provided that she has not known Man. Children who have never known either may see us as well. That is the law fixed by my mother, the price that she demanded for accepting the gift my father offered. And though her law does not function as she intended in every instance, for the most part it functions well enough."

"All right," Auk said.

"The faces we had as mortals have rotted to dust, and the voices we once possessed have been still for a thousand years. No augur, no sibyl in the *Whorl*, has ever seen or heard them. What your augurs and sibyls see, if they see anything, is the self-image of the god who chooses to be seen. You say that you could nearly make out the face of my father's concubine. The face you nearly saw was her own image of herself, her self as she imagines that self to appear. I feel confident that it was a beautiful face. I have never met any woman more secure in her own vanity. In the same fashion, we sound to them as we conceive our voices to sound. Have I made myself clear to you, Auk?''

"No, Terrible Tartaros, 'cause I can't see you."

"What you see, Auk, is that part of me which can be seen. That is to say, nothing. I came blind from the womb, Auk, and because of it I am incapable of formulating a visual image for you. Nor can I show you the Holy Hues, which are my brother's and my sisters' thoughts before they have coalesced. Nor can I exhibit to you any face at all, whether lovely or terrible. You see the face I envision when I think upon my own. That is to say, nothing. When I depart, you will behold once more the luminous gray you mention."

"I'd rather you stayed around awhile, Terrible Tartaros. If Bustard ain't going to come back, I like having you with me." Auk licked his lips. "Probably I oughtn't to say this, but I don't mean any harm by it."

"Speak, Auk, my noctolater."

"Well, if I could scheme out some way to help you, I'd do it."

There was silence again, a silence that endured so long that Auk feared that the god had returned to Mainframe; even the distant woman's voice was silent.

"You asked by what power you hear my words as words, Auk, my noctolater."

He breathed a sigh of relief. "Yeah, I guess I did."

"It is not uncommon. My mother's law has lost its hold on you, because there is something amiss with your mind."

Auk nodded. "Yeah, I know. I fell off our tall ass when he got hit with a rocket, and I guess I must've landed on my head. Like, it don't bother me that Bustard's dead, only he's down here talking to me. Only I know it would've in the old days. I don't worry about Jugs, either, like I ought to. I love her, and maybe that cull Urus's trying to jump her right now, but she's a whore anyhow.'' Auk shrugged. ''I just hope he don't hurt her.''

''You cannot live in these tunnels, Auk, my noctolater. There is no food for you here.''

''Me and Bustard'll try to get out, soon as I find him,'' Auk promised.

''If I were to possess you, I might be able to heal you, Auk.''

''Go ahead, then.''

''We would be blind, Auk. As blind as I. Because I have never had eyes of my own, I could not look out through yours. But I shall go with you, and guide you, and use your body to heal you, if I can. Look upon me, Auk.''

''There's nothing to see,'' Auk protested.

But there was: a stammering light so filled with hope and pleasure and wonder that Auk would willingly have seen nothing else, if only he could have watched it forever.

''If you're actually Patera Silk,'' the young woman at the barricade told him, ''they'll kill you the minute you step out there.''

''No step,'' Oreb muttered. And again, ''No step.''

''Very possibly they would,'' Silk conceded. ''As in fact they almost certainly will—unless you're willing to help.''

''If you're Silk you wouldn't have to ask me or my people for anything.'' Uneasily she studied the thin, ascetic face revealed by the bright skylight. ''If you're Silk, you are our commander and even General Mint must answer to you. You could just tell us, and we'd have to do whatever you said.''

Silk shook his head. ''I am Silk, but I can't prove that here. You would have to find someone you trust who knows me and can identify me, and that would consume more time than I have; so I'm begging you instead. Assume—though I swear to you that this is contrary to fact—that I am not Silk. That I am—this, of course, is entirely factual—a poor young augur in urgent need of your assistance. If you won't help me for my sake, or for that of the god I serve, do so for your own, I implore you.''

"I can't launch an attack without an order from Brigadier Bison.''

"You shouldn't,'' Silk told her, "with one. There's an armored floater behind those sandbags. I can see the turret above them. If your people attacked, they would be advancing into its fire, and I've seen what a buzz gun can do.''

The young woman drew herself up to her full height, which was a span and a half less than his own. "We will attack if we are ordered to do so, Caldé.''

Oreb bobbed his approbation. "Good girl!''

Looking at the sleeping figures behind the barricade, children of fifteen and fourteen, thirteen and even twelve, Silk shook his head.

"They're pretty young.'' (The young woman could not have been more than twenty herself.) "But they'll fight if they're led, and I'll lead them.'' When Silk said nothing, she added, "That's not all. I've got a few men, too, and some slug guns. Most of the women—the other women, I ought to say—are working in the fire companies. You were surprised to find me in command, but General Mint's a woman.''

"I am surprised at that, as well,'' Silk told her.

"Men want to fight a male officer. Besides, the women of Trivigaunte are famous troopers, and we women of Viron are in no way inferior to them!''

Recalling Doctor Crane, Silk said, "I'd like to believe that our men are as brave as theirs, as well.''

The young woman was shocked. "They're slaves!''

"Have you been there?''

She shook her head.

"Neither have I. Surely then it's pointless for us to discuss their customs. A moment ago you called me Caldé. Did you mean that, . . . ?"

"Lieutenant. I'm Lieutenant Liana now. I used the title as a courtesy, nothing more. If you want my opinion, I think you're who you say you are. An augur wouldn't lie about that, and there's the bird. They say you've got a pet bird."

"Silk here," the bird informed her.

"Then do as I ask. Do you have a white flag?"

"For surrender?" Liana was offended. "Certainly not!"

"To signal a truce. You can make one by tying a white rag to a stick. I want you to wave it and call to them, on the other side. Tell them there's an augur here who's brought the pardon of Pas to your wounded. That's entirely true, as you know. Say he wants to cross and do the same for theirs."

"They'll kill you when they find out who you are."

"Perhaps they won't find out. I promise you that I won't volunteer the information."

Liana ran her fingers through her tousled hair; it was the same gesture he used in the grip of indecision. "Why me? No, Caldé, I can't let you risk yourself."

"You can," he told her. "What you cannot do is maintain that position with even an appearance of logic. Either I am caldé or I am not. If I am, it is your duty to obey any order I give. If I'm not, the life of the caldé is not at risk."

A few minutes later, as she and a young man called Linsang helped him up the barricade, Silk wondered whether he had been wise to invoke logic. Logic condemned everything he had done since Oosik had handed him Hyacinth's letter. When Hyacinth had written, the city had been at peace, at least relatively. She had no doubt expected to shop on the Palatine, stay the night at Ermine's, and return—

"No fall," Oreb cautioned him.

He was trying not to. The barricade had been heaped up from anything and everything: rubble from ruined buildings, desks and counters from shops, beds, barrels, and bales piled upon one another without any order he could discern.

He paused at the top, waiting for a shot. The troopers behind the sandbag redoubt had been told he was an augur, and might know of the Prolocutor's letter by this time. Seeing Oreb, they might know which augur he was, as well.

And shoot. It would be better, perhaps, to fall backward toward Liana and Linsang if they did—better, certainly, to jump that way if they missed.

No shot came; he began a cautious descent, slightly impeded by the traveling bag. Oosik had not killed him because Oosik had taken the long view, had been at least as much politician as trooper, as every high-ranking officer no doubt had to be. The officer commanding the redoubt would be younger, ready to obey the orders of the Ayuntamiento without question.

Yet here he was.

Once invoked, logic was like a god. One might entreat a god to visit one's Window; but if a god came it could not be dismissed, nor could any message that it vouchsafed mankind be ignored, suppressed, or denied. He had invoked logic, and logic told him that he should be in bed in the house that had become Oosik's temporary headquarters—that he should be getting the rest and care he needed so badly.

"He knew I'd go, Oreb." Something closed his throat; he coughed and spat a soft lump that could have been mucus. "He'd read her letter before he came in, and he's seen her." Silk found that he could not, even now, bring himself to mention that Oosik had lain with Hyacinth. "He knew I'd go, and take his problem with me."

"Man watch," Oreb informed him.

He paused again, scanning the sandbag wall but unable to distinguish, at this distance, rounded sandbags from helmeted heads. "As long as they don't shoot," he muttered.

"No shoot."

This stretch of Gold Street had been lined with jewelers, the largest and richest shops nearest the Palatine, the richest of all clinging to the skirts of the hill itself, so that their patrons could boast of buying their bangles "uphill." Most of the shops were empty now, their grills and bars torn from their fronts by a thousand arms, their gutted interiors guarded only by those who had died defending or looting them. Beyond the redoubt, other richer shops waited, still intact. Silk tried and failed to imagine the children over whose recumbent bodies he had stepped looting them. They would not, of course. They would charge, fight, and very quickly die at Liana's order, and she with them. The looters would follow—if they succeeded. This body (Silk crouched to examine it) was that of a boy of thirteen or so; one side of his face had been shot away.

He had not been on Gold Street often; but he was certain that it had never been this long, or half this wide.

Here a trooper of the Guard and a tough-looking man who might have been the one who had questioned him after Kypris's theophany lay side-by-side, their knives in each other's ribs.

"Patera!" It was the rasping voice that had answered Liana's hail.

"What is it, my son?"

"Hurry up, will you!"

He broke into a trot, though not without protest from his ankle. When he had feared a shot at any moment, this lowest slope of the Palatine had been very steep; now he was scarcely conscious of its grade.

"Here. Grab my hand."

The Guard's redoubt was only half the height of the rebel

barricade, although it was (as Silk saw when he had scrambled to the top) rather thicker. Its front was nearly sheer, its back stepped for the troopers who would fire over it.

The one who had helped him up said, "Come on. I don't know how long he'll last."

Silk nodded, out of breath from his climb and afraid he had torn the stitches in his lung. "Take me to him."

The trooper jumped from the sandbag step; Silk followed more circumspectly. There were sleepers here as well, a score of armored Guardsmen lying in the street wrapped in blankets that were probably green but looked black in the skylight.

"They going to rush us, over there?" the trooper asked.

"No. Not tonight, I'd say—tomorrow morning, perhaps."

The trooper grunted. "Slugs'll go right through a lot of that stuff in their fieldwork. I been lookin' it over, and there's a lot of furniture in there. Boards no thicker than your thumb in junk like that. I'm Sergeant Eft."

They shook hands, and Silk said, "I was thinking the same thing as I climbed over it, Sergeant. There are heavier things as well, though, and even the chairs and so forth must obstruct your view."

Eft snorted. "They got nothin' I want to see."

That could not be said of the Guard, as Silk realized as soon as he looked past the floater. A talus had been posted at an intersection a hundred paces uphill, its great, tusked head (so like that of the one he had killed beneath Scylla's shrine that he could have believed them brothers) swiveling to peer down each street in turn. Liana would have been interested in it, he thought, if she did not know about it already.

"In here." Eft opened the door of one of the dark shops; his voice and the thump of the door brightened lights inside, where troopers stripped of parts of their armor and more or less bandaged lay on blankets on a terrazzo floor. One moaned, awakened by the noise or the lights; two, it seemed, were not breathing. Silk knelt by the nearest, feeling for a pulse.

"Not him. Over here."

"All of them," Silk said. "I'm going to bring the Pardon of Pas to all of them, and I won't do it en masse. There's no justification for that."

"Most's already had it. He has."

Silk looked up at the sergeant, but there was no judging his truthfulness from his hard, ill-favored face. Silk rose. "This man's dead, I believe."

"All right, we'll get him out of here. Come over here. He's not." Eft was standing beside the man who had moaned.

Silk knelt again. The injured man's skin was cold to his touch. "You're not keeping him warm enough, Sergeant."

"You a doctor, too?"

"No, but I know something about caring for the sick. An augur must."

"No hurt." Oreb hopped from Silk's shoulder to the injured man's chest. "No blood."

"Leave him alone, you silly bird."

"No hurt!" Oreb whistled. "No blood!"

A bald man no taller than Liana stepped from behind one of the empty showcases. Although he held a slug gun, he was not in armor or even in uniform. "He—he isn't, Patera. Isn't wounded. At least he doesn't—I couldn't find a thing. I think it must be his heart."

"Get a blanket," Silk told Eft. "Two blankets. Now!"

"I don't take orders from any shaggy butcher."

"Then his death will be on your head, Sergeant." Silk took his beads from his pocket. "Bring two blankets. Three wouldn't be too many. The men watching the rebels can spare theirs, surely. Three blankets and clean water."

He bent over the injured man, his prayer beads dangling

in the approved fashion from his right hand. "In the names of all the gods you are forgiven forever, my son. I speak here for Great Pas, for Divine Echidna, for Scalding Scylla, for Marvelous Molpe . . ."

The names rolled from his tongue, each with its sonorous honorific, names empty or freighted with horror. Pas, whose Plan the Outsider had endorsed, was dead; Echidna a monster. The ghost that haunted Silk's mind now, as he spoke and swung his beads, was not Doctor Crane's but that of the handsome, brutal chem who had believed himself Councillor Lemur.

"The monarch wanted a son to succeed him," the false Lemur had said. "Scylla was as strong-willed as the monarch himself but female. Her father allowed her to found our city, however, and many others. She founded your Chapter as well, a parody of the state religion of her own whorl. His queen bore the monarch another child, but she was worse yet, a fine dancer and a skilled musician, but female, too, and subject to fits of insanity. We call her Molpe. The third was male, but no better than the first two because he was born blind. He became that Tartaros to whom you were recommending yourself, Patera. You believe he can see without light. The truth is that he cannot see by daylight. Echidna conceived again, and bore another male, a healthy boy who inherited his father's virile indifference to the physical sensations of others to the point of mania. We call him Hierax now—"

And this boy over whom he bent and traced sign after sign of addition was nearly dead. Possibly—just possibly—he might derive comfort from the liturgy, and even strength. The gods whom he had worshiped might be unworthy of his worship, or of anyone's; but the worship itself must have counted for something, weighed in some scales somewhere, surely. It had to, or else the Whorl was mad.

"The Outsider likewise forgives you, my son, for I speak

here for him, too." A final sign of addition and it was over. Silk sighed, shivered, and put away his beads.

"The other one didn't say that," the civilian with the slug gun told him. "That last."

He had waited so long in fear of some such remark that it came now as an anticlimax. "Many augurs include the Outsider among the minor gods," he explained, "but I don't. His heart? Is that what you said? He's very young for heart problems."

"His name's Cornet Mattak. His father's a customer of mine." The little jeweler leaned closer. "That sergeant, he killed the other one."

"The other—?"

"Patera Moray. He told me his name. We chatted awhile when he'd said the prayers of the Pardon, and I—I— And I—" Tears flooded the jeweler's eyes, abrupt and unexpected as the gush from a broken jar. He took out a blue handkerchief and blew his nose.

Silk bent over the cornet again, searching for a wound.

"I said I'd give him a chalice. To catch the blood, you know what I mean?"

"Yes," Silk said absently. "I know what they're for."

"He said theirs was yellow pottery, and I said—said—"

Silk rose and picked up the small traveling bag. "Where is his body? Are you certain he's dead?" Oreb fluttered back to his shoulder.

The jeweler wiped his eyes and nose. "Is he dead? Holy Hierax! If you'd seen him, you wouldn't ask. He's out in the alley. That sergeant came in while we were talking and shot him. In my own store! He dragged him out there afterward."

"Show him to me, please. He brought the Pardon of Pas to all these others? Is that correct?"

Leading Silk past empty display cases toward the back of the shop, the jeweler nodded.

"Cornet Mattak hadn't been wounded then?"

"That's right." The jeweler pushed aside a black velvet curtain, revealing a narrow hallway. They passed a padlocked iron door and stopped before a similar door that was heavily barred. "I said when all this is over and things have settled down, I'll give you a gold one. I was still emptying out my cases, you see, while he was bringing them the Pardon. He said he'd never seen so much gold, and they were saving for a real gold chalice. They had one at his manteion, he said, before he came, but they'd had to sell it."

"I understand."

The jeweler took down the second bar and stood it against the wall. "So I said, when this is over I'll give you one to remember tonight by. I've got a nice one that I've had about a year, plain gold but not plain looking, you know what I mean? He smiled when I said that."

The iron door swung open with a creak of dry hinges that reminded Silk painfully of the garden gate at the manse.

"I said, you come into the strong room with me, Patera, and I'll show it to you. He put his hand on my shoulder then and said, my son, don't consider yourself bound by this. You haven't sworn by a god, and—and—"

"Let me see him." Silk stepped outside into the alley.

"And then the sergeant came in and shot him," the jeweler finished. "So don't you go back inside, Patera."

In the chill evil-smelling darkness, someone was murmuring the prayer that Silk himself had just completed. He caught the names of Phaea and Sphigx, followed by the conventional closing phrase. The voice was an old man's; for an eerie moment, Silk felt that it was Patera Pike's.

His eyes had adjusted to the darkness of the alley by the time the kneeling figure stood. "You're in terrible danger here," Silk said, and bit back the stooped figure's title just in time.

"So are you, Patera," Quetzal told him.

Silk turned to the jeweler. "Go inside and bar the door,

please. I must speak to the—to my fellow augur. Warn him.''

The jeweler nodded, and the iron door closed with a crash, leaving the alley darker than ever.

For a few seconds, Silk assumed that he had simply lost sight of Quetzal in the darkness; but he was no longer there. Patera Moray—of an age, height, and weight indeterminable without more light—lay on his back in the filthy mud of the alley, his beads in his hands and his arms neatly folded across his torn chest, alone in the final solitude of death.

Chapter 7

WHERE THELX HOLDS UP A MIRROR

Silk stopped to look at Ermine's imposing façade. Ermine's
had been built as a private house, or so it appeared—built for
someone with a bottomless cardcase and a deep appreciation
of pillars, arches, friezes, and cornices and the like; features
he had previously seen only as fading designs painted on the
otherwise stark fronts of shiprock buildings were real here in
a jungle of stone that towered fully five stories. A polished
brass plaque of ostentatiously modest proportions on the
wide green front door announced: "Ermine's Hôtel."

Who, Silk wondered almost idly, had Ermine been? Or
was he still alive? If so, might Linsang be a poor relation—or
even a rich one who had turned against the Ayuntamiento?
And what about Patera Gulo? Stranger things had happened.

Though he felt cold, his hands were clammy; he groped
for his robe before remembering that it was back in the borrowed traveling bag with the borrowed blue tunic, and wiped
his hands on the yellow one he was wearing instead.

"Go in?" Oreb inquired.

"In a minute." He was procrastinating and knew it. This
was Ermine's, the end of dreams, the shadeup of waking. If
he was lucky, he would be recognized and shot. If he was not,
he would find Thelxiepeia's image and wait until Ermine's

closed, for even Ermine's must close sometime. An immensely superior servant would inform him icily that he would have to leave. He would stand, and look about him one last time, and try to hold the servant in conversation to gain a few moments more.

After that, he would have to go. The street would be gray with morning and very cold. He would hear Ermine's door shut firmly behind him, the snick of the bolt and the rattle of the bar. He would look up and down the street and see no Hyacinth, and no one who could be carrying a message from her.

Then it would be over. Over and dead and done with, never to live again. He would recall his longing as something that had once occupied an augur whose name chanced to be his, Silk, a name not common but by no means outlandish. (The old caldé, whose bust his mother had kept at the back of her closet, had been—what? Had he been Silk, too? No, Tussah; but tussah was another costly fabric.) He would try to bring peace and to save his manteion, fail at both, and die.

"Go in?"

He wanted to say that they were indeed going in, but found himself too dismayed to speak. A man with a pheasant's feather in his hat and a fur cape muttered, "Pardon me," and shouldered past. A footman in livery (presumably the supercilious servant envisioned a few seconds before) opened the door from inside.

Now. Or not at all. Leave or send a message. Preserve the illusion.

"Are you coming in, sir?"

"Yes," Silk said. "Yes, I am. I was wondering about my pet, though. If there are objections, I'll leave him outside."

"None, sir." A faint, white smile touched the footman's narrow lips like the tracery of frost upon a windowpane. "The ladies not infrequently bring animals, sir. Boarhounds, sir. Monkeys. Your bird cannot be worse. But, sir, the door . . ."

It was open, of course. The night was chill, and Ermine's would be comfortably warm, rebellion or no rebellion. Silk climbed the steps to the green door, discovering that Liana's barricade had been neither higher nor steeper.

"This is your first visit to Ermine's, I take it, sir?"

Silk nodded. "I'm to meet a lady here."

"I quite understand, sir. This is our anteroom, sir." There were sofas and stiff-looking chairs. "It is principally for the removal of one's outer garments, sir. They are left in the cloakroom. You may check your bag there, if you so desire. There is no hospitality here in the anteroom, sir, but one can observe all the guests who enter or depart."

"Good man?" Oreb studied the footman through one bright, black eye. "Like bird?"

"Tonight, sir," the footman leaned nearer Silk, and his voice became confidential, "I might be able to fetch you some refreshment myself, however. We've little patronage to-night. The unrest."

"Thank you," Silk said. "Thank you very much. But no."

"Beyond the anteroom, sir, is our sellaria. The chairs are rather more comfortable, sir, and there is hospitality as well. Some gentlemen read."

"Suppose I go into your sellaria and turn to the right," Silk inquired, "where would I be then?"

"In the Club, sir. Or if one turns less abruptly, in the Glasshouse, sir. There are nooks, sir. Benches and settees. There is hospitality, sir, but it is infrequent."

"Thank you," Silk said, and hurried away.

Strange to think that this enormous room, a room that held fifty chairs or more, with half that many diminutive tables and scores of potted plants, statues, and fat-bellied urns, should be called by the same name as his musty little sitting room at the manse. Swerving to his right he wound among them, worrying that he had turned too abruptly and feeling that he walked in a dream through a house of giants—while politely declining the tray proffered by a deferential waiter. All the chairs he saw were empty; a table with a glass top scarcely bigger than the seat of a milking stool held wads of crumpled paper and a sheet half covered with script, the only signs of human habitation.

A wall loomed before him like the face of a mountain, or more accurately, like a fog bank through rents in which might be glimpsed scenes of unrelated luxury that were in truth its pictures. He veered left, and after another twenty strides caught sight of a marble arch framing a curtain of leaves.

It had been as warm as he had expected in the sellaria; passing through the arch he entered an atmosphere warmer still, humid, and freighted with exotic perfumes. A moth with mauve-and-gray wings larger than his palms fluttered before his face to light on a purple flower the size of a soup tureen. A path surfaced with what seemed precious stones, narrower even than the graveled path through the garden of his manteion, vanished after a step or two among vines and dwarfish trees. The music of falling water was everywhere.

"Good place," Oreb approved.

It was, Silk thought. It was stranger and more dreamlike than the sellaria, but more friendly and more human, too. The sellaria had been a vision of opulence bordering on nightmare; this was a gentler one of warmth and water, sunshine and lush fertility, and though this glass-roofed garden might be used for vicious purposes, sunshine and fertility, water and warmth were things in themselves good; their desirability could only be illustrated more clearly by the proximity of evil. "I like it," he whispered to Oreb. "Hyacinth must too, or she wouldn't have told me to meet her here, where all this would surely dim the beauty of a woman less lovely.''

The sparkling path divided. He hesitated, then turned to his right. A few steps more, and there was no light save that from the skylands floating above the Whorl. ''His Cognizance would like this as much as we do, I believe, Oreb. I've been in his garden at the Palace, and this reminds me of it, though that's an open-air garden, and this can't be nearly as large.''

Here was a seat for two, masterfully carved from a single block of myrtle. He halted to stare at it, longing to sit but restrained by the fear that he would be unable to stand again. ''We have to find this image of Thelxiepeia,'' he muttered, ''and there must be places to sit there. Hyacinth won't come. She's at Blood's in the country, she's bound to be. But we can rest there awhile.''

A new voice, obsequious and affected, murmured, ''I *beg* your pardon, sir.''

''Yes, what is it?'' Silk turned.

A waiter had come up behind him. ''I'm rather embarrassed, sir. I really don't know quite how to phrase it.''

''Am I not supposed to be in here now?'' As Silk asked, he resolved not to leave without a fight; they might overwhelm him with a mob of waiters and footmen, but they would have to—no mere order or argument would suffice.

''Oh, no, sir!'' The waiter looked horrified. ''It's quite all right.''

The desperate struggle Silk had visualized faded into the mist of unactualized eventualities.

''There is a gentleman, sir. A very tall gentleman, sir, with a long face? Rather a sad face, if I may say so, sir. He's in the Club.''

''No go,'' Oreb announced firmly.

''He would not give me his name, sir. He said it was not

relevant." The waiter cleared his throat. "He would not give your name either, sir, but he described you. He said that I was to say nothing if you were with someone, sir. I was only to offer to bring you and anyone who might be in your company refreshment, for which he would pay. But that if I found you alone, I was to invite you to join him."

Silk shook his head. "I have no idea who this gentleman is. Do you?"

"No, sir. He is not a regular patron, sir. I don't think I've ever seen him before."

"Do you know the figure of Thelxiepeia, waiter? Here in the Glasshouse?"

"Certainly, sir. The tall gentleman instructed me to look for you there, sir."

Colonel Oosik was tall, Silk reflected, though so massive that his height had not been very noticeable; but Oosik could scarcely be called long-faced. Since only he and Captain Gecko had read Hyacinth's letter, the long-faced man was presumably Gecko. "Tell him I can't join him in the Club," Silk said, choosing his words. "Express my regrets. Tell him I'll be at the figure of Thelxiepeia, and I'm alone. He may speak to me there if he chooses."

"Yes, sir. Thank you, sir. May I get you anything, sir? I could bring it there."

Silk shook his head impatiently.

"Very well, sir. I will deliver your message."

"Wait a moment. What time is it?"

The waiter looked apologetic. "I have no watch, sir."

"Of course not. Neither do I. Approximately."

"I looked at the barman's clock, sir, only a minute or two before I came here. It was five until twelve then, sir."

"Thank you," Silk said, and sat down on the carved wooden seat without a thought about the difficulty of getting up.

Hieraxday, Hyacinth's letter said. He tried to recall her

exact words and failed, but he remembered their import. She had mentioned no time, perhaps intending late afternoon, when she would have finished her shopping. The barman's clock was in the Club, no doubt; and the Club would be a drinking place, primarily for men—a rich man's version of the Cock, where he had found Auk. The waiter was unlikely to have glanced at the barman's clock after speaking to the long-faced man, whoever he was; so it had probably been ten minutes or more since he had noticed the time. Hieraxday was past. This was Thelxday, and if Hyacinth had waited for him (which was highly unlikely) he had not come.

"Hello, Jugs," Auk said, emerging from the darkness of a side tunnel. "He wants us to work on Pas's Plan."

Chenille whirled. "Hackum! I've been looking all over for you!" She ran to him, surprising him, threw her arms around him, and wept.

"Now," he said. "Now, now, Jugs. Now, now." She had been unhappy, and he knew it and knew that in some ill-defined and troubling way it was his fault, although he had meant her no harm, had wished her well and thought of her with kindness when he had thought of her at all. "Excuse," he muttered, and let go of Tartaros's hand to embrace her with both arms.

When at last she ceased sobbing, he kissed her as tenderly as he could, a kiss she returned passionately. She wiped her eyes, sniffled, and gulped, "Oh, Hierax! Hackum, I missed you so much! I've been so lonesome and scared. Hug me."

This baffled him, because he already was. He tried, "I'm sorry, Jugs," and when it seemed to do no good, "I won't ever leave you again unless you want me to."

She nodded and swallowed. "It's all right, as long as you keep coming back."

He noticed her ring. "Didn't I give you that?"

"Yeah, thanks." Stepping back, she held it up to show it

off better, although the bleared greenish lights could never do it justice. "I love it, but you can have it back anytime if you need the gelt."

"I'm flush, but I gave it to you?"

"You forget, huh?" She looked at him searchingly. "On account of hitting your head. Or maybe a god got you like Kypris did me? It's still pretty hard for me to remember lots of things that happened when she was boss, or Scylla."

Auk shook his head, and found that it no longer ached. "I've never had no god bossing me, Jugs, or wanted to either. That's lily. I never even knew about Kypris, but you were a lot different when you were Scylla."

"Some of that was me, I think. Hold me tighter, won't you? I'm really cold."

"Your sunburn don't hurt any more?"

She shook her head. "Not much. I'm starting to peel a little. The bird was pulling on the peels before he left, only I made him stop."

Auk looked around. "Where is he?"

"With Patera and Stony, I guess. That Urus beat the hoof and they took off after him. Me, too, only we came to a split in the tunnel, you know?"

"Sure. I've seen a lot of them."

"And then I thought, they're not going to look for Auk anymore, and that's what I want to do. So I sort of slowed down, and when they went one way I went the other. I guess the bird went with them."

"That was you I heard calling me."

Chenille nodded. "Yeah. I yelled until my pipe gave out. Oh, Hackum, I'm so glad I found you!"

"We found you," he told her seriously. "Why I ran off, Jugs . . ." He fell silent, massaging his big jaw.

"You saw somebody, Hackum. Or anyhow you thought you did. I could see that, and Patera said so, too."

"Yeah. My brother Bustard. He's dead, see? Only he was

down here talking to me. I was going to say he wasn't really, I just sort of dreamed it, only now I'm not so sure. Maybe he was. Know what I mean?''

The gray shiprock walls seemed to press in upon her. ''I think so, Hackum.''

''Then he went away, and I missed him a lot, just like when he died. So then when I saw him again, maybe it was a couple, three hours later, I waved and yelled and tried to catch up, only I never did. Then I got lost, but I didn't care because I was looking for Bustard, and he could've been any-where. Then I ran into this god. Into Tartaros. Mostly I call him Terrible Tartaros, 'cause I can't say the other right.''

''You met a god, Hackum? Like you'd meet somebody in the street, you mean?''

''Sort of.'' Auk sat down on the tunnel floor. ''Jugs, will you sit on my lap, the way you used to do in the old days? I'd like that.''

''All right.'' She did, laying her launcher flat, crossing her long legs, and leaning back in his arms. ''This is really better, Hackum. It's a lot warmer. Except I don't do it much any more because I know I'm a pretty good load. Orchid says I'm getting fat. She's been telling me for a couple of months now.''

He held her closer, reveling in her softness. ''She's fat. Real fat. Not you, Jugs.''

''Thanks. This god you met. Tartaros, right? He's for you like Kypris is for us.''

''Yeah, except he's one of the Seven.''

''I know that. Tarsday.''

''He's got a whole bunch of stuff besides us. The main thing is, he's the night god. Anywhere it's dark, that's a spe-cial place for him. Sleep and dreams, too. I mean, any god can send a dream if he wants to, but the regular kind that seem like nobody sent 'em are his. I call him Terrible Tar-taros 'cause you had to say terrible or the other, or Maytera'd stomp you. I'd lay he could cut up rough, but he's been a bob cull with me. He came along to show how to find you and get out of here, and all that. He's next to us right now, only you can't see him 'cause he's blind.''

"You mean he's here with us?'' Chenille's eyes were wide.

"Yeah, he's sitting right here with me, only I wouldn't try to reach over and feel. Maybe he wouldn't do anything—''

She had already, waving her free arm through the empty space on Auk's right.

He shook her, not roughly. "Don't, Jugs. I told you.''

"He's not there. There's nothing there.''

"All right, there's nothing there. I was shaving you.''

"You shouldn't do that.'' She got up. "You don't know how shaggy scared I am down here, or how shaggy hungry.''

Auk rose too. "Yeah, it wasn't very funny, I guess. I'm sorry, Jugs. I won't do it again. C'mon.''

"Where are we going?''

"Out.''

"Really, Hackum?''

"Sure. You're hungry. So am I. We're going to go out and get a dimber dinner, probably at Pork's or one of those places. After that, we can rent a room and get a little rest. He says I got to rest. After that, maybe we'll do what Scylla said, only I don't know. I'll have to ask him.''

"Tartaros? That's who you're talking about? You really met him?''

"Yeah. It's real dark in there and pretty wet. Water's sort of raining through the roof. If you saw it, you probably didn't go in, but there's nothing in there that'll hurt you. I don't think so, anyhow.''

"I've still got this lantern that Gelada had, Hackum, only there's no way to light it.''

"We don't have to,'' he told her. "It's not very far.''

"You said we were going out.''

"It's on our way." He stopped and faced her. "Only we'd be going even if it wasn't, 'cause he's got something to show us. He just told me, see? Now listen up."

She nodded, drawing Incus's robe around her.

"This's a real god. Tartaros, just like I told you. My head's not right 'cause I got a bruise in there and a big gob of blood, too, he says. He's trying to fix it, and I been feeling better ever since he started. Only we got to do like he says, so you're coming if I got to carry you."

"Wood girl," Oreb called. "Here girl!"

Silk sat up; the "girl" might be Hyacinth. If there was the least chance, one in a thousand or ten million—if there was any chance at all—he had to go. He made himself stand, picked up the bag, coughed, spat, and stumbled away. The path wound right then left, dropped into a tiny vale, and forked. White as ghosts, enormous blossoms dripped moisture. "I'm coming, Oreb. Tell her I'm coming."

"Here, here!"

The bird sounded very near. He stepped off the glittering path, his feet sinking in soft soil, and parted the leaves; the face that stared into his own might have been that of a corpse, hollow-cheeked and dull-eyed. He gasped, and saw its bloodless lips part. Oreb flew to him, becoming two birds.

He advanced another step, sparing the crowding plants as much as he could, and found himself standing upon red stones that bordered a clear pool no bigger than a tablecloth, which a path approached from the opposite side.

"Here girl!" Oreb hopped to the wooden figure's head and rapped it smartly with his beak.

"Yes," Silk said, "that's Thelxiepeia." No other goddess had those tilted eyes, and a carved marmoset perched upon the figure's shoulder. He tapped his reflected face with a finger and clapped his hands, but no monitor appeared in the silvered globe she held. "It's just a mirror," he told Oreb. "I hoped it might be a glass—that Hyacinth might call me on it."

"No call?"

"No call on this, alas." With help from a friendly tree, he walked the stony rim of the pool to a swinging seat facing the water. Here, as Oosik had said, one saw the pool reflected in Thelxiepeia's mirror, and her mirror reflected in it.

Hieraxday had been the day for dying and for honoring the dead. Crane had died; but he, Silk, had done neither. Today, Thelxday, was the day for crystal gazing and casting fortunes, for tricks and spells, and for hunting and trapping animals; he resolved to do none of those things, leaned back in the swing, and closed his eyes. Thelxiepeia was at once the cruelest and kindest of goddesses, more mercurial even than Molpe, though she was said—it would be why her image was here—to favor lovers. Love was the greatest of enchantments; if Echidna and her children succeeded in killing Kypris, Thelxiepeia would no doubt, would doubtless . . .

Become the goddess of love in a century or less, said the Outsider, standing not behind Silk as he had in the ball court, but before him—standing on the still water of the pool, tall and wise and kind, with a face that nearly came into focus. *I would claim her in that case, long before the end. As I have so many others. As I am claiming Kypris even now because love always proceeds from me, real love, true love. First romance.*

The Outsider was the dancing man on a toy, and the water the polished toy-top on which he danced with Kypris, who was Hyacinth and Mother, too. *First romance,* sang the Outsider with the music box. *First romance.* It was why he was called the Outsider. He was outside—

"I, er, hope and—ah—trust I'm not disturbing you?"

Silk woke with a start and looked around wildly.

"Man come," Oreb remarked. "Bad man." Oreb was perched on a stone beside Thelxiepeia's pool; when he had concluded his remarks, he pecked experimentally at a shining silver minnow that darted away in terror.

"Names are not—um—requisite, eh? I know who you are. You know me, hey? Let that be enough for both of us."

Silk recognized his swaying visitor, started to speak, and assimilating what had been said remained silent.

"Capital. I—ah—we are taking a risk, you and I. An—ah—rash gamble. Simply by, urp, being where we belong. Here on the hill, eh?"

"Won't you sit down?" Silk struggled to his feet.

"No. I—ah—no." His visitor belched again, softly. "Thank you. I have been waiting in the—ah—bar. Where, ump, I have been compelled to buy drinks. And—um—drink. Standing's best. Um, at present, eh? I'll just, er, lean on this, if I may. But please—ah—be seated yourself, Pa—" He covered his mouth with his hand. "Seated by all means. It is I who should—and I do. I, um, am. As you see, eh?"

Silk resumed his place in the swing. "May I ask—"

His visitor raised a hand. "How I knew I should find you here? I did not, Pa— Did not. Nothing of the sort. But while I was—rup!—sitting in that, er, whatchamacallit, I observed you to enter the room. Not the—um—one I sat in, that, ah, darksome and paneled drinking place, hey? The other. The outer room, much bigger."

"The sellaria," Silk supplied.

"Ah—quite. I, um, went to the door. Spied upon you." The visitor shook his head in self-reproach.

"It was excusable, surely, under the circumstances. I have recently done far worse things."

"Good of you to say so. I—um—waylaid that waiter. You spoke with him."

Silk nodded.

"I had, um, observed you to pass under—ah—through the arch. I had never had the, er, pleasure myself, eh? I, ah, apprehended that it was—ah, is—some sort of garden, however. I inquired about it. He, um, indicated that it was—is, I surmise—employed for, um, discussions of a—ah—amorous nature."

"You knew that I would be here, at this particular spot." Silk found it extremely inconvenient to be unable to say *Your Eminence.* "You told him to look for me here."

"No, no!" His visitor shook his head emphatically. "I, ah, anticipated you might, um, possibly have an appointment. As he had, um, inadverted. But I—ah—in addition, um, however, ah, considered that you might wish to, um, petition the immortal gods. As I, ah, myself. I inquired about such a place in this, um, conservatory. He mentioned the present, ah, xylograph." The visitor smiled. "That's the spot, I told him. That's where you'll find him. Would you mind if I, um, sat myself, now? There by you? I'm—ah—quite fatigued."

"Please do." Hastily, Silk moved to one side.

"Thank you—ah—thank you. Most thoughtful. I have had no supper. Hesitated to order anything in—ah—that place. With the wine. Parsimony. Foolish—ah—imbecile, actually."

"Catch fish," Oreb suggested.

Silk's visitor ignored him. "I've funds, eh? You?"

"No, nothing."

"Here, Pa— My boy. Hold out your hands." Golden cards showered into Silk's lap. "No, no! Take them! Others—ah—more. Where they came from, eh? Wait for the waiter. Buy yourself a bit of food. For me, ah, in addition. I am, um, in need. Of help. Of—ah—succor. Such is, um, the long and short of it. I cast myself—um. Ourselves. I—we—cast ourselves upon your—ah—commiseration."

Silk looked searchingly at Thelxiepeia, who returned his look with wooden aplomb. Was this enchanted gold that would (figuratively at least) melt at a touch? If not, what had he done to earn her favor? "Thank you," he managed at last. "If I can be of any service to Your—to you, I will be only too happy to oblige you." He counted them by touch: seven cards.

"They came to the Palace. To the—ah—Palace itself, if you can, um, credit that." His visitor sat with his head in his hands. "I was, um, dining. At dinner. In came a, ah, page, eh? One of the boys who runs with messages for us, hey? You do that?"

"No. I know of them, of course."

"Some of us did, eh? I, myself. Many years ago. We—ah—matriculate to schola. Ah—afterwards. Some of us. Fat little boy. Not I. He was. Is. Said they'd arrest me. Arrest His Cognizance! I said, ah, balderdash. Ate my sweet, eh? They—um—arrived. Unannounced. Officer—um—captain, lieutenant, something. Troopers with him, Guardsmen everywhere, eh? Looked everywhere for His Cog— Turned the whole place upside down. Couldn't find him though. Took me. Bound my hands. Me! Hands tied behind me under my robe."

"I'm very sorry," Silk said sincerely.

"They, er, carried me to the headquarters of the Second Brigade. A temporary headquarters. Do I make myself—ah—intelligible? Brigadier's house. No more—ah—titular generals in the Civil Guard, hey? No generalissimo any more. Only this, er, brigadiers. Quizzed me, eh? Hours and hours. Absolutely. Old Quetzal's letter, hey? You know about it?"

"Yes, I've seen it."

"I—ah—composed it. I didn't—ah—inform the brigadier, eh? Didn't 'fess up. Would have shot me, eh? We—ah—I'd expected trouble. Labored to phrase it softly. His— He wouldn't hear of it." His visitor looked around at Silk with the expression of a whipped hound, his breath thick with wine. "You apprehend whom I—ah—intend?"

"Of course."

"He sent it back. Twice. Hadn't happened in years, eh? The third stuck. 'How readily here might I, ah, inscribe—' Yes, inscribe. Ah, 'Let us welcome him and obey him as one of ourselves. With what delight do—shall I inscribe in its place, let us welcome him and, ump, obey him, for he is one of ourselves!' That's what got the third draft past His—ah—past the person known to us both, eh? So I—um—presume. Proud of it, hey? Still am. Still am."

"With reason," Silk told him. "But the Civil Guard can't have cared for it. I'm surprised they let you go." He yawned and rubbed his eyes, discovering that he felt somewhat better, refreshed by his few moments of sleep.

"Talked my way out, hey? Eloquent. No one speaks of me like that. Dull at the ambion, eh? What they say. I know, I know. Eloquent tonight, though. Swim or sink, and I did, Pa— I did. Go between. Peacemaker. End rebellion. Used their glass to talk to Councillor Loris. Harmless, ump! Let him go. Bad feeling in the ranks, hey? Augurs shot, eh? A sibyl, too. The—um—missive. Lay clothing, as you, er, wise. Fearful still. Terribly frightened. Not, er, shamed by the accusation—admission. Still afraid, sitting in there sipping. Looking over my shoulder, hey? Afraid they'd come for me. Sprang up like a rabbit when a porter dropped something in the street."

"I suppose that every man is frightened when his life is threatened. It's very much to Your—to your credit that you are willing to admit it."

"You will—ah—assist me? If you can?"

Oreb looked up from his fishing. "Watch out!"

"I'm tired and very weak," Silk said, "but yes, I will. Will we have to walk far?"

"Won't have to walk at all." His visitor thrust his hand beneath his cream-colored tunic. "I've, ah, informed you it wasn't me they wanted, eh? After old Quetzal, actually. The Prolocutor. His Cognizance. Signed the letter, hey?"

Silk nodded.

"They'd have shot him, eh? Earlier. Earlier. When they—ah—constrained me. That was then, hum? This is—er—the

present instant. After midnight. Nearly one, eh? Nearly one.
Late when they released me. I've said it? Suppertime—after
suppertime, really. They know your—um—profession. Vocation, hey? Mint's a sibyl. You take my meaning?''

"Of course," Silk said.

His visitor produced an elegant ostrich-skin pen case.
"On the other side, old Quetzal is, hey? Unmistakable. The
letter shows it. And there is that—ah, um—other matter. Vocation, eh? Brigadier thinks he and I might arrange an—urp
—hiatus in hostilities. A truce, hey? His word. Been one already, eh? So why not?''

Silk straightened up. "There has? That's wonderful!''

"Little thing, eh? Few hundred involved. Didn't last. But
an augur—see the connection? This augur, one of our—
ah—of the Chapter's own, crossed the lines. One side to the
other, eh? Got them to stop shooting so he could. Colonel's
son, wounded. Nearly dead. This—ah—holy augur brought
him the Pardon. So far so good? Rebels—ah—tendered an
extension. Both sides, um, sweep up bodies. Claim their
dead, hey? They did. So why not longer? Old Quetzal might
do it. Respected by both sides. Man of peace. You follow
me?''

Silk nodded to himself.

"If your, ah, supporters learn the brigadier sent me, eh?
What then? Shoot, eh? Possibly. Very possibly. So I require
some, um, document from you, Pa— From, ah, you. Signed,''
the visitor's voice faded to a whisper, "with your—ah—as
the—um—your civil title.''

"I see. Certainly.''

"Capital!'' He took a sheaf of paper from the pen case.
"These, um, fanciful leathers are not—ah—conducive to
penmanship. But the paper should help, hey? I'll hold the
ink bottle for you. Brief, ah, inconsiderable. Concise. The,
um, bearer, eh? Respect his—ah—um . . .''

"No shoot," Oreb suggested.

He handed Silk a quill. "Point suit you? Not too fine, eh? My prothonotary, Pa— Incus. You know him?"

"I met him once when I was trying to see you."

"Ah? Hm."

The pen case braced on both knees, Silk dipped the quill.

"He—ah—Incus. He points them for me. Had him do it, ah, Molpsday. Too fine, though. Hairsplitters. I shall rid myself of Incus, ah, presently. Could be dead this moment. 'Mongst the gods, eh? Haven't laid eyes on him for days. Gave him a—um—errand. Never came back. All this unrest."

Bent above the paper, Silk hardly heard him.

> To General Mint, her officers and troopers.
>   The bearer, Patera Remora, is authorized by me and by . . .

Silk looked up. "To whom did you speak? Who was this brigadier who released you?"

"Brigadier, er, Erne. Signed for me, too, eh? His side."

> Brigadier Erne to negotiate a truce. Please show him every courtesy.

The wavering tip of the quill stopped and began to blot; there seemed to be no more to say. Silk forced it to move on.

> If the whereabouts of His Cognizance the Prolocutor are known to you, please conduct the bearer to him in order that he may assist His Cognizance in conducting negotiations.

Oreb dropped a struggling goldfish and pinned it with one foot. "No shoot," he repeated. "Man hide."

> I hold you responsible for the safety of the bearer, and that of His Cognizance. Both are to be permitted to

pass unharmed. Their movements are not to be restricted in any fashion.

A truce made and kept in good faith is greatly to be desired.

I am Pa. Silk, of Sun Street, Caldé

"Capital! Yes, capital, Pa— Thank you!"

With his beak pointed to the glass roof, Oreb gulped down a morsel of goldfish and announced loudly, "Good man!"

"There is a—um—dispenser in here someplace." The visitor retrieved his pen case and took out a silver shaker. "If you require sand, eh?"

Silk shuddered, added the date, blew upon the paper, then spat congealing blood into the moss at his feet.

"I thank you. I have—ah—so expressed myself, um, previously, I, er, recognize. I am, um, in your, ah, books, eh? Your debtor."

Silk handed him the safe-conduct.

"I, ah, surmise that I can stand now, er, walk. All the rest. Taken a bit dizzy there, eh? For an, er, momentarily." He climbed to his feet, holding tightly to the chain from which their seat was suspended. "I shall partake of an, er, morsel of food, I believe. An, um, collation. Much as I should like— ah—may be imprudent . . ."

"I had a good supper," Silk told him, "and it might be dangerous for us to be seen together. I'll stay here."

"I, um, consider it would be best myself." His visitor released the chain and smiled. "Better, hey? Be all right with a bite to eat. Too much wine. I—ah—concede it. More than I ought. Frightened, but the wine made it worse. To think that we, ump, we pay—" He fell silent. Slowly his smile widened to a death's-head rictus. "Hello, Silk," he said. "They made me find you."

Silk nodded wearily. "Hello, Mucor."

"It's smoky in here. All smoky."

For a moment he did not understand what she meant.

"Dark, Silk. Like falling down steps."

"The fumes of the wine, I suppose. Who made you find me?"

"The councillors will burn me again."

"Torture, unless you do as they say?" Silk tried to keep the anger he felt out of his voice. "Do you know their names, these councillors who threaten to burn you?"

The visitor's grinning head bobbed. "Loris. Tarsier. Potto. My father said not, but the soldier made him go."

"I see. His Eminence—the man you're possessing—told me he'd talked with Councillor Loris through a glass. Is that why you possessed him when you were sent to look for me?"

"I had to. They burned me like Musk."

"Then you were right to obey, to keep from being burned again. I don't blame you at all."

"We're going to kill you, Silk."

Foliage beside the pool shook, spraying crystal droplets as warm as blood; a white-haired man stepped into view. In one hand he held a silver-banded cane with which he had parted the leaves. The other poised a saber, its slender blade pointed at the visitor's heart.

"Don't!" Silk told him.

"No stick," Oreb added with the air of one who clarifies a difficult situation.

"You're Silk yourself, lad! You're him!"

"I'm afraid I am. If you left your place of concealment to protect me, I would be somewhat safer if you didn't speak quite so loudly." Silk turned his attention back to the death-mask that had supplanted his visitor's face. "Mucor, how are you supposed to kill me? This man has Musk's needler now; he followed me here to return it to me, I imagine. Do you—does the man you're possessing have a weapon?"

"I'll tell them, and they'll come."

"I see. And if you won't, they'll burn you."

The visitor's head bobbed again. "It brings me back. I can't stay gone when they burn me."

"We must get you out of there." Silk raised the ankle he had broken jumping from Hyacinth's window and rubbed it. "I've said you're like a devil—I told Doctor Crane that, I know. I thought it, too, when I saw the dead sleepers; I forgot that devils, who torment others, are themselves tormented."

The saber inched forward. "Shall I kill him, lad?"

"No. He's as good a chance for peace as our city has, and I doubt that killing him would ensure Mucor's silence. You can do no good here."

"I can protect you, lad!"

"Before I left you, I knew that I'd meet Hierax tonight." Silk's face was somber. "But there's no reason for you to die with me. If you've tracked me through half the city to return the needler I dropped, give it to me and go."

"This, too!" He held out the silver-banded cane. "Lame, aren't you? Lame when we fought! Take it!" He threw the cane to Silk, then drew Musk's needler and tossed it into Silk's lap as well. "You're the caldé, lad? The one they tell about?"

"I suppose I am."

"Auk told me! How'd I forget that? Gave your name! I didn't know until this fellow said it. Councillors! Loris? Going to kill you?"

"And Potto and Tarsier." Silk laid Musk's needler aside, thought better of it, and put it into his waistband. "I'm glad that you brought that up. I'd lost sight of it, and it strains probability. Mucor, do you have to return to Loris right away? I'd like you to do me a favor, if you can."

"All right."

"Thank you. First, did Councillor Loris tell you about the man you're possessing? Did he ask you to find him?"

"I know him, Silk. He talks to the man who's not there."

"To Pas, you mean. Yes, he does, I'm sure. But Loris told you. Did he say why?"

The visitor's head shook. "I have to go soon."

"Go to Maytera Mint first—to General Mint, they're the same person." Silk's forefinger traced a circle on his cheek. "Tell her where I am, and that they'll come here to kill me. Then tell Maytera Marble—"

"Girl go," Oreb remarked.

The corpse-grin was indeed fading. Silk sighed again and rose. "Sheath that sword, please. We've no need of it."

"Possession? That's what you call this, lad?"

"Yes. He'll come to himself in a moment."

Silk's visitor caught hold of the chain to steady himself. "You proferred a comment, Pa—? I was taken, ah, vertiginous again, I fear. Please accept my—um—unreserved apology. This—ah—gentleman is . . . ?"

"Master Xiphias. Master Xiphias teaches the sword, Your Eminence. Master Xiphias, this is His Eminence Patera Remora, Coadjutor of the Chapter."

"Really, ah, Patera, you might be more circumspect, hey?"

Silk shook his head. "We're past all that, I'm afraid, Your Eminence. You're in no danger. I doubt that you ever were. My own is already so great that it wouldn't be much greater if you and Master Xiphias were to run up to the first Guardsman you could find and declare that Caldé Silk was at Ermine's awaiting arrest."

"Really! I—ah—"

"You spoke to Councillor Loris, so you told me, through Brigadier Erne's glass."

"Why, er, yes."

"For a moment—while you were dizzy, Your Eminence—I thought that Loris might have told you where to find me; that a certain person in the household he's visiting had told him that I might be here, or had confided in some-

one else who did. It could have come about quite inno-
cently—but it can't be true, since Loris sent someone to you
in order to locate me. Clearly the information traveled the
other way: you knew that I might come here tonight. I doubt
that you actually told Loris that you knew where to find me;
you couldn't have been that certain I'd be here. You said
something that led him to think you knew, however. In his
place, I'd have ordered Brigadier Erne to have you followed.
Thanks to some careless remarks of mine Tarsday, he didn't
need to. Will you tell me—quickly, please—how you got your
information?''

"I swear—warrant you, Patera—"

"We'll have to talk about it later." Silk stood up less steadily than Remora had, leaning on the silver-banded cane. "A
moment ago I told Master Xiphias not to kill you; I'm not
certain it would have been wrong for me to have told him to
go ahead, but I don't have time for questions—we must go
before the Guard gets here. You, Master Xiphias, must return
home. You're a fine swordsman, but you can't possibly protect me from a squad of troopers with slug guns. You, Your
Eminence, must go to Maytera Mint. Don't bother filling
your belly. If—"

"Girl come!" Oreb flew to Silk's shoulder, fluttered his
wings, and added, "Come quick!"

For a wasted second, Silk stared at Remora, searching for
signs of Mucor in his face. Hyacinth was in sight before he
heard the rapid pattering of her bare feet on the path of false
gems and saw her, mouth open and dark eyes bright with
tears above the rosy confusion of a gossamer dishabille, her
hair a midnight cloud behind her as she ran.

She stopped. It was as if the sight of him had suspended
her in amber. "You're here! You're really here!"

By Thelxiepeia's spell she was in his arms, suffocating him
with kisses. "I didn't—I knew you couldn't come, but I had
to. Had to, or I'd never know. I'd always think—"

He kissed her, clumsy but unembarrassed, trying to say by his kiss that he, too, had been forced by something in himself stronger than himself.

The pool and the miniature vale that contained it, always dark, grew darker still. Looking up after countless kisses, he saw idling fish of mottled gold and silver, black, white, and red, hanging in air above the goddess's upraised hand, and for the first time noticed light streaming from a lamp of silver filigree in the branches of a stunted tree. "Where did they go?" he asked.

"Was—somebody—else here?" She gasped for breath and smiled, giving him sweeter pain than he had ever known.

"His Eminence and a fencing master." Silk felt that he should look around him, but would not take his eyes from hers.

"They must have done the polite thing," she kissed him again, "and left quietly."

He nodded, unable to speak.

"So should we. I've got a room here. Did I tell you?"

He shook his head.

"A suite, really. They're all suites, but they call them rooms. It's a game they play, being simple, pretending to be a country inn." She sank to her knees with a dancer's grace, her hand still upon his arm. "Will you kneel by the pool here with me? I want to look at myself, and I want to look at you, too, at the same time." Abruptly, the tears overflowed. "I want to look at *us.*"

He knelt beside her.

"I knew you couldn't come," a tear fell, creating a tiny ripple, "so I have to see us both. See you beside me."

As in the ball court (though perhaps only because he had experienced it there) it seemed that he stood outside time.

And when they breathed again and turned to kiss, it seemed to him that their reflections remained as they had been in the quiet water of the pool, invisible but forever present. "We—I have to go," he told her. It had taken an enormous effort to say it. "They know I'm here, or they soon will if they don't already. They'll send troopers to kill me, and if you're with me, they'll kill you, too."

She laughed, and her soft laughter was sweeter than any music. "Do you know what I went through to get here? What Blood will do to me if he finds out I took a floater? By the time I got onto the hill, past the checkpoints and sentries— Are you sick? You don't look at all well."

"I'm only tired." Silk sat back on his heels. "When I thought about having to run again, I felt . . . It will pass." He believed it as soon as he had said it, himself persuaded by the effort he had made to compel her belief.

She rose, and gave him her hand. "By the time I got to Ermine's, I thought I'd been abram to come at all, drowning in a glass of water. I didn't even look in here," happy again, she smiled, "because I didn't want to see there wasn't anyone waiting. I didn't want to be reminded of what a putt I'd been. I got my room and started getting ready for bed, and then I thought—I thought—"

He embraced her; from a perch over the filigree lamp, Oreb croaked, "Poor Silk!"

"What if he's there? What if he's *really down there,* and I'm up here? I'd unpinned my hair and taken off my makeup, but I dived down the stairs and ran through the sellaria, and you were here, and it's only a dream but it's the best dream that ever was."

He coughed. This time the blood was fresh and red. He turned aside and spat it into a bush with lavender flowers and emerald leaves and felt himself falling, unable to stop.

He lay on moss beside the pool. She was gone; but their reflections remained in the water, fixed forever.

When he opened his eyes again, she was back with an old man whose name he had forgotten, the waiter who had offered him wine in the sellaria, the one who had told him of Remora, the footman who had opened the door, and others. They rolled him onto something and picked him up, so that he seemed to float somewhere below the level of their waists, looking up at the belly of the vast dark thing that had come between the bright skylands and the glass roof. His hand found hers. She smiled down at him and he smiled too, so that they journeyed together, as they had on the deadcoach in his dream, in the companionable silence of two who have overcome obstacles to be together, and have no need of noisy words, but rest—each in the other.

Chapter 8

PEACE

Maytera Marble smiled to herself, lifting her head and cocking it to the right. Her sheets were clean at last, and so was everything else—Maytera Mint's things, a workskirt that had been badly soiled at the knees, and the smelly cottons she had dropped into the hamper before dying.

After strenuous pumping, she rinsed them in the sink and wrung them out. Her dipper transferred most of the sink water to the wash boiler before she took out the old wooden stopper and let the rest drain away; when it had cooled, the water in the wash boiler could be given to her suffering garden.

With her clever new fingers, she scooped the white bull's congealing fat from the saucepan. A rag served for a strainer; a chipped cup received the semiliquid grease. Wiping her hands on another rag, she considered the tasks that still confronted her: grease the folding steps first, or hang out this wash?

The wash, to be sure; it could be drying while she greased the steps. Very likely, it would be dry or nearly dry by the time she finished.

Beyond the doorway, the garden was black with storm. That wouldn't do! Rain (though Pas knew how badly they needed it) would spot her clean sheets. Fuming, she put aside the wicker clothes-basket and stepped out into the night, a hand extended to catch the first drops.

At least it wasn't raining yet; and the wind (now that she came to think of it, it had been windier earlier) had fallen. Peering up at the storm cloud, she realized with a start that it was not a real cloud at all—that what she had taken for a cloud was in fact the uncanny flying thing she had glimpsed above the wall, and even stared at from the roof.

A memory so remote that it seemed to have lain behind her curved metal skull stirred at this, her third view. Dust flew, as dust always does when something that has remained motionless for a long time moves at last.

"Why don't you dust it?" (Laughter.)

She would have blinked had she been so built. She looked down again, down at her dark garden, then up (but reasonably and prudently up only) at the pale streaks of her clotheslines. They were still in place, though sometimes the children took them for drover's whips and jump ropes. Started upward thus prudently and reasonably, her gaze continued to climb of its own volition.

"Why don't you dust it?"

Laughter filled her as the summer sunshine of a year long past descends gurgling to fill a wineglass, then died away.

Shaking her head, she went back inside. It was a trifle windy yet to hang out wash, and still dark anyway. Sunshine always made the wash smell better; she would wait till daylight and hang it out before morning prayer. It would be dry after.

When had it been, that sun-drenched field? The jokes and the laughter, and the overhanging, overawing shadow that had made them fall silent?

Grease the steps now, and scrub them, too; then it would be light out and time to hang the wash, the first thin thread of the long sun cutting the skylands in two.

She mounted the stair to the second floor. Here was that

picture again, the old woman with her doves, blessed by Molpe. A chubby postulant whose name she could not recall had admired it; and she, thin, faceless, old Maytera Marble, flattered, had said that she had posed for Molpe. It was almost the only lie she had ever told, and she could still see the incredulity in that girl's eyes, and the shock. Shriven of that lie again and again, she nevertheless told Maytera Betel at each shriving—Maytera Betel, who was dead now.

She ought to have brought something, an old paintbrush, perhaps, to dab on her grease with. Racking her brain, she recalled her toothbrush, retained for decades after the last tooth had failed. (She wouldn't be needing *that* any more!) Opening the broken door to her room . . . She should fix this, if she could. Should try to, anyhow. They might not be able to afford a carpenter.

Yet it seemed tonight that she remembered the painter, the little garden at the center of his house, and the stone bench upon which the old woman (his mother, really) had sat earlier. Posing gowned and jeweled as the goddess with a stephane, the dead butterfly pinned in her hair.

It had been embarrassing, but the painter had wonderful brushes, not in the least like this worn toothbrush of hers, whose wooden handle had cracked so badly, whose genuine boar bristles, once so proudly black, had faded to gray.

She pushed the old toothbrush down into the bull's soft, white fat, then ran it energetically along the sliding track.

She could not have been a sibyl then, only the sibyls' maid; but the artist had been a relative of the Senior Sibyl's, who had agreed to let her pose. Chems could hold a pose much longer than bios. All artists, he had said, used chems when they could, although he had used his mother for the old woman because chems never looked old. . . .

She smiled at that, tilting her head far back and to the right. The hinges, then the other track.

He had given them the picture when it was done.

She had a gray smear on one black sleeve. Dust from the steps, most likely. Filthy. She beat the sleeve until the dust was gone, then started downstairs to fetch her bucket and scrub brush. Had the bull's grease done what it was supposed to? Perhaps she should have paid for real oil. She lifted the folding steps tentatively. The grease had certainly helped. All the way up!

Gratifyingly smooth, so she had saved three cardbits at least, perhaps more. How had she gotten them down? With the crochet hook, that was it. But if she did not push the ring up she would not need it. The steps would have to come down again anyway when she scrubbed them, and she itched to see them work as they should. An easy tug on the ring, and down they slid with a puff of dust that was hardly noticeable.

"Why don't you dust it?"

Everyone had laughed, and she had too, though she had been so shy. He had been tall and—what was it? Five-point-two-five times stronger than she, with handsome steel features that faded when she tried to see them again.

All nonsense, really.

Like believing she had posed, after she had told Maytera over and over that she had lied. She would never have taken these new parts if . . . Though they were hers, to be sure.

One more time up the steps. One final time, and here was her old trunk.

She opened the gable window and climbed out onto the roof. If the neighbors spied her, they would be shocked out of their wits. *Trunk* evoked only her earlier search for its owner.

Footlocker, that was it. Here was a list of the dresses she had worn before they had voted to admit her. Her perfume. The commonplace book that she had kept for the mere pleasure of writing in it, of practicing her hand. Perhaps if she went back into the attic and opened her footlocker, she would find them all, and would never have to look at the thrumming thing overhead again.

Yet she did.

Enormous, though not so big you couldn't see the skylands on each side of it. Higher up and farther west now, over the market certainly and nosing toward the Palatine, its long axis bisected by Cage Street, where convicts were no longer exposed in cages. Its noise was almost below her threshold of hearing, the purr of a mountain lion as big as a mountain.

She should go back down now. Get busy. Wash or cook—though she was dead, and Maytera Betel and the rest dead, too, and Maytera Mint gone only Pas knew where, and nobody left to cook for unless the children came.

Enormous darkness high overhead, blotting the sundrenched field, the straggling line of servants in which she had stood, and the soldiers' precise column. She had seen it descend from the sky, at first a fleck of black that had seemed no bigger than a flake of soot; had said, "It looks so dirty." A soldier had overheard her and called, "Why don't you dust it?"

Everyone had laughed, and she had laughed, too, though she had been humiliated to tears, had tears been possible for her. Angry and defiant, she had met his eyes and sensed the longing there.

And longed.

How tall he had been! How big and strong! So much steel!

Winged figures the size of gnats sailed this way and that below the vast, dark bulk; something streaked up toward them as she watched—flared yellow, like bacon grease dripping into the stove. Some fell.

"Here we are," Auk told Chenille. It was a break in the tunnel wall.

"This leads into the pit?"

"That's what he says. Let me go first, and listen awhile. Beat the hoof if it sounds a queer lay."

She nodded, resolving that she and her launcher would have something to say about any queer lay, watched him worm his way through (a tight squeeze for shoulders as big as his), listened for minutes that seemed like ten, then heard his booming laugh, faint and far away.

It was a tight squeeze for her as well, and it seemed her hips would not go through. She wriggled and swore, recalling Orchid's dire warnings and that Orchid's were twice—at least twice!—the size of hers.

The place she was trying so hard to get into was a pit in the pit, apparently—as deep as a cistern, with no way to go higher, though Auk must have found one since he was not there.

Her hips scraped through at last. Panting as she knelt on the uneven soil, she reached back in and got her launcher.

"You coming, Jugs?" He was leaning over the edge, almost invisible in the darkness.

"Sure. How do I get out of here?"

"There's a little path around the sides." He vanished.

There was indeed—a path a scant cubit wide, as steep as a stair. She climbed cautiously, careful not to look down, with Gelada's lantern rattling on the barrel of her launcher. Above, she heard Auk say, "All right, maybe I will, but not till she gets here. I want her to see him."

Then her head was above the top and she was looking at the pit, a stade across, its reaches mere looming darkness, its sheer sides faced with what looked like shiprock. A wall rose above it on the side nearest her. She stared up at it without comprehension, turned her head to look at the shadowy figures around Auk, and looked up at it again before she recognized it as the familiar, frowning wall of the Alambrera, which she was now seeing from the other side for the first time.

Auk called, "C'mere, Jugs. Still got that darkee?"

A vaguely familiar voice ventured, "Might be better not to light it, Auk."

"Shut up."

She took Gelada's lantern off the barrel of her launcher and advanced hesitantly toward Auk, nearly falling when she tripped over a roll of rags in the darkness.

Auk said, "You do it, Urus. Keep it pretty near shut," and one of the men accepted the lantern from her.

The acrid smell of smoke cut through the prevailing reek of excrement and unwashed bodies; a bearded man with eyes like the sockets in a skull had removed the lid of a firebox. He puffed the coals it held until their crimson glow lit his face—a face she quickly decided she would rather not have seen. A wisp of flame appeared. Urus held the lantern to it, then closed the shutter, narrowing the yellow light to a beam no thicker than her forefinger.

"You want it, Auk?"

"I got no place to put it," Auk told him; and Chenille, edging nearer, saw that he had his hanger in his right hand and a slug gun in his left. The blade of the hanger was dark with blood. "Show her Patera first," he said.

On legs as thin as sticks, the shadowy figures parted; a pencil of light settled on a dark bundle that stared up at her with Incus's agonized eyes. A rag covered his mouth.

"Looks cute, don't he?" Auk chuckled.

She ventured, "He really is an augur . . ."

"He shot a couple of 'em with my needler, Jugs. It got 'em mad, and they jumped him. We'll cut him loose in a minute, maybe. Urus, show her the soldier."

Hammerstone was bound as well, though no rag had been tied over his mouth; she wondered whether it would work on a chem anyway, and decided that it might not. "I'm sorry, Stony," she said. "I'll get you out of this. Patera, too."

"They were going to stab him in the throat," Hammerstone told her. "They'd grabbed him from behind." He spoke slowly and without rancor, but there was a whorl of self-loathing in his voice. "I got careless."

"Those ropes are made out of that muscle in the back of your leg," Auk told her conversationally. "That's what they got him tied up with. They're pretty strong, I guess."

Neither she nor Hammerstone replied.

"Only I don't think they'd hold him. Not if he really tried. It'd take chains. Big ones, if you ask me."

"Hackum, maybe I shouldn't say this—"

"Go ahead."

"What if they jump you and me like they did Patera?"

"I was going to tell you why Hammerstone here don't break loose. Maybe I ought to do that first."

"Because you've got his slug gun?"

"Uh-huh. Only they had it then, see? They got hold of Incus, and they made Hammerstone give it to 'em. It takes a lot to kill a soldier, but a slug gun'll do it. So'll that launcher you got."

She scarcely heard him. When she had struggled through the narrow opening in the side of the tunnel, the deep humming from above had so merged with the rush of blood in her ears that she had assumed it was one with it; now she realized that it actually proceeded from the dark bulk in the sky that she (like Maytera Marble) had thought a cloud. She peered up at it, astonished.

"We'll get to that in a minute," Auk told her, looking upward too. "Terrible Tartaros says it's a airship. That's a thing kind of like the old man's boat, see? Only it sails through the air instead of water. The Rani of Trivigaunte's invaded Viron. That's another reason for us to do like he showed us down there—"

Hammerstone heaved himself upright, throwing aside four stick-limbed men who tried to hold him down. The sinews that bound his wrists and ankles broke in a rattattoo of poppings, like the burning of a string of firecrackers.

Almost casually, Auk thrust his hanger into the ground at his feet and leveled the slug gun. "Don't try it."

"We got to fight," Hammerstone told him. "Patera and me. We got to defend the city."

Reluctantly, Chenille trained the launcher Hammerstone had taught her to load and fire at his broad metal chest. He knelt to tear off Incus's gag, snapping the cords that had secured Incus's hands and feet between his fingers.

"Look! Look!" Urus shouted and pointed, then futilely directed the beam of Gelada's lantern upward. Others around him shouted and pointed, too.

Another voice, remote but louder than the loudest merely human voice silenced them, filling the pit with its thunder: *"Convicts, you are free! Viron has need of every one of you. In the name of all the—in the Outsider's name, forget your quarrel with the Civil Guard, which now supports our Charter. Forget any quarrel you may have with your fellow citizens. Most of all, forget every quarrel among yourselves!"*

Chenille grasped Auk's elbow. "That's Patera Silk! I recognize his voice!"

Auk could only shake his head, unbelieving. Something—a tumbling, flying thing that appeared, incredibly, to have a turret and a buzz gun—had cleared the parapet of the wall and was drifting into the pit, lower and lower, an armed floater blown upwind by a wind that was none, hundreds of cubits above the Alambrera.

Chenille's launcher was snatched from her hands and fired as soon as it had left them, Hammerstone aiming at the immense shape far above the floater, directing a single missile at it (or perhaps at the winged figures that streamed from it like smoke), and watching it expectantly to observe the strike and correct his aim.

"There Auk!" thundered a hoarse voice from the floater tumbling slowly overhead. *"Here girl!"*

A second missile, and Auk was firing the slug gun that had been Hammerstone's, too, shooting winged troopers who swooped and soared above the pit firing slug guns of their own.

A minute dot of black fell from the vast flying thing Auk had called an airship. She saw it streak through the milling cloud of winged troopers. An instant later, the dark wall of the Alambrera exploded with a force that rocked the whorl.

Silk stood in his boyhood bedroom, looking down at the boy who had been himself. The boy's face was buried in his pillow; by an effort of will he made it look toward him; each time it turned, its features dissolved in mist.

He sat down on the sill of the open window, conscious of the borage growing under it and of lilacs and violets beyond it. A copybook lay open, waiting, on the sleeping boy's small table; there were quills beside it, their ends more or less chewed. He ought to write, he knew—tell this boy who had been himself that he was taking his blue tunic, and leave him advice that would be of help in the troubles to come.

Yet he could not settle upon the right words, and he knew that the boy would soon wake. It was shadeup, and he would be late at his palaestra; already Mother approached the bed.

What could he say that would have meaning for this boy? That this boy might recall more than a decade later?

Mother shook his shoulder, and Silk felt his own shoulder touched; it was strange she could not see him.

Fear no love, he wrote; and then: *Carry out the Plan of Pas.* But Mother's hand was shaking him so hard that the final words were practically unreadable; *of Pas* faded from the soft, blue-lined paper as he watched. Pas was, after all, a thing of the past. Like the boy.

Xiphias and the Prolocutor were standing at the foot of the boy's bed, which had become his own.

He blinked.

As if to preside over a sacrifice at the Grand Manteion, the Prolocutor wore mulberry vestments crusted with diamonds and sapphires, and held the gold baculus that symbolized his authority; Xiphias had what appeared to be an augur's black robe folded over his arm. It seemed the wildest of dreams.

His blankets were pushed away; and the surgeon, standing next to his bed beside Hyacinth, rolled him onto his side and bent to pull off the bandages he had applied earlier. Silk managed to smile up at Hyacinth, and she smiled in return—a shy, frightened smile that was like a kiss.

From the other side of the bed, Colonel Oosik inquired, "Can you speak, Caldé?"

He could not, though it was his emotions that kept him silent.

"He talked to me last night before he went to sleep," Hyacinth told Oosik.

"Silk talk!" Oreb confirmed from the top of a bedpost.

"Please don't sit up." The surgeon laid his hand—a much larger and stronger one than the hand that had awakened him—upon Silk's shoulder to prevent it.

"I can speak," he told them. "Your Cognizance, I very much regret having subjected you to this."

Quetzal shook his head and told Hyacinth, "Perhaps you'd better get him dressed."

"No time to dawdle, lad!" Xiphias exclaimed. "Shadeup in an hour! Want them to start shooting again?"

Then the surgeon who had held him down was helping him to rise, and Hyacinth (who smelled better than an entire garden of flowers) was helping him into a tunic. "I did this for you last Phaesday night, remember?"

"Do I still have your azoth?" he asked her. And then, "What in the Whorl's going on?"

"They sent Oosie to kill you. He just came back and he doesn't want to."

Silk was looking, or trying to look, into the corners of the room. Gods and others who were not gods waited there, he felt certain, watching and nearly visible, their shining heads turned toward him. He remembered climbing onto Blood's roof and his desperate struggle with the white-headed one, Hyacinth snatching his hatchet from his waistband. He groped for it, but hatchet and waistband had vanished alike.

Quetzal muttered, "Somebody will have to tell him what to tell them. How to make peace."

"I don't expect you to believe me, Your Cognizance—" Hyacinth began.

"Whether I believe you or not, my child, will depend on what you say."

"We didn't! I swear to you by Thelxiepeia and Scalding Scylla—"

"For example. If you were to say that Patera Caldé Silk had violated his oath and disgraced his vocation, I would not believe you."

Standing upon the arm of his mother's reading chair, he had studied the caldé's head, carved by a skillful hand from hard brown wood. "Is this my father?" Mother's smile as she lifted him down, warning him not to touch it. "No, no, that's my friend the caldé." Then the caldé was dead and buried, and his head buried, too—buried in the darkest reaches of her closet, although she spoke at times of burning it in the big black kitchen stove and perhaps believed eventually that she had. It was not well to have been a friend of the caldé's."

"I know our Patera Caldé Silk too well for that," Quetzal was telling Hyacinth. "On the other hand, if you were to say that nothing of the kind had taken place, I would believe you implicitly, my child.''

Xiphias helped Silk to his feet, and Hyacinth pulled up a pair of unbleached linen drawers that had somehow appeared around his ankles and were new and clean and not his at all, and tied the cord for him.

''Caldé . . .''

At that moment, the title sounded like a death sentence. He said, ''I'm only Patera— Only Silk. Nobody's caldé now.''

Oosik stroked his drooping, white-tipped mustache. ''You fear that because my men and I are loyal to the Ayuntamiento, we will kill you. I understand. It is undoubtedly true, as this young woman has said . . .''

In the presence of the Prolocutor, Oosik was pretending he did not know Hyacinth, exactly as he himself had tried to pretend he was not caldé; Silk found wry amusement in that.

''—and already you have almost perished in this foolish fighting,'' Oosik was saying. ''Another dies now, even as we speak. On our side or yours, it does not matter. If it was one of us, we will kill one of you soon. If one of you, you will kill one of us. Perhaps it will be me. Perhaps my son, though he has already—''

Xiphias interrupted him. ''Couldn't get home, lad! Tried to! Big night attack! Still fighting! Didn't think they'd try that. You don't mind my coming back to look out for you?''

Kneeling with his trousers, Hyacinth nodded confirmation. ''If you listen at the window, you can still hear shooting.''

Silk sat on the rumpled bed again and pushed his feet into the legs. ''I'm confused. Are we still at Ermine's?''

She nodded again. ''In my room.''

Oosik had circled the bed to hold his attention. ''Would it not be a great thing, Caldé, if we—if you and I, and His Cognizance—could end this fighting before shadeup?''

With less confidence in his legs than he tried to show, Silk stood to pull up and adjust his waistband. "That's what I'd hoped to do." He sat as quickly as he could without loss of dignity.

"We will—"

Quetzal interposed, "We must strike fast. We can't wait for you to recover, Patera Caldé. I wish we could. You were startled to see me vested like this. My clothes always shock you, I'm afraid."

"So it seems, Your Cognizance."

"I'm under arrest, too, technically. But I'm trying to bring peace, just as you are."

"We've both failed, in that case, Your Cognizance."

Oosik laid his hand upon Silk's; it felt warm and damp, thick with muscle. "Do not burden yourself with reproaches, Caldé. No! Success is possible still. Who had you in mind as commander of your Civil Guard?"

The gods had gone, but one—perhaps crafty Thelxiepeia, whose day was just beginning—had left behind a small gift of cunning. "If anyone could put an end to this bloodshed, he would surely deserve a greater reward than that."

"But if that were all the reward he asked?"

"I'd do everything I could to see that he obtained it."

"Wise Silk!" Oreb cocked a bright black eye approvingly from the bedpost.

Oosik smiled. "You are better already, I think. I was greatly concerned for you when I saw you." He looked at the surgeon. "What do you think, Doctor? Should our caldé have more blood?"

Quetzal stiffened, and the surgeon shook his head.

"Achieving peace, Caldé, may not be as difficult as you imagine. Our men and yours must be made to understand that loyalty to the Ayuntamiento is not disloyalty to you. Nor is loyalty to you disloyalty to the Ayuntamiento. When I was a young man we had both. Did you know that?"

Xiphias exclaimed, "It's true, lad!"

"There is a vacancy on the Ayuntamiento. Clearly it must be filled. On the other hand, there are councillors presently in the Ayuntamiento. Their places are theirs. Why ought they not retain them?"

A compromise; Silk thought of Maytera Mint, small and heartrendingly brave upon a white stallion in Sun Street. "The Alambrera—?"

"Cannot be permitted to fall. The morale of your Civil Guard would not survive so crushing a humiliation."

"I see." He stood again, this time with more confidence; he felt weak, yet paradoxically strong enough to face whatever had to be faced. "The poor, the poorest people of our quarter especially, who began the insurrection, are anxious to release the convicts there. They are their friends and relatives."

Quetzal added, "Echidna has commanded it."

Oosik nodded, still smiling. "So I have heard. Many of our prisoners say so, and a few even claim to have seen her. I repeat, however, that a successful assault on the Alambrera would be a disaster. It cannot be permitted. But might not our caldé, upon his assumption of office, declare a general amnesty? A gesture at once generous and humane?"

"I see," Silk repeated. "Yes, certainly, if it will end the fighting—if there's even the slightest chance that it will end it. Must I come with you, Generalissimo?"

"You must do more. You must address both the insurgents and our own men, forcefully. It can be begun here, from your bed. I have a means of transmitting your voice to my troops, defending the Palatine. Afterward we will have to put you in a floater and take you to the Alambrera, in order that both our men and Mint's may see you, and see for themselves that there is no trickery. His Cognizance has agreed to go with you to bless the peace. Many know already that he has sided with you. When it is seen that my brigade has come over to you as a body, the rest will come as well."

Oreb crowed, "Silk win!" from the bedpost.

"I'm coming, too," Hyacinth declared.

"You must understand that there is to be no surrender, Caldé. Viron will have chosen to return to its Charter. A caldé—yourself—and an ayuntamiento."

Oosik turned ponderously to Quetzal. "Is that not the system of government stipulated by Scylla, Your Cognizance?"

"It is, my son, and it is my fondest desire to see it reinstated."

"If we're paraded through the city in this floater," Silk said, "many of the people who see us are certain to guess that I've been wounded." In the nick of time he remembered to add, "Generalissimo."

"Nor will we attempt to conceal it, Caldé. You yourself have played a hero's part in the fighting! I must tell Gecko to work that into your little speech."

Oosik took two steps backward. "Now someone must attend to all these things, I fear, and there is no one capable of it but myself. Your pardon, my lady." He bowed. "Your pardon, Caldé. I will return shortly. Your pardon, Your Cognizance."

"Bad man?" mused Oreb.

Silk shook his head. "No one who ends murder and hatred is evil, even if he does it for his own profit. We need such people too much to let even the gods condemn them. Xiphias, I sent you away last night at the same time that I sent away His Eminence. Did you leave at once?"

The old fencing master was shamefaced. "Did you say at once, lad?"

"I don't think so. If I did, I don't recall it."

"I'd brought you this, lad, remember?" He bounded to the most remote corner of the room and held up the silver-banded cane. "Valuable!" He parried an imaginary opponents's thrust. "Useful! Think I'd let them leave it behind in that garden?"

Hyacinth said, "You followed when we carried him up here, didn't you? I saw you watching us from the foot of the stairs, but I didn't know you from a rat then."

"I understand." Silk nodded almost imperceptibly. "His Eminence left at once, I imagine. I had told him to find you if he could, Your Cognizance. Did he?"

"No," Quetzal said. With halting steps, he made his way to a red velvet chair and sat, laying the baculus across his knees. "Does it matter, Patera Caldé?"

"Probably not. I'm trying to straighten things out in my mind, that's all." Silk's forefinger traced pensive circles on his beard-rough cheek. "By this time, His Eminence may have reached Maytera Mint—reached General Mint, I should say. It's possible they have already begun to work out a truce. I hope so, it could be helpful. Mucor reached her in any event; and when General Mint heard Mucor's message, she attacked the Palatine hoping to rescue me—I ought to have anticipated that. My mind wasn't as clear as it should be last night, or I would never have told her where I was."

Hyacinth asked, "Mucor? You mean Blood's abram girl? Was she here?"

"In a sense." Silk found that by staring steadfastly at the yellow goblets and chocolate cellos that danced across the carpet, it was possible to speak to Hyacinth without choking, and even to think in a patchy fashion about what he said. "I met her Phaesday night, and I talked to her in the Glasshouse before you found me. I'll explain about her later, though, if I may—it's appalling and rather complex. The vital point is that she agreed to carry a message to General Mint for me, and did it. Colonel Oosik's brigade was being held in reserve when I spoke to him earlier; when the attack came, it must have been brought up to strengthen the Palatine."

Hyacinth nodded. "That's what he told me before we

woke you. He said it was lucky for you because Councillor Loris ordered him to send somebody to kill you, but he came himself instead and brought you a doctor.''

''I operated on you yesterday, Caldé,'' the surgeon told Silk, ''but I don't expect you to remember me. You were very nearly dead.'' He was horse-faced and balding; his eyes were rimmed with red, and there were bloodstains on his rumpled green tunic.

''You can't have had much sleep, Doctor.''

''Four hours. I wouldn't have slept that much, if my hands hadn't started to shake. We have over a thousand wounded.''

Hyacinth sat on the bed next to Silk. ''That's about what we got, too—four hours, I mean. I must look a hag.''

He made the error of trying to verify it, and discovered that his eyes refused to leave her face. ''You are the most beautiful woman in the whorl,'' he said. Her hand found his, but she indicated Quetzal by a slight tilting of her head.

Quetzal had been dozing—so it appeared—in the red chair; he looked up as though she had pronounced his name. ''Have you a mirror, my child? There must be a mirror in a suite like this.''

''There's a glass in the dressing room, Your Cognizance. It'll show you your reflection if you ask.'' Hyacinth nibbled at her full lower lip. ''Only I ought to be in there getting dressed. Oosie will come back in a minute, I think, with a speech for Patera and one of those ear things.''

Quetzal rose laboriously with the help of his baculus, and Silk's heart went out to him. How feeble he was! ''I've had four hours sleep, Your Cognizance; Hyacinth less than that, I'm afraid, and the doctor here about the same; but I don't believe Your Cognizance can have slept at all.''

''People my age don't need much, Patera Caldé, but I'd like a mirror. I have a skin condition. You've been too well bred to remark upon it, but I do. I carry paint and powder now like a woman, and fix my face whenever I get the chance.''

"In the balneum, Your Cognizance." Hyacinth rose, too. "There's a mirror, and I'll dress while you're in there."

Quetzal tottered away. Hyacinth paused with one hand on the latch-bar, clearly posing but so lovely that Silk could have forgiven her things far worse. "You men think it takes women a long while to get dressed, but it won't take *me* long this morning. Don't go without me."

"We won't," Silk promised, and held his breath until the boudoir door closed behind her.

"Bad thing," Oreb muttered from a bedpost.

Xiphias displayed the silver-banded cane to Silk. "Now I can show you this, lad! Modest? Proper? Augur can't wear a sword, right? But you can carry this! Had a stick first time you came, didn't you?"

"Bad thing!" Oreb dropped down upon Silk's shoulder.

"Yes, I had a walking stick then. It's gone now, I'm afraid. I broke it."

"Won't break this! Watch!" Between Xiphias's hands, the cane's head separated from its brown wooden shaft, exposing a straight, slender, double-edged blade. "Twist, and pull them apart! You try it!"

"I'd much rather put them back together." Silk accepted the cane from him; it seemed heavy for a walking stick, and somewhat light for a sword. "It's a bad thing, as Oreb says."

"Nickel in that steel! Chrome, too! Truth! Could parry an azoth! Believe that?"

Silk shuddered. "I suppose so. I had an azoth once and couldn't cut through a steel door with it."

The azoth reminded him of Hyacinth's gold-plated needler; hurriedly, he put his hand in his pocket. "Here it is. I've got to return this to her. I was afraid that it would be gone, somehow, though I can't imagine who might have taken it, except Hyacinth herself.'' He laid it on the peach-colored sheet.

"I gave your big one back, lad. Still got it?''

Silk shook his head, and Xiphias began to prowl around the room, opening cabinets and examining shelves.

"This cane will be useful, I admit,'' Silk told him, "but I really don't require a needler.''

Xiphias whirled to confront him, holding it out. "Going to make peace, aren't you?''

"I hope to, Master Xiphias, and that's exactly—''

"What if they don't like the way you're making it, lad? Take it!''

"Here you are, Caldé.'' Oosik bustled in with a sheet of paper and a black object that seemed more like a flower molded from synthetic than an actual ear. "I'll turn it on before I pass it to you, and all you'll have to do is talk into it. Do you understand? My loudspeakers will repeat everything that you say, and everyone will hear you. Here's your speech.''

He handed Silk the paper. "It would be best for you to read it over first. Insert some thoughts of your own if you like. I would not deviate too far from the text, however.''

Words crawled across the sheet like ants, some bearing meaning in their black jaws, most with none. *The insurgent forces. The Civil Guard. The rebellion. The commissioners and the Ayuntamiento. The Army. The arms in the Alambrera. The insurgents and the Guard. Peace.*

There it was at last. *Peace.*

"All right.'' Silk let the sheet fall into his lap.

Oosik signaled to someone in the outer room, waited for a reply that soon came, cleared his throat, and held the ear to his lips. "This is Generalissimo Oosik of the Caldé's Guard. Hear me all ranks, and especially you rebels. You're fighting us because you want to make Patera Silk caldé, but Caldé Silk is with us. He is with the Guard, because he knows that we are with him. Now you soldiers. Your duty is to obey our caldé. He is sitting here beside me. Hear his instructions.''

Silk wanted his old chipped ambion very badly; his hands sought it blindly as he spoke, rattling the paper. ''My fellow citizens, what Generalissimo Oosik has just told you is true. Are we not—'' The words seemed predisposed to hide behind his trembling fingers.

''Are we not, every one of us, citizens of Viron? On this historic day, my fellow citizens—'' The type blurred, and the next line began a meaningless half sentence.

''Our city is in great danger,'' he said. ''I believe the whole whorl's in great danger, though I can't be sure.''

He coughed and spat clotted blood on the carpet. ''Please excuse me. I've been wounded. It doesn't matter, because I'm not going to die. Neither are you, if only you'll listen.''

Faintly, he heard his words re-echoed in the night beyond Ermine's walls: *''You'll listen.''* The loudspeakers Oosik had mentioned, mouths with stentorian voices, had heard him in some fashion, and in some fashion repeated his thoughts.

The door of the balneum opened. Framed in the doorway, Quetzal gave him an encouaging nod, and Oreb flew back to his post on the bedpost.

''We can't rebel against ourselves,'' Silk said. ''So there is no rebellion. There is no insurrection, and none of you are insurgents. We can fight among ourselves, of course, and we've been doing it. It was necessary, but the time of its necessity is over. There is a caldé again—I am your caldé. We needed rain, and we have gotten rain.'' He paused to look across the room at the rich smoke-gray drapes. ''Master Xiphias, will you open that window for me, please? Thank you.''

He drew a deep and somewhat painful breath of cool, damp air. ''We've had rain, and if I'm any judge of weather, we'll get more. Now let's have peace—it's a gift we can provide ourselves, one more precious than rain. Let's have peace.''

(What was it the captain had said whole ages ago in that inn?) "Many of you are hungry. We plan to buy food with city funds and sell it to you cheaply. Not free, because there are always people who will waste anything free. But very cheaply, so that even beggars will be able to buy enough. My Guard will release the convicts from the pits. Generalissimo Oosik, His Cognizance the Prolocutor, and I are going to the Alambrera this morning, and I'll order it. All convicts are pardoned as of this moment—I pardon them. They'll be hungry and weak, so please share whatever food you have with them.''

He recalled his own hunger, hunger at the manse and worse hunger underground, gnawing hunger that had become a sort of illness by the time Mamelta located the strange, steaming meals of the underground tower. "We had a poor harvest this year,'' he said. "Let us pray, every one of us, for a better one next year. I've prayed for that often, and I'll pray for it again; but if we want to have enough to eat for the rest of our lives, we must have water for our fields when the rains fail.

"There are ancient tunnels under the city. Some of you can confirm that because you've come upon them while digging foundations. They reach Lake Limna—I know that, because I've been in them. If we can break through near the lake—and I'm sure we can—we can use them to carry water to the farms. Then we'll all have plenty of food, cheaply, for a long time.'' He wanted to say, until it's time for us to leave this whorl behind us, but he bit the words back, pausing instead to watch the gray drapes sway in the breeze and listen to his own voice through the open window.

"If you have been fighting for me, don't use your weapons again unless you're attacked. If you're a Guardsman, you have sworn that you'll obey your officers.'' (He could not be sure of that, but it was so probable that he asserted it boldly.) "Ultimately, that means Generalissimo Oosik, who commands both the Guard and the Army. You've already heard what he has to say. He's for peace. So am I."

Oosik pointed to himself, then to the ear; and Silk added, "You'll hear him again, very soon."

He felt that the shade should be up by now—indeed that it was past that time, the hour of first light, and time for the morning prayer to Thelxiepeia; yet the city beyond the gray drapes was still twilit. "To you whose loyalty is to the Ayuntamiento, I have two things to say. The first is that you're fighting—dying, many of you—for an institution that needs no defense. Neither I nor Generalissimo Oosik nor General Mint desires to destroy it. So why shouldn't there be peace? Help us make peace!

"The second is that the Ayuntamiento was created by our Charter. Were it not for our Charter, it would have no right to exist, and wouldn't exist. Our Charter grants to you—to you, the people of Viron, and not to any official—the right to choose a new caldé whenever the position is vacant. It then makes the Ayuntamiento subject to the caldé you have chosen. I need not tell you that our Charter proceeds from the immortal gods. All of you know that. Generalissimo Oosik and I have been consulting His Cognizance the Prolocutor on this matter of the caldé and the Ayuntamiento. He is here with us, and if I have misinformed you he will correct me, I feel certain."

With his left hand Quetzal accepted the ear; his right traced a trembling sign of addition. "Blessed be you in the Most Sacred Name of Pas, the Father of the Gods, in that of Gracious Echidna, His consort, in those of the Sons and their Daughters alike, this day and forever, in the name of their eldest child, Scylla, Patroness of this—"

He continued to speak, but Silk's attention deserted him; the door of the dressing room had opened. Hyacinth stepped through it, radiantly lovely in a flowing gown of scarlet silk. In a low voice she said, "The glass in there just told me the Ayuntamiento's offering ten thousand to anybody who kills you and two thousand each for Oosie and His Cognizance. I thought you should know."

Silk nodded and thanked her; Oosik muttered, "It was only to be expected."

"Consider, my children," Quetzal was saying, "how painful it must be to Succoring Scylla to see the sons and daughters of the city that she founded clawing one another's eyes. She has provided everything we require. First of all our Charter, the foundation of peace and justice. If we wish to regain her favor we need only return to it. If we wish to reclaim the peace we have lost, again we need only return to her Charter. We wish justice, I know. I wish it myself, and the wish for it has been planted in every bosom by Great Pas. Even the worst of us wish to live in holiness, too. Perhaps there are a few ingrates who don't, but they are very few. We wish all these things, and we can make them ours by one simple act. Let us return to our Charter. That is what the gods desire. Let us accept this anointed augur, Patera Caldé Silk. The gods desire that, too. To conform to Sustaining Scylla's Charter, we must have a caldé, and the smallest of our children know on whom the choice has fallen. If you have any doubts on these topics, my children, I beg you to consult the anointed augur into whose care you are given. There is one, you know, in every quarter. Or you may consult the next you see, or any holy sibyl. They will tell you that the path of duty is not difficult but simple and plain."

Quetzal paused, exhaling with a slight hiss. "Now, my children, a most painful matter. Word has come to me that devils in human shape are seeking our destruction. Falsely and evilly, they promise money they have not got and will not pay, for our blood. Do not believe their lies. Their lies offend the gods. Anyone who slays good men for money is worse than a devil, and anyone who slays for money he will never see is a fool. Worse than a fool, a dupe."

Oosik reached for the ear, but Quetzal shook his head. "My children, it will soon be shadeup. A new day. Let it be a day of peace. Let us stand together. Let us stand by the gods, by their Charter, and by the caldé they have chosen for us. I bid you farewell for the present, but soon I hope to talk to you face-to-face and bless you for the peace you've given our city. Now I believe Generalissimo Oosik wants to speak to you again."

Oosik cleared his throat. "This is the Generalissimo. Operations against the rebels are canceled, effective at once. Every officer will be held responsible for his obedience to my order and for the actions of his troopers or soldiers, as the case may be. Caldé Silk and His Cognizance are going through the city on one of our floaters. I expect every officer, every trooper, and every soldier to receive them in a manner fully in accordance with loyalty and good discipline.

"My Caldé, have you anything further to say?"

"Yes, I do." Silk leaned toward him, speaking into the ear. "Please stop fighting. It was needful, as I said; but it's become senseless. Stop them if you can, Maytera Mint. General Mint, please stop them. Peace is within our grasp—from the moment we accept it, all of us have won."

He straightened up, savoring the wonder of the ear. It really does look like a black flower, he thought, a flower meant to bloom at night; and because it's bloomed, shadeup is on the way, even if the night looks nearly as dark as ever.

To the ear he added, "We'll be with you in a few minutes, on the floater Generalissimo Oosik told you about. Don't shoot us, please. We certainly won't shoot you. No one will." He turned to Oosik for confirmation, and Oosik nodded vigorously.

"Not even if you shoot me. I'll stand up if I can, so you can see me." He paused. Was there more to say?

Attenuated like distant thunder, his words flew back to him through the window, an ebbing storm: *"Can see me."*

"Those who fought for Viron will be rewarded, regardless of the side on which they fought. Maytera Marble, if you can hear this, please come to the floater. I need you badly, so please come. Auk, too, and Chenille." Had Kypris possessed Hyacinth, rendering her irresistible? Could she possess two women simultaneously? For a second he pondered the question among the remembered faces of his teachers at the schola. He ought to end this, he thought, by invoking the gods; but the time-worn honorifics caught in his throat.

"Until I see you," he said at last, "please pray for me—for our city, and for all of us. Pray to Kind Kypris, who is love. Pray especially to the Outsider, because he is the god whose time is coming and I am the help he's sent us."

He let the hand that held the ear fall, and Oosik took it from him. "For which we all give thanks," Oosik said, and Oreb muttered, "Watch out."

No one spoke after that. Although Oosik and his surgeon, Xiphias, and Quetzal were all present, the bedroom felt empty. Beyond the window, a hush hung over the Palatine. No street vendor hawked his wares and no gun spoke.

Peace.

Peace here, at least; for those on the Palatine and those surrounding it, there was peace. Incredible as it seemed, hundreds—thousands—had ceased fighting, merely because he, Silk, had told them to.

He felt better; perhaps peace, like blood, made one feel better. He was stronger, though he was still not strong. The surgeon had poured blood—more blood—into him while he slept, and that sleep must have been something akin to a coma, because the needle had not awakened him. Another's blood—another's life—had let him live, though he had been certain the night before that he would die that night. Premonitions born of weakness could be frustrated, clearly; he would have to remember that. With friends to help, a man could make his own fate.

Chapter 9

VICTORY

Xiphias, it transpired, had gone to the Palace, bringing back one of Remora's fine robes. It fit Silk surprisingly well, although it carried in its soft fabric a suggestion of somber luxury he found detestable. "They won't know you outside of this, lad," Xiphias said. He, shaking his head, wondered how they could possibly know him in it.

Oosik returned. "I have had more lights mounted on your floater, Caldé. There will be a flag on its antenna as well. Most will be on you, two on the flag." Without waiting for a reply, he asked the surgeon, "Is he ready?"

"He shouldn't walk far," the surgeon said.

"I can walk around the city if need be," Silk told them.

Hyacinth declared, "He should lie down again till it's time to go," and to please her, he did.

Within half a minute, it seemed, Xiphias and the surgeon were lowering him into a litter. Hyacinth walked beside him as she had when the waiters had carried him out of the Glasshouse, and it seemed to him that his mother's garden walked with her; from the other side, Quetzal asperged him with benedictions, his robe of mulberry velvet contributing the mingled smells of frankincense and something else to the cool and windy dark. At his ears, the *frou-frou-frou* of Hyacinth's skirt and the *whish-shish* of Quetzal's robe sounded louder than the snap of Oosik's flag. Troopers saluted, clicking their heels. One knelt for Quetzal's blessing.

"It would be better," Oosik said, "if you did not have to be carried into the floater, Caldé. Can you do it?"

He could, of course, rising from the litter with the help of Xiphias's cane. A volley of shots crackled in the distance; it was followed by a faint scream, rarefied and unreal. "Men fight," Oreb commented.

"Some do," Silk told him. "That's why we're going."

The entry port let spill a sallow light; the surgeon was crouching inside to help him in. "Blood's floater was open," Silk remarked, remembering. "There was a transparent canopy—a top that you could see through almost as well as air—but when it was down, you could stand up."

"You can stand in this, too," the surgeon said, "right here." He steered Silk toward the spot. "See? You're under the turret here."

Straightening up, Silk nodded. "I rode in one of these yesterday—on the outside, when the rain stopped. It wasn't nearly as roomy as this." Corpses, including Doctor Crane's, had taken up most of the space inside.

"We took out a lot of ammo, Caldé," the trooper at the controls told him.

Silk nearly nodded again, although the trooper could not see his head. He had found the ladder he recalled, a spidery affair of metal rods, and was climbing cautiously but steadily toward the open hatch at the top of the turret.

"Bad thing," Oreb informed him nervously. "Thing shine."

To his own astonishment Silk smiled. "This buzz gun, you mean?" It was dull black, but the open breech revealed bright steel. "They won't shoot us with it, Oreb. They won't shoot anyone, I hope."

The surgeon's voice floated up from below. "There's a

saddle for the gunner, Caldé, and things to put your feet in.''

"Stirrups." That voice had been Oosik's, surely.

Silk swung himself onto the leather-covered seat, almost but not quite losing his grip on Xiphias's cane. There were officers on horseback around the floater, and what seemed to be a full company of troopers standing at ease half a street behind it. The footman who had admitted him to Ermine's was watching everything from his station by the door; Silk waved to him with the cane, and he waved in return, his grin a touch of white in the darkness.

It's going to rain again, Silk thought. I don't believe we've had a morning this dark since spring.

Quetzal's head rose at his elbow. "I'm going to be beside you, Patera Caldé. They're finding a box for me to stand on."

With as much firmness as he could muster, Silk said, "I can't possibly sit while Your Cognizance stands."

A hatch opened at the front of the floater; Oosik's head and shoulders emerged, and he spoke to someone inside.

Quetzal touched Silk's hand with cold, dry fingers that might have been boneless. "You're wounded, Patera Caldé, and weaker than you think. Stay seated. That is my wish." His head rose to the level of Silk's own.

"As Your Cognizance desires." With both hands on the rim of the hatch, Silk heaved up his unwontedly uncooperative body. For an instant the effort seemed too great; his heart pounded and his arms shook; then one foot found a corner of the box on which Quetzal stood, and he was able to hoist himself enough to sit on the coaming of the open turret hatch. "The gunner's seat remains for Your Cognizance," he said.

The floater lifted beneath them, gliding forward. Louder than the roar of its engine, Oosik's voice seemed to reach into every street in the city: *"People of Viron! Our new caldé is coming among you as we promised. At his side is His Cognizance the*

Prolocutor, who has confirmed that Caldé Silk has the favor of all the gods. Hail him! Follow him!"

Brilliant white lights glared to left and right, less than an arm's length away, more than half blinding him.

"Girl come!" Oreb exclaimed.

A black civilian floater had nosed between their floater and the troopers, and was pushing through the mounted officers. Hyacinth stood on its front seat beside the driver; and while Silk watched openmouthed, she stepped over what seemed to be a low invisible barrier, and onto the waxed and rounded foredeck. "Your stick!" she called.

Silk tightened the handle, leaned as far back as he dared, and held it out to her; the civilian floater advanced until its cowling touched the back of the floater upon which he rode.

And Hyacinth leaped, her scarlet skirt billowing about her bare legs in the updraft from the blowers. For an instant he was certain she would fall. Then she had grasped the cane and stood secure on the sloping rear deck of his floater, waving in triumph to the mounted officers, most of whom waved in return or saluted. As the floater in which she had come turned away and vanished into the twilight beyond the lights on their own, Silk recognized the driver who had returned him to his manse Phaesday night.

Hyacinth gave him a mischievous grin. "You look like you've seen a ghost. You didn't expect company, did you?"

"I thought you were inside. I should've—I'm sorry, Hyacinth. Terribly sorry."

"You ought to be." He had to put his ear to her lips to hear her, and she nipped and kissed it. "Oosie sent me away. Don't tell him I'm up here."

Lost in the wonder of her face, Silk could only gasp.

Quetzal raised the baculus to bestow a benison, although Silk could see no one beyond the glare that enveloped the three of them except the mounted officers. The roar of their floater was muted now; an occasional grating hesitation suggested that its cowling was actually scraping the cobbles.

"You said you took a floater," Silk told Hyacinth. "I thought you meant that you just, well, took it."

"I wouldn't know how to make one go." Sitting, she edged nearer, grasping the coaming of the turret hatch. "Would you? But that driver's my friend, and I gave him a little money."

They rounded a corner, and innumerable throats cheered from the dimness beyond the lights. Someone shouted, "We've gone over to Silk!"

A thrown chrysanthemum brushed his cheek, and he waved.

Another voice shouted, "Live the caldé!" It brought a storm of cheering, and Hyacinth waved and smiled as if she herself were that caldé, evoking a fresh outburst. "Where are we going? Did Oosie tell you?"

"To the Alambrera." Silk had to shout to make himself heard. "We'll free the convicts. The Juzgado afterward."

A jumble of boxes and furniture opened to let them pass—Liana's barricade.

Beside him, Quetzal invoked the Nine: "In the name of Marvelous Molpe, you are blessed. In the name of Tenebrous Tartaros . . ." They trust the gods, Silk thought, all these wretched men; and because they do, they have made me their leader. Yet I feel I can't trust any god at all, not even the Outsider.

As if they had been chatting over lunch, Quetzal said, "Only a fool would, Patera Caldé."

Silk stared.

"Didn't I tell you that I've done everything I could to prevent theophanies? Those we call gods are nothing more than ghosts. Powerful ghosts, but only because they entailed that power to themselves in life."

"I—" Silk swallowed. "I wasn't aware that I had spoken

aloud, Your Cognizance. I apologize; my remark was singularly inappropriate." Oreb stirred apprehensively on his shoulder.

"You didn't, Patera Caldé. I saw your face, and I've had lots of practice. Don't look at me or your young woman. Look at the people. Wave. Look ahead. Smile."

Both waved, and Silk tried to smile as well. His eyes had adjusted to the lights well enough now for him to glimpse indistinct figures beyond the mounted officers, many waving slug guns just as he waved the cane. Through clenched teeth he ventured, "Echidna told us Pas was dead. Your Cognizance confirmed it."

"Dead long ago," Quetzal agreed, "whoever he really was, poor old fellow. Murdered by his family, as was inevitable." Deftly he caught a bouquet. "Blessings on you, my children. Blessings, blessings. . . . May Great Pas and the immortal gods smile upon you and all that you own, forever!"

"Silk is caldé! Long live Silk!"

Hyacinth told him happily, "We're getting a real tour of the city!"

He nodded, feeling his smile grow warm and real.

"Look at them, Patera Caldé. This is their moment. They have bled for this."

"Peace!" Silk called to the shadowy crowds, waving the cane. "Peace!"

"Peace!" Oreb confirmed, and hopped up onto Silk's head flapping his wings. The day was brightening at last, Silk decided, in spite of the storm-black cloud hanging over the city. How appropriate that shadeup should come now— peace and sunlight together! A cheering woman waved an evergreen bough, the symbol of life. He waved in return, meeting her eyes and smiling, and she seemed ready to swoon with delight.

"Don't start throwing flowers to yourself," Hyacinth told

him with mock severity. "They'll be blaming you soon enough."

"Then let's enjoy this while we can." Seeing the woman with the bough had recalled one of the ten thousand things the Outsider had shown him—a hero riding through some foreign city while a cheering crowd waved big fanlike leaves. Would Echidna and her children kill the Outsider too? With a flash of insight, he felt sure they were already trying.

"Look! There's Orchid, throwing out the house."

A light directed at the flag showed her plainly, leaning so far from the second-story window through which Kypris had called to him that it seemed she might fall any moment. They were floating down Lamp Street, clearly; the Alambrera could not be far.

As Hyacinth blew Orchid a kiss, something whizzed past Silk's ear, striking the foredeck like a gong. A high whine and a booming explosion were followed by the rattle of a buzz gun. Somebody shouted for someone to come down, and someone inside the floater caught his injured ankle and pulled.

He looked up instead, to where something new and enormous that was not a cloud at all filled the sky. Another whine, louder, mounting ever higher, until Lamp Street exploded in front of them, peppering his face and throwing something solid at his head.

Oosik shouted, "Faster!" and disappeared down his hatch, slamming it behind him.

"Inside, Patera Caldé!"

He scooped Hyacinth into his arms instead, dropping the cane into the floater. It was racing now, careering along Lamp Street and scattering people like chaff. She shrieked.

Here was Cage Street, overlooked by the despotic wall of the Alambrera. Hanging in the air in front of it was a single trooper with wings—a female trooper, from the bulge at her chest—who leveled a slug gun. He slid off the coaming and dropped, still holding Hyacinth, onto the men below.

They sprawled in a tangle of arms and legs, like beetles swept into a jar. Someone stepped on his shoulder and swarmed up the spidery ladder. The turret hatch banged shut. At the front of the floater Oosik snapped, "Faster, Sergeant!"

"We're getting a vector now, sir."

Silk tried to apologize, to tug Hyacinth's scarlet skirt (about which Hyacinth herself seemed to care not a cardbit) over her thighs, and to stand in a space in which he could not possibly have stood upright, all at once. Nothing succeeded.

Something struck the floater like a sledge, sending it yawing into something else solid; it rolled and plunged and righted itself, its straining engine roaring like a wounded bull. Reeking of fish, a wisp of oily black smoke writhed through the compartment.

"Faster!" Oosik shouted.

The turret gun spoke as if in response, a clatter that went on and on, as though the turret gunner were intent on massacring the whole city.

Scrambling across Xiphias and the surgeon, Silk peered over Oosik's shoulder. Fiery red letters danced across his glass: VECTOR UNACCEPTABLE.

Something banged the slanted foredeck above their heads, and the thunder of the engine rose to a deafening crescendo; Silk felt that he had been jerked backwards.

Abruptly, their motion changed.

The floater no longer rocked or raced. The noise of the engine waned until he could distinguish the high-pitched song of the blowers. It ascended to an agonized scream and faded away. A red light flared on the instrument panel.

For the second time in a floater, Silk felt that he was truly floating; it was, he thought, like the uncanny sensation of the moving room in which he had ridden with Mamelta.

Behind him, Hyacinth gasped. A strangely shaped object had risen from Oosik's side. Before Silk recognized it, it had completed a leisurely quarter revolution, scarcely a span in front of his nose. It was a large needler, similar to the one in his own waistband; and it had bobbed up like a cork, unimpelled, from Oosik's holster.

"Look! Look! They're picking us up!" Hyacinth's full breasts pressed his back as she stared at the glass.

He plucked Oosik's needler out of the air and returned it to its holster. When he looked at the glass again, it showed a sprawling pattern of crooked lines, enlivened here and there by crimson sparks. It looked, he decided, like a city in the skylands, except that it seemed much closer. Intrigued, he undogged the hatchcover over Oosik's seat and threw it back. As he completed the motion, both his feet left the floor; he snatched at the hatch dog, missed it by a finger, and drifted up like Oosik's needler until someone inside caught his foot.

The pattern he had seen in the glass was spread before him without limit here: a twilit skyland city, ringed by sunbright brown fields and huddled villages; and to one side, a silver mirror anchored by a winding, dun-colored thread. Oreb fluttered from his shoulder as he gaped and disappeared into the twilight.

"We're flying." Incredulity and dismay turned the words to a sigh that dwindled with the black bird. Silk coughed, spat congealed blood, and tried again. "We are flying upside down. I see Viron and the lake, even the road to the lake."

Quetzal spoke from inside the floater. "Look behind us, Patera Caldé."

They were nearer now, so near that the vast dark belly of the thing roofed out the sky. Beneath it, suspended by cables that appeared no thicker than gossamer, dangled a structure like a boat with many short oars; Silk's lungs had filled and emptied before he realized that the oars were the barrels of guns, and half a minute crept by before he made out the blood-red triangle on its bottom. "Your Cognizance . . ."

"You don't understand why they're not shooting at us." Quetzal shook himself. "I imagine it's only that they haven't noticed us yet. A wind is forcing them to hold their airship parallel to the sun, so they're peering down at a dark city. At the moment our floater's presenting its narrowest aspect to them. But we're turning, and soon they'll be looking straight down at us. Let's duck inside and shut the hatch."

The glass showed Lake Limna now. Watching its shoreline creep from one corner to the other, Silk thought of Oosik's needler; their floater seemed to be tumbling through the sky in the same dilatory fashion.

Clinging to him, Hyacinth whispered, "You're not afraid at all, are you? Are we up terribly high?" She trembled.

"Of course I am; when I was out there, I was terrified." He examined his emotional state. "I'm still badly frightened; but thinking about what's happening—how it can possibly have come about except by a miracle—keeps my mind off my fear." Watching the glass, he tried to describe the airship.

"Pulling us up, lad! That's what she said! Think we could cut it?"

"There's nothing to cut; if there were, they'd know where we were and shoot us, I believe. This is something else. Was it you who held my foot, by the way? Thank you."

Xiphias shook his head and indicated the surgeon.

"Thank you," Silk repeated. "Thank you very much indeed, Doctor." He grasped the operator's shoulder. "You said we were getting a vector. Exactly what does that mean?"

"It's a message you get if you float too fast, My Caldé, either north or south. You're supposed to slow down. The monitor's supposed to make you if you don't, but that doesn't work any more on this floater."

"I see." Silk nodded, encouragingly he hoped. "Why are you supposed to slow down?"

Oosik put in, "Going too fast north makes you feel as if someone were shoveling sand on you. It is not good for you, and makes everyone in the floater slow to react. Going south too fast makes you giddy. It feels like swimming."

Almost too softly to be heard, Quetzal inquired, "Do you know the shape of the Whorl, Patera Caldé?"

"The whorl? Why, it's cylindrical, Your Cognizance."

"Are we on the outside of the cylinder, Patera Caldé? Or on the inside?"

"We're inside, Your Cognizance. If we were outside, we'd fall off."

"Exactly. What is it that holds us down? What makes a book fall if you drop it?"

"I can't remember the name, Your Cognizance," Silk said, "but it's the tendency that keeps a stone in a sling until it is thrown."

Hyacinth had released him; now her hand found his, and he squeezed it. "As long as the boy keeps twirling his sling, the stone in it can't fall out. The Whorl turns—I see! If the stone were a—a mouse and the mouse ran in the direction the sling was going, it would be held in place more securely, as though the sling were being twirled faster. But if the mouse were to run the other way, it would be as if the sling weren't twirling fast enough. It would fall out."

"Gunner!" Oosik was staring at the glass. "Your gun should bear." As he flicked off his own buzz gun's safety, the red triangle crept into view.

"Trivigaunte," Hyacinth whispered. "Sphigx won't let them make pictures of anything. That mark's on their flag."

Auk stood, unable for a moment to recall where he was or why he had come. Had he fallen off a roof? Salt blood from his lips trickled into his mouth. A man with arms and legs no thicker than kindling and a face like a bearded skull dashed past him. Then another and another.

"Don't be afraid," the blind god whispered. "Be brave and act wisely, and I will protect you." He took Auk's hand, not as Hyacinth had put her own hand into Silk's a few minutes before, but as an older man clasps a younger's at a crisis.

"All right," Auk told him. "I ain't scared, only kind of shook up." The blind god's hand felt good in his own, big and strong, with long powerful fingers; he could not think of the blind god's name and was embarrassed by his failure.

"I am Tartaros, and your friend. Tell me everything you see. You may speak or not, as you wish."

"There's a big hole with smoke coming out in the middle of the wall," Auk reported. "That wasn't there before, I'm pretty sure. There's some dead culls around besides the ones Patera killed and the one I killed. One's a trooper, like, only a mort it looks like. Her wings broke, I guess, maybe when she hit the ground. Everything's brown, the wings and pants and a kind of a bandage, like, over her boobs."

"Brown?"

Auk looked more closely. "Not exactly. Yellowy-brown, more like. Dirt color. Here comes Chenille."

"That is well. Comfort her, Auk my noctolater. Is the airship still overhead?"

"Sure," Auk said, implying by his tone that he did not require a god to coach him in such elementary things. "Yeah, it is." Chenille rushed into his arms.

"It's all right, Jugs," he told her. "Going to be candy. You'll see. Tartaros is a dimber mate of mine." To Tartaros himself, Auk added, "There's this hoppy floater that's falling in the pit, only slow, while it shoots. That's up there, too. And there's maybe a couple hundred troopers like the dead mort flying around, way up."

The blind god gave his hand a gentle tug. "We emerged from a smaller pit into this one, Auk. If you see no other way out, it would be well to return to the tunnel. There are other egresses, and I know them all.''

"Just a minute. I lost my whin. I see it." Releasing Chenille, Auk hurried over, jerked his hanger from the mire, and wiped the blade on his tunic.

"*Auk,* my son—"

He shooed Incus with the hanger. "You get back in the tunnel, Patera, before you get hurt. That's what Tartaros says, and he's right.''

The floater was descending faster now, almost as though it were really falling. Watching it, Auk got the feeling it was, only not straight down the way other things fell. Until the last moment, it seemed it might come to rest upright; but it landed on the side of its cowling and tumbled over.

Something much higher was falling much faster, a tiny dot of black that seemed almost an arrow by the time it struck the ruined battlement of the Alambrera's wall, which again erupted in a gout of flame and smoke. This time masses of shiprock as big as cottages were flung up like chaff. Auk thought it the finest sight he had seen in his life.

"Silk here!" Oreb announced proudly, dropping onto his shoulder. "Bird bring!" A hatch opened at the front of the fallen floater.

"Hackum!" Chenille shouted. "Hackum, come on! We're going back in the tunnel!''

Auk waved to silence her. The wall of the Alambrera had taken its death blow. As he watched, cracks raced down it to reappear as though by magic in the shiprock side of the pit. There came a growl deeper than any thunder. With a roar that shook the ground on which he struggled to stand, the wall and the side of the pit came down together. Half the pit vanished under a scree of stones, earth, and shattered slabs. Coughing at the dust, Auk backed away.

"Hole break," Oreb informed him.

When he looked again, several men and a slender woman

in scarlet were emerging from the overturned floater; its tur-ret gun, unnaturally canted but pointing skyward, was firing burst after burst at the flying troopers.

"Return to the woman," the blind god told him. "You must protect her. A woman is vital. This is not."

He looked for Chenille, but she was gone. A few skeletal figures were disappearing into the hole from which he and she had emerged into the pit. Men from the floater followed them; through the billowing dust he could make out a white-bearded man in rusty black and a taller one in a green tunic.

"Silk here!" Oreb circled above two fleeing figures.

Auk caught up with them as they started down the helical track; Silk was hobbling fast, helped by a cane and the woman in scarlet. Auk caught her by the hair. "Sorry, Patera, but I got to do this." Silk's hand went to his waistband, but Auk was too quick—a push on his chest sent him reeling back-ward into the lesser pit.

"Listen!" urged the blind god beside Auk; he did, and heard the rising whine of the next bomb a full second before it struck the ground.

Silk looked down upon the dying augur's body with joy and regret. It was—had been—himself, after all. Quetzal and a smaller, younger augur knelt beside it, with a woman in an augur's cloak and a third man nearly as old as Quetzal.

Beads swung in sign after sign of addition: "I convey to you, Patera Silk my son, the forgiveness of all the gods."

"Recall now the words of Pas—"

It was good; and when it was over, he could go. Where? It didn't matter. Anywhere he wished. He was free at last, and though he would miss his old cell now and then, freedom was best. He looked up through the shiprock ceiling and saw only earth, but knew that the whole whorl was above it, and the open sky.

"I pray you to forgive us, the living," the smaller augur

said, and again traced the sign of addition, which could not—now that he came to think of it—ever have been Pas's. A sign of addition was a cross; he remembered Maytera drawing one on the chalkboard when he was a boy learning to do sums. Pas's sign was not the cross but the voided cross. He reached for his own at his neck, but it was gone.

The older augur: "I speak here for Great Pas, for Divine Echidna, for Scalding Scylla."

The younger augur: "For Marvelous Molpe, for Tenebrous Tartaros, for Highest Hierax, for Thoughtful Thelxiepeia, for Fierce Phaea, and for Strong Sphigx."

The older augur: "Also for all lesser gods."

The shiprock gave way to earth, the earth to a clearer, purer air than he had ever known. Hyacinth was there with Auk; in a slanting mass of stones, broken shiprock rolled and slid to reveal a groping steel hand. Glorying, he soared.

The Trivigaunti airship was a brown beetle, infinitely remote, the Aureate Path so near he knew it could not be his final destination.

He lighted upon it, and found it a road of tinsel down a whorl no bigger than an egg. Where were the lowing beasts? The spirits of the other dead? There! Two men and two women. He blinked and stared and blinked again.

"Oh, Silk! My son! Oh, son!" She was in his arms and he in hers, melting in tears of joy. "Mother!" "Silk, my son!"

The whorl was filth and stink, futility and betrayal; this was everything—joy and love, freedom and purity.

"You must go back, Silk. He sends us to tell you."

"You must, my lad." A man's voice, the voice of which Lemur's had been a species of mockery. Looking up he saw the carved brown face from his mother's closet.

"We're your parents." He was tall and blue-eyed. "Your fathers and your mothers."

The other woman did not speak, but her eyes spoke truth.

"You were my mother," he said. "I understand."

He looked down at his own beautiful mother. "You will always be my mother. Always!"

"We'll be waiting, Silk my son. All of us. Remember."

Something was fanning his face.

He opened his eyes. Quetzal was seated beside him, one long, bloodless hand swinging as regularly and effortlessly as a pendulum. "Good afternoon, Patera Caldé. I would guess, at least, that it may be afternoon by now."

He lay on dirt, staring up at a shiprock ceiling. Pain stabbed his neck; his head, both arms, his chest, both legs, and his lower torso ached, each in its separate, painful way.

"Lie quietly. I wish I had water to offer you. How are you feeling?"

"I'm back in my dirty cage." Too late, he remembered to add *Your Cognizance*. "I didn't know it was a cage, before."

Quetzal pressed down on his shoulder. "Don't sit up yet, Patera Caldé. I'm going to ask a question, but you are not to put it to the test. It is to be a matter for discussion only. Do you agree?"

"Yes, Your Cognizance." He nodded, although nodding took immense effort.

"This is my question. We are only to speak of it. If I were to help you up, could you walk?"

"I believe so, Your Cognizance."

"Your voice is very weak. I've examined you and found no broken bones. There are four of us besides yourself, but—"

"We fell, didn't we? We were in a Civil Guard floater, spinning over the city. Did I dream that?"

Quetzal shook his head.

"You and I and Hyacinth. And Colonel Oosik and Oreb. And . . ."

"Yes, Patera Caldé?"

"A trooper—two troopers—and an old fencing master that someone had introduced me to. I can't remember his name, but I must have dreamed that he was there as well. It's too fantastic.''

"He is some distance down the tunnel now, Patera Caldé. We have been troubled by the convicts you freed.''

"Hyacinth?'' Silk struggled to sit up.

Quetzal held him down, his hands on both shoulders. "Lie quietly or I'll tell you nothing.''

"Hyacinth? For—for the sake of all the gods! I've got to know!''

"I dislike them, Patera Caldé. So do you. Why should either of us tell anyone anything for their sake? I don't know. I wish I did. She may be dead. I can't say.''

"Tell me what happened, please.''

Slowly, Quetzal's hairless head swung from side to side. "It would be better, Patera Caldé, for you to tell me. You've been very near death. I need to know what you've forgotten.''

"There's water in these tunnels. I was in them before, Your Cognizance. In places there was a great deal.''

"This is not one of those places. If you have recovered enough to grasp how ill you are and keep a promise, I'll find some. Do you remember blessing the crowds with me? Tell me about that.''

"We were trying to bring peace—peace to Viron. Blood had bought it—Musk, but Musk was only a tool of Blood's.''

"Had bought the city, Patera Caldé?''

Silk's mouth opened and closed again.

"What is it, Patera Caldé?''

"Yes, Your Cognizance, he has. He, and others like him. I hadn't thought of that until you asked. I'd been confusing the things.''

"What things, Patera Caldé?''

"Peace and saving my manteion. The Outsider asked me to save it, and then the insurrection broke out, and I thought I would have saved it if only I could bring peace, because the people made me caldé, and I would save it by an order.'' For a second or two, Silk lay silent, his eyes half closed. "Blood—men like Blood—have stolen the city, every part of it except the Chapter, and the Chapter has resisted only because you are at its head, Your Cognizance. When you're gone . . ."

"When I die, Patera Caldé?"

"If you were to die, Your Cognizance, they'd have it all. Musk actually signed the papers. Musk was the owner of record—the man whose body we burned on the altar, Your Cognizance. I remember thinking how horrible it would be if Musk were the real owner and clenching my teeth—puffing myself up with courage I've never really had and telling myself over and over that I couldn't allow it to happen."

"You're the only man in Viron who doubts your courage, Patera Caldé."

Silk scarcely heard him. "I was wrong. Badly mistaken. Musk wasn't the danger, was never the danger, really. There are scores of Musks in the Orilla, and Musk loved birds. Did I tell you that, Your Cognizance?"

"No, Patera Caldé. Tell me now, if you wish."

"He did. Mucor told me he liked birds, and he'd brought her a book about the cats she carried for Blood. When he saw Oreb, he said I'd gotten him because I wanted to be friends, which wasn't true, and threw his knife at him. He missed, and I believe he intended to miss. Blood, with his money and his greed for more, has done Viron more harm than all the Musks. Everything I've done has been trying to pry bits of the city from Blood. I was trying to save my manteion, I said; but you can't save just one manteion—I can't save our quarter and nothing else. I see that now. And yet I like Blood, or at least I would like to like him."

"I understand, Patera Caldé."

"Little pieces—the manteion, and Hyacinth and Orchid, and Auk, because Auk matters so much to Maytera Mint. Auk . . ."

"Yes, Patera Caldé?"

"Auk pushed me, Your Cognizance. We had been together in the floater, Hyacinth and I. Your Cognizance, too,
and—and others. We were coming down, and Colonel
Oosik—"

"You've made him Generalissimo Oosik," Quetzal reminded Silk gently.

"Yes. Yes, I did. He passed me the ear, and I talked to the
convicts, telling them they were free, and then we hit the
ground. We opened a hatch and Hyacinth and I climbed
out—"

"I'm satisfied, Patera Caldé. Promise me you won't try to
stand until I come back, and I'll look for water."

Silk detained him, clasping one boneless, bloodless hand.
"You can't tell me what's happened to her, Your Cognizance?"

Again Quetzal's head swung from side to side, a slow and
almost hypnotic motion.

"Then Auk has her, I don't know why, and I must get her
back from him. What happened to me, Your Cognizance?"

"You were buried alive, Patera Caldé. When the floater
crashed, some of us climbed out. I did, as you see, and you
and your young woman, as you say. The fencing master, too,
and your physician. I'm sure of those. The convicts were running to a hole in the ground to escape the shooting and explosions. Do you remember them?"

This time Silk was able to nod without much difficulty,
although his neck was stiff and painful.

"There was a ramp down the side of the hole, and a break
in this tunnel at the bottom. The fencing master and I
ducked through. Almost at once there was another explosion, and the hole fell in behind us. We were lucky to have
gotten in. Do you know my coadjutor's prothonotary, Patera
Caldé?"

"I've met him, Your Cognizance. I don't know him well."

"He's here. I was surprised to see him, and he to see me.

There is a woman with him called Chenille who says she knows you. They went into the tunnel yesterday, at Limna. They had been trying to reach the city.''

"Chenille, Your Cognizance? A tall woman? Red hair?''

"Exactly so. She's an extraordinary woman. Soon after the explosion, the convicts attacked us. They were friendly at first, but soon demanded we give them Patera and the woman. We refused, and Xiphias killed four. Xiphias is the fencing master. Am I making myself clear?''

"Perfectly, Your Cognizance.''

"We tried to dig our way out and found you. We thought you were dead, and Patera and I brought you the Peace of Pas. Eventually we stopped digging, having realized that the effort was hopeless. For a dozen men with shovels and barrows, two days might be enough.''

"I understand, Your Cognizance.''

"By then I was exhausted, though I had dug less than the woman. The others left to look for another way out. She and Patera are famished, and they have a tessera that they believe will admit them to the Juzgado. They promised to return for your body and me. I prayed for you after they had gone.''

"Your Cognizance distrusts the gods.''

"I do.'' Quetzal nodded, his hairless head bobbing on its long neck. "I know them for what they are. But consider. I believe in them. I have faith. You mentioned your quarter. How many there really believe in the gods? Half?''

"Less than that, I'm afraid, Your Cognizance.''

"What about you, Patera Caldé? Look into your heart.''

Silk was silent.

"I'll give you my thoughts, Patera Caldé. This young man believes, and he loves the gods even after seeing Echidna. I too believe, though I distrust them. He would want me to pray for him, and that's my office. I've done it often, hoping I wouldn't be heard. This time it's possible one will restore him, to prove she's not as bad as I think.''

Faint yet unmistakable, the crack of a needler echoed down the tunnel.

"That will be Patera, Patera Caldé. We've been lucky in the matter of weapons. Xiphias has a sword, and had a small needler he said was yours. You left it on your bed, and he took charge of it for you. He gave it to the woman. We found a large one in your waistband. Patera took it, surprising me again. Our clergy have hidden depths."

In spite of pain and weakness, Silk smiled. "Some do, perhaps, Your Cognizance."

"Last night before you saw me in the alley, Patera Caldé, I met your acolyte, young Gulo. He is most embarrassed."

"I'm sorry to hear that, Your Cognizance."

"You shouldn't be. His uncle is a major in the Second Brigade. One uncle of many. Were you aware of it?"

"No, Your Cognizance. I don't know much about Patera."

"Neither do I, though he was one of our copyists until my coadjutor sent him to you. He commands several thousand now. It's a great responsibility for someone so young. More join every hour, he tells me, because they know he's your acolyte."

Silk managed to swallow. "I hope he won't waste their lives, Your Cognizance."

"So do I. I asked if it was hard. He said he discussed each operation with those who would have to fight. He finds them sensible, and he knows something of war from his uncle's table talk. He fights in the front rank afterward, he says."

"Your Cognizance mentioned that he was embarrassed."

"So he is, Patera Caldé." Quetzal shook himself, lifting one corner of his mouth by the thickness of a thread. "He has captured his uncle. Our clergy have hidden depths. The older man is humiliated. It's an awkward situation, I'm afraid, but I was amused."

"So am I, Your Cognizance. Thank you."

Quetzal rose. "We'll find our own amusing, when we find our way out. May I look for water?"

"Of course, Your Cognizance."

"You won't try to stand until I'm back? Give me your word, Patera Caldé."

Silk sat up.

"Please, Patera—"

"I have to go with you, Your Cognizance. I have to find water, wash, and drink, so I can do whatever I can for Viron and Hyacinth. You've got nothing to carry water in, and all four of you couldn't possibly carry me far."

"You've been suffocated, Patera Caldé," Quetzal bent over him. "We merely thought you dead, and I shouldn't have hinted at a miracle. No god can turn back death, and if they could, no god would to please us. You were still alive when we dug you out. You revived naturally—"

Unaided, Silk staggered to his feet. "I had a cane, Your Cognizance. Master Xiphias gave it to me. I didn't need it then, or at least not much. Now I do."

Quetzal offered him the baculus. "Use this."

"Never, Your Cognizance. Councillor Lemur called me— No, I won't."

The tunnel behind them was nearly choked with earth; a trampled path led Silk to an opening in the wall. "Is this where you found me, Your Cognizance? In there?"

"Yes, Patera Caldé. But if your young woman is in there, she is surely dead by now."

"I realize that." Silk put his head through the opening, "and I believe she's in the pit with Auk, anyway; but Master Xiphias values that cane, I need it, and it's probably very close to the place where you found me." He began to work his shoulders through.

"Be careful, Patera Caldé."

The wall was shiprock, little more than a cubit thick. Beyond it lay a cavity hollowed from the tumbled soil that

seemed utterly dark. When Silk tried to stand, he found his
head capped by a rough dome; earth and small stones showered him invisibly. "This could collapse any moment," he
told the swaying figure in the tunnel.

"So it could, Patera Caldé. Come out, please."

His questing fingers had come upon stubby protuber-
ances he assumed were roots. Exploring his pockets, he discovered the cards Remora had given him and used one to
scrape away the soil. One root wore a ring. He cleared away
more soil until he could get a firm grip on the hand, tugged,
dug farther, and tugged again.

"There are new sounds in this tunnel, Patera Caldé. You
had better leave that place."

"I've found someone, Your Cognizance. Somebody
else." Silk hesitated, unwilling to trust his judgment. "I don't
think it's Hyacinth. The hand is too big."

"Then it doesn't matter whose it is. We must go."

Getting a firm grip on the arm, Silk heaved with all the
strength that remained to him, and was rewarded by a cata-
ract of earth and a dead man's embrace.

I'm robbing a grave, he thought, spitting grit and wiping
his eyes. Robbing this man's grave from below—stealing his
grave as well as his body.

It should have been at least as amusing as Gulo's uncle
the major, but was not. Holding onto the jagged edge of the
opening in the tunnel wall, he succeeded in pulling his own
partially buried body free. Back in the tunnel (suddenly very
glad of its cold, sighing airs and watery lights) he was able to
extract the corpse from the loose soil that had reclaimed it.
Quetzal was nowhere to be seen.

"He's gone to look for water," Silk muttered. "Perhaps
water could revive you the way something revived me," but
the dead man's ears were stopped with earth. As he cleaned
the pitiful face, Silk added, "I'm sorry, Doctor."

He searched his pockets again; his beads were not there,

left behind with his own worn and dirty robe at Ermine's. It seemed a very long time ago.

He wriggled back into the dark cavity beyond the tunnel wall. Hyacinth had bathed him in their bedroom at Ermine's, undressing him, and scrubbing and drying him bit by bit. He ought to have been embarrassed (he told himself); but he had been too exhausted to feel anything beyond vague satisfaction, a weak pleasure at finding himself the object of so beautiful a woman's attention. Now all her concern had been undone, and Remora's fine robe, scarcely worn, ruined.

"You returned me to life, Outsider," Silk murmured as he resumed digging, "I wish you'd cleaned me up, too." But the Outsider had doubtless been, as Doctor Crane had maintained, no more than a vein's bursting.

Or had Doctor Crane—who had thought himself, or at any rate called himself, an agent of the Rani—been in truth an agent of the Outsider? Doctor Crane had made it possible for him to proceed in his attempt to save the manteion despite his broken ankle; and Doctor Crane had freed him when he had been taken by the Ayuntamiento. It was conceivable, even likely, that Doctor Crane's skepticism had been a test of faith.

Had he passed?

Weighing that question, he dug harder than ever, making the dark, evil-smelling earth fly. If he had, he would almost certainly be tested again, after this surrender to doubt.

The card struck something hard. At first he assumed it was a stone, but it was too smooth; another half minute's work bared the new find: a slender hook. As soon as he grasped it to pull it free, he knew that he had found the silver-banded cane Xiphias had brought to Erimine's for him.

Without warning, brilliant light flooded the cavity. He turned away from it, covering his eyes.

"I see you in there. Come on out."

There was something familiar about the harsh voice, but

it was not until its owner said, "Put your hands where I can see them," that Silk recognized it as Sergeant Sand's.

Sitting the white stallion in the middle of Fisc Street, Maytera Mint surveyed the advancing ranks. Every one of those soldiers would be worth three of her best, but they were few. Hearteningly few, and the troopers from Trivigaunte had come. Just a few hundred now, but thousands more were on the way.

"Fire and fall back," she called softly, adding under her breath, "Gracious Echidna, grant that I be heard by our people but not by those soldiers." Then, a trifle louder, "Not too quickly. But not too slowly, either. This isn't the time to impress me. Don't get yourselves killed."

The first-level metal rank was practically within slug-gun range. She wheeled her stallion and cantered off, hearing the firing break out behind her, the *whiz . . . bang!* of missiles and the dull booming of slug guns.

Someone cried out.

I told them to, she reminded herself. I emphasized it in the briefing.

Yet she knew the wound had been real. She reined in the stallion and turned to look again: behind the soldiers, Rook's blocking force was straggling into position. Too early, she thought. Far too early. You never appreciated men like Bison and the captain—men who helped you make plans and carried them out—until you got something like this.

One long cable had been looped around each pillar of the Corn Exchange; it was not taut yet, nor should it have been. She risked a glance up at the towering façade, another at Wool and his bullock men, motionless in the shadows half a street away. He and they stood ready beside their animals, waiting for her signal.

The bullock men trusted her. So did the ragged men and women who were shooting and retreating as she had taught them. Shooting and dying, because they had trusted a weak woman—trusted her because Brocket had taught her to ride when she was a child.

She clapped heels to the stallion's sides. He had been used long and hard yesterday, yet he surged forward, a foaming wave of strength. Patera Silk's azoth was in her hand; she thumbed the demon.

Seeing its terrible blade split the sky, Wool's bullock men prodded their animals. The cable tightened, a slithering monster of steel and silence, Echidna's greatest serpent.

The soldiers halted and faced about at a loud command, their officer having seen Rook's force and detected the trap. They would have to attack in earnest now, but her own voice (she told herself) was incapable of launching troops against the enemy. Her voice would not inspire anyone, so her person must. She neck-reined the stallion, and the silver trumpet that was her voice in fact echoed from every wall.

Five chains away, the blade of the azoth wrecked a fusion generator, and the soldier whose heart it had been died.

Forward! Past her own disorderly line. Another soldier down, and another! Forward!

The stallion stumbled, crying out like a man in pain.

A half-dozen soldiers dashed forward. The stallion fell, too weak to stand; it seemed to her that the street itself had struck her, casting all its clods and ridges at her at once. Steel hands laid hold of her, and bios wrestled with chems in a desperate foolish fight. A woman three times her size swung a wrecking bar. The soldier she struck, struck her with the butt of his slug gun; she fell backward and did not rise.

Maytera Mint struggled in a soldier's grasp. The azoth was gone— No! Was under her shoe. He lifted her, his arms clamping her like tongs; she stamped on the azoth with all her strength, and its lancing point sheared off his foot. Smoking black fluid spurted from the stump of his leg, slippery as so much grease. They fell, and his grip weakened.

She tore herself away, stooping for the azoth, and ran, nearly falling again, pursued with terrifying speed until the façade of the Corn Exchange frowned above her and she whirled to cut down a soldier whose blazing, arcing halves tumbled at her feet. "Run! Run! Save yourselves!"

Her people streamed past in full flight, though to her, her voice was a powerless wail.

"Hierax, accept my spirit." The azoth's blade struck the first pillar, and it shattered like glass. Another, and the façade seemed to hang in air, an ominous cloud of grimy brick.

A soldier leveled his slug gun, firing an instant before her blade split his skullplate. She felt the slug tear her habit, smelled the powder smoke, and fled, slashing wildly at a third pillar without breaking stride—stopped and turned back, hot tears streaming. "You gods, for *twenty years!* Now let me go!"

The weightless, endless blade came up. The weightless, endless blade came down. And the façade of the Corn Exchange was coming down too, falling like a picture, nearly whole and almost maintaining its graceless design as it fell, its stone sills falling neither faster nor slower than its tons of brick and timber. Her right hand, still clutching the azoth, had begun the sign of addition when Rook grabbed her from behind and dashed away with her.

Chapter 10

CALDÉ SILK

"Let me go," Maytera Marble insisted Phaesday morning. "They won't shoot me."

Generalissimo Oosik regarded her through his left eye alone; his right was concealed by a patch of surgical gauze. He shrugged. General Saba, the commander from Trivigaunte, pursed pendulous lips. "We've wasted a shaggy hole too much time on this country house already, when nobody can say—"

"You're quite wrong, my daughter," Maytera Marble told her firmly. "Mucor can and does. Our Patera Silk is a prisoner in there, just as the Ayuntamiento claims."

"Spirits!"

"Only hers, really. I'd never seen anyone possessed until she began doing it to our students. I find it very upsetting." She beckoned Horn. "You've made me a white flag? Wonderful! Such a nice long stick, too. Thank you!"

General Saba snorted.

"You don't like my bringing our boys and girls."

"Children shouldn't have to fight."

"Certainly not." Maytera Marble nodded solemn agreement. "But they were, and some have been killed. They'd run off with General Mint, you see, almost all of them. I tried to think who might help me after Mucor left, and our students were the only ones I could think of. Horn and a few others are really mature enough already, more grown up than a great many adults. It got them away from the city, too, where the worst fighting was.'' She looked to Oosik for support, but found none.

"Where it still is," General Saba snapped. "Where the troops we've got out here are badly needed."

"They were fighting your girls, some of them, as well as our Army, and some are dead. Have I told you that? Some are dead, some hurt very badly. Ginger's had her hand blown off, I'm told. No doubt some of your girls are hurt as well."

"Which is why—"

"You said we're wasting time." Maytera Marble sniffed; she had acquired a devastating sniff. "I couldn't agree more. It will only take a minute to shoot me, if they do. Then you can attack at once. But if they don't, I may be able to talk to the councillors in there. They can order the Army and the Guards who are still fighting you—"

"The Second," Oosik supplied.

"Yes, the Second Brigade and our Army." Maytera Marble bowed in humble appreciation of his information. "Thank you, my son. The councillors could order them to give up, but no one knows whether there are really councillors in the Juzgado." Without waiting for a reply, she accepted the flag from Horn.

"I'm coming with you, Sib."

"You are not!"

He followed her nearly as far as the shattered gate just the same, ignoring a pterotrooper who shouted for him to stay back, and watched unhappily as she picked her way through its tumbled stones and twisted bars, somberly clad but conveniently short-skirted in Maytera Rose's best habit.

Two dead taluses smoked and guttered on the close-mown grassway between the gate and the villa. A few steps past the first, General Saba's adjutant sprawled face down beside her own flag of truce. Disregarding all three, Maytera Marble cut across the lush lawn toward the porticoed entrance, keeping well clear of the fountain to avoid its windblown spray.

This was Bloody's house, she reminded herself, this grand place. This was where the little man with oily hair had come from, the one she and Echidna had offered to her. It had been practically impossible, for a time, for her to remember being Echidna; now the image of the little man's agonized face had returned, framed by flame as she forced him down onto the altar fire. Would Divine Echidna help her now, in gratitude for that sacrifice? The Echidna she had pictured at prayer over so many years might have condemned her because of it.

But there had been no shot yet.

No missile. No sounds at all, save the soughing of the wind and the snapping of the rag on the stick she held. How young she felt, and how strong!

If she stopped here, if she looked back at Horn, would they shoot, killing her and waking the children? The children were asleep, most of them. Or at least they were supposed to be, back there beneath the leafless mulberries. The summer's unrelenting heat, the desert heat that she had hated so much, had deserted just when the children needed it, leaving them to sleep in the deepening chill of an autumn already half spent, to shiver huddled together like piglets or puppies in unroofed houses with broken windows and slug-pocked, fire-scarred walls, though most of them had liked that better than their studies, they said: had preferred killing Ayuntamientados and pillaging their dead.

A mottled green face appeared at the window next to the big door. Only the face, Maytera Marble noted with a little shiver of relief. No slug gun, and no launcher.

"I've come to see my son, my son," she called. "My son Bloody. Tell him his mother's here."

Shallow stone steps led up to a wide veranda. Before she put her foot on the last, the door swung back. Through it she saw soldiers, and bios in silvered armor. (Bios got up like chems, as she put it to herself, because chems were braver.) Behind them stood another bio, tall and red-faced.

"Good morning, Bloody," she said. "Thank you for bringing those white bunnies. May Kypris smile upon you."

Blood grinned. "You've changed a little, Mama." Some of the armored men laughed.

"Yes, I have. When we can talk in private, I'll tell you all about it."

"We thought you wanted to cut a deal for Hoppy."

"I do." Maytera Marble surveyed the hall; though she knew little about art, she suspected that the misty landscape facing her was a Murtagon. "I want to talk about that. We've knocked down a good deal of your wall, I'm afraid, Bloody, and I'd like to see your beautiful house spared."

Two soldiers stood aside, and Blood came to meet her. "So would I, Mama. I'd like to see us spared, too."

"Is that why you didn't shoot? You killed that poor woman General Saba sent, so why not me? Perhaps I shouldn't ask."

Blood glanced to his right. "A shag-up over there. *We* didn't shoot the fussock with the flag, and I want that settled right now. If there's a question about it, there's no point in talking. I didn't shoot her, and didn't tell anybody to. None of the boys did, either, and they didn't get anybody to do it. Is that clear? Will you say Pas to that, nothing back?"

Maytera Marble cocked and lifted her head, thus raising an eyebrow. "Someone shot her from a window of your house, Bloody. I saw it."

"All right, you saw it, and Trivigaunte's going to make somebody pay. I don't blame them. What I'm saying is that it shouldn't be me or the boys. We didn't do it, and that's not open to argument. I want that settled before the cut."

Maytera Marble put a hand on his shoulder. "I understand, Bloody. Do you know who did? Will you point them out to us?"

Blood hesitated, his apoplectic face growing redder than ever. "If . . ." His eyes shifted toward a soldier almost too swiftly to be seen. "Yes, absolutely." Several of the armored men muttered agreement.

"In that case it's accepted by our side," Maytera Marble told him. "I'll report to my principals, Generalissimo Oosik and General Saba, that you had nothing to do with it and are anxious to testify against the guilty parties. Who are they?"

Blood ignored the question. "Good. Fine. They won't attack while I'm talking to you?"

"Of course not." Silently, Maytera Marble prayed that she was being truthful.

"You'd probably like to sit. I know I would. Come in here, and I think we can settle this."

He showed her into a paneled drawing room and shut the door firmly. "My boys are getting edgy," he explained, "and that gets me edgy around them."

"They're my grandchildren?" Maytera Marble sank into a tapestry chair too deep and too soft for her. "Your sons?"

"I don't have any. You said you were my mother. I guess you meant you came to talk for her."

"I am your mother, Bloody." Maytera Marble studied him, finding traces of her earlier self in his heavy, cunning face, as well as far too many of his father. "I suppose you've seen me since you found out who I was or had somebody look at me and describe me, and now you don't recognize me. I understand. You're my son, just the same."

He grasped the advantage by reflex. "Then you wouldn't want to see me killed, or would you?"

"No. No, I wouldn't." She let her stick and white flag fall

to the carpet. "If I had been willing to have you die, everything would have been a great deal easier. Don't you see that? You should. You, of all people."

She paused, considering. "I was an old woman before you found out who I was, and I think I must have looked older. I was already forty when you were born. That's terribly old for a bio mother."

"She came a few times when I was little. I remember her."

"Every three months, Bloody. Once in each season, if I could get away alone that often. We were supposed to go out out in pairs, and usually we had to."

"She's dead? My mother?"

"Your foster mother? I don't know. I lost track of her when you were nine."

"I mean y—! Rose. Maytera Rose, my real mother."

"Me." Maytera Marble tapped her chest, a soft click.

"It was her funeral sacrifice. The other sibyl said so."

"We burned parts of her," Maytera Marble conceded. "But mostly those were parts of me in her coffin. Of Marble, I mean, though I've kept her name. It makes things easier, with the children particularly. And there's still a great deal of my personality left."

Blood rose and went to a window. The dull green turret of a Guard floater showed above a half-ruined section of wall. "You mind if I open this?"

"Certainly not. I'd prefer it."

"I want to hear if they start shooting, so I can stop it."

She nodded. "My thought exactly, Bloody. Some of the children have slug guns, and nearly all the rest have needlers. Perhaps I should have taken them, but I was afraid we'd need them on the walk out." She sighed, the weary *hish* of a mop across a terazzo floor. "The worst would have hidden theirs anyway, though none of the children are really bad."

"I remember when she lost her arm," Blood told her. "She used to pat me on the head and say, you know, my, he's getting big. One day it was a hand like yours—"

"It was this one." Maytera Marble displayed it.

"So I asked her what happened. I didn't know she was my mother then. She was just a sibyl that came sometimes. My mother would have tea and cookies."

"Or sandwiches." Maytera Marble supplemented his account. "Very good sandwiches, too, though I was always careful not to eat more than a fourth of one. Bacon in the fall, cheese in winter, pickled burbot and chives on toast in spring, and curds and watercress in summer. Do you remember, Bloody? We always gave you one."

"Sometimes it was all I got," Blood said bitterly.

"I know. That's why I never ate more than a fourth."

"Is that really the same hand?" Blood eyed it curiously.

"Yes, it is. It's hard to change hands yourself, Bloody, because you have to do it one-handed. It was particularly hard for me, because by then I already had a great many new parts. Or rather, I had reclaimed a great many old ones. They worked better, that was why I wanted them, but I wasn't used to the new assembly yet, which made changing hands harder. It would have been wasteful to burn them, though. They were in much better condition than my old ones."

"Even if it is, I'm not going to call you Mother."

Maytera Marble smiled, lifting her head and inclining it to the right as she always did. "You have already, Bloody. Out there. You called me Mama. It sounded wonderful."

When he said nothing, she added, "You said you were going to open that window. Why don't you?"

He nodded and raised the sash. "That's why I bought your manteion, do you know about that? I wasn't just a sprat nobody wanted any more. I had money and influence, and I got word my mother was dying. I hadn't spoken to her in fifteen, twenty years, but I asked Musk, and he said if I really wanted to get even it might be my last chance. I saw the sense in that, so we went, both of us.''

''To get even, Bloody?'' Maytera Marble lifted an eyebrow.

''It doesn't matter. I was sitting with her, see, and she needed something, so I sent Musk. Then I said something and called her Mom, and she said your mother's still alive, I tried to be a mother to you, Blood, and I swore I wouldn't tell.''

Turning from the window to face Maytera Marble, he added, ''She wouldn't, either. But I found out.''

''And bought our manteion to torment me, Bloody?''

''Yeah. The taxes were in arrears. I'm real close to the Ayuntamiento. I guess you know that already or you wouldn't have come out here shooting.''

''You have councillors here, staying with you. Loris, Tarsier, and Potto. That was one reason I wanted to talk.''

Blood shook his head. ''Tarsier's gone. Who told you?''

''Like your foster mother, I've sworn not to tell.''

''One of my people? Somebody in this house?''

''My lips are sealed, Bloody.''

''We'll get into that later, maybe. Yeah, I've got them staying here. It's not the first time, either. When I found out about you—if you're who you say you are—I talked to Loris, just one friend to another, and he let me have it for taxes. Know how much it was? Twelve hundred and change. I was going to leave you hanging, keep talking about tearing the whole thing down. Then Silk came out here. The great Caldé Silk himself! Nobody would believe that now, but he did. He solved my house like a thief. By Phaea, he *was* a thief.''

Maytera Marble sniffed. It was at once a devastating and a confounding sniff, the sniff of a destroyer of cities and a confronter of governments; Blood winced, and she enjoyed it so much that she sniffed again. ''So are you, Bloody.''

"Lily." Blood swallowed. "Only your Silk's no better, is he? Not a dog's right better. So I saw a chance to turn a few cards and have a little fun by making the whole wormy knot of you squirm. I'd got your manteion for twelve hundred like I told you, just a little thank-you from Councillor Loris, and I was going to tell Silk thirteen hundred, then double that." Blood crossed the room to an inlaid cabinet, opened it, and poured gin and water into a squat glass.

"Only when I'd talked to him a little, I made it thirteen *thousand,* because he really thought those old buildings in the middle of that slum were priceless. And I said I'd sell them back to him for twenty-six thousand."

Blood chuckled and sat down again. "I'm not really a bad host, Mama. If I thought that you'd drink it, I'd stand you a drink, even after you called me a thief."

"I was speaking of fact, Bloody, not calling names. Here in private you may call me a trull or a trollop any other such filthy sobriquet. That is what I am, or at any rate what I've been, although no man but your father ever touched me."

"Not me," Blood told her. "I'm above all that."

"But not above defrauding that poor boy because he valued the things given to his care, and was so foolish as to imagine you wouldn't lie to an augur."

Blood grinned. "If I were above that, Mama, I'd be as poor as he is. Or as he was, anyhow. I don't remember how much time I gave him to come up with the gelt. A couple of weeks, maybe, or something like that. Then when I had him crawling, I said that if he brought me something next week or whatever, I might let him have a little more time. Then after a couple days, I sent Musk to tell him I had to have it all right away. I figured he'd come out here again and beg me for more time, see? It looked like it was going to be a nice little game, the kind I like best."

Maytera Marble nodded sympathetically. "I understand. I suppose all of us play wicked little games like that from time to time. I have, I know. But yours is over, Bloody. You've won. You have him here, a prisoner in your house. The person who told me that the councillors were here told me that, too. You have me as well. You say you wanted to avenge yourself on the foster mother we found for you, and you bought our manteion so you could avenge yourself on me, because I gave you life and tried to see that you were taken care of."

Blood stared at her and licked his lips.

"You've won both games. Perhaps all three. So go ahead, Bloody. A single shot should kill me, and I saw a lot of slug guns out there in your foyer. Then the Trivigauntis can kill you for killing General Saba's adjutant, or Generalissimo Oosik can shoot you for shooting me. Possibly you'll be given your choice. Would you rather die justly? Or unjustly?"

When Blood did not reply, she added, "Perhaps you ought to ask your friend Musk about it. He advises you, from what you've said. Where is he, anyway?"

"He stayed behind after we brought the doves. He said he had a couple things to take care of, and he doesn't get into town very often. I thought maybe your side picked him up when he tried to come home."

Maytera Marble shook her head.

Blood took a liberal swallow from his glass. "I wasn't going to shoot you, Mama, and I didn't shoot her. You agreed to that already. Let's pin it down. In about an hour, the Guard could knock this house down and kill everybody. I know that. They're not doing it because they know we've got Silk in here. Isn't that right?"

Maytera Marble nodded. "Free him, turn him over to me, Bloody, and we'll go away and leave you alone."

"It's not that easy. He's here all right, right here in my house. But it's the councillors and their soldiers who've got him, not me."

"Then I must speak with them. Take me to them."

"I'll bring them in here," Blood told her, "they're all

over." Under his breath he added, "It's still my hornbussing house, by Phaea's feast!"

Potto opened the door at the top of the cellar steps and crooked his finger at Sand. "Bring him up, Sergeant. We're getting them all together."

Sand saluted with a crash of titanium heels, his slug gun vertical before his face. "Yes, Councillor!" He nudged Silk with the toe of his right foot, and Silk rose.

He fell as he attempted to mount from the second step to the third, and again halfway up. "Here," Sand told him, and returned Xiphias's stick.

"Thank you," Silk murmured. And then, "I'm sorry. My legs feel a trifle weak, I'm afraid."

Potto said cheerfully, "We're going to try to give you back to your friends, Patera, if we can get them to take you." Grabbing the front of Remora's ruined robe, he jerked Silk up the remaining step. "You'd like to lie down again, wouldn't you? Get in a little nap? Maybe something to eat? Help us, and you'll get it."

He released Silk so suddenly that he fell a third time. "Has he tried to escape again, Sergeant?"

Silk did not hear Sand's reply; he was thinking about a great many things. Among them, names.

His own and Sand's were similar—each had four letters, each contained a single vowel, and each began with an *S*. They could not be related, however, because Sand was a chem and he a bio. Yet they were related by the similarity of their names. Not inconceivably (he found it a tantalizing idea), Sand was a cognate, a version of himself in some whorl of a higher order. Many things the Outsider had shown him seemed to imply that there were such whorls.

Sand prodded him from behind with the barrel of his slug gun, and he staggered against a wall.

Since chems were never augurs, it could not be that Sand

had been meant to be an augur. Was it possible then, that he, Silk, had been meant to be a Guardsman? If he were a Guardsman instead of a failed augur, the many correspondences (already so marked) linking them would be much more perfect, and thus this inferior whorl they inhabited more perfect, too.

But, no, his mother had wanted him to enter the Juzgado, to become a clerk there like Hyacinth's father and perhaps rise to commissioner. How glowingly she had spoken of a political career, almost up until the day he left for the schola.

"This way," Potto told him, and pushed him through a door and into a gorgeous room full of lounging soldiers and armored men. "Is that the caldé?" one of the men asked another; the second nodded.

He was in politics at last, as his mother had wished.

He had pulled a chair over to her closet and stood on the seat to examine the caldé's bust on its dark, high shelf; and she, finding him there intent upon it, had lifted it down for him, dusted it, and set it on her dressing table where he could see it better—wonder at the wide, flat cheeks, the narrow eyes, the high, rounded forehead, and the generous mouth that longed to speak. The caldé's carved countenance rose again before his mind's eye, and it seemed to him that he had seen it someplace else only a day or two before.

Streaming sunlight, and cheeks that were not smooth wood but blotched and lightly pocked. Was it possible he had once seen the caldé in person, perhaps as an infant?

"Now listen to me." Potto was standing before him, his plump, pleasant face half a head lower than Silk's own.

. . . had seen the caldé outside, because even without his lost glasses he had noticed the powder on the cheeks and the flaws that the powder tried to cover—had seen him, in that case, under the auspices of the Outsider, in a sense.

Blood and Maytera Marble were sitting side-by-side when

Potto shoved Silk into the room; he was so surprised to see her that for a moment he failed to notice Chenille, Xiphias, and a drooping augur lined up against the wall.

A still handsome elderly man standing by the fireplace said, "I'm Councillor Loris. It take it you're Silk?"

"Patera Silk. His Cognizance the Prolocutor has not yet accepted my resignation. May I sit down?"

Loris ignored the last. "You're the insurgent caldé."

"Others have called me caldé, but I'm not involved in an insurrection." Potto pushed him to the wall beside Chenille.

Loris smiled, his blue eyes glinting like chips of ice; and the seduction of his craggy wisdom was so great that even a mocking smile made it almost irresistible. "You killed my Cousin Lemur, did you, Caldé?"

Silk shook his head.

Maytera Marble said, "I don't know these others, except Chenille. Shouldn't I introduce myself?"

"I'll do it," Blood told her, "it's my house." With a slight start, Silk realized that Blood was in the chair he had occupied a week earlier, and that this was the same room.

"This is Councillor Loris," Blood began unnecessarily, "the new presiding officer of the Ayuntamiento. This other councillor's Councillor Potto."

"Caldé Silk and Councillor Potto are old acquaintances," Loris purred. "Isn't that right, Caldé?"

"I don't know this soldier myself," Blood continued, and paused to sip his drink. "It probably doesn't matter."

"Sergeant Sand," Silk told him. "He and Councillor Potto interrogated me Tarsday. It was very painful, and I suppose it's quite possible they're going to do it again."

Sand came to attention and appeared about to speak, but Silk stopped him with a gesture. "You were only doing your duty, Sergeant. I understand. In justice to you, I ought to add that you had treated me well earlier."

Potto said, "We won't need you here, Sergeant. You know what to do." Sand looked at Silk, saluted, executed an about-face, and left, shutting the door behind him.

"A very handsome young man," Maytera Marble remarked. "I was sorry to hear that he behaved badly toward you, Patera."

Blood indicated her with his glass. "This holy sibyl's Maytera Rose—"

Chenille tittered nervously. Maytera Marble said, "I'm Maytera Marble, Bloody. Remember? I explained about that. Chenille and I have met, and naturally Patera knows me well."

"Patera *Silk*, she means," elucidated the small augur in the corner. "I, *too*, am entitled to the honorific, as well as my more customary ones. Caldé, I have been appointed the new *Prolocutor* of *Viron* by *Subleviating Scylla*, who during that same *theophany* confirmed *you* as its caldé. Am *I*, as I *dare hope*, the first to—"

Silk managed to smile. "It's a pleasure to see you again, Patera."

Chenille blurted, "Why weren't you dead? I've just been standing here . . . We couldn't, none of us—"

Xiphias cackled. "He's a tough one! Student of mine, too! Truth!"

Silk said, "Maytera, do you know Master Xiphias? Master Xiphias is teaching me to fence. Master Xiphias, this holy sibyl is Maytera Marble. She's the senior sibyl now at my— Of the manteion on Sun Street."

Maytera Marble added softly, "I'm also the representative of our Generalissimo Oosik and the Trivigauntis's General Saba, Patera. I've come to arrange your release."

His voice thick with mock sincerity, Loris said, "We hold the key to the crisis now, you see, the generous gods having flung the ring into our laps. How foolish are those who scorn the power of the immortal gods!"

A black shape darted through the open window, landing with a thump on Silk's shoulder. "Bird back!"

"Oreb!" Silk looked around at him, surprised and more pleased than he would have been willing to admit.

"Scourging Scylla," ignoring Oreb, Incus had leveled his forefinger at Loris, "has given *you* nothing."

"In that case, we have gained our present advantage by merit." Loris smiled. "We thank the undying, ever-generous gods for our talents."

Oreb cocked an inquiring head. "Good gods?"

"She will *destroy* all of you, should you harm *either* of the holy augurs present, or this *sibyl.* We are *sacred.*"

"We'll risk her wrath if need be. Old man, stop reaching for your sword. It's gone. Were you thinking of overpowering us?"

Xiphias shook his head. "Think I don't know there's soldiers out there?"

"You could not even if there were none." Loris took a bookend from the mantle; it shattered between his fingers with a sharp report and an explosion of snowy chips. The door flew open, revealing Sand and two other soldiers with leveled slug guns. Oreb whistled.

Potto told them, "It's all right. Shut it."

"Caldé Silk is a strong young man, but he's been severely wounded. You are an old one, unarmed, and not as strong as you suppose. Our new Prolocutor's not physically imposing. Need I continue?"

Silk said, "I can understand how you came to be in the tunnel, Master Xiphias—both you and His Cognizance. You ran for cover just as Hyacinth and I did—"

Blood interrupted. "You've got her? Where is she?"

"I don't. I had her, if you like. We were separated." Turning back to Xiphias, Silk continued, "After you dug me out of the loose soil, you went down the tunnel to look for water with Chenille and Patera, leaving His Cognizance with me—with my body, as you thought. Is that right?"

Xiphias nodded.

"Only we didn't think your body," Chenille told Silk. "We knew you were alive. His Cognizance said there was a pulse, only we didn't understand how you could be alive after getting buried like that."

Loris rattled what remained of the bookend in his hand. "What puzzles me—excuse my interrupting your conference—is your mention of His Cognizance. I take it you don't refer to our friend, but to the actual head of the Chapter? Was he in the tunnel with you, Caldé?"

"Yes, he was. Perhaps I shouldn't have mentioned it."

Potto said happily, "He's an old man. One of the patrols will pick him up, Cousin."

"A clever old man." Loris looked grim. "A troublemaker."

Privately, Silk was trying to reconcile Quetzal's telling Chenille that he, Silk, was alive with his saying that they had thought him dead. He had lied in one or the other, but why?

"Bad thing!" Oreb told everyone.

Silk ventured, "A patrol headed by Sergeant Sand—one like the patrol that arrested me originally, I suppose—must have come across Master Xiphias, Patera Incus, and Chenille. I was surprised to see them here, but I believe I understand now. Sand must have sent the other man back here with them and gone on alone until he found me, perhaps because he'd heard my voice—I'd been talking to His Cognizance. Is that correct?"

"Where is this tunnel, Patera?" Maytera Marble asked. "Are you talking about a tunnel underneath the house?"

Potto grinned at her, displaying gleaming teeth.

Blood put down his drink. "Yeah, we're right over it, Mama, and it hooks up with a bunch of others."

Loris told her, "That's the first item you ought to pass on

to your principals, Maytera. They think they have us like rats in a cauldron. Nothing could be further from the truth. We can leave this house, and them, whenever we wish.''

Blood added, ''Only I don't want to. It's my house.''

She looked thoughtful, a finger pressed to her cheek.

''Bad hole.'' Oreb ruffled his feathers apprehensively. Chenille whispered, ''Your bird was down there with us. Auk had him on the boat.''

''You're sunburned!'' Inwardly, Silk reproached his own stupidity. ''I've been looking at you—gaping actually, I suppose. I hope you'll excuse it, but I couldn't imagine how your face had gotten so red, so close to the red-brown color of a wood-carving my mother used to have.''

''She wore *nothing* on the boat,'' Incus interposed. ''Then my robe. Maytera *forced* them to give her that gown.''

Loris snapped, ''Is this germane?''

''Perhaps not,'' Silk admitted. ''It's just that Chenille has reminded me of a childhood incident, Councillor.''

Loris waved aside Chenille's sunburn, tossing the largest fragment of the bookend onto the rosewood end table at Maytera Marble's elbow. ''Marble? Isn't that your name, Maytera? The caldé just reminded us of that.''

''It is.''

''That was what this knickknack was, I'd say. Real marble from the Short Sun Whorl, precisely like you.'' For an instant, Loris's face was no longer attractive. ''I'll leave that chunk there so you don't forget it.''

''I shan't,'' Maytera Marble promised. ''It would be wise for you to keep in mind that you're surrounded by thousands of well-armed troops, Councillor. I suppose most people in my position would be inclined to exaggerate their numbers, but I won't. I'll tell you the truth, so you won't be able to say that you were deceived, or even misled, afterward. There are two companies of Trivigaunti pterotroopers, almost the entire Third Brigade of the Civil Guard, and elements of the

Fourth. I asked Generalissimo Oosik what he meant by 'elements' and he said four floaters and the heavy weapons company. Besides all those, there are about five thousand of Maytera Mint's people, with more arriving from the city all the time. They've heard that Patera Silk's in here, and they want to charge the house. When I left, General Saba and Generalissimo Oosik were afraid they might not be able to prevent them without using Guardsmen and creating more friction.''

''Fight now?'' Oreb inquired.

Smiling, Maytera Marble turned to Silk. ''That's the bird I saw hopping into your kitchen when Doctor Crane was treating you, isn't? Later on my glass, and on your shoulder like that in the garden. I knew I'd seen him before.

''No, little bird, no fighting. Not now, or not yet. But Generalissimo Oosik told me quite frankly that if there's no way to stop Maytera Mint's insurgents from attacking short of firing on them, he'll stand back and let them do it. You see, I confided to the children that your master was in here. They seem to have told a great many other people before we left the city, so the whole thing's my fault. I feel very badly indeed about that, and I'm trying to make amends.''

Blood added, ''But she won't say who told her. Or have you changed your mind about that, Mama?''

''Certainly not. I gave my word.''

Loris, who had been leaning against the mantel, left it to stand in front of Maytera Marble. ''This little conference has already run too long. Allow me to tell you what we want, Maytera. Then you can go back out there and repeat it to the Trivigauntis and Mint's five thousand rioters, if there are actually that many, which I am ungentlemanly enough to doubt. Our position is not negotiable. You accept our terms or we'll kill these prisoners, Silk included, and crush the rebellion.''

''You have *no* authority—''

Potto's fist striking Incus's cheek sounded almost as loud as the breaking of the bookend.

"So, we've come to that." Maytera Marble smoothed the black skirt covering her metal thighs. "It will be needlers and knives next, no doubt."

Silk said, "I warn you, Councillor Potto, not to do that again."

"Or you'll break my neck?" Potto's smile was that of a fat boy contemplating a stolen pie. "Beat little butcher, big butcher bark? We've had some games of strength already. If you've forgotten them, I can teach you the rules again."

Incus spat blood. "The just *gods* avenge the wrongs of *augurs*. A doom . . ."

Potto lifted his hand, and Incus fell silent.

"No hit," Oreb suggested.

"The gods may or may not," Silk murmured. "I don't know, and if I were forced to choose, I'd probably say that they did nothing of the sort."

Loris applauded with a sardonic smile; a half-second too late, Potto joined him.

Abruptly Silk's voice dominated the room. "The law does, however. Maytera told you how many troops Generalissimo Oosik has, saying—very fairly and reasonably, I thought—that she didn't want you to feel you'd been tricked when all this is over. You should have listened more carefully."

"Tell 'em!" Xiphias put in.

"I'm attempting to." Silk nodded, mostly (it appeared) to himself. "Because it will be over soon. There will be a trial, and you, Councillor Potto, and you, Councillor Loris, will hear Maytera, Chenille, Master Xiphias, and Patera Incus testify to what they saw and heard—and felt, as well—to a judge who will no longer be afraid of you."

Potto giggled and glanced at Loris. "Is this what they picked to replace us?"

Surprising everyone, Blood said, "Yeah, I didn't get it at first, but I'm starting to."

Maytera Marble told Potto, "All human things wear out and must be replaced eventually, Councillor."

"Not me!"

"I'd think you'd welcome it. How long have you toiled, worrying and planning, for our ungrateful city? Fifty years? Sixty?"

"Longer!" Potto dropped into a gilt settee.

Silk inquired, "Councillor, do you—not the authentic Potto down in your underwater boat, but you yourself to whom I speak—recall the Short Sun Whorl? Councillor Loris implied that marble could be quarried there. I don't know anything about antiques, but I've heard that it is a stone that's never found in its natural state in our whorl."

"I'm not that old."

Loris snapped, "I was about to outline our demands. I'd like to get on with it."

Maytera Marble left her chair to stand beside Silk. "Do, Councillor, please."

"As I said, they're not negotiable. The following five conditions embody them, and we're prepared to accept nothing less." Loris fished a square of paper from an inner pocket and unfolded it with a snap.

"First, Silk must declare publicly, without reservation, that he is not and has never been caldé, that Viron has none, and that the Ayuntamiento alone is its sole governing body."

To bring peace I'll be happy to, Silk told him; and only when he had completed the final word realized that he had not spoken aloud.

"Second, there must be no new election of councillors. Vacant seats are to remain vacant, and the present members of the Ayuntamiento are to remain in office.

"Third, the Rani of Trivigaunte must withdraw her troops

from Vironese territory and furnish us with hostages—whom we will name—against further interference in our affairs.

"Fourth, the Civil Guard must surrender its treasonous officers to us, the Ayuntamiento, for trial and punishment.

"Fifth and last, the rioters must surrender their arms, which will be collected by the Army."

Through bruised lips, Incus muttered, "I suggest you *pray* long and hard over this, my son, and *sacrifice*. The *wisdom* of the gods has not enlightened your *councils*."

"We don't need it," Potto told him.

"When *Splenetic Scylla* learns—"

Maytera Marble interrupted. "What have you to offer the Rani, the rioters, as you call them, and the Guard in return?"

"Peace and a general amnesty. The captives you see here, including Silk, will be released unharmed."

"I see." Maytera Marble laid a hand on Silk's shoulder. "I'm very disappointed. It was I who persuaded General Saba and Generalissimo Oosik that you were reasonable men. They listened because of the courage of my sib General Mint. And because of her victories, of which we're all very proud, if I don't offend the good gods who gave them to her by saying so. Now I find that by interceding for you I've squandered all the credit she's earned us."

Loris began, "If you think us unreasonable now—"

"I do. You say Patera Silk isn't really caldé. What good is his declaration then? What do you want him to tell the people? That the augur of the Sun Street manteion says that your Ayuntamiento is to continue to govern the city? You'll only make yourselves ridiculous."

Potto snapped, "Why didn't you laugh?"

"Caldé?" Loris smiled. "Those are our demands. The Prolocutor hasn't freed you from your vows, you said, the implication being that you want him to. Are you willing to resign this caldéship you've never really had as well?"

"Yes, I'd like nothing better." Silk had been leaning on Xiphias's silver-banded cane; he straightened up as he spoke. "I did not choose to become involved in politics, Councillor. Politics chose me."

"Good Silk," Oreb explained.

Loris returned his attention to Maytera Marble. "You heard that. You'll want to tell Oosik what you heard."

"Unfortunately," Silk continued, "the remainder of your terms are not feasible. Take the second. The people demand that government return to our Charter, the foundation of the law; and the law requires elections to fill the empty seat in the Ayuntamiento."

"We ought to kill you," Potto told him. "I will."

"In which case you would no longer hold the caldé. The people—the rioters, as you call them—will choose a new one, no doubt a much better and more effective one than I am, since they could hardly do worse."

He waited for someone else to speak, but no one did; at length he added, "I'm not an advocate, Councillors—I wish I were. If I were, I could easily imagine myself defending you on nearly every charge that could be brought against you thus far. You suspended the Charter, but I believe there was some uncertainty regarding the wishes of the old caldé, and it was long ago in any case. You tried to put down the riots, but in that you were doing your duty. You questioned Mamelta and me when we were detained for violating a military area, which could easily be justified."

"He *hit* me!" Incus exclaimed. "An *augur!*"

Silk nodded. "That is an individual matter, concerning Councillor Potto alone, and I was considering the Ayuntamiento as a whole—or rather, what remains of that whole. But what you say, Patera, is quite right; and it's an indication of the road along which this Ayuntamiento is traveling. I'd like to persuade Councillor Loris, its presiding officer, to turn back before it's too late."

Loris fixed him with a malevolent stare. "Then you won't accede to our demands? I can call in the soldiers at once and get this over with."

Silk shook his head. "I can't accede. Nor can I speak for the Rani of Trivigaunte, obviously; but I can and do speak for Viron; and for Viron all of your demands, except the one for my resignation, are out of the question."

"Nevertheless," Maytera Marble put in, "General Mint and Generalissimo Oosik may accede to them, in part at least, to save Patera Silk. May I speak to him in private?"

"Don't be ridiculous!"

"It isn't ridiculous, I must. Don't you see that General Mint and Generalissimo Oosik and all the rest of them are only acting on the authority of Patera Silk? When I report that I've seen him and tell them you've recognized him as caldé, they will certainly want to know whether he's willing to agree to your terms. They'll have to know what he wants them to do, but they won't pay the least attention to it unless I can say that he told me in private. Let me talk to him, and I'll go back and talk to Generalissimo Oosik and General Saba. Then, if we're lucky, we'll have real peace in place of this truce."

"We have not recognized him as caldé," Loris told her coldly. "I invite you to retract that."

"But you have! You've called him Caldé several times in my presence, and I could see you congratulating yourselves on having the caldé. You even called him the key to the crisis. You're threatening to shoot *him* because *he* won't agree to your precious five demands. If he's the caldé, that's only cruel. If he isn't, it's idiotic."

She raised her hands and time-smoothed face to Loris in supplication. "He's terribly weak. I've been watching him while the rest of us were talking, and if it weren't for his stick I think he would have fallen. Can't you let him sit down? And tell everyone else to leave? A quarter of an hour should be enough.''

Blood rose, swaying a little. "Over here, Patera. Take my seat. This's a good chair, better than the one you had in here that other time.''

"Thank you,'' Silk said. "Thank you very much. I owe you a great deal, Blood.'' Chenille, next to him, took his arm; he wanted to assure her he did not need her help, but stumbled on the carpet before he could speak, eliciting an unhappy squawk from Oreb.

"Get the rest of them out,'' Loris told Potto.

Xiphias paused in the doorway, showing Silk both his hands, then twisting one slightly and separating them.

Chenille kissed his forehead, the brush of her lips the silken touch of a butterfly's wing—and was gone, violently pulled away by Potto, who left with her and shut the door.

Maytera Marble reoccupied the chair beside the one that had been Blood's. "Well,'' she said.

Silk nodded. "Well indeed. You did very well, Maytera. Much better than I. But before we talk about—all of the things we'll have to talk about, I'd like to ask a question. One foolish question, or perhaps two. Will you indulge me?''

"Certainly, Patera. What is it?''

Silk's forefinger traced small circles on his cheek. "I know nothing about women's clothes. You must know a great deal more—at least, I hope you do. You got Councillor Loris to bring Chenille her gown?''

"She was naked under that augur's robe,'' Maytera Marble explained, "and I refused to talk about anything else until they got her dressed. Bloody called in one of the maids, and she and Chenille went with a soldier to find her some clothes. They weren't gone long.''

Silk nodded, his face thoughtful.

"It's too small for her, but the maid said it was the largest in the house, and it's only a little bit too small.''

"I see. I was wondering whether it belonged to a woman I met here."

"You and Bloody were talking about her, Patera." Maytera Marble sounded ill at ease. "He asked you where she was, and you said you'd gotten separated."

Silk nodded again.

"I don't want to pry into your personal affairs."

"I appreciate that. Believe me, Maytera, I appreciate it very much." He hesitated, staring through the open window at the wind-rippled green lawn before he spoke again. "I thought it might be one of Hyacinth's, as I said. In fact, I rather hoped it was; but it couldn't be. It almost fits Chenille, as you say, and Hyacinth's much smaller." The circles, which had ceased to spin, reappeared. "What do you call that fabric?"

"It's chen. . . . Why, I see what you're getting at, and you're right, Patera! That gown's chenille, exactly like her name!"

"Not silk?"

Maytera Marble snapped her fingers. "I know! She must have told the maid her name, and it suggested the gown."

"She kissed me as she left," he remarked. "I certainly didn't invite it, but she did. You must have seen it."

"Yes, Patera. I did."

"I suppose she wanted to signal that she was with us—that she supported us. Master Xiphias made a gesture of the same sort, probably something to do with swordplay. Anyway, her kiss made me think of silk, of the fabric I mean, for some reason. It seemed strange, but I thought perhaps her skirt had brushed my hand. You say it's actually called chenille?"

"Chenille *is* silk, Patera. Or anyway the best chenille is, and the other is something else that's supposed to look like silk. Chenille is a kind of yarn, made of silk, that's furry-looking like a caterpillar. If they weave cloth of it, that's called chenille too. It's a foreign word that means caterpillar, and silk threads are spun by silkworms, which are a kind of caterpillar. But I'm sure you know that.''

"I must speak to her," he said. "Not now, but when we're alone, and as soon as I can."

"Good girl!"

"Yes, Oreb. Indeed she is." Silk returned his attention to Maytera Marble. "A moment ago when you spoke to Loris, you didn't want us to leave this room. Would you mind telling me why?"

"Was I as transparent at that?"

"No, you weren't transparent at all; but I know you, and if you'd really been so worried about me, you would have asked him to let us talk in a bedroom where I could lie down, and to send for a doctor. I don't suppose Blood's got one, now that Doctor Crane's dead; but Loris might have been able to supply one, or to send someone for one of the Guard's doctors under a flag of truce, like that white flag next to your chair."

Maytera Marble looked grave. "I should have asked him to do that. I can still ask, Patera. I'll go out and find him. It won't take a moment."

"No, I'm fine. By Phaea's favor—" It was too late to call back the conventional phrase. "I'll recover. Why did you want to stay here?"

"Because of this window." Maytera Marble waved a hand at it. "Bloody had opened it while we were in here by ourselves, and I worried the whole time that someone would get cold and shut it. You must know Mucor, Patera. She said you sent her to me."

Silk nodded. "She's Blood's adopted daughter."

"Adopted? I didn't know that. She said she was Bloody's daughter. That was Hieraxday night, terribly late. . . . Do you know Asphodella, Patera?"

Silk smiled. "Oh, yes. A lively little thing."

"That's her. I'd done the wash, you see, and I wanted to

pour the dirty water on my garden. Plants actually like dirty water with soapsuds in it better than clean. It sounds wrong, I know, but they do.''

''If you say so, I'm sure it must be true.''

''So I was pouring out the water, so much for each row, when Asphodella pulled my skirt. I said what are you doing out so late, child? And she told me she'd gone with the others to fight, but Horn had sent her back—''

''Cat come!'' Oreb warned. Silk looked for it, seeing none.

''Horn had sent her home, and quite right, too, if you ask me, Patera. So now she wanted to know if there'd be palaestra on Thelxday.''

''Then,'' Silk said slowly, ''her face changed. Is that it, Maytera?''

''Yes. Exactly. Her face became, well, horrible. She saw I was frightened, as I certainly was, and said don't be afraid, Grandmother. My name's Mucor, I'm Blood's daughter.'' Maytera Marble paused, not certain that he understood. ''Have I told you Bloody's my son, Patera? Yes, I know I did, right after we sacrificed in the street.''

''He was Maytera Rose's,'' Silk said carefully. ''You, I know, are also Maytera Rose—at least, at times.''

''All the time, Patera.'' Maytera Marble laughed. ''I've integrated our software. As far as we sibyls are concerned, I'm your best friend and worst enemy, all in one.''

He stirred uncomfortably in Blood's comfortable chair. ''I was never Maytera Rose's enemy, I hope.''

''You thought I was yours, though, Patera. Perhaps I was, a little.''

He leaned toward her, his hands folded over the crook of Xiphias's cane. ''Are you now, Maytera? Please be completely frank with me.''

''No. Your friend and well-wisher, Patera.''

Oreb applauded, flapping his wings. "Good girl!"

She added, "Even if I were entirely Maytera Rose, I'd do all I could to get you out of this."

Silk let himself fall back. It was astonishing how soft these chairs of Blood's were. He remembered (vividly now) how badly he had wanted to rest in his chair, to sleep in it, when he had talked with Blood in this very room. Yet this one was better, just as Blood had promised: yielding where it should, firm where firmness was desirable. He stroked one wide arm, its maroon leather as smooth as butter beneath his touch.

"They let me lie down after I was captured," he confided to Maytera Marble. "Sand did. I'd had to walk all the way to this house, and it was a very long way. It had seemed long when Auk and I rode donkeys; and walking with Sand's gun at my back, it seemed a great deal longer; but once we arrived, once we'd climbed up through the hatch into the cellar, he let me lie down on the floor. He isn't a bad man, really—just a disciplined soldier obeying bad men. There's good in Loris, too, and even in Potto. I know you must sense it, just as I do, Maytera; otherwise you'd never have spoken to Potto as you did. That's why—one reason, anyway—I don't feel that this situation from which you're trying to rescue me is as bad as it appears, though I'll always be grateful."

"Cat! Cat!" Oreb flew from Silk's shoulder to the head of an alabaster bust of Thelxiepeia.

Maytera Marble smiled. "There's no cat in here, you pretty bird."

"You were telling me about this room," Silk reminded her, "and meeting Mucor. I wish you'd continue with that. It may be significant."

"I— Patera, I want to tell you first about meeting you. It won't take long, and it may be more important, maybe a lot more important. You still think about the day you came to our manteion, I know. You've mentioned it several times."

He nodded.

"Patera Pike was there, and you loved and respected him, but a man wants a woman to talk to. Most men do, anyway, and you did. You'd been raised by your mother, and we could see how you missed her."

"I still do," Silk admitted.

"Don't feel bad about that, Patera. No one should ever be ashamed of love."

Maytera Marble paused to collect her thoughts; her rapid scan was back, and she reveled in it. "We were three sibyls, I was about to say. Maytera Mint was still young and pretty, but so shy that she ran from you whenever she could. When she couldn't, she would hardly speak. Maybe she guessed what had happened to me long ago. I've sometimes thought that, and you were young and good-looking, as you still are."

He began a question, but thought better of it.

"I won't tell you who Bloody's father was, Patera. I've never told anybody and I won't tell now. But I will tell you this. He never knew. I don't think he even suspected."

Silk filled his lungs with the cool, clean breeze from the window. "I slept with a woman last night, Maytera. With Hyacinth, the woman Blood asked about."

"I'm sorry you told me."

"I wanted to. I've wanted—I want so badly, still, to tell people who don't know, although a great many people know already. His Cognizance and Master Xiphias and Generalissimo Oosik."

"And me." Maytera Marble's forefinger tapped her metal chest through her habit. "I knew. Or rather, I guessed, as anybody would, and I wish that you'd left it like that. Some things aren't improved by talking about them."

Oreb broke off his inverted examination of Thelxiepeia's features to applaud Maytera Marble. "Smart girl!"

"We were three sibyls, as I said. But Maytera Mint wasn't there for you Patera, so I was the only ones left. I was old. I don't think you ever grasped how old. My faces had gone long before you were born. You never realized they weren't there, did you?''

"What are you talking about? Your face is where it ought to be, Maytera. I'm looking at it.''

"This?'' She drummed her fingers on it, a quick metallic *tap-tap-tap.* "This is my faceplate, really. I used to have a face like yours. I would say like Dahlia's, but she was before your time. Like Teasel's or Nettle's, and there were things in it, little bits of alnico, that let me really smile or frown when I moved them with the coils behind my faceplate. But all that's gone except for the coils.''

"It's a beautiful face," Silk insisted, "because it's yours.''

"My other face wasn't, and what it was showed in your own every time you saw it. I resented that, and you resented my resentment and turned to me to ease your loneliness. But we were much more alike than you realized, not that I've ever cared, myself, for machines like this. I never thought they could be people, really, no matter how many times they said they were. Now I'm just a message written on those teeny gold doodads you see in cards. But I'm still me, a person, because I always was.''

Silk fumbled Remora's ruined robe for a handkerchief, and finding none blotted his eyes on his sleeve.

"I didn't tell you that to make you feel sorry for me, Patera. Neither of me were easy to love, no more than I am now. You were able to love one just the same, and not very many men could have, not even many augurs. I thought that if you knew how you came to love and not like me, it might help you some other time with some other woman.''

"It will, I know." Silk sighed. "Thank you, Maytera. With myself, most of all.''

"Let's not talk about it any more. What do you think of the Ayuntamiento's terms? Still what you told Loris?''

Silk made a last dab at his eyes, feeling the grit in the

cloth, knowing that he was dirtying his already-soiled face and not caring. "I suppose so."

Maytera Marble nodded. "They're perfectly hopeless. Not a single thing for Trivigaunte, and why should the Guard hand over its senior officers, why should Generalissimo Oosik allow it? But if we offered trials, regular ones with judges—"

"Man back!" A big hand glittering with rings had appeared on the windowsill. It was followed by a yellow-sleeved arm and a whiff of musk rose.

"That's why you wanted to stay here." Silk stood up a trifle unsteadily, helped by the cane, and crossed the room to the window. "So your son could join us."

"Why no, Patera. Not at all."

Leaning over the sill, Silk spoke to Blood. "Here, hold onto my hand. I'll help you up."

"Thanks," Blood said. "I should have brought a stool or something."

"Take mine, too, Bloody." Maytera Marble braced one foot on the sill in imitation of Silk.

Flushed redder than ever with exertion, Blood's face rose on the other side of the window. With a grunt and a heave, he tumbled into the room.

"Now for my granddaughter. She'll be easy after Bloody." Bending over the sill again, Maytera Marble clasped skeletally thin hands and lifted in an emaciated young woman with a seared cheek.

"Poor girl!"

Silk nodded his agreement as he returned to his chair. "Hello, Mucor. Sit down, please, so that I may sit. We're neither of us strong."

"Needlers're no good 'gainst the soldiers," Blood puffed. He brushed off the front of his tunic and reached beneath it. "So I'm giving you this, Caldé Silk."

"This" was an azoth, its long hilt rough with rubies and chased with gold; its sharply curved guard was more elaborate than that of the one Doctor Crane had given him at Hyacinth's urging, and diamonds ringed its pommel.

Silk resumed his seat. "I should have anticipated that. Doctor Crane told me you had two."

"Don't you want it?" Blood did not trouble to hide his surprise.

"No. Not now, at least."

"It's worth—"

"I know what it's worth, and how effective a weapon it can be in a strong hand like yours. At the moment, I don't have one, though that's the least of my reasons for refusing."

Silk settled back in his chair. "I asked your daughter to sit down, and she was good enough to oblige me. I can't invite you to sit in your house, and I'm very aware that I'm occupying your former seat; but there are many others."

Blood sat.

"Thank you. Maytera—"

"Cat come!"

It did, almost before Oreb's agitated whoop, springing lightly over the windowsill to land noiselessly in the middle of the room and glare at Blood with eyes like burning amber. Maytera Marble gathered her skirts as if it were a mouse; Silk asked, "Is that Lion? I seem to remember him."

The lynx turned its glare on him and nodded.

"Patera's been making everybody sit," Maytera Marble told Mucor. "It would be nicer if you had your big kitty sit too, Darling. I wouldn't mind him so much then."

Lion lay down obediently, dividing his attention between Blood and Oreb.

"Sphigx bless you." Maytera Marble traced the sign of addition. "I—it's rather amusing now that I come to think of it, the sort of thing the children enjoy. Patera thought I wanted this window open so your Papa could come in, and I said, no,

I hadn't even thought of it, which was the plain truth. I wanted it opened because you told me the first time, Darling, not to stay in rooms with the doors and windows shut, because you might have to drop in again, and that would make it harder. So I was happy when he opened this one, and now you've come in through it, and your long-legged kitty, too.''

"I didn't know she could take over an animal like that." Blood had his thumb on the demon. "We didn't know she had any power left till Lemur taped the caldé talking to Crane, but it sounds like she's been paying visits to both of you."

"Sneaking outside the window, Bloody? You shouldn't do that."

"I didn't."

"A listening device." Silk sighed. "I'm disappointed. I'd thought there might be a secret door behind one of these big paintings. When I was a sprat, boys' books were full of them, but I've never actually seen one."

"You knew I'd come?"

"I surmised you might. Do you want the entire thing?"

Maytera Marble sniffed loudly. "I do, Patera."

"I wish you wouldn't make that noise," he told her.

"Then I won't, or at least not very often. But Bloody's my son, and I meant I have a right to know."

"All right, the entire thing." Silk leaned back in his chair, eyes half closed. "On Hieraxday, I walked some distance through the city with His Cognizance, and from the East Edge to Ermine's; it was about evenly divided between Maytera Mint's insurgents and the Guard. I slept at Ermine's for a few hours, as I told you; when I woke up, half the Guard seemed to have gone over to Maytera Mint."

Maytera Marble said, "All of it but the Second, I'm told."

"Good. Before I was brought here, I was in the tunnels or in the cellar, so I didn't see much; but there were councillors here. It seemed likely they were directing their forces in person, and I didn't think they'd do that unless the situation was critical. Then too, you told me you'd walked out here with the children and mentioned a general from Trivigaunte—"

"General Saba. A very good woman at heart, from what I saw of her, though quite large and rather prone to obstinacy."

"I assume it was her airship that attacked us when His Cognizance and I were riding in Oosik's floater."

"Her airship's been over the city, certainly. It's been shooting and dropping explosives. It's huge."

"Your Doctor Crane was a spy from Trivigaunte," Silk told Blood. "You must know that by now. He told me once, joking, that if I were in need of rescue all I'd have to do was kill him. He had a device in his chest that let others find him and told them whether his heart was beating. He was shot Hieraxday morning, due to a misunderstanding. I imagine the attack on us resulted from a similar mix-up—the Trivigauntis had been told the Guard was opposing us. When they saw a Guard floater surrounded by officers on horseback, they attacked it."

"I don't see what this has to do with me," Blood grunted.

"It has everything to do with you," Silk told him, "and I was right about it, too—the only thing I've been completely right about. You were fighting in a losing cause; this house was about to be destroyed, and you might easily be wounded or killed. You knew about the tunnels, and no doubt you've been down there. So have I, as I've said—more than I like. I couldn't imagine your leaving this house in flames and trudging off underground unless there were no alternative."

"I worked shaggy hard to get this place."

"Don't swear, Bloody. It doesn't become you."

"I did! Your kind thinks it's easy. One wrong move and you're packed for Mainframe, day after day, and nobody to help me I could trust till I found Musk, nobody at all. It'd kill both of you in a week. Shag yes, it would! Twelve years I did it before I ever took my first crap in this place.''

"Bloody!''

"It's only a guess," Silk admitted, "and I can't pretend an intimate familiarity with your mental processes; but I'd imagine you've been looking for an opportunity to change sides since sometime last night.''

"What's the shaggy Ayuntamiento ever done for me? Worked me for payoffs and favors every month. Shut me down to make themselves look good. What the shag do I owe them?''

"I've no idea. Then—about an hour ago, perhaps—your mother entered the picture, ostensibly and no doubt principally to help me, but clearly with influence on the other side and eager to save you as well. So when I realized Maytera wanted us to stay in this room, I expected you to step from behind a picture.'' Silk smiled and shrugged apologetically.

Mucor surprised them all by asking, "Would you like me to see what they're doing?''

"I'd rather have you eat something," Silk told her, "but I don't suppose there's anything in here. Go ahead, if Lion will behave himself.''

He waited for her reply, but none came.

"Girl go." Oreb's croak was scarcely audible. "No here." Lion stretched himself on the floor and closed his eyes.

"Actually, I was surprised you didn't come sooner," Silk told Blood conversationally, "but of course you had to fetch Mucor and get her dressed—perhaps even clean her up a bit with the help of one of your maids, and I hadn't allowed for that. The point that puzzles me is that Mucor seems to have felt it necessary to send Lion ahead of her.''

"Did she?'' Blood eyed his adopted daughter curiously.

"So it seems. Oreb—my bird, up there—must have

glimpsed him or, more likely heard him, because he told us several times that there was a cat about.''

"She probably didn't realize that the soldiers wouldn't be afraid of him,'' Maytera Marble suggested.

"Bad cat,'' Oreb muttered.

"Not too loud,'' Silk cautioned him, "he might hear you.''

"It was nice of you to join us, Bloody.'' Maytera Marble smoothed her skirt. "It's to your advantage, no doubt, just as Patera says. But you're taking a big risk just the same.''

Blood stood. "I know it. You don't think much of me, do you, Caldé?''

"I think a great deal of your shrewdness,'' Silk told him. "I'd be glad to have your cunning mind on our side. I'm aware that you have no morals.''

"Colonel Oosik,'' Blood gestured with the azoth. "He's your man, from what I've heard. This General Saba's there for the Rani, Colonel Oosik for you.''

"Generalissimo Oosik.''

Blood snorted. "You trust him and you won't trust me, but I've had him in my pocket for years.''

Maytera Marble said, "Sit down, Bloody. Or are you going to do something?''

"I want a drink, but since the caldé doesn't want it, I think I'll hang onto my azoth as long as that cat's in here. Will you fix me one, Mama?''

"Certainly.'' She rose. "A little more gin, I imagine?''

Silk began, "If it's not too much trouble, Maytera—''

"And ice. There's ice behind the big doors underneath.''

"I'll be happy to. Brandy, or—'' she examined bottles. "Here's a nice red wine, Patera.''

"Just water and ice, please. The same for Mucor, I think.''

Blood shook his head. "No ice, Mama. She'll throw it. Believe me, I know.''

"Poor bird!''

"A cup of plain water for Oreb, if you would, Maytera. I believe he'll come down to drink it if you leave it on top of the cabinet."

"Plain water for Oreb." Revealing two fingers' width of silvery leg as she stood on tiptoe, she put a brimming tumbler on the cabinet. "Soda water and ice for Patera, and ice, gin, and soda water for you, Bloody. Soda water without ice for my granddaughter. It's nice and cool, though." As she placed the final tumbler before Mucor, she added, "I must say she doesn't look as if you've been taking good care of her."

Blood picked up his drink. "We've got to force-feed her, mostly, and she tears off her clothes."

"Who was her mother?" Silk asked.

"She never had one." Blood sipped his drink and eyed it with disfavor. "You know about frozen embryos? You can buy them now and then if you want them, but you don't always get what you paid for."

Recalling dots of rotting flesh, Silk shuddered.

"The old caldé, Tussah his name was, was supposed to have done it. That leaked out after he died. So I decided to give it a try. Buy myself an embryo with spooky powers. I got one of the girls to carry it."

"And you were actually able to purchase such a thing? An embryo that would develop into someone with Mucor's powers?"

Blood nodded unhappily. "Like I said, you don't always get what you pay for, but I was careful and I did. She's got the stuff, but she's crazy. Always has been."

"You engaged a specialist to operate on her brain."

"Sure, trying to cure her, only it didn't work. If it had, I'd be caldé."

"She's been my friend," Silk told him, "a difficult one, perhaps, but helpful just the same. She likes me, I believe, and the good god knows I'd like to help her in return."

Oreb caught at the phrase. "Good god?"

"The Outsider, I ought to have said."

Mucor herself said, "They're arguing about you." Her voice sounded faint and far away; the tumbler Maytera Marble had filled for her waited untouched on the low table before her.

Silk sipped from his own, careful not to drink too much too fast. "Men and women breed children from their bodies on impulse. We augurs rail against it; but although inexcusable, it is at least understandable. They are swept away by the emotions of the moment; and if they weren't, perhaps the whole Whorl would stand empty. Adoption, on the other hand, is a considered act, consummated only with the assistance of an advocate and a judge. Thus an adoptive parent cannot say, 'I didn't know what I was doing,' or 'I didn't think it would happen.' Worthless though those protestations are, he has no claim to them."

"You think I knew she'd turn out like this? She was a baby." Blood glared at his daughter. "I'm twice your age, Patera, maybe more. When you're as old as I am, maybe you'll have a few little things that you regret too."

"There are many already."

"You think there are. Women, you mean. Hy. Oh shag it, what's the use?" Blood set his drink aside and wiped his damp left hand on his thigh. "I don't care much for them. Neither would you, if you'd been in my business as long as I have. I started when I was seven or eight, just a dirty little sprat going up to men in the market. Anyhow, Mucor's the only child I'll ever have, probably."

Maytera Marble told him, "She's the only granddaughter I'll ever have, too, Bloody. If you won't take proper care of her, I will."

Blood looked angrier than ever. "Like you did me?"

"It would be better if we kept our voices down," Silk said. "You're not supposed to be here."

"I wish I wasn't." A smile twisted Blood's mouth. "That

would be the elephant, wouldn't it? Shot for trying to pick up a couple bits down at the market. Hey, Patera, you want to meet my sister? She'll give you some hot mutton.''

''Bloody, don't!''

''It's pretty late to tell me that, Mama. Or don't you think so?''

Without waiting for an answer, he turned to Silk. ''I'm going to outline a deal. If you take it, I'm in, and I'll do everything I can to get you out of here in one piece.''

Silk opened his mouth to speak.

''When I say you, that's you and the other augur, the old man, Mama here, and that big piece from Orchid's. Even your bird. All of you. All right?''

''Certainly.''

''If you don't take it, I'm out the window, understand? No hard feelings, but no deal either.''

''You could be shot going out the window, too, Bloody,'' Maytera Marble warned him. ''I'm surprised that you weren't, you and my granddaughter, before you got back inside.''

Blood shook his head. ''There's a truce, remember? And I'll stick the azoth back under my tunic. They aren't going to shoot an unarmed man and a girl that never even come close to the wall.''

''As good as a secret passage.'' Maytera Marble's eyes gleamed with amusement.

''Right, it is.'' Blood went to the window. ''Now here's what I say, Caldé. I'll come over to you and Mint, gun, goat, and gut, and try to see to it that all of us get clear. When we do, I'll sign over your manteion to you for one card and other considerations, as we say, and you can owe me the card.''

He waited for Silk to speak, but Silk said nothing.

''After we get out, I'm still your bucky. I've done plenty of favors for the Ayuntamiento, see? I can help you too, and I will, everything that I can. I've got Mucor, remember,'' Blood nodded toward her, "and I know what she can do now. Lemur's crowd never got anything half as good as that."

Silk sipped from his tumbler.

"More talk," Oreb muttered; it was not clear whether it was a suggestion or a complaint.

"Here's all I want from you, Caldé. No gelt, just three things. Firstly, I get to hang onto my other property. That means my real estate, my accounts at the fisc, and the rest. Number two, I stay in business. I'm not asking you to make it legal. I don't even want you to. Only you don't shut me down, see? Last, I don't have to pay anybody anything above regular taxes. I'll open my books to you, but no more payoffs on top of that. You understand what I'm telling you?"

Blood leaned against the window frame. "Look it over, and you'll see I'm making you as good a deal as anybody could ask for. I'm giving you my complete, unlimited support, plus some valuable property, and all I want from you is that you leave me alone. Let me keep what's mine and earn my living, and don't come down on me any harder than you do on anybody else. What do you say?"

For a few seconds, Silk did not say anything. The tramp of rubber-shod metal feet came faintly from the wide foyer on the other side of the carved walnut door, punctuated by Potto's strident tones; embroidered hangings stirred, whispering, in the cool wind from the window.

"I've been expecting to be tested." Silk glanced at his tumbler, surprised to find that he had drunk more than half his soda water. "Tested by the Outsider. He's been testing me physically, and I felt quite confident that he would soon take my measure morally as well. When you began, I was certain this was it. But this is so easy!"

Lion raised his head to look at him inquiringly, then rose, stretched, and padded over to rub his muscled, supple body against Silk's knees.

Maytera Marble shook her finger at her son. "What

you've been doing is very wrong, Bloody. You sell rust, don't you? I thought so.''

"To begin," Silk told Blood, "you must turn my manteion over to me—you're going to do that right now. If you didn't bring along the deed, you can go out that window and get it. I'll wait."

"I brought it," Blood admitted. He fished a folded paper from an inner pocket of his tunic.

"Good. My manteion, for three cards."

Blood crossed the room to an inlaid escritoire; after a time, Mucor stood as well, her mouth working silently as though she were pronouncing the labored scratchings of Blood's pen.

"I'm not much of a scholar," he said at length, "but here you are, Patera. I had to sign for Musk, but it should be all right. I've got his power of advocacy."

The ink was not yet dry; Silk waved the deed gently as he read. "Fine." He took three of Remora's cards from his pocket and handed them to Blood.

"You're to do everything in your power to end the fighting without further loss of life," he told Blood, "and so am I. If I'm caldé when it's over, as you obviously expect, you will be prosecuted for any crimes you may have committed, in accordance with the law. No unfair advantage will be taken beyond that which I just took. That's a large concession, but I make it. I warn you, however, that nothing that you may have done will be overlooked, either. If you're found guilty on any charge, as I expect that you will be, I'll ask the court to take into consideration whatever assistance you've rendered our city in this time of crisis. Am I making myself clear?"

Blood glowered. "You extorted that property from me. You took it under false pretenses."

"I did." Silk nodded agreement. "I committed a crime to right the wrong done to the people of our quarter by an earlier one. Why should men like you be free to do whatever you wish whenever you wish, guaranteed that you yourself will never be victimized? You may, if you choose, complain about what I've done when peace has been restored. You have a witness in the person of your mother.''

He gave the lynx a last pat before pushing him away. ''I wouldn't advise you to call your adopted daughter, however. She's not competent to testify, and she might tell the court about the nativity of her pets.''

''You had better not ask me to testify, either, Bloody,'' Maytera Marble told him. ''I'd have to tell the judge that you tried to bribe our caldé.''

''They're coming,'' Mucor announced to Silk. ''Councillor Loris has finished talking to Councillor Tarsier through the glass. They've decided to kill you and send your body back with the woman that killed Musk.''

Silk froze, his eyes on Blood.

Oreb squawked, ''Watch out!''

Instinctively, Maytera Marble reached out to her son, a plea for forgiveness and understanding.

His grip on the azoth tightened, and the shimmering horror that was its blade divided the cosmos, leaving Maytera Marble on one side and the hand she had held out to him on the other. It dropped to the carpet as the hideous discontinuity swung up, showering them with plaster and sundered lath. Silk shouted a warning; absurdly, he tried to shield her from Blood's downward cut with Xiphias's cane.

Its thin wooden casing exploded in blazing splinters; but the azoth's blade sprang back from the double-edged steel blade the casing had concealed, having notched it to the spine.

It seemed to Silk then that his arm moved of itself—that he merely watched it, a spectator fully as horrified as she, and fully as separated from his arm's acts. As the door flew in with a crash, that arm swung the ruined blade.

From behind Sergeant Sand and a second soldier equally large, Potto barked, *"Shoot him!"*

The notched blade slid forward, penetrating Blood's throat as readily as the manteion's old bone-handled sacrificial knife had ever entered that of a ram.

"Shoot the caldé?" Sand's hand caught the other soldier's slug gun.

Blood's knees buckled as the light left his eyes. The double-edged blade, scarlet to within a hand's breadth of the notch with Blood's own blood, retreated from his throat.

"Yes, the caldé!"

For a moment it seemed to Silk that Maytera Marble should have knelt to catch Blood's blood; perhaps it seemed so to her as well, for she crouched, her remaining hand extended to her son as he fell.

Silk turned, the sword still in his hand. Sand's slug gun was no longer pointed at him, if it had ever been. Sand fired, and the second soldier a fraction of a second after him. Potto fell, his cheerful face slack with surprise.

"Take this, Patera." Maytera Marble was pressing Blood's azoth into his free hand. "Take it before I kill you with it."

He did, and she took Xiphias's ruined sword from him, and with its crook wedged between her small black shoes, contrived to wipe its blade with a big handkerchief that she shook from her sleeve.

There was a clash of heels and a crash of weapons as Sand and the second soldier saluted. Soldiers and men in silvered armor peering around them began to salute as well. Silk nodded in response, and when that seemed inadequate traced the sign of addition in the air.

EPILOGUE

It had been hastily erected, Caldé Silk reflected, studying the triumphal arch that spanned the Alameda—very hastily. But surely this new generalissimo from Trivigaunte would understand the situation, would realize the difficulties they had labored under in organizing a formal welcome in a city still at war with what remained of its Ayuntamiento, and make allowances.

Now, this wind.

It stirred yellow dust from the gutters, whistled among the chimneys, and shook the ramshackle arch until it trembled like an aspen. Flowers covering the arch would have been nice, but that moment of searing heat on Hieraxday had made flowers out of the question. So much the better, Silk thought; this wind would surely have stripped off every petal an hour ago. Even as he watched, a long streamer of colored paper pulled free, becoming a flying jade snake that mounted to the sky.

There the Trivigaunte airship fought its straining tether, so high that its vast bulk appeared, if not festive, at least unthreatening. From that airship, it should be simple to gauge the advance of Generalissimo Siyuf's troops. Silk wished that there had been time to arrange for signals of some sort: a flag hung from the gondola when she entered the city, for example, or a smoke pot lit to warn that she had been delayed. Rather to his own surprise, he discovered that he was eager to go up in the airship himself, to see Viron like the skylands again, and travel among the clouds as the Fliers did.

There were a lot of them out today, riding this cold wind. More, he decided, than he had ever seen before. A whole flock, like a flight of storks, was just now appearing from behind the airship. What city sent them forth to patrol the length of the sun, and what good did those patrols do? Speculation about the Fliers had been dismissed as bootless at the schola, until the Ayuntamiento had condemned them as spies.

Had the Ayuntamiento known? Did Councillor Loris, who wielded what authority remained to it, know now?

Might it not be possible to track Fliers in the airship, anchor at last at that fabled city, learn its name, and offer whatever assistance in its sacred labor Viron and Trivigaunte could provide?

(Buried, he had been wherever he had thought to be.)

A fresh gust, colder and wilder than any before it, roared up the Alameda, shaking its raddled poplars like rats. To his right General Saba stiffened, while he himself shivered without shame. He was wearing the Cloak of Lawful Governance over his augur's robe; it fell to his shoe-tops and was of the thickest tea-colored velvet, stiff with gold thread. He ought to have been awash in his own perspiration; he found himself wishing ardently for some sort of head-covering instead. General Saba had a dust-colored military cap and Generalissimo Oosik beyond her a tall helmet of green leather topped with a plume, but he had nothing.

He recalled the broad-brimmed straw hat he had worn while repairing the roof of the manteion—which would be missing more shingles, surely, thanks to this wind. He had pulled that hat down so that Blood's talus could not identify him later, and it had known him by that.

(Dead by his hand, Blood and the talus both.)

He had lost that recollected hat somehow. Might not this wind return it to him? All sorts of rubbish was blowing about, and stranger things had happened.

His wound throbbed. Mentally he pushed it aside, forcing himself to fill his lungs with cold air.

The shade had not climbed far yet, but what should have been a bright streak of purest gold seemed faint, and flushed with brownish purple. The Aureate Path was empty and failing visibly, signally the end of mankind's dream of paradise, of some inconceivable fraternity with its gods. For one vivid instant he remembered Iolar, the dying Flier. But no doubt the sun was merely dimmed at the moment, stained and darkened by dust. Winter was long overdue in any event. Was Maytera Mint, who would be so conspicuously absent from this, her victory parade, cold too? Wherever she was?

Was Hyacinth? Silk shivered again.

Far away, a band struck up, and ever so faintly he heard, or seemed to hear, the sound of bugles, the tramp of marching feet, and the clatter of cavalry.

That was a good sign, surely.